VANISHED

Also by James Delargy

55

VANISHED

James Delargy

**SIMON &
SCHUSTER**

London · New York · Sydney · Toronto · New Delhi

First published in Great Britain by Simon & Schuster UK Ltd, 2021

Copyright © James Delargy 2021

The right of James Delargy to be identified as author
of this work has been asserted in accordance with
the Copyright, Designs and Patents Act, 1988.

1 3 5 7 9 10 8 6 4 2

Simon & Schuster UK Ltd
1st Floor
222 Gray's Inn Road
London WC1X 8HB

Simon & Schuster Australia,
Sydney

Simon & Schuster India,
New Delhi

www.simonandschuster.co.uk
www.simonandschuster.com.au
www.simonandschuster.co.in

A CIP catalogue record for this book is
available from the British Library

ISBN: 978-1-4711-7756-9
Trade Paperback ISBN: 978-1-4711-7757-6
eBook ISBN: 978-1-4711-7758-3
Audio ISBN: 978-1-3985-0129-4

Typeset by Palimpsest Book Production Ltd, Falkirk, Stirlingshire
Printed and bound in Great Britain by CPI Group (UK) Ltd,
Croydon, CR0 4YY

MIX
Paper from
responsible sources
FSC® C020471

To my Mum and Dad

And to all the essential workers who gave their all
for the common good during the COVID crisis

VANISHED

1

Detective Emmaline Taylor

A family was missing. They had been in the town and then they weren't. What they were even doing there in the first place wasn't yet known. No one should have been there. No one had for close to fifty years.

It had been a short, choppy flight from Perth on a twin-prop plane into the blood red dirt and streak of tarmac that was Leonora Airport before driving south along Route 49. The Goldfields Highway. An indication of what was out here. Or at least what used to be out here. The good times had long gone.

The relentless desert scrub drifted by the window as Detective Emmaline Taylor rested her arm atop the steering wheel. There was no need to move it. The road was as straight as an arrow. From here to the horizon. The kinds of roads driverless cars were built for. But she had insisted on driving herself rather than be picked up at the airport by one of the local cops. The hundred kilometres would give her time to think. Mainly about why she had been called out here. It was unusual for the Major Crime Squad to get involved in what was technically a misper case but as it involved three members of the same family, someone had classed it as a major case. Hence the need to come out here. Into the dust.

From the file that she had scanned on a plane that seemed to flit up and down through the turbulent air like a hawk swooping for prey, the place that she was looking for was called Kallayee, a town on the edge of the Great Victoria Desert. A name suspected to be Indigenous in nature but as mysterious as the family's disappearance.

The names of the family had also been in the file. Lorcan Maguire, thirty-one years old, Naiyana (pronounced Nee-Ya-Na, according to the file) Maguire, twenty-eight years old, and Dylan Maguire, six years old. Last known address given as Cannington, Perth. Married for eight years. He had worked in the financial sector and she had been a housewife, charity worker and campaigner. Not the kind of people you would expect to be living in what was essentially a ghost town.

The information she had on Kallayee was that it had been mainly deserted since the 1940s when the goldmines had run dry. The whole region had been briefly popular again in the 1970s when increasing gold prices led people to check out old sites but it was short-lived. Since then it had been abandoned and left to rot. Now it was another spot on the map, never to be returned to. But the Maguire family had returned to it. They had even been living there,

2

according to Lorcan Maguire's parents. She had skimmed through the facts to get a better idea of the timeline and environment. Surveying the entire pond before diving in. A moment's peace before disturbing the calm surface.

She nearly missed the turn-off. She had been warned that there was no sign for Kallayee anymore and that the GPS would not direct her to it, but she was still distracted by Seamus and Charlotte Maguire's statement. They had called the disappearance in because Lorcan had failed to contact them since a Christmas Day phone call. This was apparently unusual as he gave them an update every couple of days. The family – at least on Lorcan's side – was close knit. There had been less concern from Naiyana's. Emmaline wondered why. Disappointment at her choice of husband? A past dispute? The file had mentioned nothing about it. She tucked it away for later. It would all mean nothing if she could locate the family. The reasons why Naiyana might not want to talk to her family or vice versa only became a concern if there was a crime. And right now there was no evidence of one.

Just a family who had straight up disappeared. From a town that had itself disappeared long ago.

2

Nowhere

It doesn't take long for eyes to adjust to absence of light. In fact after a while it just becomes the nature of things. But the craving for daylight remains. For the sun's rays. For that vitamin D.

What the darkness also brings is loneliness. Not that I am alone down here but right now I cannot hear or see anyone. I miss the sound of other people breathing. Even the wretched snoring, which was apparently all the bed's fault. I'm going to buy earplugs. If I ever get out of here. At least I can smell and taste the rising smoke, even though the machines aren't working. But what I miss most of all is the rumbling. The reverberations that signalled life, signalled progress, ingrained into me. Part of my life out here. I can see them for what they are now. Soothing. The white noise that dulled everything else. I'm left with only the clack that reverberates around the walls like time is ticking down. And running out.

A reoccurrence of the victim mentality I've always

fought against. I am not a victim. In fact it feels fitting, considering what I have done, to be buried underground for eternity. Or until business is complete. Even if part of me still thinks it was a mistake coming here. You can run, but you can't hide. Even down here.

3

Naiyana Maguire

Hurton had been bad enough. A single street town that the white ute had flashed through in less than thirty seconds, but which at least boasted a general store/post office/bottle shop, a hardware store, a pub and something that resembled a cafe. It was a long way from Perth. Never again would Naiyana complain about living in a dead suburb. Nothing was as dead as this.

Then the black tarmac began to fade, cracking apart, the slivers filling with dust, the black fading to brown then orange, seeming to open beneath the wheels as the road lost all form, the scenery encroaching from both sides welcoming them. By the time they reached Kallayee it had pretty much gone completely.

Her sense of disappointment wasn't shared by the others. In the back seat her son was giddy with glee, his cooing accompanied by the scurp of his sweaty fingers on the window. In the front seat, her husband was leaning forward, gazing out the window like his son.

'Look at this place,' said Lorcan. 'Home.'

She raised her eyebrows at this. Another thing she would have to do herself out here. An hour every week in front of her mum's mirror with a thread. Plucking them, trying to keep them neat. Painful. She wondered again why she had agreed to this. It didn't take long for her to remember. For safety. A temporary solution, but as ever Lorcan had jumped straight into it. He never learned. Act first, ask questions later. Or not at all. And lose all their money.

'So which one, Dad?'

'Yeah, which one?' she said, turning to Lorcan.

Every dwelling looked barely habitable, falling down around themselves as if they had given up the ghost after everyone first left. Forty years ago? Sixty years ago? He had told her but she had forgotten. It looked more like a hundred years ago. There were a few isolated brick structures but mostly the town was constructed of corrugated tin walls and roofs that had rusted to match the colour of the soil as if burying themselves in shame.

Weeds clung to the foot of buildings seeking shelter and whatever moisture collected on the tin at night and rolled down the side like tears. She felt like crying. This was where she found herself.

'Stop!' said Naiyana.

Lorcan hit the brakes. The furniture loaded on the flatbed behind – beds, pots, pans and a camping stove – crashed against the rear of the cab, as if jolted from slumber.

'What is it?'

With her eyes she signalled the crossroads ahead. It was guarded by the skeleton of a long-dead kangaroo, its ribs poking up proudly from the dust.

'We should move it,' she whispered.

'What for?' said Lorcan.

'So he doesn't see it,' she said, hoping that Dylan hadn't noticed. Glancing in the rear-view she could see that his attention remained on the collapsed building they had just passed. Already exploring the ruins. Something she would have to watch for. For him this would be the best school holiday ever. Yesterday he had been in Clementine Primary surrounded by concrete, traffic-calming and cleanliness and now he was out here in the middle of a dangerous, unknown land.

'He's seen skeletons before, Nee,' said Lorcan.

'We don't need him having nightmares.'

'We can't whitewash these things. We live here now. The sooner he gets used to it, the better.'

Before she could say anything to stop him, Lorcan looked over his shoulder and called in back.

'Heads up, Dylan. Take a look at our new neighbour,' he said as he hit the accelerator.

4

Lorcan Maguire

Skeletons. A ruined town. The endless possibilities of emptiness. His son was lapping it up. This was what Lorcan wanted. He needed to sell this to Dylan as he was sure Nee was a lost cause. As soon as the Perth carnage had blown over, she would want to return. But he had plans. He had lost their first house but he would build another. Bigger and better. He would make a life out here for them. Until such a time they could return. She had given him six weeks, twelve at the most. He was banking on a lot longer.

She still blamed him. And she was right. He had overstretched on their investments and paid for it, the mortgage on the five-bedroom house bought at the market's zenith, crippling them. It had always been too big for them. Merely a statement of false affluence. When his career had peaked.

Now they were on this adventure. He knew his parents – and especially hers – saw it as a selfish pursuit. Taking a huge risk with a young child. But they didn't know the other factors. And Dylan wasn't that small anymore. Give him a tablet and he could find anything he wanted at the touch of the few buttons. Which was riskier than anything they might meet out here. Plus they had taken plenty of medical supplies, bandages and ointments, an inhaler even though none of them suffered from asthma, numbers for emergency advice, coordinates and directions to the nearest doctor and hospital even if they were an hour away. Plus it was the school holidays. They had six weeks before Dylan was due back and he could teach his son a lot in that time. How to erect a shelter, how to source water, survival techniques he had studied online and built himself a little manual of. He felt prepared. Prepared to show Nee that he knew what he was doing.

'Are we there yet?'

This wasn't Dylan of course, but Nee. Another jab for him to prove he was in control.

He peered out the window. None of the buildings looked suitable. Sweat prickled at his hairline despite the air con blasting at full tilt. He had thought that having the choice of any building would be exhilarating, almost an out-of-body experience where he would float above the town and find this rough diamond in the midst of the rubble. It wasn't proving to be the case. They were all extensive fixer-uppers.

Turning at the far edge of town he drove back to the crossroads and followed the dead boomer's nod to go right.

'Have you got an address?' asked Nee. She wasn't

looking out the window anymore but staring at him as if he could materialize their house from thin air.

'Pick one,' he replied.

'Pick one?'

Her dark eyes narrowed, the delicate Thai features contracting into something vicious. It gave the impression that she was in pain. But Lorcan knew that she was considering all the angles before committing to a response. She avoided long, drawn-out domestics, if possible. One wound, provided it was deep enough, was sufficient.

'Any one?'

Lorcan was glad of the interruption from the back seat, the childish fervour dispelling the growing mood in the vehicle.

'Any,' he replied, turning towards his son who was leaning into the front seat between them like a dog. And just as eager.

'What do you mean, any?' asked Naiyana. 'Which one did you buy?'

'I didn't buy any of them.'

'What—?'

Lorcan jumped on the grenade before it exploded.

'It's called adverse possession.'

'What is?'

'It's an old common law right we inherited from the Poms.' He could see on her face that she was lost so he continued. 'If a house is abandoned, we can take it, make some improvements and if . . . when . . . we meet a series of requirements we gain title to it.'

11

He smiled at her. It wasn't returned, her lips drawn tight. Dylan was watching both of them.

She waved her slender hand across the expanse of the front windscreen. 'There isn't much to hold onto.'

'There will be.'

A curl of her lip told him she doubted it very much.

'So we move in and just take it over? Like an army?' asked Dylan.

'Exactly,' said Lorcan. He kept quiet that they would need to hold onto the property for twelve years before they could claim title. That was a long way down the line. The main thing, according to the law, was to hold exclusive, uninterrupted and adverse possession, meaning that the owner had not given them permission to move in. Which they hadn't. And there was no one around to dispute with.

In the end the kangaroo gave them a bum steer. Turning around and passing the crossroads once again, he spotted it. The best of a bad bunch, the red brick slap-dashed with white lime or paint that had faded over time but still stood out from the rest. A bungalow with the roof caved in on one side. But there would be time to fix that. Out here it didn't rain very much. Which, of course, presented a big problem in itself.

5

Naiyana

As he backed the ute close to a front door that was hanging off the bottom hinge and leaning precariously forward like a late-night drunk angling for support, she studied the place she was to call home. That she would be forced to call home. It was nothing like the expansive, five-bedroom, three-bathroom and one fucking great kitchen that she had left behind. One with an island in the middle that she literally couldn't touch the centre of without standing on the step Dylan had for reaching the toilet when he was younger. The dilapidated state of the house felt intimidating, like it would crash around them at any point.

Dylan, however, was unbound by such worries and rushed off to check it out.

'Don't go inside,' she called out as an arm slid around her shoulder. Whether it was her edginess at the new place or at the dead surroundings, she tensed her shoulders against his grip, almost fighting to get away. She took it as a sign, trusting her body.

'Well?' asked Lorcan.

'Well, you've got a lot of work to do,' she replied.
'It'll be worth it.'

'I'll reserve judgement. First, check inside. Once I get the all-clear I'll come in.'

'Just keep an open mind.'

'It's been open since we left Perth. Believe me, if we didn't have to lie low I wouldn't be here.'

There was a pause. She knew what Lorcan was thinking. This was punishment for what he had done and for what he had tried to do to rectify it. But she wasn't entirely innocent herself. He had lost the house but she had made plenty of enemies too.

She watched as he left her side and half-lifted, half-pushed the front door open, some of the blue paint crumbling onto the front step. He stepped inside and took what he had called adverse possession of the house. More adversity they didn't need.

Grasping Dylan's hand to prevent him from following his father inside she waited for the assessment.

Dylan fought her grip, pulling strongly against her. She had never been one for exercise. The intensity of the charity and campaigning work kept her naturally slim, working until she realized that she hadn't eaten. Her genes helped too, her father and mother little pockets of dynamism. People who had suffered more adversity than she could ever dream of; who had survived a long and torturous trip here only to be faced with a wrathful government and suspicious population. But even they wouldn't speak to her now. Bloody-mindedness was obviously inherited too.

Her mind returned to the present. As did a spark of fear. It entered her body through the right side of her gut where her appendix had been removed when she was eleven, the scar pale and raised against her skin.

'Lorc?' she called out at the house.

There was no answer.

'Shall I go in and get Daddy?' offered Dylan but Naiyana retained her grip. The house had already taken one. She wasn't going to lose another.

She licked her lips. They were already beginning to crack in the dry heat. Another thing she missed about Perth. The air around here was like an oven, as if just waiting to reach critical temp, ignite and burn everything to cinders. She couldn't wait to see a beach again, feel the sea lap at her ankles, dive in.

'Daddy!' called out Dylan.

Again no answer.

She began to wonder if he had fallen down a hole in the floor, or if silently some wall on the far side of the house had collapsed on top of him. But surely she would have heard that. Nothing fell in complete silence. The saying about trees falling in woods was bullshit. Everything solid made a sound. Especially if it fell and hit that block of wood Lorcan called his head.

Letting Dylan drag her she approached the front door. Inside was dark, which was both fantastic and forbidding. It meant the roof was still intact, something that her husband could work with. Whenever she found him.

He had carefully rested the door against the inner wall but the wide split in the wood looked like a drunken mouth laughing at her stupidity and growing terror. She would have to go inside.

She pulled Dylan's hand, yanking him back with all her strength. Another few years and he would be stronger than her. 'Get into the ute.'

'I want to—'

'Wait in the ute. We have to make sure that there are no . . . animals living in there.' It was the insects she was more worried about. But Dylan was at the age where he was more afraid of things that were bigger than him than smaller.

'But I don't—'

'There's a KitKat in the esky,' she said. That finally broke the resistance, the boy pulling away from her, not in the direction of the house but in the direction of the ute and the ice-cold chocolate bar that awaited in the cooler. It would keep him occupied for a few minutes, enough time for her to figure out what the hell was going on.

She turned back to the doorway. The laughing drunk continued mocking her foolishness. She was reminded of Lorcan's grandfather, the Irishman who was unable to pronounce her name and took to calling her Neeve, a disrespect she lived with for the sake of family appeasement. He had died not long after their wedding. She had used the excuse of being pregnant to avoid going to the funeral.

'Lorc?'

She tested the front step. It was solid underfoot, maybe the only solid part of the whole structure. Again a multitude of horrors that could have befallen her husband choked her thoughts. Could she and Dylan drag him out from under a wall if needed? She doubted it. The thought of being without him suddenly seemed real and distressing. Was that a sign she loved and needed him? Or that out here he had suddenly become of use once again, that his physicality – one of the reasons she had been attracted to him in the first place – would be essential to their survival?

Leaning in she went to poke her head around the door. She would call out again before entering. As if asking permission of the previous owners so as to not disturb their ghosts.

'Lor—?'

A face popped into view.

Stepping back and almost falling off the front step, she screamed.

The face was smiling, and almost demented with glee.

Lorcan came to the front door and looked out. A grin that she thought looked almost evil was stuck on his face.

'It's perfect,' he said.

6

Naiyana

Lorcan led her into the house by the hand. Whereas Dylan couldn't pull her, her husband certainly could, the loose T-shirt he wore masking a set of broad shoulders and strong arms. The arms of a farmer as Seamus, her father-in-law, often said, though neither of them had been near a farm in their lives. In fact as far as she was aware, this was the closest any of the Maguire family had come to country living.

They left Dylan outside with the job of finishing off his chocolate bar and pulling the weeds that were growing in the crack between the ground and the edge of the building. After first checking for spiders and snakes of course. It didn't fill her with confidence that the first check was for spiders and snakes. Not a hole in the wall or a major structural defect, just that there was nothing venomous that might incapacitate or kill their only child.

Her bigger child, Lorcan, was bounding around, ultra-keen to get started. Like the obscure law about adverse possession, he had read up about renovating a house; everything from bricklaying to plastering to simple wiring. She didn't doubt that he had a basic understanding of it all but the house needed a lot of work. More than he could manage. More than both of them could manage. Especially in six weeks. Twelve at the most. However long it took for things to die down.

The living room was covered in dust, anything of value removed. The wooden floor creaked loudly but after a few tentative steps she was confident that it would hold out. As long as they didn't throw any wild parties. Which out here wasn't likely. She couldn't help but think that their crossroads kangaroo might have died from boredom.

The hallway and bedrooms were in a similar condition, the dry air and the roof maintaining them reasonably well. She suddenly found some positivity creeping in. What *could* be done replaced what needed to be done and where she found herself. This was the get-up-and-go disposition that had proved such a boon when infiltrating animal testing centres, protesting refugee conditions and campaigning for weeks on end. This was the firebrand she had rediscovered in the last couple of years after staying home to raise Dylan. The teenage Naiyana had returned. And then she had overstepped the mark. People had suffered because of it. Even Lorcan.

A final insult was out back, separate from the house. The toilet. Consisting of a tin shed over a hole in the ground. A thunderbox according to her husband. That was what she was reduced to. At least the years of disuse had eliminated any stench. A small mercy. And it had four walls, unlike the worst affected room. The kitchen. There the top part of the gable wall had collapsed, cracked from the effects of frost or extreme heat, Lorcan suggested. With it the roof had sagged losing a few sheets of tin and exposing it to the sun, the moon and the elements. The kitchen would remain semi-outdoors. Until Lorcan could get the wall and roof fixed. *After* they had cleared and swept the house and laid traps for anything that might have been lurking in the corners.

There was a house in here somewhere. Maybe a home. She could visualize it. And that was the first step. It had to be.

7

Lorcan

'A book?'

'Yeah, a book. About us setting up home out here.'

'For six weeks,' she reminded him. In return, he gave her a non-committal nod. If he could get the house up and running and Dylan into the local school – wherever that was – he could argue for them to stay until the end of term. Eighteen weeks. Then next term. And the term after that. If they liked it.

'What sparked this brainwave?' she continued.

Lorcan watched as she put the plastic crate that was filled with plates and cutlery down. After three hours of sweeping dust and dead insects from all the rooms they were transporting their stuff in from the ute, sheltering from the early afternoon sun. Already Dylan had quit, parking himself behind the wheel of the ute pretending to drive it, the window cranked down to make sure air circled, like he was a dog. It would have been embarrassing. Had anyone been around to see it.

He put his hand on the old table they had dragged

from the living room to the kitchen. It would do as a dining table. Once it had been given a good clean. They had brought enough anti-bac to suffocate the whole town. One of Nee's stipulations in agreeing to come.

'I was just thinking,' he started.

'Thinking got us into this mess.'

He pushed the box with the two-ring camping stove and cooking utensils to the middle of the table. It creaked. He would have to look at tightening the screws. No one wanted it to collapse in the middle of dinner.

'I'll take some video too as an add-on exclusive to the book. Extra content.'

This was intended to pique her interest. Vlogging was Naiyana's thing and she'd had plenty of practice in some challenging situations, recording the raids of testing centres, disrupting companies and corporations. A dangerous occupation. And he should know. He had worked for a vicious crook.

'What do you know about writing a book? You barely read, never mind write.'

'It isn't fiction. I don't have to make it up. Just tell the truth.'

'Once you fix this place up so we can live in it,' she reminded him.

'As well as.'

Lorcan watched his wife pause, shake her head and then shrug. She hadn't given up, just realized that there was nowhere to go. No common ground. They would stay at the opposite ends of this argument. But he was determined to have the last word. He had plans. Repairing the house and their family.

'Come with me,' he said, holding his hand out.

'Let's get this finished,' she protested but he spread his arms and ushered her out the front door.

Dylan was still behind the wheel of the ute, bouncing up and down as if manoeuvring over particularly bumpy terrain, shouting at imaginary people to get out of the way as he made his urgent delivery.

Turning her around, he pointed to the house that was now in front of them.

'First I'll set up the generator so that we have electricity. Then I'll mend the gable wall and fix the roof. Then I'll get to work on the inside. Plaster, tile, build furniture.'

'And water?'

'We passed a well.'

'Where?'

'Close to where Skippy keeled over.'

She tilted her head at him but it forced a smile from her, dragging the sweetness back to a face he had fallen in love with all those years ago that now only briefly returned after accomplishing all the chores an adult had to do. Your love goes to your kid first and what's left goes to your partner. Or football. Or golf.

'We can make do with the bottled water for the time being,' he said, wedging a giant plastic container of water under each arm and hauling them inside.

8

Emmaline

Suddenly the instruction to take a left at the dead kangaroo made sense. Emmaline pulled up outside the bungalow. Although it was in a state of disrepair, it was practically a mansion compared to the rest of the town.

As she exited the 4x4 and stretched legs that cried out with joy after being in a cramped airplane and behind the wheel for the last four hours, a couple of local cops filtered out from their own vehicle. She had been informed their names were Rispoli and Barker. Their crisp, clean shirts indicated they had been basking in the delights of air con while they waited for her.

As a detective from the MCS, she held rank. What she didn't know was what she would be working with.

As she walked towards them they stayed in formation on either side of the vehicle as if afraid she was going to steal it. Maybe they hadn't been expecting a dark-skinned police officer. Or maybe that was her own bias talking. Or previous experience, her dad eyed with outright suspicion even when on council business, his authority and presence questioned.

'Tell me what you know that you think I might not.'

This was a question to gauge competence. If she had been in their shoes she would tell her everything. Always assume that the new entrant doesn't know what has happened. Half-telling a story provided room for something to be left out. Possibly something major.

The older one, Barker – a senior constable, given the two stripes on his upper arm – glanced at the younger one. His lined face wore years of worry. Someone who didn't like dealing with superiors. Possibly jealousy, possibly afraid of saying the wrong thing. Or conscious of an upcoming retirement and the lovely safe pension beyond the fence. 'We have cordoned off the crime scene.'

Emmaline looked at the tape. It was shuffling in the gentle breeze holding back precisely no one from entering. But it was correct protocol. She hoped they had been smart enough not to contaminate the scene. 'Seal it, log it and step away' as her staff sergeant had taught her.

'Anything inside?'

'No bodies,' said Barker.

An instant leap to the most severe outcome. He had already made up his mind. Not good practice. Or wise at this early stage.

'And what do we know about the mispers' last movements?'

It was Rispoli's turn to speak. He was maybe a year or two younger than Emmaline and hitched his back a little straighter to answer her. Maybe a military background. Maybe good etiquette. Maybe taking his cue from his more experienced partner. She didn't get a confident feeling from either. They looked frightened, overwhelmed.

'The father's family called it in. Last contact was a phone call on Christmas Day.'

'So, ten days ago.'

There was a joint nod from the officers.

'No contact since?'

'None. The father stated that he and his wife had been scheduled to visit Boxing Day but that his son, Lorcan Maguire, phoned on Christmas Day and cancelled.'

'Pretty odd.'

'Agreed.'

'Anything on how the mispers were acting?'

Rispoli continued. 'I quote: "I could hear that wife of his in the background. There seemed to be some tension but nothing more than normal."'

Which raised the immediate question: what was normal? It meant different things to different people. Her own aunt and uncle in Cape Town fought all the time but that was what they needed to be sure that they were listening to each other. They had been

26

married forty years. And had never once disappeared off the face of the earth.

'Seamus Maguire also noted that his son asked for a couple of thousand dollars to help pay for some materials for the house. But overall, the impression he got was that the family seemed determined to make a go of it.'

So a family determined to make a go of life out here but with an underlying tension in the air. Emmaline took a deep breath. It was time for action. The last contact with the family had been ten days ago. It was time to uncover something more recent.

'I want you to dig up any transactions or use of bank cards during the last few weeks. Phone logs too. See if there has been any movement. If they're some-where else, we can track them.'

The officers nodded.

Emmaline glanced around. Something important was missing. Transport.

'Find out what vehicle they own. And put out a KLO4 on the number plate.'

Emmaline studied the house again. It would take a day or two to gather the information. Right now all she had was what was in front of her.

9

Emmaline

Emmaline couldn't believe that anyone would choose to live here. She had seen more structurally sound – and tidier – crack dens. What had it been like before they started work on it? It probably said a lot about the family. They weren't afraid of hard work, or afraid of very much at all. Coming all the way out here and building a life. It made their sudden disappearance all the stranger.

In addition it would have taken patience to build a house. A patience she lacked, perfection hard to attain and fleeting when reached. This she blamed on the ballet lessons her parents had pushed her into when she was nine years old. The only black kid in the class, wearing flesh-coloured ballet pumps that didn't match her skin colour and made it look like she was some burn victim wearing hideous bandages on her feet. Nowadays of course they made pumps for a range of skin tones. As ever, the world was twenty years behind where she needed it to be.

Ballet had been the 'in' thing at the time and her

parents – new to the country, him Black South African and her English Rose pale – had wanted Emmaline to fit in so that they could develop connections. As a result she had spent four years prancing around, pimped out for the aspiration of middle-class anonymity. But ballet was a tough gig. Where nothing but perfection was acceptable. In other arts and sports results were prized over perfection but a missed step was like murder. It eventually tore her away from ballet and left her with the stanza that achievement was more important than perfection. Which she took into her police work. How the job was done played second fiddle to getting the job done.

Overall, the house was a mess. It looked to have been ransacked, cupboards and drawers scattered across the floor, camp beds flipped onto their sides and the thin mattresses slashed. A wardrobe in what she guessed had been Dylan's room was torn apart, the contents strewn. Someone had been looking for something. Something not of obvious value either; personal items, pictures, ornaments and even a small box of jewellery untouched. As if the family had left in a hurry. Or been taken without warning.

The kitchen was in a similar state. At the far end the roof sagged, a missing sheet of tin allowing the blue sky to peep through. In the corner was a pile of swept rubble and a collapsed table. Something violent had occurred here. The blood smeared on the pieces of smashed mirror all but confirmed that.

Emmaline turned to Rispoli. He had been following

her around the house like a shadow, while Barker called in the details she had requested.

'Have you bagged and tagged a sample?'

'Already done.'

Emmaline leaned in closer. The blood was smeared across the glass and ingrained with dust, washing the threatening red to a harmless brown. The quantity wasn't enough to suggest significant injury but any loss of blood was cause for concern. Especially as no attempt had been made to clean it up. Forensics would check the rest of the house for residue. A visible patch of blood was worrisome, but a larger patch of cleaned-up blood elsewhere in the house might signal something worse.

10

Naiyana

The bed was uncomfortable, the mattress nothing but foam covered in a man-made fibre that stuck to her skin like glue.

In an attempt to foster some marital order Lorcan had pushed the camp beds together but the thick metal poles left a large crevice in the middle.

She lay back and stared at the ceiling. After unloading the ute, sweeping and tidying the house she had expected to be tired but sleep was miles away and not helped by Dylan in the other bedroom. He was complaining of noises, rattling from above and rumblings from below. She put it down to first-night nerves, the adjustment period she had feared. At least there weren't any neighbours to gripe about the crying.

As a result she was awake as Lorcan read her a bedtime story using the battery-powered lamp. A history of the town. Disappointingly it wasn't brief.

'In 1893 they discovered gold and started mining. By 1896 the town site was declared by the government and gazetted a year later. Back then the only way in and out was a bi-weekly coach from Hurton to Wisbech and on south to Kalgoorlie.'

She tried to drift off but Lorcan's chuckle woke her.

'They named the first mine "The Dark". And the second "Rattlesnake" after one of the discoverers apparently. By 1899 both were operating ten-head stamp mills, pounding the rock to extract the ore.'

As she fought for sleep against the sound of his voice, she learned that at its peak in 1905 Kallayee had a population of 1,016 people, including three pubs, a bank, a post office, a small school and two brothels. She wished some were still open. Even the brothel. For company. Someone else Lorcan could bore with this history lesson. She'd even pay the prostitutes at this stage.

'The well dried up so they capped it and built a rotunda over the top. Dropped another out near some place called Orange Lake and transported the water back to town. I'll try there first. Then I'll try uncapping the well in town. The water should be fine for washing clothes at least.'

Naiyana didn't respond, willing sleep upon herself.

'Then in 1921 there was a fatal fire at Rattlesnake. Twenty people were killed. Mining halted for three years, so people drifted away to the nickel mines at Leonora and Gwalia. That was it until increasing gold prices in the late seventies made gold mining economically viable again. But not here. So Kallayee faded into a silent existence.'

He paused. The history lesson was over but he wasn't finished.

'Do you think that the noises are ghosts?'

She swivelled around to look at him, his face itself ghostly in the pale light.

'Let's not mention that in front of Dylan.'

Lorcan nodded. 'Good idea.'

But as if he had somehow sensed that he was being talked about there was a sharp cry from the other bedroom. Naiyana stared at her husband. Neither of them said anything for a moment.

'Your turn,' said Lorcan.

'You're closer to the door.'

'By about a metre.'

She paused to see if chivalry would surmount discomfort. It had in the past. Young love.

'I'm tired,' she said.

'So am I.'

'You dragged us out here.'

It was the same blunt club she would continue to swing until it became ineffective. As much as Dylan needed time to settle in, so did she. Lorcan believed it was all worth it but she remained unconvinced. Maybe even less so than when they had left late last night to drive all the way out here.

From the other room Dylan began to cry. For Mummy. For Daddy. For anyone.

She glanced at Lorcan in case gallantry won out but his nose was back in the tablet. Reading up on more history. Or better yet, how to install a bloody window.

33

Wrapping the blanket around her shoulders, she entered the other bedroom, goosebumps on her flesh, her senses heightened.

Dylan was tossing and turning as she perched on the edge of the bed, pulling him close, trying to comfort him.

After half an hour his twisting stopped and she went to leave. If she could get a couple of hours before the sun came up that might get her through tomorrow. Life was to be taken a day at a time at the moment, future plans thrown out of non-existent windows.

As she tried to sneak out of the room Dylan woke again. The deep brown eyes that he had inherited from her spoke of a disquiet, even fear.

'It's rumbling again,' he said, quietly as if afraid to awaken a monster.

'What is, honey?'

Dylan didn't answer. But in the silence she heard something too. A rumble like something was stirring in the belly of the earth itself. Hungry to eat. Closing her eyes she tried to identify the source but almost as soon as she did it seemed to disappear, leaving her wondering if she had imagined it entirely.

11

Emmaline

The rest of the house was clean. Of blood or excessive bodily fluid at least. Nothing that random daily existence couldn't account for.

After that it was a case of inspecting the rest of the town for evidence that something untoward had taken place. At present, the case remained a misper. Times three.

The team had increased by one. Anand, another constable from Leonora, had been dragged in from two days' leave to help, wearing a sour expression as befitted the rapid change of plans. They spread out like ants, using the Maguire house as the nest.

From what she had read, Kallayee was a goldrush town that had given up a modest few veins. Like a heroin addict's arm they had been stabbed relentlessly, gold transported out and opiate transported in, something greatly appreciated with nothing else to do in the evening but reminisce about lost opportunities.

Gwalia, a town beside Leonora, had the only real claim to fame. It had once been visited by an American president. Back then Herbert Hoover had simply been a young geologist, sent there to develop his company's latest find into a working concern. He had eventually become manager of the new mine and shipped in a load of Italian labourers who were hired cheap and laid off just as cheaply. As the Italian immigrants filtered south looking for work, they had eventually crept into Kallayee and for a time the official language became an Italian–Australian mix that was incomprehensible outside the town. It explained the long-dead store with the name 'The Italian Press' in fading writing above the door.

She stuck with Rispoli as she scoured the town. Her opinion of it remained the same: no place for a young family to live. The tin shacks that hadn't fallen over were close to doing so, the wood dwellings frayed and split, all uninhabitable. The few brick constructions had been gutted a long time ago. Around every corner, she expected to fine a lone, wizened stockman resting on a barrel, his feet up watching all the action unfold in his long undisturbed town, waiting to tell his tale to someone. But rarely in this business was everything laid out in one neat polished script. Everything had a dog-ear somewhere, a wrinkle that needed to be smoothed out.

Emmaline had a question to ask. And not about the case.

'Rispoli. Sounds Italian.'

The young constable turned to her. 'I can see how you made rank.'

36

The accompanying smile lifted his cheekbones and involved his whole face. Even his ears seemed to rise. A handsome face, pleasing to her eye. Set free from Barker's rigid deportment, he was emerging from his shell.

'Related to anyone who used to live here?'

'My mum did one of those ancestry trees once.'

'And?'

'We came from Leichhardt in New South Wales. And before that Abruzzo in Southern Italy. My great-grandfather moved the family out here to Kalgoorlie. Never made it up to Kallayee. Not officially anyway.'

'What do you mean?'

'It means that he might have worked the mines. But not according to any government records. Near impossible to tax his kind of iterant working back then.'

He nodded his head towards her. 'I guess your family weren't originally Aussie.'

Emmaline stopped in her tracks and turned to him, sharply at the waist, flicking her head. Her recently shorn locks prevented the whip she desired.

'Why do you say that?'

The young officer stopped. His lips moved, no words came out. A dash of colour came to his tanned cheeks.

'I didn't mean . . . I . . . It was . . .'

He was backtracking rapidly. His eyes flicked this way and that. Trying to get out of the snare he had triggered.

Emmaline tried to hold her glare but failed. A smile

eased across her face, basking in the endorphin rush, essential to keep her going through this strung-out day.

'It's okay.'

'I wasn't saying . . .'

Emmaline put him out of his misery. 'My dad's from Cape Town and my mum's from London. They moved out here when I was two. She got offered a good job and Dad was happy to try somewhere warmer. Simple as that. No drama. No running away. Just a better job and a better life. Like your great-grandparents.'

'No,' chortled Rispoli, shaking his head. 'They were running away.'

'From?'

'A story for later.'

They shared a smile. Emmaline wondered if this could go somewhere, a primal urge taking over. Something that society suggested she should be ashamed of. But she wasn't. There was nothing wrong with fishing; hunting, catching and letting go.

As they entered yet another shed, the sun poking holes through the tin, allowing dust motes to dance in the brilliant bursts of energy, she asked him what he knew about the town.

'Dead goldmining town. A few good shoots but mostly famous for the mine collapse in 1921. Killed around twenty people. Then another two in the riot against the mining company after. The government even cordoned off a few houses, in case they sank into the collapsed mine.'

To Emmaline it sounded a lot like what had happened in the family home. Had there been a collapse? Did that explain the roof and wall? Scaring them into leaving in a hurry? But why not collect their valuables? Why not get in contact?

'There is, of course, also the legend that the town is cursed,' said Rispoli.

'Is that your official opinion?' she asked as they left the shack.

He smiled. 'Soon it might be our only line of enquiry.'

She smiled back but hoped it didn't come to that. As a rule she steered away from superstition. Her mother was a superstitious woman, the house decorated with feathers and trinkets, abiding customs that her father obeyed in public and had always encouraged Emmaline to disobey in private.

Indeed, the town itself seemed to exist in some kind of limbo, between what it had once been and vanishing back into dust. Her mother might even have relished the almost spiritual silence. It wasn't on any map and there were no road signs directing traffic to it. The government had done everything it could to prevent anyone living here. But it was an easy edict to defy. Emmaline looked at the scrub beyond the town, sand dunes and gibber plains, a hard, closely packed surface of pebbles, populated by a few weary eucalyptus trees, mulga shrubs and deep-rooted spinifex grass all adapted to low rainfall and high temperatures. There was nothing but barren land, no government or police keeping watch. And nature abhorred a vacuum.

The first discovery was made by Anand, his energetic cries dragging the four of them behind a house with a roofless coal shed. There they found a quad bike with its tyres slashed. Petrol in the tank. In poor condition, the seat worn, the throttle grip and gear bar rubbed smooth from excessive use and sparkling in the sun, clean unlike the sandy, oily engine.

As Barker issued a request for a check on its origin, a second, more significant discovery was made close by. A patch of reddened earth. Likely blood. In larger quantities than was found in the house. It reminded her of the aftermath of a western. A duel at high noon.

It meant three things.

That Forensics needed to be called. To test if the blood samples matched.

That something had happened here. Something bad.

And that, for a town that had been dead for forty years, a lot of blood had been recently spilled.

12

Lorcan

Dylan didn't sleep the next night either, again complaining about rumbling. He had wanted to persuade Dylan that it was his imagination but even he felt it. Naiyana too. A rumble that seemed to come and go without rhyme or reason. He had even gone to check the generator a couple of times to make sure it wasn't automatically switching on at night. Even though it lacked capacity to do so. Nee pushed him to find a reason for the unnerving phenomenon. There was only one explanation he could think of. A water source or aquifer beneath the town. Untapped for decades.

The sleep Dylan failed to get at night was recovered during the day when the rumbles seemed to disappear, which was comforting for the child but less so for him and Nee, slaving all day to try and get the house in order.

With continued dry weather he abandoned mending the roof to drive out to the uncapped well near Orange Lake. This would give him a good idea of the state of the water table. Plus, if he could draw water there it would save having to dig through a century of dirt and uncap the original well.

Orange Lake was about five kilometres south of town, a faded wooden signpost signalling the way. Standing all on its own was a small tin shack. There was no lake. Just dry, scorched land stretching into the distance. Dragging open the door, light filtered through the rusted tin. Inside, a stone wall surrounded the well but it had cracked and partly collapsed down the hole it protected. Above it, the metal bucket attached to the pulley was cracked too, virtually useless for collecting liquid, but Lorcan dropped it anyway.

He fed the rope slowly through his hands waiting for a distant, welcome splash. He wasn't confident. The whole shack smelled bone dry, no hint of moisture in the air.

After twenty torturous seconds there was a sound. The solid, dry clang of metal hitting rock. Raising the bucket slightly, he lowered it again, faster this time to allow for the bucket to bounce off the offending rock in case it was merely an obstruction. Still no splash. Just the clang of metal on rock. A third time confirmed the insult. The well was dry. Which meant they were currently stuck in the desert without water.

NAIYANA

With Lorcan gone and Dylan fast asleep, she continued to tidy and organize, sweeping each room twice using the small hand-held vacuum that they had packed to get into the corners, having to stop regularly to empty the container. It was frustrating in two ways. In having to vacuum, something she had never enjoyed and which she usually farmed out to Dylan for pocket-money, or Lorcan on the promise of sex, and in the feeling that she was fighting a losing battle.

She was pleased with one thing. The mirror that her mother had passed down to her and which had been passed down from her own mother had survived the journey, wrapped in five layers of bubble wrap and tucked between her knees in the cab. She had never lived anywhere without it hung up. Her family watching over her. A giant eye to keep them safe. The nail on the kitchen wall held firm. Immediately the room felt brighter, more like home. More subconscious than physical. But Naiyana didn't care. Any sliver of joy was something to cling to at the moment.

13

Lorcan

He pulled the horizontal shutters back and let the well breathe. Not that it had been exactly starved of oxygen given the multiple holes in the wood. Sand and dust had practically filled the old well. The cap would be somewhere underneath. How far underneath he didn't know.

The winch that would have perched on top like a metal sawhorse was long gone, so he reached down and stabbed a spade into the sand. It was loose, not compacted like he had feared. At the top at least. He started to dig, the sand collapsing in and around each spadeful. He continued his Sisyphean battle, his feet settling into the sand, swamping his trainers.

Footsteps approached from behind him. In the shimmering haze, his wife and son approached.

'If it isn't the Irish Mario,' she laughed.

Lorcan looked down. He smiled too. From her perspective it would look like he was stuck halfway down a pipe trying to exit the level. If only disappearing was that easy.

'Any water?' she asked, glancing down the well.

'I hope so. Orange Lake was a bust.'

'How far down do you have to go?'

He checked his progress. He had only removed a few inches of material.

'Your guess is as good as mine.'

The look on her face suggested that she wasn't keen on her survival relying on guesswork.

'I'm taking the ute to town,' she said. 'See what they have, food-wise.'

The nearest town, Hurton, was ten kilometres as the crow flew. But a crow didn't have to deal with the treacherous dips, gullies, rises and scrubland of the outback. By road it was a thirty-kilometre round trip. And given the state of the tarmac, speed limits were unlikely to be broken.

Lorcan nodded. 'You taking Dylan?'

'Wasn't planning to. He can help you.'

'I'll let him wander around.'

She gave him a hard look. 'Don't let him wander too much.'

On cue, he watched his son poke his head into a half-collapsed shack across the road.

'Dylan, stay out of there!' he shouted, his voice carrying across the empty street.

The boy turned, guilt smeared across his face, shuffling closer to them but gazing back at the shack. The childish temptation to explore was hard to resist. And it never truly left. Lorcan could attest to that. Moving out here was a chance for them all to explore. And renew.

* * *

Naiyana took the ute and left in a cloud of dust. He watched it fade into the cloud like a magic trick. He turned to instruct Dylan to help him with the well but his son was lying in the shade at the front of the shack swooping his Matchbox cars through the sand, flicking them off a ramp. Lorcan left him to it and returned to the well.

After thirty minutes, his sweaty shirt abandoned, he adjudged his progress. He was now four feet down, his hands choked further up the handle as the space became tighter, bucket after bucket of sand and dirt dumped over the side.

Another hour and he was seven feet down and unable to see over the rim. It should have provided him some solace from the heat but noon had brought the sun nearly directly overhead, peering in at him. Looking up, the entrance seemed to narrow, the walls tightening as if closing in. A flick of panic sent his heart rate sky-rocketing. Suddenly it occurred to him that he was standing in a hole, on top of a cap that was over a hundred years old, in the desert with only his six-year-old son around to help. This wasn't smart. 'About as smart as trying to lose weight by chopping off your arm', a phrase he had used many times to caution investors in his previous job. It was time to get out.

He clambered out of the well into the sun. He felt like a mole, squinting in the bright light. Dylan was standing by the well looking agitated. As if he had sensed his father's panic.

'Given up on stunt racing?' asked Lorcan, with a smile, riding the curious wave of joy at making it out alive. As if he had escaped death somehow.

'I seen someone,' said Dylan, his gaze fixed down the street in the direction of their house.

'Mum?'

'No.'

'Where?' asked Lorcan.

At this Dylan grabbed his hand and pulled. Urgent. Insistent. Lorcan let him lead, his son's short legs churning the sand.

'Dylan, this isn't one of your special friends, is it?' Lorcan recalled Bennie and Ixsell, the pair of characters that his son had invented previously. Apparently a lot of only children did the same. For company. They had disappeared a year ago and Lorcan had to admit he was glad when they had left. He didn't need his kid to be a fantasist. Not out here.

'No,' said Dylan, adamant.

Lorcan let his son lead them behind the shack that he had been poking his head into earlier. There lay a mound of dirt that had been excavated when levelling the ground. From the top, most of the town could be seen.

'Over there,' said Dylan, pointing.

Lorcan followed the finger. He looked for the ute and for Nee but neither seemed to be there. The town was empty.

'I don't see anything, Dyl.'

'It was there.'

47

'What was?'

'A person.'

Lorcan studied his son's face. He looked stressed, his eyes drawn and strained. The lack of sleep might have been somewhat at fault but there was nothing that indicated that he was lying. Or joking. There was no laughter in Dylan's expression. Besides, for a kid, a joke was only fun if there was an immediate pay-off.

'We can find them!' Dylan grabbed his wrist and tugged it.

Down the back of the hill they passed through the back of another property, parts of an ancient Hudson Eight rusting in the backyard, through to the main street. Lorcan was beginning to worry. As far as he knew Dylan had never been in this part of town. Not with him anyway. Maybe with Nee, but it was unlikely. She had shown no propensity as yet to explore town, happy to confine herself indoors.

They crossed the empty street and passed along the side of a house, the slatted wood of a collapsed fence underneath his feet.

Then he saw it.

And laughed.

In the distance and leaning up against an outhouse was an old coat-rack, some trapped tumbleweed wrapped around the top resembling a head. In the distant heat haze he could see how it would have fooled a six-year-old, looking like a man passing time, leaning against his shack. The 'hairy panic' had been quite literal.

'It's just a coat-rack, Dyl.'

Dylan shook his head. 'That's not him.'

But Lorcan had had enough. He didn't need a wild-goose chase. He had a well to dig out, plus a roof and generator to fix. And he was falling behind.

'No one's here.'

'But there was, Daddy.'

The tables turned and Lorcan began to drag his son. The argument continued as they reached the main street again. A rumble filled the air, this time accompanied by a swell of dust. Naiyana stopped, the bags of groceries balanced on the passenger's seat beside her.

'What are you both doing here?' she asked. 'I hope you aren't getting into any trouble.'

Lorcan shook his head wearily. 'Dyl thought he saw someone.'

'I did see someone,' he protested.

'Dylan, we've been over this.'

'But I did.'

Lorcan turned to his wife. 'Have you seen anyone around, Mummy?'

Naiyana looked at him and then her son. She looked sad to disappoint him. 'No, I haven't.'

'I did!'

Dylan broke free of his grasp and ran off towards their house.

'We don't need Bennie and Ixsell coming back,' said Naiyana.

'No, we don't,' agreed Lorcan. 'It was just heat haze. I haven't seen anyone.'

'No one else is stupid enough to be out here,' said Naiyana, the words as biting as the heat.

14

Lorcan

There was no doubting the rumble any longer. Dylan might have been imagining people in town but he wasn't imagining the noise. It growled like an angry dog buried deep in the earth. A warning, according to Nee, but she would have taken anything as a cue to leave. Lorcan wanted more than anything to believe that the noises were psychosomatic. But if they could all hear it, that was impossible.

Dylan shuffled noisily. He was awake again. Which meant they all were awake again.

'We need to consider moving back.'

There it was. Nee's thoughts made public. Fuelled by lack of sleep and exasperation.

'We talked about—'

'Can we move back, Daddy?' interjected Dylan. The hope in his face was unmissable. A chance to see his friends again. But friends could be made anywhere. Especially when you were young.

He glared at Nee for broadcasting her thoughts

publicly, before smiling at his son. 'Put your head-phones on and listen to some music.'

Dylan looked at him, paused, then nodded, the giant black headphones engulfing a significant portion of his head.

He refocused on Naiyana. 'What did you say to him?'

'I didn't say anything,' she replied. In much the same plaintive manner that Dylan had done earlier when insisting that he'd seen someone in town. A trait either learned or inherited from her.

'You must have.'

'He's not stupid. He understands that this isn't living.'

'It's survival for a little while, then we can live. We can become a family again. We were too disconnected in Perth. We were consumed by our jobs in the day, then Dylan in the evening, before trying to catch up on the work we missed looking after him.'

'So your cure is to force us together? In a ghost town we can't escape from? *That's* unnatural. Our whole presence here is unnatural. No one should be forced to live in the desert. The people who came out here all those years ago had to. They had to find gold to buy food. We have money.'

'We're also running though. Remember that.'

Lorcan left in the morning without exchanging a word with Naiyana. She could tinker with whatever she needed to in the house to keep her busy. He had work to do.

As he climbed into the ute he gazed over at his son. He had occupied a mound of piled earth to the side of the house and had brought all his vehicles to the party.

'What have you got there, Dyl?'

Dylan put the yellow dumper truck down on what looked like a road carved into the hill that led to the beginnings of a cave dug into the earth.

'A mine,' he said, obviously pleased with himself.

'Looks good.'

'I need another dump truck though. The digger has to wait until the first one goes and comes back before it can load again.'

Lorcan smiled. His son had developed an entire business, excavating clay from the hole and transporting it to the bottom. An impressive enterprise, hindered by a lack of equipment.

'Want me to see if I can get you another?' he asked, refusing to chide himself for attempting to buy his loyalty. Dylan's happiness was a key component of any long-term success out here.

'Yes!' said Dylan. 'And a crane if there is one. And a monster truck.'

'A monster truck?'

'Yes. To get home after work.' Stated as if it was the only and obvious answer.

Lorcan smiled and put on his sunglasses. 'I'll see what I can do.'

15

Lorcan

Though there was little danger of meeting anything coming the other way he stuck to the middle of the fissured track that wound towards the main road and then on to Hurton. The tyres crackled as they met the fractured edges as if driving over a massive sheet of bubble wrap. He reminded himself to pick up a spare tyre or two. He didn't want to have to trek to town across the scrub and there was no chance of hitching a ride. There was also no chance of the road being repaired and he wondered why the government had not just dug up the road when they were closing Kallayee down. Probably cheaper to let it rot, he suspected, as another deep scar tried to wrench the steering wheel from his hand.

Reaching the main road he turned towards Hurton. With the improvement in the surface and less chance of being pitched into the scenery, his thoughts drifted back to Naiyana and her pleas to leave. He couldn't let her poison their son against this before they had given it a real shot. It was verbal sabotage. Just when he was trying to fix things. He would prove that he was capable of creating a home for them out here.

There were only a few people on Main Street, but given the silence of daytime Kallayee it was like a bustling city. He pulled to the side of the road outside a place called Mallon and Son's Hardware, the sign above the double doors freshly painted and firmly attached to the red-brick building.

He expected a mom-and-pop store rather than a franchise. What he found was the focus of attention. The old attendant at the till – most likely Mallon – halted his conversation with a younger man – likely Son – his hand drifting under the counter. To reach for a weapon. Or for an alarm of some sort.

He was a stranger and strangers around here were noticed. He gave both men an obligatory nod and orientated himself. The store exceeded his expectations. It had everything he needed: tools, materials, screws, nails. Pulling his tablet from his pocket he flicked through to the page he wanted. Building a wall. He needed about a hundred bricks to be on the safe side, cement mix, club hammer, trowel, sand. He went to follow a link to another site offering advice but found the 'Device not connected to the Internet' page. Something he would have to get used to out here. Lack of coverage, lack of connectivity.

'Can I help?'

Lorcan glanced to his side. Son was standing close to him, his look one of curiosity rather than helpfulness.

In the background Mallon was monitoring progress from his perch behind the counter like an owl.

'I just need to pick up some bricks, cement and sand.'

'What is it that you're looking to do?'

'Repair a gable wall.'

'I see. Where?'

Lorcan paused. Why did that matter? He glanced at the counter. Mallon had his ear wedged to a landline phone but Lorcan couldn't hear what he was saying. His senses piqued. Were they going to jump him on the way out? Rob the out-of-towner? Did they think he had rolls of cash in his pockets?

'A place I have.'

'Not in town.'

'No, not in town,' confirmed Lorcan.

There was a momentary pause before Son shrugged, seeming to accept the conversation was headed down a blind alley. Lorcan breathed a sigh of relief. He had expected more of an interrogation. Son pointed at the tablet. Lorcan wondered if he had ever seen one before.

'You want the password?'

'You have Internet?' asked Lorcan.

A frown crossed Son's previously unconcerned face. 'Hurton's remote, man, not ancient,' he said, taking the tablet and dashing a number into the settings before passing it back. 'For customers only, mind.'

'Customers only,' repeated Lorcan before refocusing on what he needed.

16

Emmaline

It could have been mistaken for a rock poking through the dust.

As they waited on Forensics to arrive – ETA was an hour – the four officers scoured the area near the patch of blood. The priority was locating a weapon. That's when Emmaline had reached out for the sand-covered rock only to find that it was metallic and almost perfectly rectangular.

A phone.

Holding it with her thumb and forefinger only, she pressed the button on the side of the Samsung. The screen lit up asking for a swipe code. There was no signal and the battery read ten per cent. This meant that it had been on the ground long enough to have been camouflaged with a dusting of sand but not so long for the battery to have run completely out of charge. Maybe a week ago and clearly dropped in a hurry.

The other officers stood around her, staring at the phone.

'Check it for prints?' asked Barker.

'Do you have a kit with you?'

'I have an older kit for latents,' said Anand, making for the police-marked 4x4 he had arrived in.

While they waited, Emmaline aimed the phone towards the sun, studying the screen.

'Put an evidence bag on that,' she said, pointing to a large, flat-topped rock. Rispoli followed orders and placed the bag on the rock. Emmaline placed the phone on top of the bag.

'I think I know whose phone this is.'

'How?' asked Rispoli and Barker in conjunction.

'The repeat pattern on the main screen. The grease and sweat from the owner's fingers as they unlock it. Over and over again. Pressing too hard. Instinct or anger. Reinforcing the pattern. An L.'

'For Lorcan,' said Rispoli.

Emmaline nodded as she lightly swiped an 'L' pattern on the access screen. The screen altered to a photo of Naiyana and Dylan Maguire, the mother swinging the child by the arms, both of them happy. A photo taken from the Kaarta Gar-up lookout, high on Kings Park, Perth CBD visible in the background.

Amongst the text messages there were a few Lorcan had sent to his family before Christmas, confirming that they were okay and trying to settle in. Nothing about the state of the house, just updates about the family. There were a few calls from anonymous numbers that would have to be checked but zero in the last seven days. Amongst the videos there were a number detailing the family's previous existence in Perth, at their old home, a fancy detached house that diametrically contrasted the hovel they had lived in before their disappearance. Videos of the family on the beach and on holiday. More recent ones had Lorcan Maguire exhibiting the house explaining what he was going to do with it, from putting in windows to painting, plus a couple focusing on repairing the gable wall and roof. Clearly an attempt to catalogue building a life from scratch. Another YouTube generation family, happy and smiling on the outside but striving for a dream that was built on unsafe foundations. Especially given the territory. The videos were part of the con, dreams narrated to obscure the reality.

The documents folder contained a bevy of saved Internet pages and downloaded How To manuals but it was amongst the voice recordings that she found the most important clue. The last thing recorded on the device. A garbled incoherent message, the voice male – probably Lorcan's. There was real terror in his tone, his sentences clipped, his breathing short and sharp.

'We have to leave, Dylan. Before they come back.'

In the background there was a fainter voice, that of a child crying and resisting. Dylan.

'We'll go to town. Quick!'

'Where's mummy?' asked the fainter voice.

'She's gone.'

After that was silence. Until the recording cut out.

The deathly hush of the town was unnerving. As if in mourning for Lorcan and Dylan's lives.

Emmaline looked at the others gathered around her. Their expressions suggested they were almost too scared to break the continued silence but, like her, analysing what they had heard. Like, who was the 'they' Lorcan had mentioned, and what did he mean when he had said that Naiyana was 'gone'? Did he mean taken? Or killed? When was it recorded and why had it cut out? And finally, who were they running from?

What wasn't in doubt, with this recording and the quantities of blood, was that this almost certainly was a major crime.

Anand returned with the fingerprint kit only to be greeted with silence.

'I wasn't gone that long,' he protested.

'Copy that recording and everything from the phone for me,' she said to Barker. 'Ask Forensics to retrieve any relevant fingerprints from it. Then get the data to our Tech team. See if we can build a timeline.'

17

Emmaline

The sun was going down fast, racing for the horizon as if fleeing in shame. Or maybe it had an engagement later. Emmaline would have liked one too. Something quick and meaningless. No pressure, no commitment. Open-ended. There was something liberating about open-endedness. Especially in a profession where the pressure was always on to tie up everything.

Forensics had been and gone in two hours. Efficient. Dr Rebecca Patel's forte. Conversation was strictly for discussing facts. And without the test results she didn't have any yet.

Anand and Barker were driving the couple of hours back to their families in Leonora. Rispoli was heading in the same direction.

'Need a lift?' he asked.

Emmaline looked at the Maguire house in front of her. She had nowhere booked in Leonora and no real reason to go there. Apart from Rispoli. Handsome, tall and distinguished. With a hint of charm. An honesty too in his eyes. But although a hook-up sounded good, it was not smart. She had few rules but one was – almost – sacred: never on the first day.

'I'll stay here.'

'In Hurton? They've what they call a B&B, but it's more a storage shed out the back of Miller's place, the painter and decorator.'

'No, here. I'll kip in the car.'

'You can't.'

'I've had worse.'

Emmaline wanted to stay. They had the phone and the panicked message but no bodies, no evidence of foul play other than the blood. She felt drawn to stay.

Rispoli glanced at his feet, then met her eyes again. 'Give me an hour. I'll see what I can do.'

With that he hopped in his car and drove off, the dust rising to meet the rapidly darkening sky. Emmaline was alone. She was used to being alone. Others weren't, trying to scare her that some imaginary clock was ticking down on her chance to have a child. She wasn't even in her thirties and yet all her aunts and uncles were waiting for 'the good news' at the beginning of every phone call. As if her becoming a detective in the MCS wasn't good news. But for her relatives, the MCS was merely a precursor to her real job. Not to say there hadn't been times when she had found herself alone at night looking into sperm donors and IVF and wondering if she could go it alone with a child. Given her previous relationships she might be better off going it alone. She needed a man to accept her. Who knew when to be close and also when to be distant. It was a tricky balance. Just like any baby she might one day conceive, she needed any long-term partner customized a little, not too much, just the edges rounded so that they didn't grate on each other too much like a pair of tectonic plates. Not that there were too many of those around Australia. The earth didn't move much around here. Which only got her thinking about sex again. And abandoning her rule of not sleeping with someone on the first day. If Rispoli ever returned. If he didn't she would have to consider setting up house out here like the Maguire's had.

In the end, he returned after an hour and a half, dragging a caravan that Emmaline was amazed had survived the haul. He parked it in a free space a few plots away from the Maguire house.

He exited with a smile. 'It's not the Ritz.'

Emmaline walked around the outside. It didn't take long. There was room for one. Two at a squeeze.

'Are we sharing?' she asked, her instincts overruling common sense. A few hours and it would be midnight, so technically the second day. A loophole she had exploited before.

'Do you want me to?'

She caught his eyes, dark like hers but with a hint of warming hazel. They held her stare. Long enough for common sense to regain control.

'Let's raincheck that. Once we find them.'

He smiled. 'As an incentive.'

Emmaline smiled back. He knew how to play the

game. It was better when they knew how to play the game.

With a wave and unhurried exit, in case either of them changed their mind, Rispoli left.

Taking a last look around, she entered the caravan. The revolting aroma of cigarettes hit her instantly, like the air itself had turned sour. That a smoker had lived there was further evidenced by the unnatural yellow of the roof and piss-coloured tinge to the cushion fabric. Emmaline cracked open the window – two inches before it caught on the latch – and settled on the narrow couch that encircled a chipped MDF table.

The caravan was stocked with a kettle, coffee and some packets of dry noodles. Enough for tonight at least. It's what had taken Rispoli the extra half-hour, she supposed. She smiled. She could add thoughtful to the positives. He was putting forward a strong case. After making some chicken noodles that tasted like warm cardboard but filled her stomach, she settled in to read the file of documents on the Maguire family that she hadn't got to on the plane.

Lorcan Maguire was up first. Perth born and bred. His most recent job was with a company called INK Tech which offered financial advice, investments, stock options, as well as a sideline in buying up companies in financial difficulties and asset-stripping them. Employed for eight years with a couple of promotions. And then suddenly, last month, he'd been made redundant. Streamlining. A disappointing tale but all too familiar. He had apparently received a reasonable redundancy payout. Which, she assumed, he was using to finance this move and the house repairs.

But there was something else. An add-on to the story. After he had left, a glut of information had been reported as missing from INK Tech's system. Suspicion had been raised that Lorcan had taken the information to sell to a rival. Or to blackmail the company. A court case regarding criminal misconduct had loomed briefly but was dropped as it couldn't be proved that he did it or that he did it maliciously.

Something else caught Emmaline's eyes. The owners of INK Tech. Georgios and Nikos Iannis. Well-known in Perth circles. Both with a chequered past. Criminal records for fraud and extortion. They had used jail terms to gain qualifications in finance and cleaned up their act. But there was always a little dirt under the mudguard. Prison had made them smart. Emmaline wondered if it had removed their propensity for violence.

18

Naiyana

The house was done. Or at least she had done everything she could. *You can't polish a turd*, she thought to herself, as she took a walk. Through *her* town, a thought which filled her with a strangely uplifting sense of importance. A broken kingdom was still a kingdom after all.

She would walk and vlog. If Lorcan could write a book maybe she could vlog about life in town. At least fucking YouTube wouldn't bow to some sweaty bastard in a suit stuffing dollars in its G-string and get her channel shut down like the test centres ones. Those had been genius. Well planned, perfectly executed. But illegal.

There was only one problem. Dylan, tagging along, pausing every few seconds to investigate something. And constantly talking over her monologues.

'Mum, Mum, film me!'

The tug on her arm distorted the camera shot.

'Dylan, not now,' she berated him.

'When?'

'Later.'

'You said that five minutes ago. I want to be in it.'

Naiyana wasn't having it. She was still unsure over showing her own face in them. In case it was seen by the wrong people. People who might want to harm her. Words were powerful and all she had. One hundred and ten pounds with arms like matchsticks does not a fighter make.

Her words and looks had won Lorcan over. Though handsome, a good earner and a good father she always wondered if she had sold herself short. When she had first met him she had been a touch broken-hearted. And fried-out from the non-stop social justice campaigning and the many protests across the state and further wide. Each battle like a war. And though her wounds couldn't be seen they were there. She was weakened. He was a solid and undemanding choice.

Then motherhood took over, creating a bubble she found it hard to escape from. More love-stuck than love-struck. Then a couple of years ago she had bumped into a former colleague and now campaign head who had asked her to get involved again. Only this time, she had something tangible and personal to fight for. Her child. And herself. She desired real change. Having Dylan had instilled in her the sense that she could do anything. She could create life so what could stop her? But there was one thing she had lost from her teenage firebrand years. The stop button. The tap could be turned on but not off. This unrelenting forcefulness made her popular in the community. A driving force. But she had taken it too far. Marches and protests were fine but she needed more. She demanded infiltrations and graffiti. Politics and smearing. Which led her to become a pariah, although she thought of herself more as a martyr, for she had been right. But it had hurt people.

She aimed the phone down the street. The road arrowed perfectly straight almost all the way to the horizon where it twisted off deeper into the outback, towards Orange Lake and after that, she had no idea. And had no intention of finding out.

The emptiness seemed a fitting end to a first chapter. She would upload it when she got to Hurton tomorrow. Squeezing her eyes tight and opening them she let them readjust to the real world, brighter than the screen, the colours sharper and more intense than the digitized version. The realization that she actually was here, and not viewing this barren town on a computer screen back in civilization, hit her with a thud of sadness. She would be back amongst the living some-time soon, she promised herself. But right now it was time for dinner. She glanced around. Dylan was nowhere to be seen.

'Dylan?' she called out.

There was no answer. Not even an echo, nothing of significance for the sound waves to bounce off. There was nothing for miles.

She swivelled around to look towards the cross-roads. She searched for a speck of movement amongst the disused buildings. Nothing. Sliding the phone into the pocket of her shorts she called out again. More urgently this time, trying to muster concern more than anger. And failing.

'Dylan, get out here now!'

Again there was no response.

Moving to the nearest house, a wooden bungalow that was missing one entire side wall, she peeked inside.

'Dylan?' she called out again, only to be met with silence.

It was the same in the next broken shack.

'This isn't funny, Dylan.' Concern had now turned into a deep, hollow worry that echoed inside her.

She looked at the doghouse that adjoined the shack. It was still standing, better constructed than the shattered dwelling it was attached to. She didn't think Dylan would have crawled into it but he could have. So she checked, squeezing her head inside and nearly vomiting with the musty smell of hot, stale air and straw bedding that had turned to dust.

She stood up fast, squeezing her eyes shut, this time to fight the dizziness. Her legs and arms felt numb.

'Get out here now, Dylan!' Anger had turned to fear. This was a game of hide and seek she was not enjoying. Hide and seek was tolerable only in a safe and controlled environment. Where she knew every place Dylan could hide and she could delay the search to sneak another sip of wine.

She passed on to the next building, her cries for Dylan growing more frantic. Her desperation was building as was her hatred of this town. There was something else too. The sense that there were eyes on her. Watching her every move. And taken her son.

Moving back to the middle of the street, she looked around again. But there was nothing. Nobody and nothing. But she knew there was. She could feel it. There was something here with them. In Kallayee.

Her veins froze and her muscles seized. Maybe Dylan had been right. Maybe he had really seen someone in town. Suddenly it felt as if each grain of sand was an eye watching her, looking, judging. A million eyes. A million judgements. She took a breath, the fiery air choking her lungs. Was she going crazy? Was there something creeping up from below the ground, a toxic gas from some long-forgotten mine that silently blanketed the town? She had read about that sort of thing before. Carbon dioxide or monoxide. Or maybe that was a hallucination as well. Maybe they were all slowly going crazy.

Or maybe they were being haunted by the ghosts of the people who had once lived there. The collapsed mine. The twenty dead miners. A shiver ran down her back at the thought, enough to loosen her muscles. Taking another breath she chided herself for getting caught up in paranormal nonsense. Dylan was here. Somewhere. It was just her and him. In this town.

19

Emmaline

It was too dark to explore a town that was filled with dilapidated houses on the brink of collapse. And it was too early to sleep, so Emmaline drove to Hurton, careful to avoid running off the road. That was another angle to consider. That the family had simply driven off the road and been killed. Or maimed. Or trapped. Sending up some eagle eyes might be the way to go. A light plane out of Leonora or Kalgoorlie. Something for her to follow up on tomorrow.

There was only one place open in town. A pub that had seen better days, the brick crumbling and one of the porch lights flickering like a drunk passing in and out of consciousness, but better than nothing.

All eyes fell upon her as she entered. She recognized the stares, a mix of curiosity, lust and suspicion, all in equal measure.

She took a seat on a stool that squeaked under her as if protesting the disruption to its evening of quiet inaction. At the far end of the bar, two men in baseball caps sat on similar red-topped stools, while a third stood between them. Their conversation had paused in favour of visually undressing her. There were further mumblings from the booths beyond but it was too dark to see into them.

The barman left his perch along the back counter and stepped forward to meet her. His eyes betrayed the same suspicion, his eyelid half-closed on one side. His mouth slightly drooped too. On the same side. Bell's palsy. Not severe but noticeable close up.

'Got any vodka?'

'Yep.'

'Good vodka?'

'It all does the same job.'

Emmaline smiled. 'A double. Dash of pineapple juice. And ice.'

As she waited for her drink she awaited the questions. There were always questions for a young, attractive, single woman in a pub. What was up for grabs was whether they would be inquisitive or intrusive.

'Where are you from?'

It was the guy standing up between his friends who broke the ice.

'Out of town,' said Emmaline meeting his narrowed eyes.

'Out of country, more like,' said the guy, bathing in his friends' laughter.

Emmaline met the comment head-on as her drink arrived. Lacking a straw she stirred it with her finger as she replied. 'Nope, Australian. What's your excuse?'

'Excuse for what?' asked the guy, confused, a look on his face as if wondering whether he had left the gas on at home.

'For that dumb look on your face. And that haircut. Was your mum drunk when she did it? Or just angry that you didn't pull out when you promised?'

The guy's friends exploded in laughter, one spitting out his beer over the bar, the cascade just missing the barman.

Emmaline swivelled on her stool and waited for the guy to charge over. He was tall but skinny. Manageable. She had studied a number of forms of self-defence. It was only smart to in her job. Sometimes she had to ask questions that riled people. Sometimes she just liked asking questions that riled people.

But the guy was being held back by his still chuckling friends, seething but subdued by the offer of another beer. They were dropkicks, neither smart nor gonna make it very far. She turned her attention to her reason for being here.

'Any of you know the Maguire family?'

The question was met with murmurs that suggested knowledge but no outright response. Interesting but not incriminating.

Emmaline was used to being treated with suspicion. Because she was a cop or because of her skin colour. Some even considered it a kind of novelty. As if they were surprised she was able to do the job.

'You can't find them?' came an anonymous voice from a side booth.

'I have news for them,' said Emmaline, wanting to avoid disclosing the circumstances. News of the disappearance didn't need to be broadcast yet. There were formal channels for that.

'So are you a postwoman or a cop?' said one of the three from the end of the bar. One of the seated ones. As ugly as his mate, features bent out of shape.

'Right now I'm tired and pissed off. They lived out in Kallayee.'

Met with more murmurs but nothing substantial, she returned to her drink, the vodka cheap and nasty as was the pineapple juice. Enough to get the job done. But she wouldn't drink too much. She had the guys at the end of the bar to keep an eye on.

As she nursed the dregs and weighed up having a second against the perilous drive home, she felt a presence beside her. She turned around to find a guy with a pair of sparkling blue eyes that contrasted a worn, tanned face that made him look older than he was. Outdoor work maybe. A farmhand. A high-wire guy maintaining the electricity lines. A painter–decorator. Possibly Miller who owned the shitty B&B Rispoli mentioned.

'*Are* you a cop?'

Emmaline paused. She didn't detect any accusation or bitterness in the question. She nodded.

'Haven't seen you before,' he said.

'Do you get many cops calling with you?' she asked.

'That would be telling. Another?' he asked, tilting his head towards her nearly empty glass.

Emmaline shook her head. Half an hour and she'd attempt the drive home. 'You go right ahead, though.'

He did. He was handed a foamy beer that threatened the lip but stayed in the glass. He nodded at the seat. 'Mind if I?'

Emmaline waved her hand in invite, overhearing some protests from the far end of the bar. But those three had lost their right to speak to her. Informally. Formally she retained the right to speak to all of them anytime she liked.

'The name's Matthew. Or Matty if you want.'

Emmaline took the offered hand. It was calloused and meaty. She squeezed it to show she wasn't intimidated.

'Emmaline.'

'Nice name. Unusual.'

'Unusual to have a nice name?' she asked.

'Unusual to hear it.' Matty sipped his beer. 'Do you always try to wind people up?' he asked, nodding to the far end of the bar.

'Only if I'm bored. Or fucked with.'

Matty smiled. 'I'll try and do neither then.'

'Then we might just get along,' said Emmaline.

'What brings you here?' he asked, taking another sip.

'The Maguires. Do you know them?'

'Not as such. I saw them around town. Heard some things.'

'What kind of things?'

'Usual small town stuff. Gossiping. Speculating. The

father came in to buy materials at Spider Mallon's place.'

'Often?'

'Every couple of days. Maybe just to get away from there. To not go mad, you know? Like cabin fever.'

'Does that happen a lot out here?'

'Been known to,' said Matty with a knowing nod.

'What was he like?'

'I only spoke to him once. He seemed guarded, I suppose, but you would be if you didn't know anyone. He just came in to do business and got out. He was always glancing over his shoulder though, as if he thought he was being watched.'

'What did the wife and kid do when he was getting the materials?'

'That was the odd thing,' said Matty. 'You never saw them together. It would either be him or her in town. Her less often. And only to buy groceries.'

'How often?'

'Only a couple of times.'

'So she bought in bulk?'

'You'd have to ask Darcey at the store. But I doubt it. You don't keep nothing in bulk around here. Except the golden stuff,' he said, raising his half-empty glass.

Emmaline wondered about the grocery shopping. Maybe Naiyana Maguire drove further afield to get supplies. To Leonora or Wisbech perhaps. To pick up specific items, stuff to make them feel at home.

'And the boy?'

'Sometimes he was with them, sometimes not.'

'Any sign of trouble? Aggro?'

Matty laughed. 'Like what? They didn't spend every living minute together so maybe they argued, maybe they didn't. Or maybe they didn't have to live in each other's back pocket.'

He was of course right. Most trouble wasn't an explosion. It was devious and cunning, bubbling slowly underneath the surface before revealing itself in all its destructive glory. Like a volcano.

'Did you spot anyone else new in town?'

'What? Apart from you?'

Emmaline smiled and looked to the end of the bar. The three guys were whispering amongst themselves. Her senses warned her that they were planning something.

'I'm sure this town is no stranger to police,' she said.

Matty tilted his head and pursed his lips suggesting that she was correct in that assumption.

'You seen anyone new, Bill?' asked Matty.

The barman answered without moving from the back counter, surveying his domain. 'Some tourists, some farmhands. One insurance salesman. And one guy who was lost. All dressed up for an interview. He'd gotten Kallayee and Kalgoorlie mixed up. Poor bastard.'

Matty and Bill shared a laugh. But Emmaline had another question. 'Did anyone pay the Maguires a visit? A getting-to-know-the-neighbours deal?'

'Nothing I've heard,' said Matty.

Emmaline glanced at Bill. His face was impassive, helped by the frozen nerves on one side of it.

'But that's not to say that someone couldn't have,' continued Matty as he made his excuses to go to the dunny. As he went to leave, Emmaline stared at his face, drawn again to his cool, blue eyes. His most redeeming feature. They exhibited a coldness, however, that suggested he might have been capable of meeting and threatening the family. But of shamefacedly bragging to the cops about it? Hard to tell. She couldn't discount the possibility that someone in town had something to do with the family's disappearance. But what would they have done with them? Kidnap them? Kill them?

A few punters started to file out of the pub behind her. Towards home she surmised as she doubted there was a nightclub worth its salt within a hundred kilometre radius.

As she kept her eye on the three men stubbornly hovering at the end of the bar there was a tap on her shoulder. The woman was in her sixties, with dishevelled grey hair. Her face beamed, her kindly demeanour supported by a night on the sauce.

'You got a picture of them?' she asked.

'The family?'

'Yeah, love.'

Emmaline pulled out her phone and brought up a picture. The three of them together, in a semi-formal pose. Dressed smartly but relaxed. Donated by Lorcan's family.

She tapped the phone with one wavering finger. 'I've seen him.'

Emmaline perked up. 'The father? Where? When?'

'Before New Year. Last Tuesday, I think.'

'The twenty-eighth?'

'Yeah, love. In Wisbech.'

'Wisbech? What was he doing?'

The silver-haired woman shrugged. 'Talking to someone.'

Emmaline scrolled through the photos and found one of Lorcan's entire family. 'Any of these people?'

The woman studied the photo closely, tongue poking through her lips in concentration. She shook her head. 'I only saw the back of his head. Black hair. Neatly cut.'

'Nothing else?'

She shook her head. 'I only saw his face,' she said, pointing at Lorcan. 'But I recognized him from town. From Mallon's. The hardware place.'

With that she left, aiming for the door and barely making it through. Given her state of inebriation she wasn't an entirely reliable witness statement but it was something. Who had Lorcan Maguire been meeting in Wisbech last Tuesday? Not his family, so a friend? Or someone from INK Tech? Matty had said that he seemed defensive, always checking over his shoulder. Did they follow him back to Kallayee? Was this the cause of the panicked recording on the phone?

Her thoughts were interrupted by Matty's return

but her mind remained abuzz. She was suddenly desperate to reread the files, convinced she had missed something.

'I have to head back,' she said to Matty.

His raised eyebrows intimated that he had another suggestion. 'You can stay at mine. I'm right around the corner.'

Emmaline smiled. Dismissed any flicker of temptation. She instigated her rule. 'Not tonight.'

Matty grinned. 'But another night?'

Finding her car keys in her pocket, Emmaline said, 'Who knows? I could be around for a while. Until I talk to the Maguires anyway.'

She glanced at the three dropkicks at the end of the bar looking for a reaction. Failing to get one, she headed for the door.

'Here's my number,' said Matty, passing her a thin matchbook, the name and number of the pub written in green on a grey background. Basic.

Emmaline looked inside. There was only a sliver of six grey-topped matches inside. 'There's no number.'

Matty took another sip and smiled. 'Just call the pub. I'm usually here.'

Emmaline smiled and slipped the book into her pocket.

20

Naiyana

Naiyana searched from building to building, calling out for her son but finding the loneliest reply of all. Silence.

Desperation crept in. She checked her phone. Out of habit. She knew she had no signal to call Lorcan or the police.

Leaving one building, she caught a flash of something up ahead. Possibly a figure, possibly not. Ignoring the voices that warned her against following the mysterious figure, she did, stumbling over broken fences and rubble buried in the dirt.

Reaching the house, the figure had disappeared from sight, so she followed her instinct on where it had gone. Where Dylan had gone.

She kept calling out. Still Dylan didn't return her pleas. He was punishing her and maybe she deserved it. She had been ignoring him while she played on her phone and now it was his turn for a game. A cruel game.

It was only a shortness of breath that made her

pause, leaning on a fence that bent under her weight but resisted just enough to support her. She looked around again. The entire town seemed to be holding its breath, waiting for her next move, as if playing hide and seek too.

Squeezing her eyes shut she tried to block everything out. She took a deep, arid breath that almost choked her. It rebooted her senses. She flashed open her eyes. There had been no figure. And even if there was, it wasn't Dylan. A six-year-old boy couldn't outrun her.

Sucking in more air she decided to return to the house. Hopefully Lorcan had returned. They could search together. Plan and search. She felt so desperate she didn't even care that she needed Lorcan. She was independent and strong but fear was fear. And fear was selfish. It was always better to wade through deep shit with a partner in tow.

Back at the house, there was no sign of their white Toyota. She fought the crush of disappointment as she stepped inside the front door. She pondered her next move. Walking across the scrub to Hurton to get a signal seemed like folly. But viable folly. Proactive folly.

Her thoughts were interrupted by the noise. Not the low rumbling that plagued them at night but something else. A rustling. Like an animal hunting for food. It was coming from inside the house. Maybe the figure in town was real. Not human but animal. Coming from the bedrooms. An insistent growl, angry or hungry. She grabbed a knife from the kitchen. To defend herself. To attack.

She crept down the hallway trying to keep quiet but the old floorboards made it impossible. The noise had switched from rustling growl to a squeak. A litany of all the savage animals it might be flashed through her head, but none of them squeaked. What squeaked in the desert?

Easing open their bedroom door she could immediately see that it was empty, the beds still a mess from this morning, the evening sun poking through the simple wooden shutters that Lorcan had erected to keep the light out.

There was one room left. As she approached Dylan's door she prepared herself for anything. Four legs, two legs, hairy, scaly, wild.

She pushed the door open. What she found made her drop the knife, narrowly missing her foot as it embedded in the floorboards. Dylan was in bed, his eyes closed but thrashing around as if in the midst of a nightmare, the bed squeaking in pain as his weight shifted across the worn springs.

Naiyana sat on the edge of it and touched his forehead. He wasn't feverish at least. Just a tired boy catching up on the sleep he wasn't getting at night. She sat there until the darkness swamped them both, quick and oppressive. Lorcan still wasn't back. Her sense of apprehension switched from her son to her husband. Where was he?

21

Lorcan

He hadn't lasted long in the pub. The stares and the whispers that swirled around the musty air were too much. A few galoots had asked outright who he was and what he was doing but he had ignored them. An older woman with silver hair had even attempted to chat him up but it had all seemed like one big joke being played at his expense. So he had bought himself a few tinnies and found a remote spot between Kallayee and Hurton to drink them in peace, the ute looking out over a deep gorge, something he wanted to come out and explore in the full light of day.

As he chucked another empty into the scrub, his thoughts turned to his life and what he – they – were doing here. He had hoped it would bring them all together. Striving for a common goal. A surfeit of space and freedom without the unrelenting pressure of work. But as far as he had run, it was still on his mind. What he had done. Whether it had been right. Whether it had been necessary. It had burnt a lot of bridges and brought a lot of heat. He had torn up his career for the sake of some petty revenge. Destroying companies seemed ingrained in the family DNA, like one giant succubus, feeding off despair.

They would be looking for him. They had previous in hunting people down which he had only learned at the tribunal. These were not people to mess with. Crooks. Violent crooks. But what was done was done. No turning back. No contact. But that was a fallacy. There was always contact. While they still had their mobile phones there would always be contact. Earlier today, while in Hurton, Phil had texted that he wanted to come see him. What Lorcan wondered was why? As a concerned colleague? Out of curiosity? Or an ulterior motive? It was a long way to come for a catch-up. He believed he knew why Phil wanted to meet. To find out if he had the information. Or if he was selling it.

22

Naiyana

She eventually fell asleep beside Dylan, her unease over her husband's whereabouts defeated by exhaustion. It didn't last long. The all too familiar rumble returned like a woodpecker chipping at her skull. But this time it seemed different. The sound was not coming from deep inside the earth but through the air. The chug of an engine. Faint but definitely not her imagination at play. Lorcan was back. She felt relief but also anger. Where had he been? How dare he leave them out here alone for so long? The questions replaced the woodpecker by tapping at her brain. She waited for the engine to draw closer, followed by the creak of furtive footsteps in the hallway. But the sound didn't get any closer. In fact, it disappeared.

Now she was wide awake. With Dylan sound asleep she ventured outside. The air had a chill but remained temperate. She found no sign of Lorcan or the ute.

But she was sure she had heard it. Using the light from the gibbous moon overhead she walked towards the crossroads, only the whisper of the wind in the air and the crackle of sand underneath her sandals accompanying her. She felt a strange peacefulness out here alone, looking for her husband as if looking for love once again.

As she approached the crossroads the peacefulness began to wane. What if it wasn't Lorcan but someone else?

Maybe they could help her find Lorcan.

Or maybe they wouldn't. She was out here all alone. Defenceless.

Reaching the crossroads she contemplated if she wanted to find the source of the noise or if it was best to conclude she was crazy. Crazy but alone. It was a close call. She had an aunt in Geelong who had been committed to an asylum, so madness may run in the family, if that kind of shit was hereditary.

She looked up and down the dirt thoroughfares leading from the crossroads but there was no movement and no noise. Her only company was the kangaroo skeleton. But even it had a role. As a local landmark. Her role was less clear. Mother, yes. Wife, sometimes. Cleaner, no thanks. Was this a sign that she needed to go back to Perth? Rediscover her purpose? At least there she had the Internet to fall back on for answers. Out here she was crippled into ignorance and isolation.

Her thoughts were disturbed by the familiar rumbling. The mysterious noise that was knocking Dylan – and all three of them, really – out of sorts. She wanted to return to the house and Dylan and bed but she needed answers. It was time to solve this mystery. Ignorance was not a state she enjoyed. Orientating herself towards the sound she made for a tin and brick dwelling by the side of the road.

23

Emmaline

The drive back had been precarious, with only a faint crescent moon to guide her.

And there wasn't much to come back to, just a dour, empty caravan that seemed to reek even more, as if the previous tenant had snuck in after she'd left and helped themselves to a pack of twenty.

She regretted not asking Matty back. All that awaited her here was work. Fun, but not FUN.

While she had been in the pub a couple more files had arrived on her phone from HQ. Four YouTube vlogs posted by Naiyana Maguire under the username NeeM999. The report also noted a further one hundred and twenty-three relating to previous campaigns Naiyana had been a part of. They had all been banned and taken down. Emmaline would get to them another time. What happened while Naiyana was in Kallayee was her focus right now.

Rather than concentrate on house repairs like Lorcan's amateur videos, they focused on the struggles of moving there. The first two were narrated only, but by the third she was on-screen. They had been given the title: *Outback Motherhood*. They were styled as a raw account but managed with an experienced and skilful touch, hiding the full story, the pep in her voice betrayed by a tiredness around her eyes that make-up couldn't hide completely. Trying to force the narrative.

The vlogs were mementos of the family's life there. Shots of the town, colourful skylines and abandoned shacks to go along with a commentary on the hardships, before in the third video Dylan made an appearance, playing with his toy trucks on a mound of dirt, not acknowledging the camera, his face unseen.

At the end of the same video, Lorcan could be heard, telling Naiyana to put the phone down and help him with something, irritation in his voice and in her answer. It hadn't been edited out of the otherwise professional vlog, possibly on purpose. It gave a sense that all was not well, that nerves were frayed, mother and father – and even Dylan – perhaps withdrawing from each other.

In the final video, a more honest piece about the lack of showers and tips on how to wash using a bucket and cloth, the video captured a rising brown swirl in the background. A small dust devil, which would have been the most interesting thing in the wide shot but Emmaline had spotted something else. She paused the video and squinted at the screen. The paused shot showed a scene of the house for the first time, Lorcan on the roof hard at work laying bricks.

But behind it all, deep in the background there was something else. A figure in the distance spying from around the side of a house, the dark shape of a head and shoulders that when she carried on the vlog slid around the corner and disappeared again. Rewinding and playing it again only made her more certain. Someone was there. Not Lorcan, and not Naiyana who was capturing it all on her phone. It might have been Dylan checking out the town, let loose by his parents. She had no one left to confirm it with. That was the problem.

24

Emmaline

The figure in the vlog and the question of who Lorcan Maguire might have met in Wisbech plagued Emmaline the whole night, her sleep intermittent before the yearning for answers forced her to drag the thin curtains open and let the morning light flood in.

She ordered Barker, Rispoli and Anand back in to search the town. There was something here that would explain the disappearance, she was sure of it. The ground couldn't just have opened up and swallowed the family despite the many mines and the history. She wanted every inch searched.

So they returned to exploring buildings, slowed down only by the need to check that the structures wouldn't fall on their heads. This was still Barker's number one bet on what had happened to the family, even though from the videos Emmaline thought it unlikely that they had been big into group activities.

Once again she teamed up with Rispoli. Their first date had been scouring abandoned buildings, so why not repeat it on the second.

Near the crossroads came the first building of interest. A tin and brick structure when it had been intact but the front wall had given out, the remaining walls unable to support the roof which lay at an angle, the rear desperately clawing the wall, the front biting into the dirt.

'Over here,' she called to Rispoli.

'What is it?'

'I want to check under this building.'

'Why? It's collapsed.'

'Yeah, I think it collapsed recently.'

'What makes you so sure?'

'It isn't covered in dust like it would be if it had been in this position for a long time.'

'Maybe a gust of wind swept it clean.'

'Maybe.' Emmaline worried that although the family might not have been into group activities, they might have just got unlucky. Calling the other two over, Rispoli and Anand each grabbed the front of the tin roof and lifted it, jackets wrapped around their hands to counter the sizzling heat and sharp edges of the exposed metal. It came up intact. But barely.

Sliding onto her stomach, she peered under. Dark. And dusty. Lacking the unmistakable stench of decaying flesh. A positive sign.

'You sure you want to go under there?' asked Barker, perched on one knee beside her.

'Not sure at all,' said Emmaline. 'But I have to.'

Reaching out she started to claw her way under, pushing chunks of destroyed brick and stone out of the way. As the light diminished the temperature rose. Thirty to a hundred in a second. It was like crawling into an oven.

'I hope you've got your tetanus shots,' shouted Barker after her. Helpful as ever.

Emmaline slid a little further in, moving as fast as she could. She didn't want to be under here any longer than needed. No one had called out for help when it had been lifted and the air held no indication of death. She didn't want to be the first to cause either.

'Have you still got it?' she asked, choking in the dust.

'We're good,' said Rispoli, his voice strained. It didn't fill her with confidence.

With the roof angle and the space closing in, she got flat onto her stomach, dragging herself over an old, bone dry wooden stanchion that tore at her blouse as if trying to stop her from venturing any further.

From behind, Barker ordered her to hurry, backed by muted grunts from Rispoli and Anand, the tin oscillating above her now, brushing the crown of her head.

She had crawled to the middle of the building now. Her eyes scanned the darkness and she reached out for the brush of clothes, flesh, anything. She found nothing.

'I'm coming out,' she announced, backing up rapidly, her head scraping the rusted tin, tasting the flakes of oxidized metal in her mouth. An awkward and hasty retreat back into the light.

The instant she was clear, Rispoli and Anand,

supported by Barker, dropped the sheet roof with a crash, turning away from the cloud of dust.

'Anything?' asked Barker, flexing his arms, his hands a fiery red.

Emmaline shook her head, enduring a mixture of relief and disappointment. The family had not been crushed by the collapsing building. But they were still missing.

The search resumed. A couple of plots along from the collapsed house, Emmaline pushed a piece of sheet metal aside and entered another crumbling building. There the inner wall had partly collapsed turning the ground floor into a single room. There was no furniture inside. No bodies either, but she could see that it had been one of the fancier houses in its time, with a kitchen that had been gutted apart from an old yellowing refrigerator. She checked inside. The family weren't entombed within.

'How was the caravan?' asked Rispoli as they made their way to the next dwelling.

'It looks and smells like a smoker's lung,' said Emmaline.

'Webster was a sixty-a-day man.'

'Was?'

'There's a reason it was available on such short notice.'

That ended the conversation. Briefly.

'I went into Hurton last night,' she admitted.

'A hive of activity, I bet.'

'I found out a few things.'

'Such as?' asked Rispoli as they entered the next building. It was wooden but the walls remained solid. It was also better furnished than most of the others as if the occupants had recently vacated, much like the Maguires.

'The family were rarely seen together. Spotted on their own in town mostly.'

'While the other remained here?'

'I assume so. The father also met with someone apparently. In Wisbech.'

'Family?'

'No.'

'So who?'

'We need to find out . . .' said Emmaline. The sentence tailed off. She moved to one of the abandoned cupboards and looked at the floor.

'This has been moved,' she said.

'I'm sure it got moved all the time,' said Rispoli, peeking into the kitchen.

'No, it's been moved recently. Look at the marks in the dust.' Underneath the low-heeled legs of the cupboard were marks indicating lateral movement, the fading brown of the wood underneath exposed. 'Help me,' she said as she dragged the cupboard to the side following the path of the marks. It revealed a hole in the floor, neatly cut into the wood and rounded at the edges.

Using her phone to cast a light she made out a set of roughly hewn steps. It reminded her of basements she had read about in newspapers. Ones where the products of incestuous relationships were kept. Or kidnap victims.

'Call Barker and Anand. We're going down.'

25

Emmaline

Progress was as slow down here as it was up top. They first had to make sure that the buttresses planted along the tunnel were sound. Emmaline comforted herself that they had been standing for maybe a hundred years, so she and Rispoli would have been mightily unlucky to have them fall on their heads at precisely this moment. But anyway, each was checked as they moved along.

The question had been floated as to whether to bring in a specialist team, but consensus was that getting in specialist miners or cavers would take too long. Besides, there might be nothing down here but lost hopes from a century ago.

That theory was revised somewhat by the discovery of the supplies. Cans of soda, bags of crisps and snacks that most definitely did not exist a century ago. Including a number of Chunky Peanut Butter KitKats. Someone had been down here. Recently.

Emmaline, with Rispoli following, increased her pace, calling out the names of the family but getting nothing but an empty echo in return. There was a chance that they had stumbled upon the tunnel and decided to go for a stupid and reckless adventure. But that didn't account for the fact that the cupboard had been replaced over the entrance.

From behind her, Rispoli called out again. His heavy voice bounced straight back at them. They had reached a dead end, but a dead end littered with empty chocolate bar wrappers, metal detectors and a pair of ear-defenders. And something else. Two machines that although ingrained with soot and dust, were very much modern in design. One looked like a red bin with a short conveyor belt underneath it; the other some sort of grinding machine with wheels and a hammer. Both were attached to a small generator. It was a processing line of some sort. The bin was full of small rocks.

'What do you think?' he asked.

'Looks like a mining operation. Small scale. Load the rocks to crush them and then feed the material into this bin using the looped hose to wash and recycle the water.'

'Looking for gold?'

'Probably given the area we're in.'

'There can't be much.'

'Enough to warrant trying. Enough to warrant leaving the machines behind.'

'Unless they're planning to come back,' said Rispoli.

'If they do they are in for a surprise,' said Emmaline. 'Get Forensics in here. Check the equipment, check the rubbish left behind. Let's find out who these people were.'

'What if it was the family?'

'It means we still have the same question to answer. What happened to them?'

26

Lorcan

He slept in the ute all night. It gave him space to breathe. That was the irony of Kallayee. All this space but still he found it claustrophobic. He was trapped in his own head, his past misdeeds holding him hostage.

Naiyana was ignoring him too. She'd cooked breakfast for herself and Dylan only. If this was her chosen method of punishing him he was happy with that. No shouting, no screaming. Especially given his simmering hangover. He had always found silence the easiest punishment. For a short while anyway. Let the storm pass. Besides, if she continued not to talk to him he could always do something worse that would make her scream at him. You don't stay together for eight years and not know what triggers the other person's fuse. A skill learned by all humans from an early age. Where are the boundaries? What can I get away with before my parents – or spouse – are forced to intervene?

She didn't even have a go at him for not getting to

work immediately. A weird feeling of tranquillity hung over everything this morning. As if he went away for one night and she had been turned into a zombie.

At least Dylan wasn't ignoring him. So after lugging the cement and bricks into place to start work on repairing the gable wall, he took a break with his son, learning how his mining operation worked. The digger filled the truck, which left for town for the gold and diamonds to be removed before returning, the hole getting slowly deeper and deeper, the lorries trailing dirt out by the tonne. It was amazing what the boy had picked up from television and books, his mind like a sponge.

'It's a big-time operation, son, isn't it?'

'Very big. And it will get bigger once you buy me more trucks.'

Lorcan smiled. 'For that you need to help Dad.'

So he bribed Dylan to help mix the cement, shovelling in the sand as he turned it over and over, instructing his son to add water when necessary. It was hard but gratifying work, the cement making a satisfying wet slop as it fell onto the sheeting.

He glanced in the kitchen window. Nee was busy at the table still ignoring him. The edge of a large plaster sneaked out from underneath the shoulder of her top.

'Dylan? Did something happen yesterday? To Mum?'

The boy was easing water into the hole in the centre of the wet cement creating a muddy lake. He stopped and looked away. A telltale sign of guilt.

'What is it, Dylan?'

'We had a fight. Mum was doing her video and I wanted to be in it but she said no and so I ran off.'

'Where?'

'Home. I waited but she didn't come back for ages. I fell asleep, but I heard her come in.'

So that was why she was distant, thought Lorcan. She had been terrified she'd lost Dylan and he hadn't been there to help. Hurt herself doing so. She was recovering from the shock. And the anger towards him. She was right to be angry at him.

'I had another nightmare too.'

'The rumbling again?'

The boy nodded. 'Mum wasn't there.'

'She probably went back to her own bed,' said Lorcan. 'You're a growing boy. It's a tight squeeze both of you on one bed.'

'No, she wasn't there. She wasn't in the house.'

Lorcan stopped shovelling, the grey mixture settling into a shapeless blob on the metal he had scavenged from a collapsed building across the road.

'I don't know where she went, Daddy.'

'I'm sure she was just getting some air, Dyl,' said Lorcan, though he wasn't sure at all.

27

Emmaline

More officers were dragged in – requisitioned from Kalgoorlie and Perth – and the whole town thoroughly checked, building to building right to the outskirts. Fourteen other tunnels had been found. All either empty or collapsed. And not recently.

At the end of it, the conclusion was that the family, or their bodies, were nowhere in town.

A fresh KLO4 for the family or their vehicle was reissued statewide and a plane was sent up to check the major thoroughfares for any crashed utes.

As those were out of her hands, Emmaline's focus switched to finding out who Lorcan Maguire had met in Wisbech. She started with questioning the people at his former job.

INK Tech was based in an industrial park in Welshpool, a short skip south of Perth Airport. It was a basic building with grey prefab walls and an all-encompassing dreariness. All of the capital had clearly been spent on the hardware inside, rows of state-of-the-art computers and servers droning in the background.

She first met with Nikos Iannis, the joint owner. His brother, Georgios, the co-owner, was unavailable as he had been confined to hospital for the last three months with a particularly virulent type of bone cancer. The prognosis wasn't good. So Nikos was in sole charge and immediately she could see that he had enough personality and bulk to command ten businesses, the giant of a man unable – or unwilling – to rise from his desk as Emmaline was led inside by his secretary.

She took a seat. Introductions were forsaken. She had done that already over the phone.

'You recently made Lorcan Maguire redundant, didn't you?'

At the mention of his name, Nikos's self-satisfied smile vanished. Emmaline continued. 'What can you tell me about him?'

'That he was a snake,' spat Nikos.

'You said "was",' she noted. 'Do you know something we don't?'

The smile returned. There was a calculating menace behind it. 'I probably know a *lot* of things you don't, Detective Taylor.'

'That's not an answer, Mr Iannis.'

'Should I have my lawyer present?'

'This isn't a formal interview but if you wish—'

'I said "was" only because he *was* my employee. Now he isn't.'

Emmaline ran with it. 'What was he like?'

'I told you what he was like.'

'When he *was* employed with you. Before he was made redundant.'

Nikos drew a breath that struggled to enter lungs crushed by the fat weighing in his chest. 'From what I hear, he had been underperforming for the last year. As if he was bored of the work. Then after a warning his work had picked up again. Probably because he wanted to stay in the job while stealing my information.'

'What was the information?' asked Emmaline.

'Client data. Numbers.'

'Financial information?'

Nikos's face turned to stone. 'I don't think I need to answer that.'

'No, but it might help.'

'What makes you think I want to help?'

There was a pause as they stared at each other.

'Why was he let go?' asked Emmaline.

'Business pressures. We needed redundancies. He just missed the cut. I actually had sympathy for the bugger. We gave him to the end of the month and another month's wages on top. Pretty generous I'd say. Then we found that we had a chunk of data missing.'

'Why do you think he stole it?'

'Only a few people had access to it. It was him.'

'The court didn't agree.'

'It couldn't be proved for certain,' said Nikos. 'But that works both ways.'

'What do you mean?'

'Reasonable doubt.' Again the dark eyes flashed menace.

'Did you see him again?'

'Lorcan? No. Not after court. We were too busy warning our rivals off purchasing stolen information. In case he tried to sell it to them. Now they're all over us.'

Emmaline had seen the newspaper reports. INK Tech was under intense media fire for losing sensitive client data.

'You shouldn't have gone to court,' said Emmaline.

Nikos didn't respond, the cold stare suggesting he didn't need to be reminded. Maybe his lawyers had even warned him against it at the time but in a throwback to earlier years, he couldn't let a slight pass. But now, as a proper, law-abiding businessman it was a reputation rather than a body that took a hammering.

'I'll need to question some of his colleagues.'

Nikos frowned. 'Be sure and let me know if they know anything.'

A check of the comings and goings of the employees in the last two weeks revealed nothing of interest. After that she interviewed the rest of the employees on an informal basis and got blank faces from them all. The overall consensus was of Lorcan being a colleague rather than a close friend, none of them offering any new information and that they didn't socialize outside of the office.

As she sat there afterwards packing up her notes,

she watched the office in crisis mode, phone calls with tense clients, desperate reassurances offered that their data was safe and that all steps would be taken to ensure it stayed that way. She wondered just what effect the loss of the data and the ill-advised court case had on the company. Nikos – and the stricken Georgios – would have lost a lot of money. They might even lose more in lawsuits and claims should the stolen data ever leak. Was that enough to threaten Lorcan? Or worse?

For the moment it was another dead end.

28

Naiyana

She rounded them both up in the living room. A family meeting. She had an announcement that had taken her all day to work up to.

'I want to make a go of it.'

'Our marriage?' spat Lorcan. The grimace that followed suggested that he regretted the comment immediately. She hadn't spoken to him all day. He knew better than to wade in with a joke. The situation was delicate. More now than it ever was.

'This move. We should make a go of it.'

Her husband's grimace turned into what looked like a slightly reticent smile. 'Are you sure?'

She raised an eyebrow as if to warn him not to push it.

'Dyl, go and play in your room for a bit,' said Lorcan. The boy looked at both his parents before scuttling off, content to be dismissed from boring adult talk.

'What brought this change of heart?' asked Lorcan.

'Are you upset at it?'

'No, it's just . . . sudden.'

She moved closer to him, taking his hands in hers.

'It's—' she started, looking around the plain living room, her attempts at scrubbing the walls clean having left a number of unsavoury holes in the plaster. 'I don't want to quit this like we had to quit Perth. It's time to gut it out. Stay away from the city for a while.'

'What do we do about Dyl though? He's still having nightmares.'

'He had nightmares sometimes in Perth, too. They aren't going to suddenly stop now we're out here.'

'But he didn't wake up every night. They seem to be worse out here, more vivid.'

'He's just moved to a strange, new place so of course he will have strange, new dreams. Just give it time. We have to give this place time.'

She touched her husband's face, offering him the demure, shy smile she knew he couldn't resist.

29

Emmaline

If there was intrigue surrounding Lorcan's departure from INK Tech, there was scandal with Naiyana's. He had been accused of stealing data, which had adversely affected a small company temporarily. Her machinations on the other hand had nearly taken down a national institution.

Brightside Foods – with the slogan 'Always look for the Brightside in Life' – was a legendary Australian brand manufacturing everything from TV dinners to 'Brightside's Best', their luxurious, top-of-the-range offering. And it was their product that Naiyana had forced off the shelves.

The company had created a new range of baby food for the mass market, something that was going to revolutionize the product. *Not that the babies would much care or notice*, thought Emmaline.

The problem was that one of the ingredients, a preserving agent, was banned in most countries but in its form was allowed in Australia. Naiyana had been instrumental in working through the charity to organize boycotts and virulent online campaigns disparaging the new product. The bad publicity and national outcry had succeeded in getting it forced off the shelves. Much like in Lorcan's case, however, the company's other products took a collateral hit as well and had resulted in Brightside Foods coming close to folding and the layoff of a significant number of workers from their main plant just outside Perth.

The matter had even come to the attention of Chester Grant, the local MP and Labor party darling, who was getting gip from all sides, from the workers for loss of jobs, from the business for loss of earnings and angered campaigners for the threat to the public. The file noted that there were also some barely veiled threats on social media, calling Naiyana another snowflake campaigner with nothing better to do than ruin the lives of others. The whole mess had upset a whole lot of people.

Naiyana had even found a poisoned cat on their front step in the weeks after. At the time it was considered a threat against her but from what Emmaline knew it might have even been a threat against the husband. Though given what Lorcan swiped, a rat might have been more appropriate.

This had been a few weeks before the family had moved. Lorcan's redundancy and her sudden claim to fame. They were a family that on the surface were nothing out of the normal but yet they had managed to cause massive upheaval on two fronts and then disappear. That was not normal. A run-of-the-mill suburban family with a lot of enemies.

30

Lorcan

Lorcan wasn't sure which version of his wife he preferred. The complainer or the tyrant. As the complainer he could ignore her grievances and go off and do his own thing in his own time. As the tyrant, however, she was on him constantly, demanding an increase to the pace of the repairs, insisting he turn the dive into the bloody Taj Mahal overnight.

The tyrant was also changing her mind constantly and expecting him to acquiesce. She knew she was in the position of power as he was desperate for this move to work. He was the instigator; she was the whip. But the redundancy money was quickly running out, his trips to Hurton and further afield more frequent, Dylan tagging along at her request. Getting him out of her way so she could dabble with the house.

He had repaired the gable wall. Amateurish but not bad for a first attempt. Then she had demanded the roof be sorted. So he did. Again it was no Dome of the Taj Mahal but it should keep out any rain. He had followed the manuals to the letter. Next, he would tackle the windows. An expensive and delicate job.

He was just clearing away the remaining cement into a temporary shed he had constructed out the back when Nee appeared at the door.

'The living room. When are we getting cupboards? And a sofa?'

'Any particular style?' he asked sarcastically.

'Pine would be nice.'

She had ignored his sarcasm. 'Is that necessary for—?'

'It would be nice.'

He knew what that meant. That meant, yes it was necessary. Make it happen. He wondered if she was being deliberately obtuse. That this was her ultimate revenge for him staying out drinking all night. More punishing than mere silence. As his grandfather had often said, there was a thin line between being the perfectionist who liked things done right, and being the gobshite who forced everyone to adhere to that impossible standard.

'I meant to tell you when you were in town, but you had the ute and there was no signal.'

'I'll have to go to Kalgoorlie.'

'Take Dylan with you. Make it a road trip.'

'I don't want to babysit him while I figure out what I need. I'm not a DIY expert, remember?'

'That's obvious,' she replied.

Quick and painful. He tried to come up with a snappy reply but was thwarted.

'Look, I want to do this but if I'm going to live in the desert, then I want to live like Priscilla.'

'Priscilla wasn't a complete bitch though, was she?' Lorcan was smart enough not to say this out loud.

'Make it an overnighter. Down in the afternoon, back the next afternoon. Maybe you can even take yourselves fishing or something.'

'And leave you here?'

'At least I'll get some sleep. And maybe he will too.'

31

Emmaline

Emmaline had just landed in Leonora and got into her car for the drive back to her lonely caravan when she got a call from MCS HQ. It was Zhao with two pieces of news. Firstly, that the blood types found in Kallayee didn't match. This meant two separate victims, or at least two injured parties, and secondly, that they had received information from the Maguires' credit card company and bank. Lorcan's phone was still being worked on.

Lorcan's card had last been used in Hurton on 28 December, at Mallon's hardware store. Naiyana's last expenditure was earlier than this, on 25 December in Hurton. Grocery store. Last minute items for Christmas dinner, guessed Emmaline.

The bulk of the card expenditure didn't raise any questions. Hardware products and groceries. The things necessary for survival; food, water and shelter. Heat wasn't as much of an issue during the summer.

The overnight stay in Kalgoorlie on 19 December was different. It was about a five-hour round trip and according to the records, a load of DIY furniture and some other bits and pieces – including a harness – were purchased then and the day after, Monday 20 December. Five hours was a long day trip but for a family on a budget – both were in overdraft by the time of their last recorded expenditure – it made more sense to come back. Unless the overnight stay was a cover for something else.

A call to the motel – a bottom-of-the-range one on the Red Line north of the city – confirmed that a Lorcan Maguire had stayed there on the nineteenth. And not alone. Emmaline's interest peaked. Was he meeting someone about the stolen information? Selling it to a rival or back to INK Tech? But if so, INK Tech would have called off the lawyers threatening the other companies. Unless Nikos was trying to cover his tracks. He was a man with experience in that field.

But no, Lorcan had been accompanied by a small boy. The owner confirmed Dylan's description. This seemed to blow a hole in her theory. Maybe the over-nighter was because Lorcan didn't want to do a five-hour round trip with the kid in tow. Maybe there was nothing sinister about the overnight stay at all.

But it did mean that Naiyana had been left alone in town. Had father and son fled to Kalgoorlie after a fight? Seamus Maguire had noted that there had been some tension. And there would certainly be tension without a functioning house to live in.

32

Naiyana

Complete silence.

But inside she was a melange of noise, fear and anticipation, her guts churning and occasionally being unable to resist a yelp from the build-up. The butterflies made her feel light-headed as she swayed from her perch on the camping bed. This was anticipation she hadn't felt in ages. The same anticipation that she felt when they'd taken BS Foods to court. She hoped to feel the same sense of accomplishment at the end.

For the first time in six years, she was spending the night alone. No Lorcan and no Dylan. And though there were nerves there was excitement too. For which she felt a little guilty. But only a little. There was only a little harm in wanting them gone. It was only natural to want a break, to want something different. Maybe that was cold and callous but when life was difficult you had to adapt and change. That was natural. This might be the start of a new dawn, the precipice so close. What lay ahead was unknown and that was exhilarating. She had never done anything like this before. These feelings – this – wasn't something she could vlog about. Not ever.

From the silence came a faint scratching sound, like something was tearing at the picture she had constructed of herself over the years. The vigilante housewife, the outback mother, the loving parent and wife. The scratching ripped a corner from the perfectly embossed photo. It was perfect no more. It was time to see what was underneath.

33

Emmaline

The caravan was as she left it. Infused with nicotine and sadness. Holding onto the last few days of a sick old man, and parked close to a dilapidated house infused with the last few days of a strong-willed family. She had again refused to take a hotel room in Leonora. She would slum it here until she got some answers. Stay close to the beating heart of the mystery. Build and maintain a bond with it.

She was as alone as Naiyana Maguire had been on 19 December when her husband and son had been in Kalgoorlie. Had it been Lorcan's decision to stay over, or her decision to have some space? She'd never been married so Emmaline felt she was grasping a little, but marriages were like long-term relationships made formal. With a kid as the rubber stamp.

She had always feared being confined by a baby. Her social life was vibrant – as much as being in the force allowed anyway. She had a litter of friends, she went to pubs and clubs and bars but as time went on she had found herself unable to switch off, her police radar constantly scanning for signs of trouble. She had seen what trouble could do, so her mind was attuned to ascertaining where it may occur. It was a problem to which she had found only one solution. An alcoholic solution that dulled her senses but which often led to overconsumption. The window was slender. Too little and the thoughts persisted, too much and she had a tendency to lose control. It had happened before and she'd regretted it. Not in having slept with someone she shouldn't have – but that alcohol was involved in the decision.

The glow of the computer screen waited for her. Sleep waited too but the couch/bed wasn't comfortable enough to make it anything other than a necessity. The only other option was Hurton. Maybe she could have a few and hook up with Matty. It was the one advantage of working around the state, a 'no-tie fly-by'. There was no need to have a loved one, if love was at the tip of her fingers. There when she wanted it and gone when she didn't.

From somewhere far away the sound of dingoes baying rose, disrupting her consciousness. When had they started? Had they been howling for a while and she had only just noticed? The plaintive howls reminded her of a lot of things – drinking, sex, loneliness. She hadn't heard them last night but being north of the dingo fence they were to be expected. They would go where they sensed food. Which she might count as for a hungry pack of animals.

The howling continued, rising and falling, almost

echoing around the bare caravan, a hollow wail of loneliness. Were they catching her scent and slowly approaching? Was this what Naiyana had experienced? If so, it hadn't scared her off. She had stuck around. Until after Christmas at least.

Emmaline decided to get to work. Bury herself in the notes and ignore everything else. The sooner the case was solved, the sooner she could get back to bright lights, clubs and opportunities.

These pleasant thoughts were interrupted by a scratch at the door. One single scratch. The dogs were on the hunt, looking for prey.

Drawing her gun she approached the door. She didn't need them scratching on the caravan all night. She would go out and warn them off. Fire a shot. If she needed to.

As she reached for the scooped handle, she felt a sudden stab of paranoia. Her sense of unease grew. Firing a warning shot was stupid. An overreaction. All she needed to do was make some noise and they would back off. She was the one in control. Outside, the baying continued, as if the animals were calling to each other. Calling her to join them. Tempting her to come out and play.

The handle felt cold as she turned it. Taking a deep breath she shoved it open.

The night air flooded in, fresh and clean compared to the stale, rancid caravan. There was no dog at her door. A quick glance either way confirmed that none were waiting to pounce.

Now unhindered by the aluminium shell, the baying seemed to increase in intensity. Like there was an orchestra in progress somewhere beyond Kallayee, one dog seeming to conduct the rest. Something was happening. Emmaline needed to know what.

Following the sound, she quickly found herself outside the confines of town, scrambling her way over many sand dunes and the gibber plains, past the lonely clumps of eucalyptus and mulga shrubs. She kept walking, the dingoes drawing her closer like Sirens on the desert sea, her gun raised, anticipating an attack. Right now she didn't feel like a predator at the top of the food chain. She knew she should have turned back for the safety of the caravan but they kept calling to her, feeding into her weakness, the lure of the unknown, speaking to her obsessive nature. Maybe Naiyana had been lured by the same thing but without a gun to protect her. Surely she wouldn't have been that stupid.

As the moon dipped behind one of the few clouds in the sky, the outback suddenly grew dark. Emmaline froze. More stupidity. She had left her torch behind. Was something in town turning her stupid, some malevolent force luring her to her death? It certainly felt like it, the air noticeably cooler out here in the bush, no brick, no tarmac, no tin roofs to trap the heat. Her breath lightly misted the air in front of her.

The cloud and the darkness passed as she inched over an open and sandy crest. In the near distance

123

she saw them, their eyes glaring in the moonlight, almond-shaped with an almost blue-green reflection, their gathered breath like a fog. The pack of ten dingoes were all sandy yellow, their coat colour determined by the desert they lived in, their ears pricked and furtive, aware of the stranger in their midst.

The pack had surrounded something, some guarding, some eating. The baying grew louder, evolving into short, harsh barks. She had never heard a dingo bark before and though she wasn't scared of dogs, these wild animals were something different altogether. She held no qualms over shooting them if they attacked. From this distance across the sandy scrub she was confident that she could hit a person. But a dog? They would move faster. In a straight line maybe but fast. A fast, narrow target to aim at.

She moved closer. The dingoes began to part, the barks turning into decrying howls of unfairness. Akin to a gaggle of monosyllabled teenagers having to give up something they had fought for. Emmaline wondered if she was putting herself at risk over some poor kangaroo or camel, but sensed that she wasn't.

The ground shifted beneath her feet as she descended the bank, burying into the cool sand. She got close enough to see that she was right. The dingoes weren't protecting a kangaroo or camel. The body had been torn apart, the soft belly and thighs targeted, the skull savaged to get to any available flesh. A bloodied rag that looked like a shirt and something grey lay against the golden sand. A bone. Possibly a forearm. Detached from the main body.

Emmaline held her eyes on the body and held her guts tight. Instinct told her that she had found Lorcan Maguire.

34

Emmaline

Emmaline had seen dead bodies before. But never one ripped apart by wild animals. In her head, in the space where there should have been logic and planning there was nothing, neither the inclination to throw up, nor the capacity to determine what to do next. Even the howls and cries had faded into inconsequence. Finally a thought emerged from the morass. A callous thought but a thought nonetheless. Would the animal's interference affect the assessment of how the victim died?

That thought allowed others to charge forward. Slowly her wits returned. She raised her guard again, the dingoes keeping their distance but not retreating further than the skiff of trees surrounding the dune she was at the bottom of. She reached for the phone in her pocket. As she assumed, there was no signal. She would have to leave the body to get help but didn't want to in case any remaining evidence was further destroyed.

Aiming into the sky she fired off a shot. The silence of the night exploded with a sharp crack. The dingoes scattered. Hopefully it would bring someone to investigate, and she could get them to guard the body, or better yet raise the alarm.

The report from the gunshot died away. There was a return to guarded silence. From the shelter of the trees the glowing eyes watched her, awaiting her next move. If no one came she would have to wait it out until daylight when maybe the dogs would leave her alone.

Needing to stay awake and with nothing else to do she made a quick study of the scene. Along with the once off-white shirt were a pair of ripped khaki knee-length shorts, the crotch a mass of blood, the victim no doubt savagely emasculated. The clothing told her that he had tried to escape during daylight. A small, scuffed backpack covered in cartoon dragons lay ripped open near the body with no food inside. Unless the contents had been scavenged by the dingoes. It suggested he – and Dylan, whose body was unaccounted for – were fleeing from something. And that Lorcan didn't make it far, only a couple of kilometres from Kallayee.

The arm bone lay apart from the body, gnawed at given the rough edges. It was broken too, a nasty fracture, the marrow licked clean. She wondered if the dingoes' teeth could do this but she doubted it. It certainly wasn't the cause of death. The neat round bullet hole in the shirt proved that. Near the middle of the chest, the fibres singed at the edges.

It took ten minutes of close study for the stench of

decaying flesh to cause her to step away from the scene as a cloud swept over and covered both dead and alive in an eerie darkness.

She would be blamed for not finding the body sooner but the area was vast and they'd had no leads. She had to both thank and curse the dingoes for leading her here. She'd been lucky to find the body at all. She could only hope that Forensics could make something of it.

Taking a seat on the side of the dune, she commenced her cold and lonely vigil. Someone would have heard the gunshot. They would be rushing to investigate. Surely.

The dingoes stayed too, holding their own vigil, stalking around the edge of the trees, waiting to see what the interloper was going to do, waiting to see if she would leave and let them scavenge what remained.

35

Emmaline

Daylight. The sun rose turning the land and everything on it from black to violet to orange to yellow like a bruise slowly fading in time. Emmaline was certain that the memory of this night wouldn't fade quickly.

No one had responded to the gunshot. There had been no shouts, no search parties.

With the rising sun came the heat. Her problem remained. A dead body and ten hungry animals. Ready to pounce and reclaim their meal. An idea arose. From her pocket she fished out the matchbook Matty had given her. His number. That had been a new experience, like some hard-boiled noir where the leading man gives his number to a damsel in distress. But Matty was no leading man and she was no damsel in distress. Just a damsel with a problem she now knew how to solve.

Gathering some twigs and dried leaves from a straggle of trees the dingoes weren't huddled in, she constructed a small fire near the body. Splitting the six matches in half to give herself two attempts, she struck three in conjunction. The grey-topped matches fizzled into life. Placing them beneath the kindling of dried spinifex grass, it caught immediately, smoking for a few seconds before bursting into flame. She piled on more twigs and a couple of dead branches, watching as they blackened and finally caught fire.

Praying that the unnerving presence of fire would hold the dogs off for a while, Emmaline sprinted back to the caravan, over the sand dunes, rocks and tufts of spinifex, her legs running through treacle. Reaching it she grabbed her keys and sped off in the 4x4 barrelling towards Hurton, one eye on the road and one on the phone. Close to Hurton, one bar flashed up. Braking suddenly and searing two dark tyre marks into the tarmac she called it in, her breathlessness causing a slight panic at HQ as if she was the one in trouble. She assured them that she was just fine. But that Lorcan Maguire wasn't.

Hanging up, she dragged the vehicle around and headed back to Kallayee, back to where she hoped the fire was still warding off the hungry scavengers.

36

Emmaline

The fire had been on its last legs by the time she returned to the scene. A few of the braver animals had inched closer only to scatter again upon her arrival. Rather undignified, she had face-planted down the dune for the last few metres, her weary legs giving up.

From there she sat, regained her breath and waited for backup. First came Rispoli, Barker and Anand. MCS were dispatching a team to help, backed up by dedicated admin support based at HQ.

Forensics arrived soon after. Emmaline watched as they did their thing, the crime scene manager organizing the common approach path, the metal plates slowly sinking into the sand as if being eaten by the hungry desert. Other SOCOs swarmed around the body, collecting samples, photographing, some writing on pads, some working on tablets, another sketching the scene. It was as if Emmaline had warded off one attack only to let Lorcan succumb to these albino vultures.

Rispoli approached her with a steaming cup of coffee.

'Long night?'

Emmaline took a sip. It burnt her tongue but her body saluted the caffeine.

'How did you find him?'

'A pack of dingoes.'

Rispoli raised his eyebrows. 'Lucky.'

'Luckier if we had found him earlier.'

'What do you reckon happened?'

'I think we can assume that this connects with the message we found on Lorcan's phone. Someone was after him. They already had Naiyana. He fled and made it to here.'

'And Dylan?'

'His backpack is at the scene. He's not.'

Even to her it sounded like a blunt summary of what had happened. Seeing the team leader step away from the scene, Emmaline got up and approached. Pulling the hood from her head, she could make out Dr Rebecca Patel, her dark hair shiny with sweat that streaked her face.

Making for the off-road vehicles that were parked on the far side of the dunes, Rebecca pulled a bottle of water from a cool box and swigged it. No coffee for her.

'What do we know?' asked Emmaline, shielding her eyes from the vicious reflection of the white smock.

'Facts?' asked Dr Patel.

'Facts.'

'It wasn't a dingo attack that killed him but I'm sure you already knew that.'

Emmaline nodded. 'I was the one under attack.'

'I doubt that.'

She suddenly remembered that Rebecca Patel didn't do jokes. Nothing should lighten the mood. Maybe she was right.

'We have one male, around thirty years old. Missing a significant amount of flesh.'

'The dingoes?'

Dr Patel stopped, a look of abject sympathy on her face. 'That is not a fact. The examination and any teeth marks will determine exactly.'

A waste of time, thought Emmaline but kept it to herself.

'But an assumption can be made—' said Emmaline.

'Can be made by you, Detective.'

Emmaline pressed on. 'Any initial determination on the actual cause of death? And date?' She fully expected it to match the date of the frantic phone message – a week ago, 30 December. Lorcan hadn't even made it to the New Year.

Before Dr Patel could shoot her down with assumptions not being facts, Emmaline jumped in. 'And I want your assumptions.'

'But they might not make the report.'

'I can live with that.'

Dr Patel paused as if she was weighing up her whole career in that instant.

'Shot. Once in the chest. No powder residue on the entry wound,' said Dr Patel, sipping the water.

'So not a suicide?' asked Emmaline, the caffeine in her system suddenly hitting the right spots, her muscles abuzz.

'There is residue on the victim's two remaining fingers. But in my opinion the victim fired a gun during a separate instant. His death was definitely not a suicide.'

'What type of gun?'

'Hard to be a hundred per cent sure as yet but my *assumption* is a rifle.'

'The type of gun that might be used to ward off dingoes?'

Dr Patel considered this for a moment. 'Yes. And the type of gun that makes suicide difficult unless you have very nimble toes. And he was still wearing trainers.'

'Time of death?'

'A week or so given the state of the body, plus the advanced decay from exposure to the heat. We've been lucky. Any longer and the evidence would have all disappeared.'

'What about the broken bone? A defensive wound from a bullet?'

Dr Patel shook her head. 'No. There is a lack of soot for that to be the case.'

'So?'

'It is badly fractured. Blunt force probably. A heavy impact.'

Dr Patel delivered this coldly, the ice water now flowing through her system, doing the same job as the coffee was for Emmaline. Wakening her to a murder case.

Emmaline returned to the scene and found the Forensics team removing the body for further examination. Thankfully the remoteness of the location had prevented any media attention as yet. But that was sure to come soon. Like the blowflies that sense a rotting corpse, the press would come.

Rispoli, Barker and Anand joined her at the side as Forensics underwent their final provisions. Emmaline filled them in on what she had learned so far. She would have to fill in whoever MCS sent out too. But her boss, Detective Inspector Angela Moore, had made it clear she was in sole charge. *Solve the case.*

'How sure are we it's Lorcan Maguire?' asked Rispoli.

'Ninety-nine per cent,' said Emmaline.

'More than what's left of him, anyway,' said Barker. It didn't get a laugh.

'So he was shot out here?' asked Anand, looking around the scene. 'And no one came to check?'

'I performed an impromptu experiment last night,' said Emmaline. 'I can confirm that no one came to help me.'

'Hurton is still over six kilometres away. Maybe they didn't hear it.'

'There's little to block the sound,' said Rispoli.

'Maybe it was someone from Hurton,' said Barker.

It was something Emmaline had started to consider. The people in Hurton hadn't been inviting for the most part, unco-operative about what they knew about the family, all except for the drunk woman and Matty. And that was no reason to rule either out.

'It adds weight to the message on his phone,' said Rispoli.

She nodded. 'Someone came after them. And in the recording, he said that Naiyana was already gone.'

'So her body is out here?' asked Anand, joining Barker in looking around as if Naiyana's body would suddenly rise from the sand.

'Or somewhere,' said Emmaline. 'All we know is that whoever was after Lorcan Maguire caught him. And maybe Dylan too.'

According to the message Lorcan had been escaping with his son. But he was nowhere to be found.

37

Lorcan

It had been a long drive back. With a stop-off in Wisbech for ice cream. All in all it had been a delightful road trip. Father and son together. He had picked up everything he needed – a cupboard, chairs and a second-hand sofa. He felt like he had achieved something significant. It was time to build on that. Literally. He had even managed to find a play park for Dylan to tire himself out and sleep in the cab while he nipped off to run an errand.

On returning to Kallayee, Dylan immediately resumed operations in his thriving mine. Naiyana though had seemed distracted, acknowledging the successful haul of goods but when he had suggested getting started with constructing the cupboards she had waved it off for another day. As if she wanted the house to herself. Maybe she was nesting. He was sure that was a thing he had read somewhere. Getting used to a place. Making it your own. Feeling safe and secure. Whatever the reason he was happy to oblige. The well was waiting for him.

While Dylan had slept he had stopped by an outdoor store and picked up a climbing harness. Securing it and strapping himself in, he lowered himself into the well. He continued to dig, filling buckets that he winched out using the old pulley that he had found, the harness making digging somewhat awkward but a damn sight safer than his weight collapsing the cap and plunging to his death.

An hour in, the earth began to rumble, low but insistent, dust crumbling from the stone sides, choking the air. His first thought was that the well was collapsing but aside from the shower of dust the old blocks remained intact. His second thought was a low-flying plane overhead, so he looked up and searched for it. This was something he found himself doing on occasion, casually following the planes across the sky until the horizon or his vision gave out. But there was no plane in view. This rumbling was coming from underground again, but during the day this time instead of at night.

From his time at school, he knew that West Australia as a whole was not known for major earthquakes apart from a large one in Meckering in 1968 and a smaller one in Kalgoorlie in 2010. There were also a lot of active volcanoes stretching from Melbourne to Mount Gambier but no eruptions in five thousand years. So he was pretty confident that he wasn't digging down into a magma chamber.

Ignoring the rumble for the moment he continued to fill another couple of buckets, but the rumbling failed to cease. Levering himself out of the well awkwardly – something that would get better with practice – he took the harness off and went hunting.

Putting his ear to the ground he felt the reverberations through it. He walked towards the other side of the road and put his ear to the sand once again. He might have been mistaken but it felt stronger.

Moving another few metres away from the well, further from their house, he tried again. This time the reverberations were accompanied by laughter.

'What are you doing, Daddy?'

He turned to find Dylan staring at him, the yellow dumper truck clasped in his hand.

'Searching for something,' he said.

'Can I help?'

Lorcan nodded. He continued to move and check, Dylan doing the same behind him, moving past the crossroads. The noise was definitely stronger in this quarter of town but where was the source? He had checked out most of these buildings before – even the recently collapsed one – when he'd gone scavenging for anything useful.

A fruitless hour later he gave up. As he turned to go back home, a foil wrapper floated past him sparkling in the sun. He trapped it with his foot and picked it up. It hadn't been faded with the sun. Recent. He wondered if it was one of Dylan's. At that age kids had little or no concept of littering, leaving things behind like a marker to reassure them that they had been there before and that the path was safe. But the wrapper was for a Chunky Peanut Butter KitKat. A type Dylan detested.

Resuming the hunt, he entered the nearest house. It was a solid wooden structure, one that he might have considered as their base but for the inner wall that had collapsed turning two bedrooms into one and causing irreparable damage to a hallway wall that a strong puff of breath could knock over.

The rumbling was powerful here, shaking the wooden slatted floor as if he was standing on one of those massage plates at the gym. The cupboards rattled as if the town was being shelled, shaking the house to its foundations. Then he noticed something. A cupboard that was out of place, the skid marks in the dust showing that it had been moved. Had Dylan done this? And why? But even empty it was a sturdy piece of furniture, too much for a scrawny six-year-old to move on his own. Had Naiyana moved it? She had taken to walking around town to film her vlog, sometimes even at night, according to Dylan. Had she been here checking out furniture to take? Possible. But scavenging wasn't his wife's MO.

38

Lorcan

He put his hand on the cupboard. It was vibrating, almost buzzing like a generator but more powerful. As if something was alive inside. Which was possible. Lorcan opened the cupboard and jumped backwards. With his eyes closed. Only when he had retreated a safe distance did he take a peek. He expected to see something large and deadly. But inside there was nothing but a fine, floating dust like magician's smoke.

Following the tracks in the dust, he inched the cupboard to the side. It revealed a hole in the floor. Big enough to enter. With a pitch-black tunnel beyond. Without the cupboard hindering it, the rumbling sound increased in voracity. There was something down there. He wondered if it was some odd geological force, an anomaly never before discovered. That would be perfect for his book, a mystery solved.

He was still considering this when he returned to the house to get a torch.

Naiyana was inside, editing a vlog on her phone.

It took three attempts to get her attention, like she was on another planet entirely.

'I found a tunnel.'

She looked up at him and frowned. 'What do you mean?'

'A tunnel in one of the houses. The rumbling we keep hearing is coming from it.'

Naiyana paused as if lost at what to say. Then she found the words. 'What about the well? What about plastering the walls? Getting that furniture made?' she said, pointing to the boxes propped in the corner.

'You told me not to bother.'

'I didn't mean go off potholing, or whatever you're doing. Besides having a hole in the basement isn't unusual. Look at Coober Pedy and those places, houses with personal mines dug into the basements.'

'For opal mining. This isn't opal mining. It sounds like something is growing down there.'

Naiyana glanced around, lowering her voice as if afraid Dylan would hear. 'Focus on our house, Lorcan, rather than some adventure. I already have one kid to deal with.'

'I'm checking it out,' he insisted.

'And what if it's some kind of underground aquifer?'

'That would be a good thing.'

'Not if you fall into it.'

'I won't . . .' he started but realized it was a losing battle. Grabbing the torch, he moved for the door. Act now, talk later.

She interrupted his march. 'I'm meeting an old friend

tomorrow. And will check out the school in town too. For Dylan.'

Lorcan turned. She had tried to bury the bad news up front. 'What old friend? Not one of the charity lot?'

She gave him a faint shoulder shrug.

'You know that's not wise, Nee.'

'Don't lecture me about what's not wise. You're about to wander down a hundred-year-old tunnel cut into someone's basement,' she said, mockingly.

Lorcan had no comeback to this. So he left the house with harsh words warning him that he should concentrate on fixing the house.

The tunnel was dark. The torchlight illuminated buttresses and joints that were solid but antique. The rumbling had disappeared, replaced by the clap of his footsteps. The construction was old but the smell was new, moisture in the air that made him wonder if it was indeed an aquifer. But in addition to the moisture was the unmistakable smell of hot oil. Worked oil. Industry. Maybe an open, underground oil deposit. If such a thing was possible. His geographical and geological knowledge didn't extend that far.

After ten minutes of careful manoeuvring, his torch-light fell on a small generator attached to what looked to be a red sifting device, conveyor belt and a grinding machine with wheels and a hammer. New machinery, not from the 1970s when this town was supposedly abandoned for the last time. He touched the side of the grinding machine. It was still hot. Someone had been down here. Mining. And recently. Lorcan felt his nerves take over. Suddenly he felt like he had stumbled upon something that he shouldn't have.

Who could be here? What were they looking for? And were they finding anything? In his educated opinion there were only two reasons to be down a hole in the middle of nowhere: drugs or gold. He didn't want to be caught up in either of those possibilities alone and unarmed.

It meant his exit was infinitely more rapid than his entrance speed, the torch bobbing in front of him, expecting at any moment to be confronted by person or persons unknown. Clambering out of the tunnel he tripped and skidded across the floor, smearing his shirt in fine dust.

Finding his feet, he scrambled out of the house. What now? His immediate thought, the smart thinking was to go back, tell Nee what he had found, pack everyone up and get out of there. But what had he found? Who had he found? Maybe he should be certain before he alarmed her and Dylan. So he darted across to the tin shack opposite and waited to see who – if anyone – would return.

39

Emmaline

They gave her Oily and ZZ. Both more than competent detectives. Oily was in fact Olly Treeston and got the nickname from his excess hair gel. ZZ was so called because DI Moore forgot his real name, Zhao Zheng, at a briefing once. ZZ was easier and it had stuck.

The discovery of Lorcan's body had launched the case to Number One priority. She and Oily were to work it on the ground supported by the local cops, while ZZ would cover the Perth side, deskbound since the motorcycle accident two years ago that paralysed him.

Oily had brought with him information. Or a lack of information. An investigation into the machines found down the mine had yielded nothing, the serial numbers scrubbed, making identification of the dealer impossible.

Forensics had more to report. The body had been confirmed as Lorcan Maguire's. But as well as Lorcan's blood being on his shirt there was also what they described as a significant amount of another type.

Matching Dylan's according to his medical records. They were now working on the assumption that the boy had been there but was now missing, probably injured.

A search for the shell casings was under way but nothing had been found yet, the sand being swept carefully, layer after layer.

What had been noted was a faint pair of parallel grooves in the sand leading over the hill of the crest that the wind had not quite obscured. There was no chance of determining a tread pattern in the soft sand but the width of the tyres had been estimated. Belonging to a Utility Vehicle or a 4x4. Emmaline had sent Oily, Barker and Anand back to hunt for the origin of the tracks. If the vehicle had driven over dirt or even some gibber plains, there was a chance they might find a tyre imprint that could be sampled and matched.

What was determined was that the grooves didn't proceed any further onwards after Lorcan's body. This seemed to disavow the theory that Lorcan had been moved after the incident. The offending vehicle had therefore turned and veered back onto the track leading towards the main highway. Entirely through sand. Either a lucky decision or an expert driver. The tracks didn't return to Kallayee, as if it had no business there. Whoever was in the truck had killed Lorcan Maguire and left. Job done. They were also key suspects in the disappearance of Dylan and Naiyana Maguire.

Emmaline's focus was now on finding them.

146

40

Emmaline

Emmaline gathered her team together back in Kallayee. The hunt for viable origin tracks before the dunes had been a washout and any chance of finding them on the tarmac out of town or nearer Hurton had been wiped out by the sheer volume of traffic over the last few days, polluting the scene without even knowing.

It was time to consider their options. The Forensics team had erected a temporary phone signal booster so mobile phone technology reached Kallayee for the first time. To celebrate this momentous occasion, she got ZZ on the line for a conference.

Oily though was up first. Emmaline knew he would have studied the case thoroughly. He was a fastidious character, his mind tasked with challenges his body could no longer cope with, middle age making him ever more rotund by the day, his athletic youth long behind him. The only endurance events he undertook now were with the all-you-can-eat breakfast buffets in the cafe across the street from HQ.

'Are we thinking that someone from INK Tech –

namely Nikos Iannis – got his revenge for the stolen data?'

Emmaline watched Barker glance at Rispoli and Anand, confusion etched on his face. She had already picked him out as a clocker. Nine to five, family before profession. Not that she held it against him. But she expected him to stay up to speed.

'So a professional hit?' asked Zhao, over the phone. He had been in the same academy class as Emmaline, a First Gen Aussie, his family proud of him becoming an officer. They had spent time and hard-earned money educating him, a new life for the family. In many ways similar to her. The motorcycle accident had hit them hard. Even more than for Zhao himself.

'I would read it that way,' said Oily. 'Maybe they found out that he was selling the information.'

'Or desperate to stop him before he had the chance.'

'But what about Naiyana and Dylan Maguire?' asked Emmaline.

'Use them to try and get the location of the information?' offered Oily. The lack of conviction in his voice betrayed a lack of conviction in his own theory.

'Why not take Lorcan then? What would lead them to believe that she had the info?'

Her questions were met with blank stares. It was time to slide down another path.

'We do know that Naiyana had her own problems. With the companies she was protesting against.'

'So are you thinking that someone in . . .' started Rispoli, before tailing off.

'Brightside Foods,' said Anand, the most junior member of the team and itching to get involved.

'Brightside Foods . . . did the same thing? Tried to get revenge on Naiyana for almost collapsing the company? But we're still left with the same questions.'

'Yes,' said Emmaline. 'When, where and why.'

'Plus, it would be a major risk exacting revenge in such a high profile way.'

They all agreed on that. But it couldn't be ruled out. Yet.

'We also have the MP, Chester Grant,' said Emmaline.

'That populist SOB,' said Barker, 'would flog his granny for a few cents.'

'He was closely tied to Brightside Foods,' said Emmaline.

'He was shilling for them,' added Barker, forthright.

'He's lobbied on their behalf on a number of occasions,' said Zhao, clarifying Barker's slur.

'So the discovery of Lorcan's body and disappearance of Naiyana and Dylan might be troubling for him,' said Oily.

'They were possible votes after all,' said Rispoli.

'Not likely after what had happened though,' said Emmaline.

'Then there would be no harm in seeking revenge, would there?' noted Rispoli.

Another avenue that couldn't be ruled out. The investigation was turning into something much like the desert out here. Heated, faceless and containing any number of tracks and paths to get lost down.

41

Naiyana

She met Leona in Wisbech. It was the next sizeable town along from Hurton, heading south towards Kalgoorlie. She had always been close to Leona, their children around the same age, inviting constant comparison of progress that leads to knowing each other, that leads to friendship. A kind of Six Degrees of Kevin Bacon friendship. But Leona hadn't brought Giulia along with her today given the distance and given that this was in the books as a 'client' visit in Kalgoorlie.

Wisbech had been chosen for safety. A sort of halfway house concession between not meeting former colleagues as Lorcan had wanted, and revealing their actual location. She had even called Leona from a payphone to be certain.

It was a mutually beneficial meeting. She intended to pump Leona for information on the latest situation. Leona would do the same. But Naiyana was confident she was smarter.

Sitting in a quiet corner of the almost empty café,

she waited for Leona to arrive and watched Dylan in the play park across the street. He was sprinting around the rubberized surface, scrambling up ladders and across rope bridges, bouncing and spinning and jumping, full of the joys of life. She willed it to last. When he got older, those moments would become fewer. But not entirely gone. There were always chances to play. You just had to know where to look.

'Nee!'

Leona was skittering across the cafe, her arms outstretched. Using some kind of innate sonar she managed to avoid the other tables, her narrow hips and elongated frame assisting with the skilful manoeuvring.

'Lee!'

There was a hug. Naiyana's face pressed into her shoulder, a warmth in the hug. Old friends meeting.

'How are you? How's life outside the big city?'

'Perth's not that big,' said Naiyana, more to dampen her own inner pining than the truth.

'Compared to everywhere I passed on the way here it is.'

Leona threw her head back and laughed. She always got a kick out of her own jokes, as if she herself was surprised that she had managed to come up with something so witty.

Leona glanced around. 'This town looks okay though. Better in real life than it does in your vlogs.'

Naiyana's smile became wry. 'If only I lived some-where as metropolitan as this.'

'I thought the place in your vlogs looked emptier.'

Naiyana stopped the chit-chat. It was time for serious business.

'Is the heat still bad?'

'It is summer after all,' said Leona, accompanied by the thrown-back head and unrestrained guffaw.

'Seriously, Lee.'

Leona pursed her lips and nodded. 'We're still getting threats.'

'Towards the charity?'

'And towards you.' At this Leona looked around the cafe furtively, then back to her. 'The owners of BS Foods,' she chortled at the derogatory nickname Naiyana had conceived during their pursuit of the company, 'have been to HQ looking to contact you.'

'And?'

'And what? We haven't given them an address.'

'You don't have one.'

'True.'

'Did they say what they wanted?'

'No, but I guess they are in damage control. They changed the ingredients like we asked. Apparently it tastes like dog food now. Cheap dog food,' she laughed, head thrown back.

Naiyana wondered what BS wanted with her. She supposed that getting her to endorse the altered product might generate positive publicity for a company that was trying to repair its reputation and sales figures.

'We also had a protest outside HQ from some of

the people who lost their jobs. That was a fun day,'
said Leona. This was accompanied not by a laugh but
almost a glare.

'So you're saying that the shitstorm is ongoing?'

'Blowin' strong.'

Despite the continuing stormy weather front,
Naiyana felt a pang at not being back there to do
anything about it. She was missing an opportunity to
turn something bad into something good. Her main
goal in the first place. But also the drive that had led
her into this mess in the first place. So fuck BS Foods.
The loss of jobs was regrettable but acceptable collateral damage. They were the ones who had tried to
force a dangerous product onto the market.

'Chester Grant has also been in contact,' said Leona.
'Well his office has, to be more accurate.'

'What does the slimy bastard want?'

'Not sure. Probably the same as BS.'

Naiyana nodded at this. No doubt the weasel was
getting a stick up the arse from BS and his now jobless
constituents.

'There might be another reason for our esteemed
MP getting in contact,' said Naiyana, unable to hold
it back.

'What?' asked Leona, intrigued.

'I can't say. Other than it might be to do with BS.
BS on top of BS,' said Naiyana and sniffed a laugh.
'But on another topic, what do you think of the
vlogs?'

'Outback Motherhood? I love them!' said Leona.

'But you need to be more than a voice behind the camera. We should see you.'

Naiyana thought so as well, but that would bring risks. But wasn't life all about risks? She had taken so many already that she could tolerate another few. As long as no one found out the location of the town, it would be a massive fuck-you to BS Foods and Chester Grant.

42

Emmaline

The afternoon brought with it a report from Tech on Lorcan's phone. Naiyana's was still offline and missing.

The date of the final, frantic recording was confirmed. The thirtieth of December at 17:03.

The rest of Lorcan's movements had been analysed – when his phone had been within range of the mast 14 km north of Hurton anyway. Like most in the area it was a super mast but didn't quite have the span to reach Kallayee. It never needed to before.

Emmaline ushered Oily and Rispoli into the caravan, a very non-hi-tech base for the investigation. Fittingly it was falling apart like the town itself. Barker and Anand had been sent into Hurton to question the locals as to whether they had heard a gunshot sometime in the afternoon of 30 December. Or last night. And to garner any further information on the family's movements during their sixteen days in town. That was all. Sixteen days. Emmaline couldn't help but think that the family seemed to stir up a world of shit wherever they went.

'So this is what we know. We have Lorcan – and presumably the family – leaving Perth on the twelfth December. An overnight in Kalgoorlie before passing the towers around Kanowna and Menzies and arriving in Hurton on the thirteenth. After then it goes dark until the fifteenth when his phone connected and a matching credit-card charge was made in the local hardware store in Hurton. One call to his parents. Five minutes.'

'According to them it was nothing urgent,' said Oily. 'Confirmation that they had arrived, found a place, were settling in, etc., etc.'

'Then he was in Hurton again on the sixteenth. More expenditure on materials.'

'So we can assume that they didn't quite know what they were getting into,' said Rispoli.

'Possibly on a number of fronts,' said Emmaline, thinking about the missing data and the boycotted baby food.

She continued. 'Then on the nineteenth Lorcan Maguire – and his son – stayed overnight in Kalgoorlie, purchasing more materials there including the DIY furniture still present in the house, returning on the twentieth. On the twenty-first Naiyana Maguire's card was recorded as being used in Wisbech. In a cafe in the afternoon.'

'There is expenditure on her card for ice cream with three toppings, suggesting either she has a sweet tooth or Dylan was with her,' said Oily.

'Then we have Naiyana's card back in Hurton on

the twenty-second, purchasing groceries and gas. The phone signal puts her back in Hurton again on the twenty-fourth. But there is no spend on the card that day.'

'So she just visited Hurton?'

'She doesn't have to be in town to be in range of the mast,' noted Rispoli.

That was something for Emmaline to consider. Not all of the movements had to necessarily relate to Hurton. She could have been meeting other people. Or heading to other places.

'On the twenty-fifth there's a confirmed visit to Hurton and expenditure on her card.'

'Then forward to the twenty-seventh when Lorcan's phone appears in Hurton. Making a call to an unknown number,' said Rispoli.

'The bank card was not used though.'

'Maybe he was scared to max it out. It was border-line by that stage.'

Emmaline nodded in agreement. 'On the twenty-eighth the phone is picked up in Wisbech. No spend again. So if he wasn't spending money, my guess is that he was meeting someone.'

'But we don't know who?' said Oily.

'We don't,' admitted Emmaline.

After a pause to digest this, Rispoli continued, 'On the twenty-ninth there is contact with Naiyana's phone. Hurton again. Bank card not used.'

'Finally we come to the thirtieth,' said Emmaline. The records showed it had been a busy day. For both parents. 'First of all, Lorcan's phone is picked up in Wisbech in the morning before falling off radar at eleven twenty-four. Presumably heading back to Kallayee as that was where we found the phone.'

'With the message,' added Oily.

'Yes. So he had driven there in the morning only to spend no money and then return. So the question is – did he spot someone in Wisbech? Maybe the net was closing in? I'd been thinking that he may have come back from Wisbech to find Naiyana was gone. Like in the message. So he felt that he had to take Dylan away immediately. But he was caught. But –' Emmaline looked at her colleagues '– Naiyana's phone is picked up in Wisbech on that same afternoon. There's an active signal from 2:27 to 3:33.'

'Could he have had both phones?' asked Oily. 'He switched one off and the other one on?'

'But why would he have both?'

'If Naiyana was in Kallayee, she would have had no need for a phone,' said Rispoli.

Emmaline nodded. 'She would also not need one if she was already gone.'

'Or taken?'

'When Lorcan was in Wisbech,' said Oily.

'So the message on Lorcan's phone was faked? He already knew that she had gone?' said Rispoli.

'It didn't sound faked.'

'No, it didn't,' admitted Emmaline. 'We have three options. One, Lorcan Maguire took both phones to Wisbech knowing that his wife was gone. Possibly looking to cover his tracks. Two, he took both phones for an unknown reason and returned to Kallayee to find his wife gone. Or three, he returned to Kallayee and Naiyana then left to go to Wisbech herself.'

She let that sink in before concluding, 'What we do know is that the thirtieth is the last day either of the phones was in contact with a tower.'

'So were they both meeting people in Wisbech?' asked Rispoli.

Oily spoke up. 'ZZ organized warrants and matched locations with Nikos Iannis's phone and those of his work colleagues. No correlation, no overlap of location.'

'Unless they met in Kallayee, of course,' said Rispoli. 'By accident or design.'

'In the dead zone,' said Emmaline. It had never rung truer.

43

Emmaline

'They also checked Internet history,' said Oily, opening another document on the laptop.

'Never a good thing,' said Rispoli, shrugging his shoulders in a 'You know how it is' kind of way that made Emmaline smile.

Oily continued regardless. 'Mainly "how to build" stuff, but also something more disturbing – a number of "how to kill" searches.'

'Are we talking termites, cockroaches, spiders?' asked Emmaline.

'Probably, but the research centred on what poisons to use to get rid of them.'

'Anything that could kill a human?'

'Any poison could kill a human with the right dosage.'

'Let's canvas places from Kalgoorlie to Hurton to enquire if they sold poison to anyone fitting Lorcan Maguire's description.'

'That will take a while.'

'Has to be done,' said Emmaline. If someone sold

Lorcan poison it would give them a lead on Naiyana's demise. If not her location.

'There were also various searches on mining and digging for gold.'

'So he was using the mines,' said Emmaline. 'Was that the reason they moved here specifically? Did he know something?'

'There is also the question as to where he sourced the equipment,' said Rispoli.

'I've looked it up. Plenty of sources for small-time gold mining. If you hit the right seam.'

'If you got lucky.'

'Could Naiyana be in one of the mines? Poisoned?' asked Rispoli.

'We searched them pretty thoroughly,' noted Oily.

'But not *all* mines.'

Emmaline piped up. 'Get me the most thorough list you can. Find out if we missed any. Include Hurton and beyond.'

At this rate she would need to sequester the entire MCS to help. Lorcan Maguire could have poisoned his wife and stashed her in one of the mines. It might explain the 'she's gone' comment. But knowing or suspecting this did nothing to narrow down the expanse of the search. And it certainly didn't explain why Lorcan was shot in the desert and Dylan was missing.

'They found another video recording too. Dated twenty-second December. Badly corrupted but Tech worked their magic on it. Here.'

Oily cranked the volume and tapped play. The screen remained pitch black. Emmaline was about to joke that Tech's magic was nothing to write home about when the sound of careful footsteps and rasped breathing filled the caravan. Though the blackness of the screen remained undiminished the footsteps halted, breath held. Another sound arose. A distant voice, maybe two voices, unclear but present. There and gone. The rustling of movement and breathing returned as if the person holding the phone was moving rapidly. Then the recording ended abruptly.

'Nothing else?' asked Emmaline.

'No, they passed the recording through modulation to try and clean it up. This is the best we have. According to them the voice is almost certainly male and Australian. From Brisbane-Gold Coast direction they determine. A long way from home.'

'There is also a subtle tick in his speech,' noted Rispoli. 'Like he's chewing gum.'

'The echoes indicate it was recorded in an enclosed space.'

'The same tunnel the mining equipment was in?'

'That might explain the darkness. Either that or the phone was kept in his pocket. Out of sight,' said Emmaline.

'What if they were trapped somewhere down a mine? Maybe Lorcan got out with his son and tried to escape. They had to leave Naiyana behind. Or she was already dead.'

'Have they played it to Lorcan's family?'

'Yeah,' said Oily. 'No one recognized the voice.'

'But we do know that the phone was out of signal range at the time of the recording,' said Emmaline. 'The question is whether someone had come out to visit the family. And if that visitor was welcome or not.'

'Someone from INK Tech or Brightside?'

Or Chester Grant, thought Emmaline but kept him out of the equation as yet. She recognized the growing desperation within the caravan. They had found Lorcan's body but the overall sense was that they were already too late. This was the overriding emotion of being a police officer in her experience – arriving too late to prevent bad things from happening. Only there to piece together the aftermath and create one final snapshot of a person's life. But once a mirror was broken it couldn't be put back the same way it had been. The cracks were always there.

'Do we put the recording out nationally?' asked Rispoli. 'See if anyone recognizes it?'

'Or keep it to ourselves for now in case these people killed Lorcan Maguire and took Naiyana and Dylan hostage,' said Emmaline.

'We haven't received a ransom request though, have we? Which would be odd for a kidnapping.'

She couldn't fault the logic. She was glad to have Rispoli on her team. Given the rapidly increasing workload she needed about twenty competent officers like him. But she was left with four. Plus Barker.

She noted, 'Plus we have Naiyana's blood in the house. And Dylan's on his dad's shirt.'

'And more near the quad bike with the slashed tyres,' said Anand.

'Which, according to Forensics, doesn't match Naiyana's,' said Oily. 'Or Lorcan's or Dylan's.'

'But it matches someone's. Just nobody in the system.'

'So *do* we go public with the recording?' asked Rispoli, looking to Emmaline.

The risks remained. What if someone was holding Naiyana and Dylan? What if going public forced them to kill both? But minus a ransom demand and given Lorcan Maguire's murder, the blood found in the house and the blood found in town, they needed a solid lead. Identifying this unknown voice on a dead man's phone was a solid lead.

Emmaline took a deep breath, almost tasting the years of Papa Webster's cigarettes on her tongue. 'Send it out. We'll hope for the best.'

Not a situation any investigator wanted to be in, she thought.

44

Lorcan

Naiyana cooked dinner on the camping stove. They could make the rest of the house a mansion but until there was a working cooker it would always look temporary. He had never appreciated before how the kitchen was the most essential part of a house. You could sleep on the floor, sit on beanbags, even shit in an outside dunny and manage, but minus a cooker it all felt transitory.

Eggs and beans. Breakfast for dinner. Naiyana said she was going into town tomorrow for more groceries. He knew that she hated this cooking, cleaning bullshit. So did he. They had employed a cleaner in Perth. Once a week for fifty bucks. Worth it to not have to worry about it. Affluent times.

She was on her third glass of wine, her hand not quivering yet but not far off. Normally he would say something about taking it easy with the booze but not tonight. Her falling asleep was part of the plan.

'What was the school like?' he asked, trying to instigate a non-fractious conversation.

'Yeah, okay,' she said, mumbling. 'Nothing like Clementine. Old, dusty and decayed – but fine.'

'Doesn't sound good for Dylan.'

'He'll manage. He'll make new friends and . . .' The sentence drifted away. The wine was taking effect. Suddenly she was reanimated, a new topic broached. 'Are you sure that no one knows we are here?' she said, taking a large gulp.

'I'm sure,' said Lorcan. 'Why?'

'I just . . . wanted to know.'

'What about you?'

'No one,' she said, followed by another gulp.

Lorcan narrowed his eyes, trying to drill into her skull. 'Nee?'

'I was just wondering.'

'You didn't reveal anything to your friend? Or in one of your vlogs?'

'No.'

'Did someone reply to them?'

'No.'

'Maybe you should be more worried about who might already be with us.'

'What do you mean by that?' she asked, with an overexaggerated frown.

'Nothing,' said Lorcan.

'You want to go back to that tunnel, don't you?' she said, the glass finding wine-stained lips that had turned a glorious red.

He said nothing. Which said plenty.

'Don't leave us here.'

'I'll just take a look.'

The rest of the dinner passed in silence. As did the half-hour before she passed out on the sun lounger in the living room. Lorcan put a sleepy Dylan to bed and left. He would be back before she awoke.

45

Lorcan

He took up his previous spot in the tin shack opposite the tunnel house. The air was a little colder than previous nights but his nerves kept him warm, hands pressed to his legs to stop them from jerking up and down.

Just before midnight he heard it. The rumble of an engine, coasting slowly into town. A minute later, the moonlit shadow of a dark coloured ute came into view, its headlights off. A stealthy approach. Experienced. It backed up to the door of the wooden structure and three figures emerged. All male given their height and breadth. Working in the darkness they began to unload items from the back, carrying them inside, sometimes needing two of them to heft whatever it was.

Lorcan didn't interrupt them. He had seen spy movies before. It was best to gather information before deciding upon any action. Find out who they were and what they were doing. Determine if they were friend or foe. Caution swayed him more towards the latter than the former. His immediate concern was that these people were working for Nikos and were here to do something bad to him. But if they were they would have no need for the tunnel and the equipment. From what he had read Nikos and his brother exercised concise not convoluted punishments. This dash of common sense relaxed him. That and the Browning .22-250 rifle sat by his side. He had been offered it at a good price by a guy outside Mallon's yesterday. He had been suspicious at the start as the guy, who introduced himself as Matty, knew that he was living out at Kallayee – word had obviously spread – and said he might need it to shoot dingoes or anything else threatening his property. At the time, Lorcan had wondered if it was a subtle warning but the guy took $200 and gave him the rifle and a few shells. He had yet to fire it and as he sat there staring at the rifle he wondered if he had been taken for a ride. He had only fired a gun once in his life. At a clay pigeon shoot organized by INK Tech. Maybe that training would come back to haunt Nikos Iannis. But first things first. He had to find out who these people were and what they wanted. He turned his focus back to the house across the road.

The unloading was completed in fifteen minutes and the three men disappeared inside the building. The focused glare of headlamps erupted from the window holes, darting around as if they were making sure the room was clear before eventually disappearing.

Lorcan waited for five minutes before following. Sneaking inside, he immediately saw that the cupboard covering the hole had been moved. For a moment a chill passed through him. What if they had spotted anything out of place? Had he touched anything? Would they be able to tell? What if they were actual spies, their mission secret and illegal? The British government had used some places out here for nuclear testing in the 1950s and 1960s. Maybe there was something down there that had been left behind. Uranium or plutonium. Fanciful but possible.

He stood at the tunnel entrance. Murmured speech echoed through it, faint and distorted. In no language he could identify. He wondered if they were foreign spies. The thought scared him even more.

It was time to make a decision. Should he go down after them? In the narrow tunnel the rifle would be constrictive and he wasn't sure how well prepared they might be. It appeared a slick operation so he had to assume they had rigged defences of some sort.

His deliberation paid off. Suddenly a faint light appeared, growing stronger by the second. One of the three men was returning.

Lorcan panicked. He looked around the room. The contrast of its sheer darkness was all-encompassing. He lost all sense of thought and direction. Where was the door again? How far? Was there anything in the way? The light drew closer. He had about twenty seconds. Remembering the way, he made for the door and darted around the side of the building. He pressed himself against the wall, hoping that the clouds continued to swallow up the moon. For ever would be long enough right now. A stranger passed him on the way to the ute; tall, bearded and slim, almost ghoulish, his limbs seeming to grow as if absorbing the darkness. The figure freewheeled the truck across the road into an old shed that Lorcan had never thought of checking. Even if he had, the truck looked battered enough to pass for having been left there for fifty years. Throwing a cover over it the figure walked by him again and disappeared back down the tunnel.

This time it didn't take Lorcan long to consider whether to follow or not. There was no fucking way he was going in. He would retreat to his viewing spot. Take up sentry duty. With his rifle.

He pressed his phone to his ear and listened to the recording he'd made. The rasps of breaths, the echo of the walls. And the voice. Confirmation that they weren't alone in town.

After ten minutes the low rumbling began in earnest, vibrating under his feet. The noise that had plagued them since arriving. Confirmation that these men had been here since his family came to town. Without breaking cover. Meaning that they were determined. Meaning that it was a major operation of some kind. Machines carted in and rock broken. All for what? Gold? Diamonds? Opals? And persisting in this heat and with this level of secrecy indicated success of some kind. Lorcan wanted to know. So he kept watch.

An hour before dawn the three men re-emerged,

171

breaking up to silently perform prescribed tasks. Well-drilled.

As well as the tall, bearded figure from earlier, the gathering dawn allowed him to ascribe details to the other two, the shortest one packing fat under a shirt that was glued to his body with sweat and a bald head that caught the fading moonlight. The other one had darker skin than the others, a little younger and in better shape, sporting a full head of sweeping, unkempt hair.

The bearded one – who seemed to be in nominal charge – retrieved the ute from under the cover and backed it to the door. Loading took half the time of unloading, a dusty blanket covering the flatbed dulling any stray thud or clang.

The other two climbed in and the ute crept back out of town with its lights off, the driver clearly confident of the way. Kallayee returned to how it had been. Empty.

46

Naiyana

Her head was pounding. Her bloody husband wasn't helping, pacing around the bedroom as excited as Dylan after a sugar-rush. The sun wasn't even up yet.

'There's three of them.'

'Three of who?'

'Three guys. Miners. Or spies.'

'Keep your voice down,' she said, as much for her benefit as Dylan's. 'What three guys?'

'In the tunnel.'

Naiyana frowned. 'Have *you* been drinking?'

'I saw them with my own eyes, Nee. They drove in with the lights off and headed down the tunnel. Ten minutes later that bloody rumbling started. The leader seems to be a tall guy with a beard. There's a short, stocky one and a dark-skinned one. Maybe Aboriginal.'

'You can't say that,' she said, rebuking him.

Her husband seemed to ignore her. 'I don't think they are spies but they did nuclear tests out here in the fifties and sixties. At Maralinga and . . .' He stopped there. Even he must have recognized how crazy it sounded. 'I think they are mining for gold, diamonds or opals.'

Naiyana took a moment to take it in. 'How does it affect us?'

'What do you mean?'

'They aren't disturbing us, are they?'

'No, but we don't know anything about them. Plus they have gone out of their way not to interact with us. There must be a reason for that.'

'They've obviously met you before,' said Naiyana.

Lorcan ignored her. 'We should leave,' he said.

'I thought we'd been over this. We weren't going to run.'

'That was before we knew we weren't alone.'

'I'm sick of running, Lorcan. Where do we run to next? The moon?'

She stared at her husband for an answer. She didn't want to be dragged around the country like some under-supported witness protection stooge. If it was a choice of fight or flight, she was choosing fight.

'I'll watch them again, tonight.'

Naiyana shook her head. 'They don't want us to know they are there, so we pretend we don't know.'

Her husband's eyes darted to the doorway. She could tell that he was looking to escape this conversation without replying. If he said nothing, it wasn't a lie.

'Lorcan?'

'What?'

'We don't disturb them, they won't disturb us.'

'How do you know that?'

'I don't. But they haven't bothered us so far, so why would they now?'

47

Emmaline

The autopsy report on Lorcan Maguire's body was ready the next morning. Emmaline drove to Hurton to get some breakfast and make the call. Again the local population – plus a few reporters – were out in force to watch the new arrivals. Partly curiosity and partly a desire to get them into the shops to spend money. It was a hard fact that many of these towns relied on the tourist dollar and right now she counted as a working tourist.

She called Oily. He was in Kalgoorlie with the pathologist, Dr Arthur Collins, who greeted her over the phone as if meeting a new friend.

'It's nice to meet you, Miss, Mrs or Dr Taylor. Whatever it may be.'

'It's Detective,' said Emmaline. 'What did you find?'

'I take it you want to skip the obvious.'

'Which is?'

'That Lorcan Maguire was murdered. Gunshot wound to the chest.'

'Have you got a make and calibre of the weapon?'

'Point 22 Winchester shell. Likely fired from a hunting rifle. A quite common combo around these parts for killing animals and pests.'

'And people.'

'Yes. But fortunately rarely people. It was fired from a distance of about four metres, which rules out suicide, despite the gunpowder residue on the victim's remaining fingers.'

'On that. Have you a time frame for when the victim might have fired a gun?'

'Given the continued presence of residue, I'd say recently.'

'And he'd been dead for about a week when we found him?'

'The results indicate so. Though we have to account for accelerated decomposition due to exposure to high temperatures which allow the bacteria to thrive.' This information was delivered in a friendly but cold fashion, like a priest giving last rites, the ritual to be respected but the edges lightly smoothed. The results matched Dr Patel's initial observations. Emmaline would have to remind her next time that sometimes facts could be immediately known. She wouldn't like that at all.

'And the fractured bone?'

'A radius bone. Forearm. Nasty fracture suggesting blunt force trauma from a large object.'

'Like a crowbar? Sledgehammer?'

'Bigger. Most likely a vehicle. Possibly bull bars as a culprit. A lifesaver if you hit an animal, a killer if you hit a human, but I digress,' said Dr Collins.

'So a ute?' asked Emmaline, thinking of the family's vehicle.

'Or any 4x4 or off-road vehicle,' said Dr Collins. 'If you can locate the vehicle and it hasn't been thoroughly scrubbed you might even find evidence of human material, blood, skin or hair, still present.'

'Anything else?'

'The toxicological report brought up nothing unusual in his system, no drugs, no alcohol, though of course the dingoes contaminated some of that too.'

Emmaline didn't need that visual circling her head again. Not this early in the morning.

Dr Collins continued. 'Blood that matches Dylan Maguire's registered blood group was found on the shirt at the scene.'

'Enough to suggest death?'

'Any amount of blood loss could suggest death, Detective. But it's not in worrisome quantities if that's what you are getting at. Naiyana Maguire's blood type was present too. Again not enough to necessarily suggest death, but enough to indicate injury.'

Emmaline thought back to the house and the broken mirror. A family raided, maybe even burgled. Things get out of hand, Naiyana is killed and the father grabs the son and runs before being chased down in the desert by the burglars. Or Naiyana and Dylan taken as hostages. Maybe by the voice in the tunnel. But Lorcan had recorded the video eight days before the final frantic message, so the presence of whoever this voice belonged to hadn't immediately frightened the family off.

48

Emmaline

Her next call was to Perth. ZZ and the others were looking into Lorcan Maguire's dealings, pre- and post-redundancy, and a team led by Neil Templeton, another detective from the MCS, was looking into the charity and the scandal that forced Naiyana Maguire out of a job.

It was the latter team that brought news this morning. A Leona Sanchez had come forward admitting to meeting Naiyana in Wisbech on 21 December.

An interview had been set up for noon. Emmaline told them to make it one and she would be there.

Emmaline entered the interview room to be greeted by a slim woman in her forties with lines on her face that foundation could not cover. Despite her exotic-sounding surname she was pasty white and looked like she would burn at the sheer mention of the word sun. Her demeanour was a little agitated, her long fingernails scraping her palms.

After formalizing greetings and informing Mrs

Sanchez that this interview was being recorded, Emmaline settled into the questions.

'You said you met Naiyana Maguire in Wisbech?'

'On the twenty-first of December. In the Half-Door Cafe.'

'And on any other occasion since she left Perth?'

'No, just that once.'

'Has anyone else from the charity met with her?'

'No.'

'No?'

'Not as far as I know.'

There was nothing that suggested Leona Sanchez was a liar but Emmaline decided to push her.

'Why didn't you speak up before?'

Leona Sanchez's agitation materialized into a persistent hand tremor.

'We didn't chat about much, just the latest . . . the fallout from what she – we – had done.'

'And what was the fallout?'

'You must have read about it, Detective?'

Emmaline kept quiet and waited for Leona to expand on her own question.

'It was in the papers, online, on the news even. The boycott of Brightside Foods, the recall of their new baby food line? Over a hundred jobs lost? The protests outside our office? The things sent to Naiyana—?'

Emmaline pounced. 'What kinds of things?'

'Online threats mostly. And two letters with dog shit in them. One with human. It was too much heat for the charity. It was adversely affecting donations. They told Naiyana to leave.'

'And what did you think?'

'I think they should have supported her,' said Leona, the tremor now paused. She had found Leona's backbone. Loyalty to her friend. 'Instead they threw *her* out. Nee was in the right. *We* were in the right.'

'So you want her back?'

'Yes, I want her back. But she had to move away. Into hiding.'

'Is that what she said?'

'Yes.'

'So she didn't want to go?'

Leona shook her head. 'No. We both knew she couldn't cope with being in the middle of nowhere. She was just so full of energy. And now . . .'

'Now?'

'I don't know. No one can find her. The police are around asking questions. It must mean that it's serious.'

Leona's eyes closed, the renewed tremor threatening to knock the glass of water off the table.

Emmaline didn't need her breaking down so changed the subject. 'On that day – the twenty-first – did you chat about anything specific?'

'I updated her on the whole shitstorm, nothing specific, just that it was still a shitstorm. We talked about how she and the family were doing.'

'And what was the impression you got?'

'She was coping. Trying to cope. It was a massive change for all of them.'

181

'Did she seem distressed?'

'No. Maybe bored and a little sorry for where she found herself. I was sorry for her too. We talked about the vlogs. I told her to make sure no one could identify the town.'

'Because of the threats?'

'Yes. This scandal affected a lot of people, Detective. Including that sleazeball MP.'

'Chester Grant.'

'Yes. I told her that his office had been in contact.'

'What about?'

'They didn't say. Probably arse-covering. Getting Nee to do a photo shoot with BS Foods and their revised product.'

'And was she interested?'

Leona bit her lip. 'I don't know. But she did hint that she knew something about him.'

Emmaline frowned. 'Like what?'

'She didn't say.'

'She didn't mention anything?'

'No.'

'But it sounded important?'

'Seemed to be.'

Emmaline made a note to contact Chester Grant. To see why he wanted to get in touch with Naiyana Maguire so badly.

'Just a few more questions, Mrs Sanchez. Could anyone have followed you? Did you use your credit or debit card anywhere?'

'For fuel, yes.' With this Leona's eyes flashed wide.

The tremors returned. And the self-blame. 'You don't think that someone could have . . . And I led them to her. And Lorcan. And Dylan.' She couldn't hold back her tears any longer.

'Did you tell anyone else about the meeting?' asked Emmaline.

Leona continued crying and didn't answer.

'Mrs Sanchez?'

'Just in the office. I thought the others should know she was okay. Was that wrong too?' she asked, tears now dripping freely from her lined face.

49

Lorcan

Lorcan looked at the boxes of furniture lined up in the living room. This was the easy part of fixing up the house. No Internet manuals needed, just a simple set of stick-figure instructions. However, it was excruciatingly boring given what he knew was taking place just past the crossroads.

Naiyana ducked her head into the room. 'How are you getting on?'

He stared at the box in front of him – a rocking chair – and didn't respond.

'I'm going to get some groceries. More ice for the box. Dylan is drawing in the kitchen.'

'Take him with you.'

'He's happy where he is. And I need to get away.'

He looked at her. They both knew why she needed to get away. To come to terms with the fact that they weren't alone.

He listened to the engine cough into life and the crunch of the tyres on the sand, before both sounds faded away leaving silence again. He opened the cardboard box – a jumble of pieces. He had no interest in it.

He headed to the kitchen to check on Dylan. He was giving some anonymous superhero a decidedly garish cape, his tongue poking out.

'I'm going out for a while. Stay here.'

The head lifted from his work. 'I'll come too, Daddy.'

Lorcan went to say no. Then thought about it. No harm in having a lookout. Just in case.

The house was still. No ute. No lights. And no rumbling. He put his finger to his lips to warn Dylan to stay quiet but the silence gave him no reason to suspect that the three men were lying in wait.

Carefully easing the cupboard away from the hole following the precise lines, he heard Dylan coo as the tunnel was exposed.

He prepared to enter. 'Now, you keep watch up here. If you hear a truck, shout down the tunnel for Daddy and then run and hide.' The stupidity of posting his six-year-old son as lookout became overly apparent to him but there was no one else.

'I don't want you going down there, Daddy.'

'It's okay. I'll only be fifteen minutes.'

'No!'

'Dylan, fifteen—'

'I want to come too.'

Lorcan looked at his son. Through the fear was a determination not to be left behind.

'Stay behind Daddy then.'

He switched on the torch and entered the tunnel.

50

Emmaline

After Leona's admission the charity was interrogated again. It was quickly discovered that Naiyana's location had been leaked to Chester Grant's office. They had been in touch under the pretext of contacting Naiyana for a discussion about the revised baby food and someone had thought they were being helpful by letting them know that she had moved to the Wisbech area.

Emmaline contacted Chester's office to arrange a meeting but he was unavailable all afternoon. Even to the police.

So taking advantage of being in the city, Emmaline decided to visit Nikos Iannis again. Oily joined her.

Nikos lived in a stylish, detached house in Applecross, his view of the Swan River obstructed by the really expensive houses. So near and yet so far. Which must have been galling for him. Still he wasn't doing so bad, the red slate, two-storey, an impressive property, with a swimming pool tucked under the trees at the back. In the wide driveway was a 4x4. With bull bars.

After giving their names to the intercom, a buzzer opened the gates, Nikos not bothering to leave the house to meet them, indicating his disrespect through nonchalance.

Approaching the 4x4 Emmaline spilled her keys from her pocket. Kneeling on the gravel, she surreptitiously checked the bull bars for any residue. For blood, hair or dirt, as Dr Collins suggested. Fumbling them further under, she glanced at the underside. It was clean. Recently washed. She supposed that people like Nikos didn't get to run a successful company or afford a house like this without having some smarts. And being utterly ruthless.

As she gathered her keys and looked up Nikos was standing in the doorway in a dressing gown, open down the front to reveal a chest that was flabby but glistening. Freshly shaved.

'Find anything down there?' he asked, with a grin.

'No work today?' Emmaline responded.

'When you're the boss you can choose when to go in. Maybe you'll get the chance someday.'

'Once I learn how to tie a dressing gown.'

Nikos rolled his eyes. 'What is it you want, Detective?'

'To talk about your past.'

Emmaline already knew about it. Nikos and Georgios Iannis had made their money in the shady world of debt collection, specializing in clients who had defaulted. The provision of financial advice was the reputable face of the business. Their MO, however, was mugging businesses that were in trouble and even some that weren't. There were rumours that these negotiations were fraught and in some cases, violent, the use of roughhouse tactics suspected but unproven. Beatings, leanings and breakings.

'We can talk about that out here,' said Nikos, not moving from the doorway.

'You and your brother are no strangers to violence, are you?'

'Have you come to give me a history lesson or ask a question? If it's A, I'm not interested. If it's B, I'd like to have my lawyer present.'

Oily stepped in. 'We have statements from people in your office that there were lots of anxious meetings in the days following Lorcan Maguire's redundancy.'

'There were. Looking for the information he stole.'

'Allegedly stole. Which you since haven't found.'

'No.'

'You don't seem all that worried. Especially considering we found Lorcan Maguire's body,' said Emmaline.

'What do you expect me to do about it?'

'He was shot, Mr Iannis.'

'And what? You think it was me? We were, and are, furious at the theft but more for allowing it to happen. We got negligent and it cost us. Greatly.'

'But you admit trying to contact Mr Maguire to get the information back?'

'We tried via the court.'

'And when that failed you tracked him down and sent out someone to meet him. Is that right?'

Nikos glared at her, trying but failing to disguise the look of guilt.

'All we want is to save the company,' said Nikos, less boisterous now, treading carefully. 'We had lawyers threaten other companies off buying the info. But we still don't know if he was flogging it. It hasn't turned up. Yet.'

'Which means that it was lost or is still out there somewhere. Maybe on a disk,' said Oily.

'Which you would kill to get your hands on,' said Emmaline.

'Kill is a big accusation, Detective. We're the ones who lost out in all this shit.'

'Apart from the dead man, of course.'

'I had nothing to do with that,' said Nikos, curtly.

'The house had been turned over. As if someone was looking for something.'

'I have nothing to say about that.'

'There was little in that house of value apart from that information,' said Emmaline. 'It sure seemed like professionals were sent in to search and destroy. I'm sure you know a few.'

'I'm sure I do too,' admitted Nikos.

Emmaline continued. 'They found nothing so used Naiyana Maguire as leverage to get Lorcan to tell them where the information was hidden. Her blood was found in the house. Lorcan then escaped with his son before he was caught and killed.'

'*Are* you accusing me of something?' asked Nikos. 'Is the answer, B? Do I need my lawyer?'

190

'I'm sure you will,' said Emmaline. 'But we're just covering all angles at the minute. Yours is one of the sharpest ones. Animosity breeds revenge. Doesn't it, Mr Iannis?'

Nikos Iannis curled his lips into a snarl, stepped back and shut the door.

51

Lorcan

Dylan kept bumping into his legs, making them both stumble. His son was obeying the order to stay close to the letter. It had been a slow five-minute shuffle so far, ears trained for any stray noise that might indicate they weren't alone.

'I'm scared, Daddy.'

'We'll be there soon.' Lorcan wanted to check the machine's output. If there was gold, diamond or opal then he would be able to detect fragments somewhere. Or at least he thought so anyway. And if it was uranium or plutonium? Well the three men who'd been here last night hadn't donned any special equipment to ward against radiation so he had ruled that out.

'Can we go back?'

'A little further. You can be my brave boy,' said Lorcan. Thankfully the darkness shielded Dylan from seeing that his father's own bravery was paper-thin.

His reassurance lasted for thirty seconds. Then the tears started.

'I want to go back, Daddy. I don't like it down here.'

Lorcan took another few steps and stopped. The crying bounced off the walls, surrounding him in despair. This had been a stupid idea. Bringing Dylan down here. He would have to come back alone. When Naiyana took Dylan to town next time. Tomorrow hopefully.

'Okay, let's go back,' he said, nudging Dylan back towards the exit.

The light hurt his eyes for a few seconds after they emerged from the tunnel. His skin prickled with the heat and the fact he hadn't been able to definitively prove what the men were mining.

He manoeuvred his son into the open air, the heat instantly cranking from mildly irritating to almost unbearable.

Holding his son close he gazed up and down the street to see if they had been watched. They hadn't.

One small, green bearded dragon was perched on a rock by the collapsed fence, its tongue flicking, tasting the fear in the air. Lorcan could taste it too.

52

Emmaline

In the late afternoon, Emmaline retreated to MCS HQ in Northbridge and secured a conference room that looked out over the banks of rapidly emptying desks.

She was working on what Naiyana Maguire might have on Chester Grant. According to Leona Sanchez, Naiyana had been both excited and secretive at their meeting. It suggested she knew something important, rather than minor gossip.

Family, previous schools or employment had proven a bust. The Maguire family had never lived in Chester Grant's constituency.

An affair between the two was possible but unlikely. Both were married – although that was not much of a barrier in Emmaline's experience – but her determination to make BS Foods suffer had caused Chester to suffer as well. If they had been having an affair they had disguised it well.

The only thing that linked the two of them was Brightside Foods. Brightside had been founded in the

1970s by a WA farmer called Herbert Palmer who had a vision to create quickly prepared meals based on what grew on his land and create a self-sustaining business. It had worked. By the time he died in 2003 Brightside Foods had grown into a huge nationwide enterprise, no longer just supplied by the family farm but many others around Australia, branching into many different arenas of food preparation and supply. A success story. Until recently.

After Herbert's death, and according to the newspaper reports, the rapid increase in size had forced the business to be altered from family owned to floated, allowing future wealth to be up for grabs. She wondered who owned it now.

Checking the companies register online she discovered that forty per cent of the shares were held by a company called AG Solutions. Emmaline had never heard of them and their directors were unlisted. But AG Solutions were themselves owned by AG Holdings, for which the directors were again unlisted. Down and down she followed, the rabbit hole getting ever deeper. And that's when she found it. Under AG Holdings and another company called AG Future was AG Decade. Owned by Abilene Grant.

Emmaline's interest was piqued. A quick search revealed that Abilene Grant was the mother of one Chester Grant. It meant his family held a significant amount of shares in Brightside Foods. A factor that would not necessarily be incriminating in court but in the papers would have been a landmine, what with

Chester using his position to push their agenda in parliament. And if Naiyana Maguire had learned this during her research, she might have used it against Chester Grant.

It was now six o'clock. Given that Chester had been unavailable due to afternoon meetings and it was no longer the afternoon, she called his office again. Again she was fobbed off with a prepared response that all queries should come through the standard channels.

Emmaline wasn't about to back down. 'This isn't a standard issue. It involves the murder of Lorcan Maguire and the disappearance of two other people. If you call that standard then you're in the wrong job.'

To this the secretary spluttered a little, thrown off course momentarily before regaining her composure. 'Let me . . .'

The line went quiet for nearly a minute before the secretary reappeared.

'Can you make it to Claremont in fifteen minutes?'

Fifteen minutes was a push but Emmaline wasn't going to turn down the opportunity.

Fourteen minutes later she found herself in another well-to-do area of Perth, on the opposite bank to Nikos Iannis, but a house that displayed all the same trappings of wealth right down to the gold-tipped gateposts and marble pillars.

The first thing she spotted was the white SUV in the driveway. A Toyota, like the Maguires'. Except newer. Again she used the well-practised key trick to study the bull bars. Again spotlessly clean. How people found the time to keep their vehicles so immaculate, she would never know. Hers was permanently covered in dust and bird shit.

Looking up, there was no mass of freshly shaved chest blocking the doorway. A besuited Chester Grant invited her inside, onto a white leather sofa that gleamed as the evening sun poked through the patio doors. In front of her lay a mahogany desk and mounted display cabinet that contained a vast number of rifles.

'They're all antiques,' noted Chester Grant as he helped himself to a glass of port. Emmaline had declined the offer. He might have been winding down for the evening but she still had work to do.

The colour of his well-fed but handsome face matched the port on his lips, tainting his full but perfectly trimmed beard.

'Why did you want to meet with Naiyana Maguire?' asked Emmaline.

If her question had upset his equilibrium he hid it well, slowly taking another sip and savouring it in his mouth.

'To try and get this horrendous issue resolved to the satisfaction and benefit of both parties.'

'And what would have been to the satisfaction and benefit of both parties?'

'Brightside Foods have always been willing to compromise, Detective. To gradually alter the ingredients in the *offending* product to something more widely regulated.'

'But this wasn't enough for Naiyana Maguire?'

'She was on a crusade to do good.'

He said this with a brusqueness that made it sound like it was a bad thing, revealing an anger and frustration directed at Naiyana Maguire, almost like he'd forgotten she was missing. After a second, he glanced back up as if he had realized his mistake, offering a sympathy that seemed all the more false now.

'But obviously this whole thing is horrendous.'

'For you or her, Mr Grant?'

'Hey, that's not—' he started.

Now that Emmaline had him flustered she switched paths. 'Why choose you as the mediator?'

'My job is to mediate. To represent the people in my constituency. And people include companies. They have to be treated as such as they are the main employers. Happy people are working people. And that is one thing I stand for, most of all.'

Emmaline let him espouse his political bullshit. She wasn't one of his constituents.

'So did you meet with her?'

He took another sip of port.

'No, she didn't want to. Then everything blew up. It's a shame. Brightside Foods weren't doing anything wrong. The ingredient wasn't banned here yet they were punished by this circus trial.'

Emmaline wanted to ask what punishment the

Maguire family had suffered in this so-called circus trial but left it.

She had also noted the slight pause before he answered. It had been a simple yes or no answer but it had caused him to hesitate, using the port as cover.

'I want to know if you met her *after* everything had blown up. Since she moved out of Perth.'

'No.'

A quicker, stronger denial this time.

'Did anyone from Brightside Foods meet with her?'

'I don't know.'

'Despite your close connection?'

'What do you mean?'

'I'm referring to the rumours of a connection between you and Brightside Foods.'

The abundance of colour in Chester Grant's face drained. Nothing the port could do about that.

'What rumours?' Squeezing his eyes shut, he rephrased the question. 'I mean, what connection?'

'That you are close.'

'They are the major business in my constituency. The biggest employer. Biggest taxpayer.'

'More than that.'

'I'm not keen on this line of questioning, Detective.'

'People are generally not happy with any line of police questioning, Mr Grant.'

'I think you want to accuse me of something.'

'I think you are afraid of being accused of something.'

'What could I be accused of, Detective?'

'Something that might cause a scandal.'

Chester Grant paused, studying her as he swirled his port as if weighing up what exactly she was implying, for fear of suggesting something that implicated him further.

'There are always scandals, Detective.'

'This is not a scandal, Mr Grant. This is a murder investigation.'

'Well, unless you are arresting me for it, I think you should leave.'

That was fine with Emmaline. She decided to keep what she knew to herself. It might come in useful later. To rustle a few cocked feathers.

53

Naiyana

Naiyana was happy. Today had been a good day. And she had this place to thank. The rock bottom that had spawned this upsurge.

'You look like you just won the lottery.' Her husband was at the table fiddling with a small electric heater. For the chillier evenings. No doubt he would try and burst her bubble. He had accused her in the past of being insufferable when she was happy, impossibly chirpy. Forcing everyone else to query what was missing in their lives. But that was not her fault. It was theirs.

Dylan was sticking close to her, feeding off her energy, helping her pack the groceries into the old cupboard and stuffing food into the cool box.

Lorcan threw down the screwdriver. He looked worried and frustrated. She didn't want to ask what was wrong. He would tell her soon enough. She intended to relish her own high while it lasted.

'What do you want for dinner, little man?' she asked, ruffling Dylan's hair.

'Snags!'

The expected answer.

'Try the bottom of the bag,' she said.

She watched him dig to the bottom and pull out a packet in each hand, grinning. Removing the plastic, she stabbed holes into the sausages with a fork before placing them into the pan.

Dylan helped her prep the hot dog buns, liberally buttering them so that the sausages would be swimming in a sea of fat. This was more like a proper family. Making food together. Then just like that, it all came crashing down.

'We were down the tunnel today, Mummy.'

She flicked her head towards Lorcan, who visibly winced.

'It was dark and I was scared.'

Naiyana drew a long breath. 'Why don't you go and get your toys from the backyard?'

'But I was telling you—'

'Can you get them, please?' The remnants of her good mood allowed the smile to look genuine. Dylan nodded and ran off.

Lorcan got in first. 'There was no rumbling. They weren't there.'

'That doesn't matter. They might have been. And you took our son?'

'It was safer if he was with me.'

'Safer? It was better when we thought the rumblings were ghosts. Ghosts might be scary but they aren't dangerous.'

'We can't just avoid the elephant in the town,' said Lorcan. 'They obviously have a greater purpose here than we do. It might be dangerous if we interrupt it.'

'And going down that tunnel unannounced aids that?'

'I was trying to confirm what they are doing.'

Naiyana shook her head. When had her husband lost all his sense? But it gave her an idea of her own.

'What if we announce our presence here?'

Lorcan looked at her as if she was the one who had taken leave of her senses.

'We let them know *we know* that they are here,' she continued.

'I don't know about that, Nee—'

'They knew about us long before we knew about them. If they were going to murder us, or attack us, they would have done so already.'

The mention of murder didn't seem to give her husband much comfort. In honesty it didn't give her much either.

54

Emmaline

Emmaline made it back to Kallayee by eleven. An overnight in Perth, in her own bed, had seemed the logical decision but she had wedded herself to this caravan until the case was solved. Plus, the journey had left her exhausted enough to sleep, even on the thin, uncomfortable pull-out bed. She intended to get six hours at least, determined not to beat the sunrise this morning.

As she pulled up to the caravan she saw the door ajar. Not how she had left it. Drawing her gun she slid out of the vehicle and checked for any sign of movement from the nearby structures. There was none. Sneaking up to the back window she peeked inside. Nothing but darkness. If they had been attempting to rob her – the dropkicks from the pub came to mind – they would be seriously disappointed at the very least. Putting her back to the thin aluminium, she swung around to the far side. Sitting in the dirt, leaning up against the side was a dark, huddled figure. Naiyana. She hoped. Had she escaped and come back to where she knew? But why here and not Hurton or Wisbech? Had she been imprisoned somewhere close? And why would she not make her presence known to the cops holding the perimeter of the town?

After another check that the coast was clear she inched forward and nudged the figure. There was an unladylike snort. The figure raised its head and she met the flashing blue eyes of Matty. Emmaline lowered her gun. But not all the way.

'How did you get in here? This is a crime scene.'

'Parked the quad a little outside town and walked. It was easy. Security is lax,' he said with a smile.

'And the door?'

'That caravan needed to be aired out.'

That Emmaline couldn't disagree with. She made a note to tighten security. For town as a whole, her caravan included.

'What are you doing out here? I thought you lived close to the pub.'

'I took a wrong turn,' he smiled.

'You nearly did,' she answered, holstering her gun. 'Why are you here?'

'It's nice to see you too.'

'That doesn't answer my question.'

'I have information. Tracy Marley's son said he saw that woman – Naiyana Maguire – with a man.'

'In Hurton?'

'Outside.'

'Right, let's go see him!'

'In the morning. Bobby Marley –' Matty nodded

in agreement as Emmaline screwed her face up, '– is only twelve.'

Emmaline went to step inside the opened door. She turned to find him watching her. There was a moment's pause. 'Are you coming in?'

Emmaline didn't feel so tired anymore.

55

Emmaline

She woke to find the caravan stifling hot. The sun was burning through the paper-thin curtains and there was someone squeezed into the narrow bed beside her. Where she should have felt drowsy she felt invigorated. Nothing like a reminder of the pleasures of the flesh to appreciate a new day and a chance to do it all over again.

Sitting up in bed she began to drag her clothes on as Matty slowly stirred.

'Morning,' he said, groggily.

'Get fixed up,' she answered. 'We're going to see Bobby Marley.'

'Breakfast?'

'After. I'll treat you if this turns out to be a solid lead.'

As he dragged his shirt over a hairy torso that was beginning to sag around the gut, she asked him a question.

'You said you had a quad. Did you sell another one? To Lorcan Maguire?'

He shook his head. 'I'd never sell Betsy.'

'Betsy?'

''Cause it's always a gamble if it will make it from A to B,' he said and flashed a smile, his eyes glowing in the rising sun.

'Anyone you know sell one recently?'

He shook his head, as she tucked the gun into her side-holster. 'Why do you ask?'

It was her turn to shake her head. 'Let's go, otherwise we'll be having lunch, not breakfast.'

Taking her 4x4 – she wasn't about to ride shotgun on the back of his quad – and following his directions, they made it to the near side of Hurton and up an unmarked lane leading to a building that reminded her of a typical prairie house from a TV Western, wooden pillars and a wide porch, cracked steps leading up to the front door.

Matty performed the introductions, getting Tracy Marley to bring a zombie-like Bobby to the door, bleary-eyed from being woken up early during his school holidays.

'Tell her what you told me, Bobby.'

Bobby blinked sleep from his eyes then told a story of being out on his mountain bike – an early Christmas present from his uncle – and seeing Naiyana Maguire with a man, off the main road, near to the gorge that ran east to west out the back of town and contained numerous abandoned mine openings.

'What did he look like, Bobby?'

He shrugged. 'I could only really see her. She was pretty. Very pretty.'

'Nothing on him?' asked Emmaline.

'They were sitting in a white Toyota. He had a beard. But it was too dark to see inside.'

A white Toyota. Which matched the Maguire's vehicle. And Chester Grant's.

'Nothing else? You didn't get closer?'

The boy shook his head. 'I didn't wanna get in trouble. Mum says if I get in trouble I'll lose the bike.'

The description might have been vague but it seemed to confirm that Naiyana Maguire had met someone. With a beard. Lorcan Maguire didn't have a beard. Neither did the almost baby-faced – and chested – Nikos Iannis.

Chester Grant did.

56

Naiyana

Naiyana held up the piece of paper. 'We'll leave a note.'

Lorcan laughed. 'Why don't we just bake them a pie like good neighbours do?'

She ignored his mocking. She was determined to go through with this.

'We'll leave a note written from all of us, to show them that we're harmless.'

She put the paper in front of Dylan who scrawled his signature, his tongue poking out the side of his mouth in concentration, the amateurish style of the note enhancing the non-threatening nature of it.

'I don't know if this—'

'We don't want to just walk up to their doorstep, do we? A note is best. Some form of pre-emptive communication. They obviously know we're here, they just don't know that we know.'

Lorcan sighed. 'As long as we aren't in town after. We'll watch from a safe distance and see what they do.'

LORCAN

Lorcan left the note pinned to the cupboard. Although wary of this plan he didn't have an alternative. Other than running. Which he still considered the best option.

They then drove out of Kallayee, on to the small hill that overlooked the town, parking behind some trees, obscured from view as the sun went down.

When Dylan had asked what they were doing he had told him that they were stargazing. And in fact, the clear night and arrangement of stars took his mind off what was going to take place below.

But as the night pushed on, his focus turned from the sky to the tunnel to his own house, expecting to see it ransacked or go up in flames. The best-case scenario was that the miners got spooked and fled. But why would they? To them *they* were the intruders. And if they burnt the house down? Maybe that would be for the best. It would mean Nee had to agree to leave.

At eleven, the men rolled into town, lights off, just a shadow crawling along the street. They alighted as before. Lorcan waited for the explosion of movement. He didn't have to wait long. The flailing torches and hurried exit from the building were a huge contrast to the military precision he had witnessed previously, suggesting discovery of the note. From this distance he couldn't hear anything, but the waved arms and furious pacing indicated alarm. And that was troubling.

Riling up the neighbours was a bad idea. Especially if you didn't know them. And they had access to tunnels to bury you in.

Lorcan glanced over as his wife and son slept in the passenger seats. He wondered how she could be so at peace with this.

57

Lorcan

He had watched the men intently as they eventually returned to the tunnel. He forced himself to stay awake through the small hours before finally, just before dawn, the men had reappeared and left as normal.

He watched the sun cast a warming yellow glow over the buildings, his eyes closing, nervous energy replaced by lethargy. It was over, time to shut down for a while. His eyelids felt like stone.

'Are you going to check?'

It was Nee's voice, speaking in a whisper. For a second he convinced himself it was a dream but the hand on his leg shook him back to full consciousness.

'Why me?' he said in a forceful whisper.

'I thought—'

'You can think again. It was your idea.'

He watched her try and come up with a reason not to. And fail. He had won the argument. But as she crawled into her jacket and left the ute, he felt like a coward. But it didn't make him call her back.

He watched as she scrambled down the hill and

back into town, tracking her progress all the way. He waited for the surprise attack. That somehow one of the men had stayed behind. He wondered what he would do in that instance, convincing himself that he would help but also recognizing that the presence of forethought revealed his true nature.

She entered the tunnel house and disappeared. His toes itched to move, to start a chain reaction that would force him out of the ute and down to help her, but the rest of his weary body refused to comply. He stared at the building, willing her to come back out.

A head appeared from the door. Then a body. His wife, waving at them. Lorcan allowed himself a breath but didn't move for another full minute, making sure it wasn't a wave indicating trouble.

Easing down the hill, he pulled up outside the tunnel house. The bumpy descent had woken Dylan. Naiyana got into the vehicle and held up the note. There was writing scribbled below theirs.

'They want to meet. Here. Tonight,' she explained.

'Why not somewhere more public?' asked Lorcan. 'Like Hurton. It shows they have something to hide.'

'We know that already,' said Naiyana. 'We're all hiding.'

'But if we meet them here, what would stop them from killing us?'

'They could have killed us anytime in the last ten days.'

Lorcan shook his head but knew when he was beaten. 'I preferred it when you were cynical.'

58

Lorcan

Not much got done during the day. How could it with the meeting hanging over their heads? Like a date with the electric chair. Lorcan fiddled with constructing a box bed for Dylan – they were hoping that it would help him sleep better – and when the pressure inside the house grew too much, he had tinkered with the ute. Checking the oil, water and tyres. Just in case they needed to leave in a hurry. He had all but given up on the well, at least until a time they might be alone in town again. But Kallayee as a permanent residence was looking less and less appealing. Too crowded.

His final act was to load the rifle, making sure the coast was clear before going to their bedroom and reaching high up into the space between the eaves and the wall and pulling it down. He didn't want to be fiddling around with shells if the time came.

Dinner was unappetizing, the conversation stilted. Nine p.m. rolled around. Meeting time. At the crossroads like in an old western. Lorcan wasn't keen on that. People got shot in westerns. The Good guys as often as the Bad.

Despite it being only a couple of hundred metres away, he insisted on driving. For easy escape if needed, which Naiyana accepted.

They pulled up to the crossroads at quarter to nine and waited.

At almost nine on the dot, the rusted ute pulled into town, its lights off as it sidled down the moonlit dirt street like a cowboy, stopping on the far side of the crossroads, thirty metres away, laying claim to its side of town.

Neither side exited their vehicle.

Nothing happened for a few seconds. Lorcan glanced out the side windows checking for any ambush. Then the leader got out of the rusted ute followed by his two companions. Lorcan performed a visual check for weapons but realized he didn't really know what he was looking for. Bulges? Awkward stances? He turned to find Naiyana glaring at him. She obviously wanted him to get out first but that wasn't part of his plan, so he watched as she opened the door and stepped into the night, taking Dylan with her.

Now he moved, sliding the Browning rifle out from under the driver's seat, stepping out and, using the door as cover, quickly sliding it down his pants leg, shuffling to catch up with his family. He ignored Nee's look of disgust. She was unaware of the reason he had to stall. Best that she didn't know, given her stance on guns. He focused on the three men, keeping his hand close to the butt of the rifle, ready to draw.

'Nice of you to meet us,' said the lead guy. His accent had a hint of Queensland about it. Lorcan had worked with a few guys from Brisbane but had never actually been. 'We've been neighbours in town for a while, so I suppose we should meet.'

'Who are you?' asked Lorcan.

'We don't need names, do we?'

'Neighbours normally exchange names.'

The bearded man smiled, teeth shining. 'I'm Ian.'

'We really doing this?' sneered his stocky, bald companion. Again a Queensland twang, but with a staccato caused by the persistent chew and clack of gum.

'Let's be friendly, Mike,' said Ian.

The third man introduced himself. Of Indigenous descent as Lorcan had thought. 'I'm Stevie,' he said, looking to Ian for reassurance. Another Queenslander. An invasion of them.

'I'm Naiyana.'

'Not your real name,' said Lorcan.

'And this is Dylan,' she continued, twisting sideways to reveal Dylan cowering behind her.

'And you?' asked Ian, looking at Lorcan.

Lorcan grit his teeth. 'Lorcan.' He felt exposed now. Despite the rifle.

'These are the men who are digging. That made that tunnel,' said Dylan, looking up at his dad.

The focus switched to the boy. There was a look

of bewilderment on Ian's face and concern on the others'.

'Perceptive child,' said Ian, but there was no congratulations in his tone.

The tension was almost unbearable. Lorcan's hand moved further down the butt of the rifle. How quickly would he be able to draw it? He still felt they should have remained in the ute and conducted the meeting from there.

'Why are you here?' asked Naiyana.

'Mineral analysis.'

'Bullshit,' said Lorcan, nerves causing him to unwittingly externalize. All eyes were on him now. Shit. He went all-in. 'If it was mineral analysis you wouldn't be sneaking in and out at night. Plus, it would be a bigger operation.' He wasn't sure what he was doing provoking them like this. From the look on Nee's face, she wasn't sure either.

'It's an exploratory concern,' said Stevie, calmly.

'And do you have a permit?'

'Do you?' asked Ian. 'Kallayee is off-limits without one.'

Ian delivered this with charm, every word, be it a threat, accusation or general conversation, bound by a casual bonhomie. He continued.

'Look, we are all here together. Attempting similar things. You are here to make something above ground and we are trying to make something below ground.'

Naiyana turned to Lorcan. 'It might be useful to have someone else here watching our back.'

'I agree,' said Ian. 'We can work separately *and* in collaboration with each other.'

Lorcan didn't know what to say. He had assumed that as soon as the meeting happened – and assuming they weren't murdered – that Nee would join him in jumping on the first train out of here. But she seemed to be in full agreement with Ian's plan.

So the six of them stood there, facing each other in the waning heat of the evening with a tentative arrangement in place. But how much could he trust an agreement with strangers?

They were probably thinking the same thing.

59

Emmaline

After a breakfast with Matty that she paid for – and a bunch of gawping stares and reporters' questions that she didn't – Emmaline had spent the rest of the morning looking for anyone in town who might be able to corroborate what Bobby Marley had said and provide her with a better description of Naiyana's acquaintance.

Nearing the end and having the square root of bugger-all to show for it, a call came through from HQ. Queensland police had a name for the voice on Lorcan's phone.

'A Mike Andrews. Originally from Brisbane. Forty-five years old. A scientist.'

'How sure are they?'

'Pretty sure,' said Zhao.

'Who ID'd him? A relative?'

'No relationship as far as we can tell. They recognized it from television. I've sent you the link.'

Confused, Emmaline clicked the link on her phone. It was a news report from a local channel in

Queensland. Late September last year. A balding man was standing in front of an office block, clearly enraged. He was in his mid-forties but looked older given the angry furrows across his brow. He was protesting his lay-off vehemently, his excessive chewing causing a clack every few seconds that the microphone thrust close to his mouth only exacerbated.

The accent matched. The gum chewing as well. His name flashed up in the ticker at the bottom of the screen. Mike Andrews.

'Find out what you can—'

Zhao interrupted. 'Already done.'

Emmaline should have expected as much.

'Let go from Skyline Industries in late September.'

'What do they do?'

'Act as consultants to everyone from mining companies to property developers to government agencies. Using satellite data to image the land.'

'Sounds . . .' She wanted to say boring but couldn't. She was currently in the midst of a fruitless door-stepping campaign.

'His family – parents only as he is a bachelor – say he upped sticks and left last November. Didn't tell anyone where he was going.'

'Good work, Zhao. Inform the rest of the team.'

Another question materialized.

'He mentioned "lay-offs" in the clip. That suggests more than one. Find out who else might have been laid off. I doubt he would work the tunnels alone.'

With that she let Zhao go do his thing. They had

a name now. And an occupation. But not a reason why. And nothing to suggest a link between Mike Andrews and the Maguire family.

Her thoughts were interrupted by Anand shouting, 'We got one,' from across the street.

Anand was right. They did have one. But Jacob Inglot had less information on the matter than Bobby Marley had. He informed them about seeing Naiyana Maguire parked just off the road out of town as he headed west towards the arid patch of dirt he called his farm. Out past the goldfields and just short of Dredger's Gully. She was alone but obviously waiting for someone. Jacob hadn't stopped to find out who as he was about to run out of gas and needed to get the twenty kilometres to his place and fill up with the jerry can.

'How did she seem?'

'Hard to tell. She kinda turned her face as if she was obscuring her identity, but as I was being tracked by a cloud of dirt the size of Mount Augustus, she might have been protecting herself from the onslaught. Certainly not distressed. She didn't even attempt to flag me down.'

'No other vehicles?'

'Nope. I didn't pass any either.'

'And when was this?'

'Around Christmas.'

'Date?'

'No thanks, I'm married,' grinned Jacob revealing

more than a few missing teeth. 'Twenty-third maybe. Is that helpful?'

Emmaline was considering that. It didn't confirm who Naiyana Maguire might have been waiting on, if she was indeed waiting on someone. But what was strange was to be west of Hurton, on a road that eventually led to nowhere. An odd place to meet a work colleague who would have to drive all the way from the highway through Hurton and out the other side.

She had just said 'Thank you' to Jacob Inglot when HQ called again. Mike Andrews wasn't the only person let go at that time. A friend of his – confirmed as such by both families – called Stevie Amaranga had been let go too. And he had disappeared around the same time as Mike. Without informing anyone where he was going. Both had simply vanished off the map.

She now had a voice and two names. One had definitely been down the tunnel and Emmaline now suspected the other had been with him. The gold dust residue found by the machines suggested they'd had some success.

'Any more on why they were let go?'

'Business downturn. Budget cuts.'

'It seems to be a theme.'

'It's always the arse end of the tapeworm that falls away first when the nutrients dry up,' said Zhao.

Emmaline laughed. 'How long have you been cooking that?'

'A couple of hours. The pair were given two weeks' notice and a month's redundancy.'

'Do you know what exactly they did for Skyline?'

'Satellite imaging. On the data analysis side.'

'For any particular region?'

'Queensland. Surat Basin mostly.'

'Not the Great Vic then?'

'Seems not.'

'So why go there?'

'Beats me.'

'Get onto someone at Skyline and get them to check what Mike and Stevie were researching before they left. See if they were scoping out other regions before they were let go.'

The list of suspects was now increasing. Mike Andrews and possibly Stevie Amaranga the latest additions. More avenues leading from the barren desert and trailing off towards the horizon.

60

Naiyana

The tension was unbearable. Peeking outside regularly to check if any of the miners were in town, and if so where. The knowledge of each other's presence hadn't dispelled the suspicion. It had made it worse.

Both sides knew that each were there illegally. The government would not look kindly on either of their activities but the worst that could happen to them as a family was that they'd be told to move on. Maybe accompanied by a slap on the wrist or a fine. They would be able to sneak away without too much fuss and before anyone in Perth could react. Ian, Mike and Stevie could be in worse trouble with the law. Minus a permit, they were effectively stealing from the government.

Even Dylan kept asking where the miners were. He wanted to show off his own amateur mining operation. They had become his heroes, his allegiance hanging firmly in the balance. She had warned him not to talk to them. Not that Dylan would listen. After all he had seemed to know about their presence before they did. The people that he claimed to have seen in town, and that both she and Lorcan had scoffed at, had been all too real.

With Lorcan loudly bolting together the box bed he had promised to do two days ago, Naiyana went vlogging. She needed some alone time. Just her, her phone and her thoughts.

It was another day of azure skies, a single fleck of black interrupting the beautiful monotony, the wedge-tailed eagle flying solo on its way home. Following and filming it until it was out of sight, she found herself at the house with the tunnel, staring at it even though she knew she should maintain a business-as-usual approach.

As she continued to film, the miner called Mike appeared from the house, startling her. His first reaction was to cover his face as if exposed, as surprised as she was.

'Put that away,' he said, with a clack like snapped bones.

'It's pointed upwards.'

'Put it away,' he insisted.

61

Mike Andrews

Regular fresh-air breaks had been sold as one of the positives about the family knowing of their presence. That and the fact they could work during the day now rather than just at night.

But Mike Andrews wasn't so sure. He preferred the anonymity. His appearance was too distinctive, what with his bald head and bulging gut. Now there were cameras. He tried to keep his calm. He unwrapped and threw in another stick of chewing gum. It usually helped.

This was the first time he had bumped into any of the family members since last night's meeting. He had hoped they would abscond after but here they were. Recording.

At least it was her. Even with eyes adjusting to the brightness of the day he could see that she – Naiyana – was pretty. The kind of woman he was into. But he was ten years and fifty pounds too late for that, even if the mining work was drawing weight from him hand over fist.

Stevie and Ian joined him outside, not even bothering to cover their faces. Fucking stupid. Especially Stevie. He could be linked to Stevie.

The silence was broken by Ian offering a hello and Naiyana moving off quickly, her phone shoved into her shorts pocket. Mike followed her with his eyes as she strode away from them. Another problem with being stuck down a dark tunnel. Starved of pretty sights to see.

'Back to work,' said Ian.

'I'm still on break,' said Mike, flicking his penknife open and digging at the dirt under his nails. Reminding Ian that he wasn't in sole charge. That this was a joint operation.

Ian and Stevie tried to stare him down. Fuck them. They were built for this type of shit. Skinny and fit. All he did was frequently blind himself with sweat. Both stared at him then turned to leave. He took one last look at the glorious blue sky and Naiyana's even more glorious arse before following. The tunnel and the gold was the reason they were there after all. Not the family. Think of the end game, as Ian was fond of saying. Mike's end game was a long holiday and setting up his own company. A fresh start. Be his own boss.

They weren't crooks – apart from Ian – just opportunists. Skyline wasn't going to do anything with the data. They were focused on large-scale operations not this small-scale shit. But with some luck – and the imaging data had eliminated some of that – and hard graft, they could get moderately rich. And he wasn't a greedy man. Moderately rich was good enough for him.

Analysis of the images had identified that there was an eighty per cent chance Kallayee could bear fruit. It had all the positive markings. The trace of a giant old riverbed underneath leading to the possibility of placer deposits and a chance to free-mill gold. They just had to find the right tunnel. And after a couple of abortive attempts they had struck gold. Literally. A workable mine in good condition. Abandoned for at least forty years and probably closer to ninety. So any real right to ownership had lapsed. In his opinion. The government could take a running. Stevie was with him in that. His position was that something abandoned for this long should return to a state of nature. And nature was there to be looted.

62

Emmaline

The reports flooded in. Providing many different angles to look at. Mike Andrews, Stevie Amaranga, Chester Grant, Brightside Foods, INK Tech, Nikos Iannis, the stolen information. The search into any poisons Lorcan Maguire might have purchased was inconclusive: no card payments detected but they were unable to rule out cash payments. Anything was possible, even rat poison, secreted in her meals each day.

An operation led by ZZ had revealed that Lorcan Maguire did not have a security box opened under any of his, Naiyana's or Dylan's details where the stolen data might be stored.

Thorough searches of their house in Kallayee and the foreclosed house in Perth had revealed no hard disks or electronic storage of any kind. No rival company had reported being offered the material. Though it was acknowledged they likely wouldn't report it if they had.

Not that any of this might have stopped Nikos

Iannis from pursuing the matter. The disrespect alone would be enough to make him contemplate further courses of action, and it was obvious from meeting him that he did not trust Lorcan Maguire's denial. So much so that he may have even arranged for people to travel all the way out to Kalgoorlie and beyond to meet him.

She moved on to Chester Grant. He had been adamant that he hadn't met with Naiyana Maguire. But given the connection between his family and BS Foods she was sure there was more of a story to tell. Securing a hard-fought warrant through DI Moore and the magistrates, she had been granted access to a diary of his movements and meetings before and after Christmas.

Her life in the caravan was now a sobering mix of sex and paperwork. The former was more agreeable but she had left Matty this morning with no promise on future plans. It would be left to chance. Unlike this investigation.

Chester's movements didn't immediately trigger any alarms. Dates and times. Meetings with troubled constituents. With business leaders. With family. All scheduled and timed. Official duties interspersed with personal. An expenses report was attached to the diary. Since last year's front-page scandals over false or exaggerated claims, all politicians were keeping meticulous records. And Chester Grant was no exception. But something jumped out at Emmaline. His expenses report included a trip claimed for that didn't match his calendar. A flight to Kalgoorlie, a hire car and two hundred kilometres on the clock. Way outside his constituency. On 30 December. It had been marked as WB. Which Emmaline assumed stood for Wisbech. In the direction of Kallayee. A stupid error but one that could easily be made by a man both greedy for money and desperate to keep his job.

Why Wisbech? There was only one answer. Naiyana Maguire's phone placed her in Wisbech on the thirtieth too. Did they meet to discuss what happened next? Or was it an attempt to get her to keep quiet that went south? Or a trap. Maybe he'd found out her location and sent people to silence her.

Whatever had happened on that same day Naiyana Maguire had vanished. Tomorrow she would talk to Chester again. And get some answers.

63

Mike Andrews

Even for an involuntary bachelor like himself, it was weird to spend Christmas Eve stuck down a baking hot tunnel digging for gold. It was like a story from a children's book. But what would the moral be? With hard work you get what's coming to you? Nah, not that. Fuck the system? Better but not great. There is no greater reward than cheating the system? More like it.

Mike appeared into the light, swapping the flavourless gum in his mouth for a new piece. Ian and Stevie were out there already, enjoying the breeze and the shade.

From the back of one of the nearby houses the father, Lorcan, emerged, as if he had been lying in wait all this time. His phone was up, either recording himself or them. What was up with this family and their need to record everything? What was so special about doing fuck all?

'What are you doing?' he asked, with a clack of gum, stepping towards Lorcan, ready to take the phone by force if it pointed towards him. He felt much more at ease disarming him than his wife. Not that he wouldn't mind getting his hands on her . . .

'Just recording the town. The sights and sounds.'

Ian intervened before Mike could. One step ahead. This was his job. Smoothing things over. The people person, him and Stevie the scientists.

'What for?' asked Ian.

'A book.'

Horripilation caused the mass of hair on his back to rise. Stevie looked as tense, the tendons in his wiry arms twitching. Words implicated. Videos too.

'About?'

'About life out here.'

There was a pause. Mike waited for Ian to grab the phone and chuck it. Finally Ian spoke. 'Just keep away from here.'

Lorcan glanced at them all as if about to defy the order, before he walked on, his movements stiff. He seemed to be as tense as they were.

'Are you going to allow that?'

'I don't like all these videos,' added Stevie.

'It's under control,' said Ian, trying to exert that insufferably calm authority.

'How can it be?'

'We have to learn to live together.'

'I didn't agree to become part of some sexless orgy,' said Stevie, looking at Mike.

'We have to keep it together, guys,' said Ian. Another of his all-inclusive but condescending phrases. As if he was some cult leader. Drink the Kool-Aid and shut up.

With Lorcan gone Ian dragged the burner phone from his shorts. One of many he had insisted on picking up in Brissy before they came here. For emergencies. 'I have to go to town now.'

'What is it?'

'A sale. A good price. You two get back down there.'

'And what do we do about him?' asked Mike, watching Lorcan stand in the middle of the crossroads and spin in a circle, the phone thankfully pointed at the ground.

'Forget about him. I'll deal with it.'

64

Emmaline

Emmaline hit the road early, racing against the sunrise to catch a flight back to Perth. The darkness kept its grip this morning. As if it knew something bad was going to happen.

From Leonora Airport she called Chester Grant's office to arrange an urgent meeting. It was a Saturday so she had hoped to encounter a clear diary but his secretary informed her that the Honourable MLC for Curtin was busy all day, visiting a local factory.

'At Brightside Foods by any chance?' asked Emmaline.

'I am not at liberty to divulge that,' said the secretary, delivering a practised line to fob off nosy reporters.

'I'm flying to Perth now, so tell him to free up some time.'

'He is busy all day, Detective.'

'Tell him I want to talk to him about Wisbech. That should free up some time.'

*

On the plane she browsed a report stating that the search for Naiyana and Dylan Maguire had widened to all states. It had been ten days since their likely disappearance. Their photos were now spread across the country. It wasn't one of Naiyana's best in Emmaline's opinion, dressed elegantly as if for some social event but with a smidge of tiredness around her eyes. A photograph that had highlighted the stress of the Brightside Foods battle.

On landing, she was picked up by Neil. And received a call from Zhao.

It was as Emmaline had suspected. Mike Andrews and Stevie Amaranga had accessed data both for the Murchison Goldfields north of Gwalia and the Great Vic Desert as a whole. A lot of data. Enough according to Skyline to keep a dozen analysers busy for six months. But Mike and Stevie had obviously found something in the data to convince them that Kallayee was worth the money and effort to explore.

Zhao also noted that Skyline themselves were making moves to return to the region because of the find. Once the murder investigation had concluded. Move the bodies out and the machinery in. Breathing life back into the dead town.

Mike and Stevie's bank accounts had been checked too. Both were a few cents in credit, the redundancy money long gone. Indeed their lives seemed to follow much the same path as the Maguires, the town drawing them in, bleeding them dry and spitting them out the other end. Dead in Lorcan Maguire's case.

The accounts had been abandoned since the start of December. Their phone records had been accessed as well, a warrant granted given the positive identification of Mike's voice on a dead man's phone, but the records stopped at the start of December too. Last location: Brisbane.

From there Emmaline guessed they had driven across country to here. A pair of desperate men with a crazy idea. A crazy idea fuelled by data that had proved to be correct but of which they couldn't have been sure at the time. Nothing in their past indicated a propensity towards violence but the absence of communication and lack of money marked them out as desperate.

Had they struck it lucky, then killed the witnesses? Were they living somewhere off the proceeds, untaxed and off the grid?

As she made it to the MP's office, Emmaline told Neil to have the Kallayee team investigate the local gold markets. Dig up what they could about new contacts in town selling gold. Show them Mike's and Stevie's photos.

65

Emmaline

The office was on the sixth floor of a high-rise that looked out onto North Perth, the suburbs sprawling lazily into the hazy distance. Relaxing. Better than the view from her shitty caravan.

The plump secretary in the horn-rimmed glasses informed her boss of Detective Taylor's arrival. Being announced in this way still made Emmaline feel a little odd, as if her entry should be accompanied by some ominous theme music and spark of lightning to go along with the title.

Escorted inside, Emmaline found Chester Grant secure behind his desk, no glass of port in his hand, his Armani suit looking pressed and immaculate, the whirring blast of the air con doing its job.

'Thanks for meeting me,' she said, even though she knew he hadn't really had a choice. The mention of Wisbech made it a certainty.

'I want this sorry affair solved, Detective.'

'That's what I'm trying to do. If you tell the truth.'

'Which is?'

Emmaline lunged immediately. No point holding back. 'That you were in the same town as Naiyana Maguire on the thirtieth of December. That you indeed met her. That the meeting wasn't recorded in your diary.'

Chester Grant stared at her for a moment, before turning towards the view. He took a deep breath. Emmaline sensed that he had been preparing a defence and this was the opening speech. In the end it was short.

'It was an oversight on my part.'

'A very big oversight, Mr Grant. Some might even call it a lie.'

He fixed his eyes on her. They were cold, dark and unflustered, capable of anything. 'A lie is a huge assertion. It was an oversight, that's all.'

Emmaline could see that his defences needed to be rattled.

'Was the fact that you are set to inherit a significant stake in a huge company also an oversight?'

He remained silent so she continued.

'Who owns a company called AG Solutions, Mr Grant? Which itself is owned by AG Holdings? And AG Future? And AG Decade? Who is AG? Whoever it is owns forty per cent of Brightside Foods. So they might do just about anything to someone who threatened it.'

He turned from the view to stare at her. His jaw was tense. She could almost hear the beard hair bristle. 'Those are owned . . . The *companies* are owned by

my mother. And managed by a financial advisor. I
have no say in how they are run or what they might
invest in.'

'But do you inherit these companies when she dies?
Is it true that the shares constitute the bulk of your
family's wealth?'

'What do you want to know, Detective?' he said,
his tone now sharp, seeking to get to the point. To
find a way to avoid it, no doubt.

'As I explained – the truth.'

Rolling his tongue over his upper front teeth he
sucked air through them with a sharp squeak. 'You
haven't told anyone?'

'I haven't made it public if that's what you are
concerned about. But these things have a habit of
coming out.'

Chester scowled at this. In that moment with the
scowl and the thick beard, there was something
animalistic about him, as if he wanted to tear the
room apart.

'When did you meet her?' asked Emmaline.

'On the thirtieth. Like you said.'

'Why?'

'We needed that photo shoot. She had been the face
of the whole shitshow so we needed her onside. To
prove that Brightside had taken appropriate action.
A good news story.'

Emmaline wasn't sure if she bought it. It was a long
way to travel to accomplish what a phone call could.
For a busy man. For a man with a family at Christmas.

'To lift the share price.'

'To stabilize it.'

'Or bump it so you could divest your stock. Rid yourself of the possible headache.'

Chester didn't answer this, so Emmaline continued.

'Why hide the meeting? So you could deny being personally involved if something happened?'

'No,' he said but his vicious gaze had returned to envy the freedom outside the window.

'What happened at the meeting, Mr Grant? Did she realize that the ingredient change wouldn't be immediate but gradual? Did she reveal that she knew all about AG Holdings and the others? Your mother's involvement. Your involvement.'

'Nothing happened!' he barked. 'She refused to go along with the photo shoot or any publicity. She stayed for five minutes and left. Like she was in a hurry to get somewhere else.'

'Can you prove that?'

'What?'

'That she only stayed for five minutes.'

'I was back in time for a meeting that afternoon.'

'A real meeting?'

'Yes, a real meeting. But I'd rather not have you poking around asking for an alibi from them.'

'I'm sure you wouldn't, Mr Grant, but I wouldn't be doing my job if I didn't.'

Chester Grant looked more than a little riled at this. Emmaline pounced.

'Did Naiyana Maguire threaten you with releasing

details about the ownership of the shares? Did it make you angry? Did you threaten her?'

'No. Yes . . . She said she knew about them.'

'What did she want?'

'Nothing! That was the problem. She just grinned like a bloody cat. Like she enjoyed holding this sword over me. I offered her money. I offered to sweep the whole Brightside thing away. Get her a good job here in Perth. But nothing. She didn't want anything but to see me suffer.'

'So she was principled. An endearing quality to most people. Did that make you angry?'

'Are you trying to say I'm not principled?'

Emmaline refused to let him settle. 'So you were scared that she would make this info public? What did that cause you to do, Mr Grant?'

'Nothing.' Chester's ruddy face was now purple.

'Did you let other people know where she was?'

His mouth opened wide, the accusation freezing him like a wax model. The 2019 Condemned Man Collection.

Then his head shook furiously. 'No one.'

'Not even Brightside Foods?'

'I told them there was nothing more I could do.'

'And how did they react? What did they do?'

'As far as I'm aware, nothing. And that's the truth.'

'That seems to be in short supply these days,' said Emmaline.

66

Lorcan

The crash woke them all. It sounded as if, instead of coming down the chimney on Christmas night, Santa had blown a hole in the wall.

Lorcan knew what it was immediately. An attack. The miners had waited until they were asleep and defenceless. But he was prepared. Jumping out of bed, he reached up into the eaves and grabbed the rifle. Fully loaded.

'Dylan's room,' he ordered Naiyana who was staring at the rifle.

She didn't move so he grabbed her arm. Meeting a wailing Dylan at the doorway, he pushed them both inside and slid the camp bed across the door.

'What is—?' started Naiyana.

'They are trying to—' He stopped there. No need to say any more. Not with Dylan in the room. There was a crack from inside the house. A gunshot. He knocked the safety off the rifle. It was time to hope it worked, and that he'd know how to use it. This was it. The end of the world.

Resting the rifle on top of the overturned bed, he waited for one of the bastards to come into view. And aim for what? The head? A limb? Having the rifle was both bane and saviour. It meant he could defend his family but it also meant he might be forced to use it.

His finger grew slick on the trigger. No one came into view. After a minute he wondered if they'd doubled back and were tracking around the house to the window. He and his family would be fish in a barrel.

'The truck,' he whispered, waving them across the room, dragging Nee who dragged Dylan, like a human chain. Sliding the bed away, he advanced down the hallway, the rifle barrel jolting up and down. Get to the truck and get away. Keep going until they ran out of gas or road.

They passed the entrance to the kitchen. They were close to the front door now. The keys were in his pocket. Safe.

'Wait!' cried Naiyana, stopping suddenly, acting like an anchor.

'We have to go,' said Lorcan, trying to pull her and Dylan with him.

'The kitchen,' she said, pointing.

He glanced towards the kitchen. Shards of brick and a new piece of tin were scattered across the floor. What had happened became apparent. The new part of the gable wall had collapsed taking the sheet from the roof. They were not under attack from the miners but their own house.

He didn't know where it came from but he started to laugh, releasing a swathe of pent-up nervous energy. Still the laughter came, a roar that filled the now broken house.

67

Naiyana

Her husband's laughter had disappeared by mid-morning. Christmas Day in a shattered house was not the plan. Daylight exposed the full extent of the damage. The repaired gable was missing and the hole in the roof had reappeared. All his work ruined. All her work in the kitchen ruined. Back to square one.

First off they tried to placate an upset Dylan with Christmas presents. More miniature industrial machinery for his mining operation. But what he now hankered for was a gun just like his father's. It was back in the eaves, ready for the next home invasion.

As they both studied the kitchen, she asked, 'Where did you get it?'

'From a guy in town. I thought we might need it. To shoot animals.'

'Or ourselves,' she said, nauseous at her own morbid humour.

'It's even more important now. What we have is a symbiotic relationship with those men. They said it themselves. But we are the lowest rung. They have the money. They have the numbers. And we have Dylan to think of.'

'No. Get rid of it.' She didn't need any 'accidents'. And didn't need Dylan getting his hands on it.

'You're not listening,' he said.

'*You're* not listening.'

'I am. If you insist we stay here and make a go of it then I'm keeping the gun. Marriage is all about compromise.'

It was about love and respect as well, but she said nothing. She would let him have this minor victory.

'I'm going into town,' she said.

'Again?'

'I want a Christmas dinner and I can't cook in there. I'll see if anywhere is open. So get to work fixing that mess or get writing that book. Make some money.'

'I will.'

'Don't tell me, show me.'

'Dad said he can help out,' he said glancing away, obviously embarrassed. 'Until my other plans come through.'

Naiyana narrowed her eyes. She wondered what these plans involved. But at present, she didn't have the willpower to listen.

'They want to visit,' he added.

'Your parents? Here?'

'Yeah. Tomorrow. Boxing Day.'

'Why?'

'I think they're worried about us.'

'You mean, they want to stick their nose in.'

'That's not—' whined Lorcan.

'I think you better tell Ian and that lot. Warn them to stay out of sight,' said Naiyana, heading out the door towards the ute.

68

Emmaline

Checks confirmed that Chester Grant did have a meeting on the thirtieth with Kilbourne Associates. A quick call confirmed his attendance, proving he was back in Perth by late afternoon. Greg Kilbourne had plenty of questions about why the police were requesting these details. Emmaline didn't answer, but the questions would have left the clear outline of a smoking gun. What she did learn was that Chester had no chance to get out to Kallayee itself, do anything untoward and get back in time to attend the meeting. Although killing Naiyana made sense. She held a lot of damaging information on him. Information that might ruin a career he held dear. With Lorcan and possibly Dylan Maguire caught up in it as witnesses.

Next up was investigating the local gold market. With Mike Andrews's and Stevie Amaranga's accounts static since early December it meant cash had been attained by other means.

By the time she joined them, Rispoli, Anand and

Barker had been to three dealers around Leonora checking on sudden influxes in amounts or quality of gold. They convened in a coffee shop in the afternoon, huddled around a table.

'We showed them photos of Mike Andrews and Stevie Amaranga. No positive IDs,' said Rispoli.

'Which leaves us with?' asked Emmaline, recovering from the flight with a double espresso that was powering through her system.

'We still have a few more to try. Official dealers that is,' said Rispoli.

'How many unofficial?'

'Your guess is as good as mine.'

'But no leads so far?'

Anand was flicking through his notepad. The scribble on the pages looked very neat and assured. 'One of them – Gord Sawyers – informed me that there are finds all the time. Here, there and everywhere. He was pretty unhelpful.'

'We focused on the last few months. Who came in and sold what,' said Barker, 'but apparently there is no follow-up to check that the place stated as the discovery site is the actual discovery site.'

'So this might happen a lot?' said Emmaline.

Barker nodded and shrugged.

Rispoli spoke up. 'What we know is that they have to present ID when making a sale. Their name is noted. So given that we know when they left Queensland and that they had to buy the equipment, set up and start mining, the selling could only have begun in the last six weeks to a month.'

Emmaline continued. 'So we need to identify anyone who has started and finished their gold trading career abruptly in the last month.'

69

Lorcan

'Happy Christmas!'

Lorcan shouted down the tunnel. Not that they would hear him over the noise of the machines, hard at work, making money. Money that he could do with getting some of.

In a show of good faith he had brought some chocolate cake. It was two days past its sell-by date but still edible. He was about to enter when the bald one, Mike, appeared at the entrance, his face set in a scowl that seemed to be an almost permanent fixture.

Backing him up was Stevie, thin as a whippet, wearing a look of suspicion.

'What do you want?' asked Mike, snapping the gum in his mouth and glancing behind Lorcan as if to check he hadn't brought a cavalry.

Lorcan thrust the cake towards them. 'It's Christmas.'

'Happy Christmas,' said Mike, without cheer.

Stevie stepped forward and took a piece, wolfing it down, before swigging from a bottle of water tucked in his belt. 'Thanks,' he said, offering a thin smile.

Mike glared at him as if he had done something taboo, before reaching for a piece and scoffing it.

'Where's Ian?' asked Lorcan, peering over their shoulders into the darkness.

Mike looked to Stevie, his mouth full.

'Town,' said Stevie.

'Oh. How's work?'

'Good.'

'Getting much?'

By now Mike had finished the cake. 'You don't need to concern yourself with that.' Christmas was over.

'What are you digging for?'

'I'll ask you the same question.'

'I'm just curious,' said Lorcan, flashing them both a faux-friendly smile. 'About what you're doing.'

'Best that you don't know,' said Mike, throwing a new piece of gum into his mouth.

'You probably wouldn't understand,' added Stevie.

'I read up about gold mining and extraction earlier. Diamond mining too. I have a degree in Business Management.'

This caused Mike to laugh loudly. A cruel laugh. 'Very good,' he said not hiding the sarcasm. 'Not very relevant to mineral extraction though, is it? Not much call for typing a hundred words a minute down here.'

Lorcan bit his tongue. He wanted to keep this on friendly terms. 'Is Ian off selling your find?'

'How about you go back and fix that broken wall?' said Mike with a grin that Stevie struggled not to match.

Lorcan felt his own face work into a frown. Friendly terms being stretched.

'What are you going to do now?' asked Stevie. 'Get out of town?'

'Is that what you want?' asked Lorcan, harsher than intended.

There was no immediate answer, but Mike's lazily raised eyebrows suggested that was their preference.

'We just need you to leave us alone,' said Mike.

'I could, and I could get back to fixing the wall and the roof if I had money,' said Lorcan, feeling his stomach knot.

He could sense the temperature of the room suddenly plummet. The iciness in Mike's glare returned and only the tap on the shoulder from Stevie got him to turn and head back down the tunnel. Lorcan didn't follow them.

70

Naiyana

Mrs Blanchard had only been in the shop because she needed to pick up butter for her own mashed potatoes. Naiyana persuaded her that she was only going to be a couple of minutes, rounding up a makeshift Christmas dinner of packaged turkey, ham and tinned potatoes. It wasn't Michelin star but it would have to do.

The only thing that made it remotely appetizing was her hunger. The shock of the collapsed wall, and the sudden appearance of the rifle had gone from her system and now her nervous energy needed to be replenished.

As she fought the broken road on the drive back to Kallayee a funnel of dirt approached from ahead. She slowed as the truck passed. It was Ian, his arm flopped out the window of the decrepit ute. She wondered where he was heading to. She had as many questions about his motives as her husband but she wanted to forget about him – about them – for now. It would be hard but there was Christmas to celebrate.

To make the best of. A horrible situation to be in, having to make the best of something at what was normally considered a joyous time of the year. Only Dylan had been remotely happy, ploughing on with his dirt mining. She wondered what present she could possibly get that would make this Christmas a happy one.

She knew what wouldn't make it happy.

She flagged Ian down.

71

Lorcan

After his cold shoulder at the mine, Christmas Day had been spent making plans. His dad had transferred enough money to fix the wall and the roof only. He didn't dare ask for more. You don't beg Santa for more at Christmas. What he did realize was that he missed his parents. He had itched to break free of them when younger but it was true what they said about missing something when it was gone. Despite being surrounded by his wife and child he felt alone.

He wasn't alone for long. At around eight there was a knock on their door.

He glanced at Naiyana who shook her head.

'Who is it?' she asked.

'Your neighbours,' came the reply. Ian's voice. Warm, but insistent.

Lorcan stiffened and moved for the bedroom and the rifle. Naiyana intercepted him.

'You can't answer the door with a rifle,' she whispered. 'Why are they here?'

'Why don't we just ask?'

Lorcan watched her approach the door and open it, as he stayed just out of sight.

He heard Ian wish her a happy Christmas and Naiyana respond before inviting him in. Two more sets of footsteps followed. All three strangers were in their house. Shit. He let her lead them into the living room before he joined them, standing in the doorway, within sprinting distance of the rifle. He was glad Dylan was tucked up in bed.

The tension in the room was thick, each side staring at the other. Lorcan wondered if they were armed.

'I hear there are visitors planned for tomorrow,' said Ian, his face again betraying a calculated cunning.

'Who told you . . . ?' said Lorcan, looking at Nee. She didn't hide her guilt.

'We don't need any others in this relationship,' replied Ian.

'It wasn't planned. They just want to see the new place.'

'We need you to put off anyone from coming out here. It's best for all of us.'

The sentence was again accompanied by a cat-like narrowing of his eyes. Lorcan read a very real threat in them. But where fear should have led him to cower, his own anger began to rise. How dare they come into his house and threaten him and his family by their mere presence.

'Do you think that I wanted them to see this mess? I had to beg them for money.'

The miners stayed quiet. He wondered if Mike and Stevie had shared his earlier request with Ian. He decided not to leave it to chance.

'It might be time that some of the wealth was shared around.'

'Meaning what?' asked Ian.

'Lorcan, don't—' started Naiyana.

He cut her off. 'This needs to be said. I feel I'm being backed further and further into a corner.'

'You chose the corner,' said Mike.

Ian glared at Mike to shut him up. He turned his attention to Naiyana. 'Are you all okay? The boy? Got enough food?'

'They're okay. We're fine. Happy Christmas!' spat Lorcan.

'Bully you, mate. We're stuck down a hole,' said Mike.

'You chose the hole,' said Lorcan. 'Plus, you're making money.'

'Through hard work,' noted Stevie.

'We can all work hard. If given—'

'Look,' said Ian, his hands up, conciliatory. 'Things are tense, I get that. This is still a getting-to-know-you period. But whether we like it or not we are in a sort of . . . shared relationship.'

'Symbiotic,' offered Stevie.

Ian clicked his fingers and pointed at him. 'Symbiotic relationship.'

'More parasitic,' muttered Mike, punctuated by the ritualistic snap of gum.

'Mike . . .' said Ian.

'What are they giving us apart from a headache?'

'My parents asked to come. It wasn't planned,' said Lorcan.

'We prefer plans,' said Mike.

72

Emmaline

After finishing her double espresso and agreeing a plan, Emmaline joined Rispoli on the visit to the next dealer.

He drove, Emmaline happy to take the passenger seat and enjoy the town as it passed by. She quickly decided Leonora was quite pretty, wide double-lane roads, nourished single-storey houses and scrubbed commercial properties, spread out lazily, luscious trees poking over the top like curious residents. There seemed nothing hurried about it.

Rispoli pointed out the dominating blood-red veranda of Tower Street, the grand White House Hotel and the Information Centre and Library with its symmetrical porches and columns, red and yellow as if wishing to blend into the scenery.

As they reached the top of the street an enormous rumble rattled the glass in the windows, a massive road train passing through, the ground shaking as if an earthquake was rolling through town at its own gentle pace, disturbing the peace rather than damaging it.

The final place of note on his inadvertent tour was the Leonora Alternative Place of Detention, an old mine workers' hostel which had, up until 2014, been used as an immigration detention centre for asylum seekers.

'Fucking shameful. Sometimes you could hear them at night. Crying. Wailing. Like there was a banshee on the loose.'

Emmaline could only nod. 'If the government had their way they'd be stuffed down the mines rather than in hostels. Out of sight, out of mind.'

There was a moment's pause.

'Do you always end your tours this way? Does a downer get you more tips?'

Rispoli laughed. 'I do it for the love of it. Not the money.'

'Clearly.'

They both laughed, the warm air settling in her lungs.

'How's the caravan?' he asked, glancing over at her.

'It reminds me of my student house,' said Emmaline, thinking of Matty, their bodies sprawled on the U-shaped couch/bed.

'That must have been bad.'

'When you're a student you don't much care.'

'But you're not a student now.'

'You don't think that I could pass for one?'

'I think I'm not answering that question.' Another shared smile. Relaxed.

'Does it not get lonely out there?'

She wondered what he was fishing for. An invitation? Maybe he had heard about her and Matty. Not that she would be embarrassed, just that it might affect any future hook-up between her and Rispoli. If there were any.

He pulled up outside a house on Hoover Street, the business nothing more than a prefab steel building in the yard with a couple of chairs, a desk and a safe inside.

The dealer's hopes of a sale were dashed as soon as they introduced themselves, his open, expressive and blotchy face tightening to pinched as if they had barged in and shat on his Sunday lunch.

She left it to Rispoli to explain that they were not investigating anything he might have done wrong. It didn't ease the dealer's suspicions.

'We're looking for anyone new who might have been here in the last few months. Maybe a one-off. Probably selling a sizeable amount,' said Emmaline.

The dealer kept his eyes on them as he unlocked a desk drawer and pulled out a notebook.

'No computer?' asked Rispoli.

'I'm hardly the bloody Mint, am I?'

'Mind if we take a look?' asked Emmaline.

'If you think you can read it,' said the dealer, grinning as he handed the notebook over. It was lined with figures and squiggles that were impossible to read never mind decipher.

She passed it back. The dealer ran his finger down the page. Then flipped back one. Then another, his digit scanning as if reading Braille.

He tapped the page. 'Here,' he said, flipping it round to show them. 'Fifteenth of December. One point five eleven troy.'

'Troy?'

'Troy ounces,' said the dealer with a haughtiness of knowledge. 'From fifteenth century England. It differs from the standard avoirdupois ounce—'

Emmaline cut him off. 'In terms we understand, please.' The 'please' grated on her tongue.

'It means forty-seven grams of twenty-one carat gold. Dust and small nuggets. I paid out two thousand. Made over seven hundred on the deal.'

Emmaline pointed at a symbol scrawled in the side panel. She knew what it looked like but wondered why it was there.

The dealer sneered. 'It's a cock, surely you've seen one before?'

Rispoli stepped forward as if to defend her, but she put her hand up.

'Is that something you have to clarify to many women?' said Emmaline, arrowing her head towards his crotch. 'Misshapen or just tiny?'

The dealer sneered at her.

'What does it mean?' asked Rispoli.

'It means that they were cocky.'

'In what way?'

'See the blank space before the WA on the page? West Australia was all he gave when I asked him where the gold came from.'

'And you didn't push it?'

'Not for seven hundred bucks.'

'Does that happen much?'

'Occasionally. Some people are secretive. Some have rings or heirlooms to sell. I don't want their life story.'

'Name?' asked Emmaline.

The dealer looked closely at the page. 'Ian King. He provided an ID.'

Rispoli started to work through his notepad for matches as Emmaline asked for a description.

'Tall, bearded. Wore a beanie hat that covered his hair.'

'In this heat?'

'I trade gold, not fashion advice.'

'Here!' said Rispoli, holding out his notepad to her. 'The name Ian King has come up before. Twice at other buyers. Selling significant amounts.'

Returning to the car they asked Zhao to run the name through the system. As they waited for a response, they got in touch with Barker and Anand for an update.

'Have you come across any deals made by an Ian King?' asked Rispoli.

There was a rustle of pages across the line before Barker responded. 'Yeah. One off Hoffmann, two near Remington. Decent amounts according to the dealers.'

'Did you get a description?'

'Tall with a beard.'

'And a beanie?'

'You got it.'

'Thanks,' said Emmaline. 'Keep on it.'

'Will do,' said Anand, from the background as Barker rung off.

'It's as if he was going from dealer to dealer to stay somewhat anonymous,' said Emmaline.

'Or looking for the best price.'

Zhao called. 'Ian King doesn't match with anything we have.'

'Shit,' said Emmaline.

'But there was an Ian Kinch who did a couple of stints for theft, including minor assault.'

'And how do they link?'

'Ian Kinch is a Queensland native. Born in Cairns. Did time in Capricornia Correctional Centre in Rockhampton. Mainly petty stuff but the assault he got done for took place around Miles. The Surat Basin.'

'In the same area where Mike Andrews and Stevie Amaranga worked for Skyline,' said Emmaline.

'Exactly,' said Zhao.

'Do we have a photo and a description?'

Before she finished the sentence there was a ping on her phone. A photo and description of Ian Kinch. In the picture there was no beard. His face was striking, angled and chiselled, his blue eyes piercing even in the police photo, his jaw held firm, unamused but certainly not scared. A solid nine. Six-one and a hundred and seventy pounds. Without a beanie his brown hair was tousled perfectly, as if it had been styled for the mugshot.

It wasn't conclusive proof that Ian Kinch was working with Mike Andrews and Stevie Amaranga but considering that gold was being traded without Mike's and Stevie's presence it meant there had to be a third party. And Ian Kinch fitted that bill. He was the face and the muscle. They were the brains.

73

Mike Andrews

It was a bagful of crocodile shit idea. The problem was he didn't have an alternative. Ian was still convinced that they should try and live alongside the family. Mike stuck by his remark that they were parasites. Lorcan begging for money had proved that. It would only get worse now the house had collapsed. If he found out the true amount they were bringing in then he would demand a piece of the action. And they had worked hard for it. They were the ones who stole and studied the readings, who came all the way out here, who put their savings into buying the machines, who dug out two tunnels before this one, who camped down them. They were the ones putting themselves at risk from the law. Or the collapse of a hundred-year-old tunnel. Lorcan had taken no risks.

'Aside from poking his nose in our business,' said Stevie, as they gulped down water, wishing it was beer.

'A poked nose can soon be bloodied,' said Mike, allowing the undercurrent of menace to drift freely in the afternoon air, the penknife blade worked under his nails.

'We don't antagonize them,' said Ian.

'But they can antagonize us?'

'They're loose cannons,' said Stevie.

'Parasites *and* loose cannons. Nothing about this is good for us. If I had wanted a screaming, bawling family tagging along . . .'

'We can use them as cover if we need to,' said Ian.

'Why?' said Mike, instantly suspicious. 'What are you expecting?'

'Everything,' said Ian. 'I've been inside. Expect anything and your arse is covered.'

Mike wasn't keen on prison talk. Being an unabashed pessimist he foresaw complications in everything. Which was beneficial when undertaking experiments but not so constructive on a practical level. Daily he fluctuated between being sure that they were going to jail and convinced that they would get away with it. Ian had already accused him of having a borderline personality disorder. 'Nobody's perfect,' he had replied.

A drone came into earshot. From overhead. Immediately they picked up their things and ducked for cover like they were in a war zone.

'There you go. We duck for cover but they stay out in the open,' said Mike, the echo of his gum clacking. 'And I swear there's been more planes lately. Flying low enough that I can hear them in the tunnel.'

'Less of the crazy,' said Ian, admonishing.

'The only thing crazy is being here with that family still around.'

'He has a point, Ian,' said Stevie.

Mike knew that his friend would side with him. They had worked together at Skyline for three years, bound by similar interests in complex board games and in getting ahead. But Skyline had other ideas. So he and Stevie found another way.

'You have two options,' said Ian. 'Leave or continue digging. And we've hit a good seam so it would be a shame to stop now.'

'Quit while you're ahead,' said Stevie.

'You can,' said Ian. 'I won't stop you. But you don't get any money until I finish.'

'Why?' said Mike.

'To keep your mouths shut.'

'That's not fair.'

'It is compared to the alternative way of keeping your mouths shut,' said Ian, letting the threat hang. He continued, 'No one quits halfway through. I won't quit on you, you don't quit on me.'

It was a see-through move, playing on how shoddily Skyline had treated them. Then came the carrot.

'How about tomorrow we head to a motel for the day – get some sleep and some action?'

The bribe was as obvious as the ludicrously over-sized 'Big Cassowary' statue in Mission Beach but the offer of a bath, bed, booze and babes compared to a cold bivvy bag under the stars was a winning combo. His concerns could wait another night at least.

74

Emmaline

If they didn't have conclusive proof before, the latest info from Queensland changed that. Ian Kinch's movements for the last two months had been tracked.

He had disappeared at the start of October, at almost exactly the same time as the two scientists. This had been confirmed by his social media blackout – his Facebook silent, his Twitter account closed – his bank account untroubled.

Mike's and Stevie's family and friends had been helpful, concerned about their loved ones. And even more concerned now that the police were making enquiries.

Most recalled a guy fitting Ian Kinch's description, good-looking and quick-witted, a new mate that Mike and Stevie had hung around with since Skyline had let them go. An odd bunch given how introverted Mike and Stevie were compared to Ian. For a few weeks before their disappearance they had been hitting clubs and bars every few nights. As if they were trying to blow all their redundancy money. As if it was their last night on earth. Their friends had been worried about the influence this new guy seemed to have but couldn't deny that Mike and Stevie deserved some release.

Emmaline was now convinced that there were three miners in Kallayee. She imagined a timeline. Knowing that Skyline had given them the boot, they went out to blow off some steam and fell in with Ian. They got to talking, maybe about opportunities or just work in general. Ian then persuaded them to steal the data, or Mike and Stevie knew about the data already but didn't know what to do with it. At this stage the first seemed more likely. An outgoing and street-smart Ian Kinch would have gained influence over the intro-verted scientists. Maybe he even appointed himself head of the crew, a dangerous but intriguing devel-opment for the previously reserved pair. Ian learned what the data could do. He hatched a plan and sourced the mining equipment, the serial numbers scrubbed. Ian Kinch was the face, Mike Andrews and Stevie Amaranga the brains, studying the data, surveying and picking the target. Kallayee might have been a lucky first stab or maybe they had tried a few locations in mid- to late November, before settling on Kallayee.

Weeks of hard graft had been put into the tunnel. A vein found, fortune struck. Then the Maguire family had shown up and interrupted them. So why didn't Ian Kinch scare them off immediately? He had previous convictions for theft and minor assault after all. But the family had lived alongside them for more than a couple of weeks. Did it take that long for someone in the family, possibly Lorcan Maguire, to uncover the mine? Then he was chased and killed? But what about Naiyana and Dylan? The still un-answered question.

Finally she had a lead. Now that they could place the three miners and the family together in Kallayee, Emmaline needed to find out where the miners had gone.

75

Emmaline

But even before she could consider looking into the miners' current whereabouts, something else came to light. The whereabouts of Nikos Iannis. On 30 December. His image had been captured on CCTV at a petrol station north of Kalgoorlie. Not his usual hunting ground. A city animal exclusively. Emmaline could think of no reason to be out there other than a meeting with Lorcan Maguire. And whatever might have followed.

In two hours she was back in Perth. Oily briefed her. Nikos had said nothing so far, other than to request his lawyer.

'Want to take it?' asked Oily.

There was no doubt about that.

In the interview room, Nikos sat behind the table, dressed in black slacks and a shirt that was unbuttoned at the neck. His arms were folded, leaning back in the seat in a come-and-get-me pose.

'You again?' said Nikos. Then he turned to his lawyer, a stately-looking man, his red tie neatly pinned. 'She's the one pestering me at my home.'

'You invited us in, Mr Iannis,' said Emmaline.

''Cause I thought you were a stripper,' said Nikos. '*Before* the boob job.'

Emmaline smiled. 'Are you the *After* shot then?' she said and nodded towards the open shirt and prominent man-boob cleavage.

With a stony silence descending after, she ran through the formalities of where they were and who was present, the lawyer announcing himself as Vasilios Drakos, from the firm Drakos and Galanis. He was in his sixties, with thick eyebrows that shielded his face like a sun visor, oddly jet black as opposed to his nearly pure grey hair.

Emmaline jumped straight in. 'Do you know why you are here, Mr Iannis?'

'The same reason we all are, Detective. Failed to win the lottery.'

'You have been identified on CCTV at a petrol station just north of Kalgoorlie on the thirtieth of December,' said Emmaline, pushing the image towards him. The resolution wasn't perfect, but with Nikos practically staring at the camera, it was clear enough for identification.

Nikos studied the page. Emmaline waited for the denial. In preparation for this, Rispoli had already interviewed the petrol station owner who had identified Nikos too.

Vasilios got to work. 'My client does not wish to—'

'Yeah, it's me,' said Nikos.

Vasilios turned to him. 'You do not have to—'

276

'I know what I don't have to do, Vasi,' he snapped. He faced Emmaline again. 'I was out there.'

'On the thirtieth?'

'I'll take your word for that.'

'What were you doing out there?'

'Whale-watching.'

'Mr Iannis, may I remind you that this interview is being recorded.'

Nikos laughed. 'Okay, snake-whispering. I heard it was a good area to find them.'

'Are you referring to Lorcan Maguire?'

Nikos stayed quiet, smirking.

'How did you find him? Through one of his work colleagues?'

Having lured her with some information, Nikos clammed up, basking in having Emmaline scramble for more, a wry smile on his face. Emmaline supposed this interview room was no different to hundreds he had been in before. Now he was studying the corners, looking for anything to distract him. She had just the thing, something he hated most of all – disrespect.

'You wanted to talk to him about the missing infor-mation, didn't you? You wanted to find him. For making a complete fool out of you.'

Nikos's head whipped sharply around. This had stung. He wouldn't be able to resist biting back.

Spotting the danger, Vasilios attempted to interrupt. 'My client hasn't confirmed he was even there. We would need a line-up, a focused—'

It was Emmaline's turn to interrupt. 'But I get the

feeling he fooled you again? Didn't he?' A thin smile crept onto her face, one designed to antagonize Nikos.

Nikos's nostrils flared. His teeth clamped shut. He looked to Vasilios, silently asking him to shut this down.

'Did you pay him money, Mr Iannis? To get back the information. But he double-crossed you? Maybe he'd already sold it to someone else. His double pay-off for your company's hard work. For your hard work. That wouldn't look good, would it? Fleeced by one of your employees. Some geek behind a desk. It would look like you were losing your grip without your brother in control. But there's not much he can do from a sickbed, is there? Can't hold his little brother's hand anymore.'

'These aren't questions—' said Vasilios, but Nikos had had enough, his face blazing red with anger.

'He swore he didn't have it,' said Nikos.

'Nikos, you don't—' started Vasilios but his comforting hand was batted away. Nikos had a rep to defend.

'He said he'd destroyed it.'

'And you believed him?'

'It was hard to believe anything that rat bastard said.'

'That "rat bastard" was shot dead soon after, Mr Iannis.'

He shrugged. 'These things happen. He should have been more afraid of me.'

'What does that mean?'

Nikos went quiet again, his rep defended to those in this room and on tape. There was anger but no fear. He was confident that he couldn't be linked to Lorcan Maguire's death. He had spilled the motive but knew that Emmaline lacked any evidence.

The door knocked. Neil Templeton passed her a sheet of paper. It made for some interesting reading.

'You've threatened people before haven't you, Mr Iannis? What do you want to tell us about Georgina Harbles?'

Nikos said nothing.

'What has this got to do with—' said Vasilios.

'Demonstrating that your client has prior in this area,' said Emmaline. 'Significant prior. Miss Harbles had a case against INK Tech for harassment regarding threats issued over social media. Personal, nasty stuff. Then the company she went to work for had a fire. The building burnt down with a guard inside. It looked like arson but it couldn't be proved. It had all the hallmarks of a message not to mess with the Iannis family.'

'Allegations, Detective. Never proved,' said Vasilios, finally allowed to finish a sentence. 'I ask that you either charge my client, or let him go. He has co-operated fully. Even if it was against my council.'

76

Emmaline

After Nikos had been discharged – they had nothing firm to hold him on – Emmaline had Zhao set up a conference call with Rispoli and the others in Leonora. It was time to strategize angles of attack. And defence. They had managed to limit the information leaked to the press regarding Lorcan Maguire for three days, but the result of the nationwide voice request had leaked and the newspapers were now asking if Mike Andrews was the main suspect. This had led to people in Queensland talking and now the press wanted to know if Stevie Amaranga was under suspicion too. Which meant calls from their families that ranged between pleading and apoplectic that their progeny would never do such a thing. Thankfully Ian Kinch's name remained out of any discussion for the moment. But worst of all the press wanted an update on the progress of the investigation. And Emmaline had nothing but strands.

'So do we treat Andrews and Amaranga as our main suspects?' asked Rispoli. 'They were in Kallayee, we know that. Andrews for certain. Do we add Ian Kinch to that list?'

'We need to find out where they are now,' said Emmaline. 'We know that they left in a hurry. That equipment was worth something and they abandoned it.'

'They're probably together. Lying low,' said Oily.

'We're covering phones, cards and any significant gold transactions,' said Zhao. 'But we fear that they are clever enough to use burner phones, pay in cash and keep any transactions away from reputable dealers.'

'So what do we tell the press?' asked Barker, chewing on a sausage roll.

Emmaline decided. 'That Mike Andrews and Stevie Amaranga are currently persons of interest and we are appealing that they come forward in order to eliminate themselves. We keep Ian Kinch out of it for now to see if he slips up. Make him think that we don't know about his involvement.'

'What about the other angles?' asked Rispoli.

'We have evidence of Nikos Iannis being in the region on the thirtieth and that he met up with Lorcan Maguire.'

'In Kallayee?' asked Anand.

'Somewhere north of Kalgoorlie, at least. Whether he made it as far as Kallayee is unknown. Wisbech is very possible. A meeting about the stolen information. What we do know is that Nikos was unhappy with the outcome.'

'Unhappy enough to do something about it?' asked Rispoli.

'Given his record we have to assume that's a possibility,' said Oily.

'Nothing we can pin him on yet,' noted Emmaline. 'The voice message on the thirtieth proves that he wasn't killed at the meeting, meaning that if they did meet, Lorcan was free to leave after. But that doesn't mean that Nikos let it go.'

'What are you getting at?' asked Rispoli.

'Maybe he had someone follow Lorcan. From the meeting place.'

'It's pretty easy to spot a tail out here,' said Barker.

'Maybe the tail wasn't immediate. Maybe Nikos watched him head north and had people search the area. There aren't that many towns.'

'But a big area,' said Barker.

'We need someone to have seen Nikos in the immediate area. And we haven't,' said Oily.

'But we do have sightings of strangers in Hurton,' said Emmaline. 'Rispoli, did we get anything on that?'

'Nothing. Bill, the owner of the Rack in Hurton, confirmed what he said already. A couple of tourists, a door-to-door salesman and a guy who had mistaken Kalgoorlie for Kallayee. He was backed up by two other customers. One said he knew you. A Matty Reicheld.'

Emmaline blanched a little at the name. At Rispoli knowing the name. It was an involuntary reaction, one she chided herself for. She had nothing to be ashamed of, unless Matty had something to do with the murder. And nothing pointed to him being involved. As yet.

'The salesman gave the full patter, apparently,' continued Rispoli. 'An insurance man down on his luck.'

'And the interview guy?'

'Neither Bill nor the others could give us a composite of his face.'

'But do we believe the story?'

'I certainly wouldn't be employing him if he can't even get the right town,' said Barker, with a grunt.

'Could it have been Nikos Iannis?' asked Emmaline.

'Both noted that this guy was slim and pale,' said Rispoli.

'Not words that describe Nikos Iannis,' said Oily.

'So maybe it wasn't him but someone he sent,' said Emmaline. 'A professional job.'

There was momentary silence as that sunk in. But there was one more angle.

'That leaves Chester Grant,' said Anand.

Emmaline nodded. 'We've a similar situation with him. He confessed to meeting briefly with Naiyana Maguire in Wisbech on the thirtieth. According to him it was a short, unproductive meeting and he does have a confirmed alibi later that afternoon.'

'And he couldn't have killed her and fled?' asked Oily.

Emmaline had only considered Chester dangerous from the pen side of matters rather than the sword. But he was certainly big enough and capable enough. Especially with his career on the line.

'We can check. Call in some officers from Kalgoorlie to help,' she said to Zhao. 'We also have local witnesses who saw Naiyana meeting a guy with a beard around Hurton. A description that could fit Chester Grant.'

'And Ian Kinch,' said Rispoli.

'And about half the male population out here,' added Anand.

Which was correct. Rather than narrowing the possibilities they were expanding them.

'Stick to Mike Andrews and Stevie Amaranga as persons of interest. We don't mention the others publicly at the minute,' said Emmaline.

'That will make it look like we're floundering,' said Oily, his finger on the corporate pulse as ever.

'DI Moore will just have to sell it.'

'And who is going to tell her that?'

The silence around the table told Emmaline that she was up to bat.

77

Emmaline

Emmaline watched on next morning as DI Angela Moore gave the press conference, straight-batting most of the questions. It didn't look like fun at all, the press trying to knock her off-stride, jabbing her for a response, repeating questions to see if her answer varied. It was like a police interview except instead of being questioned then tried, she was being tried in public. Emmaline wondered if she had reached her ceiling in the MCS. Every position above this involved rules and dictums. Nasty, nasty PR. Saying and doing the right things. Towing the company line. She liked living with some abandon. She could only imagine the delight the press would have with her love life.

The conference was still in full swing when she got a call from Rispoli. The wreckage of a car crash had been found on a back road outside Hurton called Dredger's Gully. A ute from what could be determined.

The plane and car couldn't go fast enough. Making it to Hurton she and Oily passed through in a flash following live directions from Anand until the phone signal gave out.

Carrying on they found Rispoli waiting for them at the next junction. Tailing him, they wound over a bumpy outback track until they came to a tight bend in the road. There, Barker and Anand were corralling tape around trees and cordoning off a large area. Beyond lay a patch of dirt before the landscape disappeared sharply.

Emmaline exited the car. As she passed under the tape, Rispoli joined her and Oily.

'It was spotted from the air,' said Rispoli, pointing at two people gawping from behind the hastily erected tape. Emmaline didn't recognize them. 'They were in a light aircraft, passing low along the gorge. They called it in.'

'Have we got a make or model? Does it match anything we have?' asked Emmaline.

'See for yourself.'

Rispoli led them to the edge. A gorge was cut into the red earth, extending down a hundred feet into scrub. Hidden from the sun, hidden from the world. Near the bottom of it a blackened scrap of metal nestled amongst the scrub.

'Make and model aren't immediately obvious,' said Rispoli. 'We're lucky it didn't start anything bigger.'

The truck had burnt up almost completely, scorching the trees around it but keeping the scenery mostly intact. It sat black against the red and green landscape like a chunk of basalt amongst sandstone.

'At the start we thought that it was dumped years ago but the breakage in the foliage is still green in parts. So I reckon it went over the edge not that long ago. We left it alone and called you and Forensics.'

'Good shout,' said Emmaline. 'Who wants to come check it out?'

They all did but she chose Oily, as the most experienced. Donning latex gloves and shoe covers they scrambled into the gorge taking a circuitous route, rounding the mulga shrubs and stepping over the dry spinifex that used the shade and relative cool to grow thick along the sides.

The first thing she noticed was that the number plates were missing. Front and back. Possibly something nefarious or simply that they had been removed and bolted onto a similar vehicle to use what was left on the road tax. The next thing she noted was that the truck had burnt up pretty thoroughly but the blaze had been contained. It suggested an accelerant but she would get that confirmed later.

Making it to the cab she peeked inside. The rich smell of burnt flesh lingered. Faint but present. Enough to make her stomach curdle. Her heart quickened. Two bodies. Of adult proportions. Age or sex was impossible to immediately determine as both were not much more than bone and singed flesh.

Oily joined her at the opposite window.

'What do you see?' asked Emmaline.

He glanced around. 'Neither body is strapped in.'

'Yes. But they're still inside the wreckage.'

'Could be the seat belts burnt in the fire.'

Emmaline screwed up her face in thought. 'But why didn't they try and free themselves when the fire started?'

Oily shrugged. 'Knocked out in the crash? And who are they? Naiyana Maguire you think? Plus someone else?'

One of the skeletons looked short enough to possibly have been Naiyana Maguire but all Emmaline was certain of was that she had another two bodies in the vicinity of Kallayee, dead under suspicious circumstances. Making three in total.

Wary of disturbing the scene any further, they hiked with some difficulty back to the top. She convened Oily, Rispoli and Barker together; Anand was still securing the scene.

'What would anyone be doing all the way out here?'

'A hell of a wrong turn,' offered Oily. 'Maybe some locals out for a good time, then bang, they go over the side of the gorge. Possibly high.'

'It's a long way from nowhere,' said Barker.

'And even if you were heading to nowhere, this isn't the route you'd take!' added Rispoli.

'We need to know if anyone has been reported missing, locally,' said Emmaline.

'Way ahead of you,' said Barker. 'There was one case in 2004 that was solved and a cold one from 2006 but nothing recent.'

'Was this Naiyana making a run for it?' asked Oily.

'Maybe she was kidnapped and they drove over the edge?' said Rispoli.

'So a Thelma and Louise?' said Barker, grinning.

'But it's not a severe enough drop,' said Oily. 'They couldn't guarantee it was going to end in death.'

Emmaline turned towards the gorge. 'What if it isn't Naiyana at all but those miners? Maybe they got caught up in whatever happened to the family. They witnessed it and were chased to their deaths?'

'A wrong turn in a place they were unfamiliar with?' said Oily.

'And unfortunate enough to both be knocked out while the truck goes up in flames around them?'

78

Lorcan

His dad's money had run out quickly. On bricks, a replacement sheet of tin and a roof beam. Three bottles of cooking gas, too. And food. His dream was turning to dust, or to be more precise getting covered in it. The book idea was out the window too unless there was a drastic upturn in fortune. He hadn't written one word. Besides, no one was going to buy a self-help book where the main character made such a piss-poor attempt to overcome adversity. Even Naiyana had abandoned her vlogs. When he had asked why, she had said she wasn't getting enough subscribers to make it worthwhile. Lorcan thought it was boredom, the same shots, the same people. They were stuck in the whirlpool, circling ever so slowly towards the plughole. As if the malaise of the situation was creeping into their psyches. He guessed that if they talked honestly, both would admit that they underestimated the difficulties they would encounter.

But they weren't talking. Naiyana was constantly going back and forth to the town claiming to have forgotten to pick up something. But he knew the truth. She just wanted to get away from him. He had disappointed her. The move had been a failure.

Even Dylan had noticed that they weren't talking to each other. This morning, he had explained in a devastatingly honest way that it felt like he had two separate parents. Something which he complained about but had learned to play to his advantage, his mining operation in the dirt hill expanded and extensively equipped, the different mines connected by roads and even a base at the bottom where the dirt was being sifted by a bent colander salvaged from the kitchen.

Lorcan was trying to work up the motivation to repair the gable wall again. Instead he sat and watched Dylan from the shade. It felt as if they were slowly wasting away in this desert, that the sand and dust was smoothing all the edges off them, their lives now bland and uninteresting. A daily slog that was as monotonous as the sky overhead. Even a perfect blue became boring after a while. He missed the irregular beauty in a cloud, edges and colours that gave the eye something to focus on, something new to appreciate. It was as if they were in stasis, waiting for something to happen, something to spark them into action, living under the same – collapsed – roof but enduring separate existences.

He watched as another load left the mine and was delivered to the foot of the hill. He glanced down the road beyond the crossroads and wondered what was happening in the actual mine. They were raking it in, he was sure of it. There was no other reason for putting up with his bullshit.

Last night Nee had again told him to leave them alone. Out of nowhere. As if she had been peering into his innermost thoughts, some shred of some tele-kinetic connection remaining between them. She admitted that she was nervous of them. And that it should make him nervous too. But he was sick of being nervous. After fucking up so many times, some-thing had to go right eventually. The law of averages said so.

'Wait here,' he told Dylan.

The boy looked up at him. 'Where are you going, Daddy?'

'To conduct some business.'

He waited outside the wooden building. He had plenty of time to wait today. Nothing was going to be built. Chalk it up as a rest day. Christmas leave.

He heard them before he saw them. Mike and Stevie.

'Those women last night . . . *dios mío* . . . but that Naiyana . . .' said Mike, letting out a long whistle followed by the familiar clack of gum.

'I prefer my women larger,' said Stevie.

'I know you do,' laughed Mike.

They exited the building out into the sun. Seeing Lorcan they paused, the chatter between them coming to an abrupt halt.

'What about Naiyana?' asked Lorcan.

Mike's mouth clamped shut. Stevie averted his eyes. Lorcan knew they were discussing his wife. For which he supposed he should be flattered, considering that she was his wife and not theirs but somehow he felt cuckolded by the gossip.

'Naiyana from yesterday,' said Stevie. He looked at Mike. 'A stripper at a place we went to.'

'Then an all-you-can-eat and motel with clean sheets,' said Mike, stifling a burp. 'Still feeling the effects today.'

'But still stuck down a hole in the middle of summer,' said Lorcan, making a show of basking in the stifling sun.

'We might be dirty,' said Mike, 'but we're making money.'

'I can get my hands dirty too,' said Lorcan, making a subtle bid to help. One he could easily retreat from if prospects weren't favourable.

'And you should be,' said Mike.

Lorcan's hopes raised that maybe there was something. That the ice was melting.

'By fixing that roof,' added Mike with a laugh and an annoying clack of gum.

'I mean down there,' said Lorcan, arching his head towards the tunnel.

'Barely room for three,' said Mike, throwing another piece of gum in his mouth.

79

Emmaline

A wrong turn in a place they were unfamiliar with?

Oily's words stumbled around her head.

She returned to the dirt road and the tyre tracks. The rest of the team followed.

'Do we inform the press?' asked Barker. In the near distance, Anand was babysitting the two amateur pilots.

'Is it only those two?' asked Emmaline.

'They came straight to us.' Barker pointed at the female. 'Mrs Ullathorne was an officer in Kalgoorlie for ten years. That's her son with her.'

'You think they can keep it quiet?'

'If we ask nicely,' said Barker.

'Can you do that?' asked Emmaline.

Barker narrowed his eyes, affronted, and went to ask the witnesses to hold a moratorium on the information. For now. It was all they could do. They couldn't lock them up or gag them. The remote nature of the scene would give them a few hours before word leaked out.

Emmaline returned to the tracks, studying the road and the patch of dirt.

'What are you looking for?' asked Rispoli.

'What do you notice about these?' she said.

There were a few shrugs, all eyes on the road and the tyre tracks that veered from it.

She put them out of their misery. 'They don't swerve off the track violently, do they? Something you would expect if the occupants were being chased. It's more of a gentle arc. Adding to this is a lack of understeer. The front tyres haven't washed out and pushed ahead. So the corner was taken slowly. And given the slow speed I think we can rule out a breakage or mechanical fault. This was by decision rather than accident.'

She returned to the tracks nearer to the cliff edge.

'These are also clean, no sign of tyre spin.'

'Which means?' asked Oily.

'Look at the road. The tracks are indistinct, tyres fighting the whole way, accelerating faster than the grip allows. Then here at the edge the tracks are clearer, no spin, as if the truck stopped and rolled over the edge gently.'

She looked at them. 'How many people have been walking over the scene?'

'Me, you, Oily, Barker and Anand,' said Rispoli. 'Though Anand was with the witnesses so you can probably count him out.'

'Do you see these prints?'

Emmaline pointed to what looked like the heel of

a boot, then further towards the edge, the toe of another boot print, faint but present.

'Ours?' asked Oily.

'They move right between the tyre tracks, which suggests someone was pushing the ute. They attempted to sweep them away with a branch like raking a bunker after a shot but they weren't thorough enough. They wanted to get away.'

'So someone else was here?' asked Rispoli.

'Seems that way,' said Emmaline. 'Here's what I think. Whoever did this drove the ute out here with the occupants already dead, or at least unconscious. They got out, placed the victims in the front seat, started the fire and pushed it over the edge. And drove away.' She paused, then carried on, 'It was a two-person job. One to drive the ute, one to drive the getaway vehicle.'

'Professional,' said Rispoli with a hiss of admiration.

Emmaline nodded. 'Not the work of amateurs anyway.'

80

Lorcan

Neither Mallon nor his son were keen on future payment plans. Cash for goods only, credit denied. Besides, Lorcan doubted that he had any credit. For ever indebted. He had the brick, tin and beam but had foolishly left the bag of cement partially open and the swirling wind had carried the bulk of it off to distant climes and other houses in need of repair.

Money was the problem. The miners weren't budging. He had been subtle, then less subtle. Which left only one option. A last resort. He had been scared to do it before but it had been three weeks so maybe Nikos was desperate. There was a chance he could get something for nothing. That would serve Nikos right.

Finding the sole payphone in Hurton, he phoned Phil.

'I'll meet you.'

'When?'

'Tomorrow, Durston Park in Wisbech. Bring money.'

'How much?'

'Tell him if it's not enough, I keep it.'

'Okay.'

'And just you, Phil. Not him.'

'Got it.'

Lorcan hung up. His entire body was shaking, the battle-weary army of regret fighting the amped-up army of need. He put his hand on the post box outside of the grocery store to steady himself. A place where post was collected and delivered three times a week. A lonely postal route.

'Mr Maguire?'

Lorcan didn't recognize the voice. The armies inside his body called a temporary truce, banding together against a common threat.

The man approached with a smile that was hidden by his beard. At least Lorcan thought it was a smile. It might have been a sneer of hatred. His suit was light grey and probably torturous to wear on a summer day like this. Had Nikos found out where they were and sent someone?

A hand shot out. Lorcan let it hang there.

'I know your wife,' said the bearded man. That didn't help Lorcan's understanding. Or his nerves. 'Well, I've met her. I hear you have a child.'

Another blast of nerves triggered through his body. Lorcan was caught between fight or flight.

'How do—?'

'I'm Greg Williams. I teach at the school.'

The school. Dylan. Naiyana had checked it out. The build-up of blood in his muscles drained suddenly leaving him woozy. And ill.

'When will one of you be visiting the school? We need time to register Dylan, complete the paperwork, etc. We're looking forward to having him. He's lucky. We have two brand new computers this term. Thank goodness for hardship grants!'

Lorcan put his hand up. 'Wait, has my wife not already been to see it? Last week?'

Greg Williams shook his head. 'No. She said she'd visit before Christmas but she never did. We were installing the new machines right up to Christmas Eve. They go perfectly with the new mobile.'

'So the school isn't run-down?'

Greg looked a little offended at this. 'It could do with some more work of course, but compared to most buildings . . .' he said, glancing around the town for comparison.

Lorcan, however, was lost in his own thoughts. Nee had stated that the school seemed okay, old, dusty and definitely not modern. The opposite to what this guy was saying. Had she seen it from outside? But the new mobile would surely have been obvious. It had been back when she didn't want to stick around, so was it merely a ruse to persuade him to leave?

Or a ruse to meet up with someone else? Someone from the charity? That MP? BS Foods? He knew all too well that illicit meetings could be arranged.

Moving hadn't improved their personal lives any more than the work-child-work-sleep pattern had in Perth. In fact, it seemed they had even more secrets than before.

81

Lorcan

Lorcan peeked in through the shutters. Naiyana was with Dylan, reading a story to him while relaxing on the plastic sun lounger. He decided not to confront her about the school. Not now. He might need to blow off some steam after his next job. One last attempt to wrangle his fair share of the profits from the neighbours. Targeting Ian this time. Their leader. If that failed then blackmailing Nikos was a runner.

Eventually, the three men came to the surface, joking amongst themselves, their day done.

'Again?' sighed Mike, wrapping his used gum in paper and shoving it in his pocket. 'You got nothing better to do?'

'It looks like I don't,' sniped Lorcan, before focusing on Ian, who was wiping his grimy face with a cloth. 'Good day?'

'G'day to you,' smiled Ian, joking.

Lorcan forced a smile. 'No, was it a good day down there?'

Ian's smile dropped to a rueful shake of the head.

'Nothing?'

'Very little.'

'That's a lie.'

Ian frowned.

Lorcan continued. 'If it was you wouldn't be giggling like idiots. And now you're off to a motel for the evening?'

Ian's face was emotionless, his sharp eyes dulled, giving nothing away. But in the background Mike couldn't resist a gloating nod.

'Whereas we barely have enough to eat.'

'It was the same for us when you came to town,' said Stevie. 'Stuck down there while you swanned around the place like you owned it. Just go back to Perth. There's nothing for you here.'

It was a brutal and honest summary but also something beseeching in the request. As if a subtle warning. But Lorcan was having none of it.

'There is something. Down there.'

'Which we are best placed to extract,' said Mike. 'Much as I'm sure you know how to do something else – not house-building obviously – so go do that and leave us alone.'

Lorcan ignored the jibe. He swung towards Ian who retained his passive, calculating expression.

'You're obviously in charge,' he said, glancing to see the scowl on Mike's face. 'We need help.'

82

Emmaline

It had been a struggle to get both the Forensics and the Recovery teams out here to this remote patch of earth, Rispoli, Anand and Oily guiding them at set points along the route like a crime-scene version of the road train she had seen in Leonora yesterday.

As they shuffled out of the way to a neutral position, Barker discovered a cluster of empty tinnies nestled in a clump of bushes. Recently discarded given the lustre of the metal. Emmaline got him to bag them up and give them to Forensics to check. For all she knew, this was a local drinking spot but it was worth checking out given what was discovered nearby.

After that Emmaline joined the teams in the gorge and watched on as the wreckage and surrounding area was sampled and swabbed, evidence cut and bagged from the scene, videos and photographs taken from every angle, including from the air, the chopper staying high to avoid unnecessarily raising dust and sand.

Unfortunately, the commotion had attracted more bystanders. The press had latched on, clogging up the roads and their engines with dirt in their desperation to be first on scene. The recovery trucks called to retrieve them had only added to the chaos.

With the exterior evidence logged, the burnt-out roof of the cab was cut open with a pair of lifesavers and the two bodies – no smaller third body was found – photographed in situ before being hoisted clear of the wreckage and the gorge. The early prognosis matched what Emmaline had determined: the bodies had been strapped in the front seat given the lack of movement, remnants of the seat belt seared onto their clothes and skin. But they hadn't been unconscious.

'Shot?'

'Both of them,' said Rebecca Patel, her face mask pulled down, unsteady on her feet due to the steep embankment.

'Your initial assumptions?'

Dr Patel didn't even put up a fight this time. 'One bullet wound each. JDD was shot in his chest.'

'JDD?'

'John Doe, the Driver,' said Dr Patel before continuing. 'Given the entry wound it is likely to have caused extensive damage to the heart muscle and lungs at the very minimum.'

'Self-inflicted?' asked Oily. His thorough but stupid question was summarily ignored by Dr Patel.

'JDP – John Doe, the Passenger – has a gunshot wound to the skull. Entry point just above the left eye. It was a catastrophic injury. There's no exit wound. Death was likely instantaneous.'

'Both male?' asked Emmaline.

'Provisionally it would seem so but I'll only confirm that once they are on the slab. They have been burnt extensively but the fire wasn't wholly catastrophic.'

'So they were killed, then placed in the vehicle. It was then set on fire and pushed over the edge to make it look like a crash.'

'It's hard to make it look like a crash when both have potentially fatal bullet wounds,' noted Dr Patel.

'Any idea on which one was killed first?'

Dr Patel shook her head. 'Impossible to determine at present. Securing an ID is our first priority.'

'Agreed,' said Emmaline.

Dr Patel returned to the burnt-out ute and Emmaline watched her crew perform a final sweep of the vehicle in situ before the Recovery team took over. The chopper lowered, whipping up dust and sand and the two bodies, bound like mummies, were winched up to the chopper for a speedy return to Leonora. The living wouldn't be so lucky, having to wade through an assembly of beached vehicles and eager press. But not down here in the gorge. Emmaline stood back as the Recovery team calculated how they were going to remove the vehicle from the scene.

Emmaline was performing calculations of her own. She now had two murder scenes. Within a few kilometres of each other. And no idea which incident had happened first.

Were the miners – if these were indeed the miners – killed by Lorcan Maguire? Who was then murdered by Ian Kinch in revenge. But why would Lorcan Maguire take such a desperate step? Had Mike and Stevie attacked Naiyana and killed her? Is that why they hadn't found her body yet? Lorcan then had discovered – as noted on the phone message – that his wife was gone and wreaked his savage revenge.

Or what if the order of death was the other way around? Lorcan Maguire had been killed first for some reason. Possibly by Mike and Stevie. Had this in turn led Ian Kinch to kill his fellow miners to wipe out any witnesses? That still left Naiyana and Dylan Maguire unaccounted for.

And what if Ian Kinch was one of these bodies? Killed by Mike or Stevie in an argument over money that spun out of control? If Ian was doing the selling it would have been easy for him to skim some from the sales. And equally possible for Mike and Stevie to siphon gold from the haul. Either of these could have led to a fatal argument.

Or finally, was an outside factor involved in all this? After all, none of them were hardened criminals. Even Ian Kinch couldn't be classed as a hardened criminal. More a schemer. But schemes can easily turn deadly.

83

Naiyana

Eight years of marriage meant that Naiyana Maguire knew when her husband was up to no good. There was a Machiavellian stench that oozed from his entire being when he had a plan. Especially when he had been on the up. Suggesting that she be the stay-at-home parent as he made more money. In business dealings and bonuses. In buying the massive house. All of which came to an end when INK Tech had let him go and the bank had foreclosed on their home. Some things were too big to manipulate. Now he was on his knees and scrapping like she had never seen before. The desperation was worrying. What was he capable of?

He had waited until he thought she was asleep before sneaking out of the house. There was only one place he would be going this late.

Ian, Mike and Stevie had shifted to days rather than nights as, according to Mike, it was easier on them and their body clocks. He had stepped into the middle of the road to talk to her as she passed in the ute, his greedy eyes matching his greedy gut. Definitely not her type.

Lorcan had just stepped into the tunnel when she caught up with him.

'Lorcan.'

'Shit!' The torchlight scrambled around the hole as he stumbled down the last few steps. The light turned and shone in her face. 'What are you doing here, Nee?'

'What are *you* doing here?'

His voice turned insistent. 'If that lot can use the equipment, then so can I. It's not rocket science.'

At this he turned and started to creep down the tunnel. It was an attempt to lose her but she tiptoed down the steps and caught up with him.

'Don't do it, Lorc.'

'I have to try. It's better than the alternative.'

'What's the alternative?'

'You don't want to know.'

She wondered what he meant. The stench of sneakiness. Cryptic and mysterious.

'Do you even know how to work the machines?' she asked, staying low so as to not crack her skull on the rock or beams overhead.

'No, but again, it's hardly rocket science. I just need to do this for a couple of nights. A week at the most. Get us in the black. Then we can move. Somewhere with running water, electricity and an indoor toilet. Get back on the ladder. That's what you want too. Deep down. I know it.'

There he was again, trying to put words in her

mouth. But she wasn't that person anymore. Still, there she was as ever, blindly following him down a deep, dark tunnel.

After ten minutes they reached the end, the light from the torch focusing on a pair of odd-looking machines, Lorcan yelping in glee as if he had just won the jackpot.

She watched on as he went to work, feeling his way around them as if he was the Fonz, searching for the sweet spot to jolt the machines miraculously into life.

'Face it, you don't know what you're doing,' she said, feeling the desperate urge to leave but needing the torch.

A flick of a button and the generator burst into life, filling the tunnel with a rumble she could feel in her sternum. Another button and the red barrel machine started to hum, a symphony building. Another minute and the arms of what must have been some sort of grinding machine went to work, adding the final falsetto to the piece, the brutal crunch of rock.

Her pleas to leave now fell on soon-to-be deaf ears. Her head quickly began to pound as she watched her husband check the conveyor belt at the end of the barrel before shovelling more crushed rock into it, the jet of water washing the material, sifting and sorting before being recycled.

He bent down and checked the conveyor belt again, the torchlight reflecting off something. Grabbing it he held it up to the light. It was a chunk of gold, a tiny nugget. The light caught his ear-to-ear grin. She hadn't seen him this happy in a long time and a part of her didn't want to ruin his moment but this was crazy and dangerous. Ian, Mike and Stevie would not abide this.

She smelled the smoke first. It was impossible to see in the darkness of the tunnel, Lorcan's torch focused on the conveyor belt and feeding rock into the crusher. At first she thought that it might have been the stench of pulverized rock but there was a distinctive oily aroma to it. Then in that instant a second source of light appeared in the tunnel, the crusher spouting a burst of flame from underneath.

'Lorcan!' she cried but hearing anything in the riotous tunnel was impossible. His focus was on the belt, holding up another nugget, gloating. Then he saw the flames. He stood up, a good six inches taller than her, his face suddenly obscured by smoke.

Cutting the generator, with the flick of a button he moved towards her. And he didn't stop, pointing behind her urgently. For a moment she had a sinking feeling of childhood dread that a monster lurked behind her. Turning there was nothing but a darkness that was soon dispersed by the torchlight. They fled, the smoke drifting out with them, hoping to not make a wrong turn.

84

Naiyana

They made it out into the fresh air, coughing up the darkness from their lungs. The town was silent. And not just because her ears were ringing.

'Are you okay?' Lorcan asked her, his voice dulled, as if she was at the top of a mountain and he was shouting from the bottom.

She was far from okay but she was alive.

'I told you!' Her shouting brought on another coughing fit.

He didn't respond. Maybe he couldn't hear her. She shouted louder.

'Another failure. How much did you get?'

He dug the tiny nuggets of gold from his pocket but Naiyana was far from finished.

'First you build a wall that collapses on us. Then you try and choke me to death. What next? Are you going to shoot us with that rifle?'

Lorcan put the gold away and turned on her. 'At least I'm trying.'

'I'm trying too.'

'Why did you lie about seeing the school?'

Naiyana felt her breath jam in her chest. She wondered how he knew this but he wasn't finished.

'Where were you, Nee? You're always off doing something. Never around here helping out.'

'Maybe the same place you are when you're supposed to be off getting materials. Accompanied by a few tinnies.'

'Only one or two. It's not as if there is any entertainment at home.'

'What do you want? A bloody nightclub? We gave all that up.'

'But we don't have to,' he said, the anger turned to pleading.

'What? Is Nikos Iannis just going to go away? Is Chester Grant? Are BS Foods?'

It was a shouting contest in the middle of an empty street in an empty town. No winners. Just losers.

85

Mike Andrews

Mike tried but failed to waft the smoke from his face. The crusher had caught fire overnight. Switching it on, nothing happened. Something had melted within the motor was Ian's less-than-expert opinion.

'How did this happen?' said Stevie.

'One guess,' said Mike.

'We don't know that,' said Ian. 'It could have been a short circuit. How much will it—?'

'Of course we know. Who else knows about this set-up?' said Mike, waving his hand around.

'It will cost *us*,' said Stevie, answering Ian's question. 'It melted through a few transistors and damaged the gearing so we need to replace those too.'

'Which you can pay for,' said Mike, looking at Ian.

'How's that?' asked Ian, giving him a look that Mike didn't often care for considering Ian's oft-mentioned past, but he wasn't going to lie down on this one.

'You are not doing your job in protecting the equipment. Which is an extension of your role as protector.'

'You want me to stay here and guard it at night?'

'No, just put a bear-trap down. Let it chew through his leg,' said Mike, ending it with a clack of gum that mimicked the sound of a leg being broken.

'You got one handy?'

'You're the one with the contacts, supposedly.'

Ian waved this off. But Stevie jumped in. 'To be fair, Ian, Mike's right. You're letting things get out of control. If we were tougher they would get out of town.'

'Since when did you two fancy yourselves as the muscle?'

'Since you stopped,' said Mike. He could feel the power pulsing through him. He and Stevie were the enforcers now, an exhilarating role reversal. 'There are only two reasons for having you around, Ian.'

'Oh, and what's that?'

'Negotiation and enforcement. And now we're experienced enough to do the negotiating. We have the merchandise, people will come to us.'

'You know nothing about enforcement,' said Ian, pacing closer.

Mike looked to his friend for backup, but Stevie's support was confined to dissenting words only. He looked around for something to defend himself with but their rifle was by the entrance steps.

'You need us,' said Mike, the power in his voice gone.

'Oh, I need *you* now?' said Ian, towering over him. 'The gold is here, the machines are here. I could have two illegals down here tomorrow. I'd get more work and less gip.'

'Look, he's only saying that we need to control that family,' said Stevie, keeping his distance.

'And if we throw them out what happens then?'

Mike couldn't find the words. This time Stevie wasn't helping him out.

'Nothing? Let me tell you then. If they go, there's a chance they yabber. And what control do we have then? Remember, keep your friends close and enemies closer.'

'Unless you get rid of them entirely.'

Both Ian and Mike looked at Stevie. The unspoken had been uttered, leaving a bitter taste. It was disgusting. It was horrible. And now that it was out in the open, it was a possibility.

86

Lorcan

Given what had happened, Lorcan was glad to get out of Kallayee. He wasn't enamoured about meeting Phil but he was keen to hear Nikos's answer. A hard 'Yes' and they could move to Vic or New South Wales for a while. Maybe even abroad. Distance themselves from Nikos and the rest of the Perth shit and start over. Somewhere more populated.

A 'No' and the options were less clear. He could try Ian again but he would be lucky to get a hello from them. They would also guard the equipment to avoid a repeat performance. 'No' also meant staying in Kallayee . . . unless they were forced out. That was another option. Get Ian to kick them out. Then Naiyana would have to leave. Where to could be decided later.

The meeting was in Durston Park in Wisbech. Far enough from Kallayee to feel safe but close enough to get to in a couple of hours. He might even head to a pub after for a spell. Clear his head and his wallet with a couple of cold ones.

It was 12:10 and Phil was late. Not a huge problem. Lorcan had time. Plenty of time. Phil was coming a long way after all. On reflection, it might be nice to see him. A familiar face. They could reminisce about the Murray River fishing trip that ended with them all in the drink trying to retrieve the tinnies that were floating away on the current. Good times. Before Phil had left INK Tech for another Nikos-backed venture.

'Lorcan Maguire.'

He recognized the voice. The bravado and the confidence. The imposing figure plumped himself onto the bench, the polo shirt unbuttoned to reveal a neatly shaved chest. His dark brows arched towards his nose. Meaning business. Meaning Nikos Iannis.

Phil had stabbed him in the back. The bastard. For money, probably. He had a mortgage and a mail order bride to take care of.

Lorcan glanced around, though he didn't know who exactly he was looking for. Georgios Iannis was in the hospital. If needed he could make a run for it . . .

'Let's make this quick,' said Nikos. 'Do you have it?'

Lorcan had been thrown off course. He had scripted to the word the story he was going to tell Phil. Lying to Nikos would be more difficult.

'Do *you* have it?' said Lorcan. 'The money?'

'It's a lot of money, Lorcan.'

'It's good information.'

'Is that the line you've been pitching to other companies?'

317

Lorcan kept quiet. He tried to compute how to play this. The playbook was scrambled now.

'Do you have the information?'

'Do you have the money?' repeated Lorcan.

Nikos grinned. 'Not here. I'm not carrying around that much. But I suspect you don't have the info with you either.'

Lorcan felt the chill crawl down his back. He felt exposed, as if Nikos was suddenly in the driving seat. That he knew something Lorcan didn't. It was true that he didn't bring the information with him. A precaution. Maybe subconsciously he knew Phil would betray him. He also knew Nikos's and his brother's rep. Playing hardball. So Nikos probably wasn't enjoying being on the other end of the stick.

'Two-hundred thousand,' said Nikos, calmly.

'Four-hundred.'

'Two.'

'Three-hundred.'

Nikos raised his eyebrows. It was a look of pure malevolence. It was clear that Lorcan was pushing his luck.

'Okay, two-hundred,' said Lorcan. Price agreed, the next part of the plan he was sure of. Keeping his voice controlled and confident, he said, 'Back here, two days. Eleven a.m.'

'Not here,' said Nikos. 'Somewhere quieter.'

Lorcan shook his head. He wasn't going to agree to that.

87

Emmaline

Once the vehicle and bodies had been recovered, Emmaline scrambled back to the top of the gorge. The police tape remained, as did a gaggle of reporters. Oily was speaking to them, offering his assistance but giving them little. A crashed vehicle. Two occupants. Unknown identity. Too early to say if they were linked to the murder of Lorcan Maguire or just a tragic accident.

She rounded up her local team: Rispoli, Barker and Anand.

'Any chance of witnesses to the crash?'

'Out here, unlikely,' said Barker.

'Nearest dwelling?'

Anand checked his tablet. 'Ulysses Hitchens. About six clicks that way,' he said, pointing further up the gorge.

'Let's go ask.'

On the way, Anand informed her and Rispoli – Barker had remained behind to help Oily finish up – that Ulysses was a little crazy.

'Says who?'

'Everyone. He has been for a while. He used to be a professor but his brain curdled in the heat.'

'A professor of what?'

'Astronomy. That's all he does now. Checks the sky for supernovas.'

'And that's a job?'

'He's retired,' said Anand. 'And be wary of his UFOs.'

'His what?'

'Ulysses's Fucking Observations. The lights in the sky he's always ringing in to the station about.'

'Recent lights?'

'Nope. For years.'

Ulysses Hitchens's place was essentially a massive glass conservatory with a simple wooden shack bolted on the front. The place was a shambles but the view, out over the gorge, was magnificent.

Ulysses answered the door in a shirt and shorts. He was around seventy years old and sported a magnificent white beard and hair that made him look like some biblical version of God in casual attire. On holiday perhaps.

'Yesss?' he asked, drawing the word out.

'I'm Detective Taylor from the Major Crime Squad, and these are Constables Rispoli and Anand from Leonora.'

Ulysses glanced at her and then the others. 'I believe I have talked to the constables before.'

Emmaline nodded. 'We've found a crashed vehicle about six kilometres back along the gorge. We're trying to pinpoint a date for the incident. Do you recall anything suspicious in the area in the past few weeks?'

'What kind of suspicious?'

'Movement. New people. Old people. Noises . . .'

'A fire,' added Rispoli. 'You might have been able to see it from your conservatory.'

'If I'm in the conservatory I'm looking up, not around, young man. I don't have time to look around.'

'This would have been a sizeable blaze,' said Emmaline. 'You might have seen the glow.'

'We get a lot of brush fires around here, miss. Unless the radio tells me to get the hell out, I ignore it,' he said, with a flourish of his hands.

'So you haven't seen or heard anything recently?'

'Oh, I didn't say that,' said Ulysses. 'I've seen lights.'

In the background Anand coughed. The UFOs he had warned about.

'Where?' asked Emmaline, treading carefully.

'Around the Keenan Run. One of the old tracks on my land.'

'What night was this?'

'It went on for a few nights, not just one. Days too. I could hear the engines. Trying to steal fence posts or cables, I guess. Copper in them, you see. I tried to get to them to warn them off but I can't move too good these days. Takes an age to get in and out of my car.'

'Where is this run?' interrupted Emmaline.

Ulysses pointed out towards where the ute was found. 'The night lights came from over there. The engines came from there,' he said, pointing the opposite direction.

'Are you sure?'

'My sight and hearing are all I have left, miss. I trust them implicitly.'

'Thank you. If we have anything further . . .' She paused. 'You don't happen to own a quad bike do you by any chance?' she asked, thinking of the one with slashed tyres in Kallayee.

Ulysses shook his head. 'No, I don't. Though I probably should. I might be able to catch the copper-stealing bastards then.'

88

Mike Andrews

Mike was upset. He wanted to give Lorcan Maguire a piece of his mind too. And a smack in the face. But Ian had outwitted them.

'You have me here as the face of this operation. So let me do my job.'

Mike felt his chest tighten. He had no counterpunch. His own words used against him.

'What are we meant to do then?' asked Stevie. 'The crusher's broken. I guess we could break some rock manually . . .'

Mike met Stevie with a scowl. He didn't want to be down the tunnel splitting rock all day.

'Clean the equipment then,' said Ian.

'You can piss off,' said Mike.

Ian glared at him. 'I don't care what you do. But you're staying out of this,' he said, striding out of the house.

LORCAN

Lorcan was still distracted by his earlier meeting with Nikos. With the promise of a showdown in two days. The money in exchange for the information. A tempting offer.

'Lorcan?'

Also too distracted to spot Ian before he peered through the window.

Lorcan rolled off the lounger and made for the back of the house, hauling Dylan with him. He listened as Naiyana met Ian at the front door.

'I just want to talk,' said Ian. He didn't sound angry, though his tone carried a hint of frustration that Lorcan was wary of. Grabbing the rifle from the eaves and holding it helped. He was glad of its unwavering support.

'Okay, let's talk,' he heard his wife say, sticking up for her family.

'Just you,' said Ian. 'You seem to be the only one with sense out of the two of you.'

Lorcan wanted to defend himself against this slight, but couldn't muster the words or actions.

'And not here,' said Ian. 'Somewhere quiet.'

'What do you mean, quiet?' asked Naiyana.

'There will be things said about your husband – and my team – that your child doesn't want to hear,' said Ian. 'Best this is done in private.'

There was a palling silence. Lorcan wasn't keen on this, his wife going off with some stranger. *But better her than me*, he reasoned.

'Lorcan?' said Naiyana.

He stayed silent and held onto Dylan tighter.

'Okay,' said Naiyana. 'I'll follow you in our ute.'

'No, we go in mine,' said Ian. 'That way your husband has transport should something happen to Dylan.'

It was a statement loaded with threat. Was something going to happen to him when Ian and Nee left? Were the other two going to come and take him or Dylan? Should he take his son and leave? Get a head start? Or should he follow them?

He stayed in the bedroom as he heard the rattle of the miner's ancient ute as it pulled away. He wondered what to do next, silently asking the rifle for help.

89

Emmaline

They followed the directions Ulysses gave them for the sound of the engines. The Keenan Run was barely worth the name, traversed at little more than walking pace from the far side of Ulysses's house, down a small incline, up the other side, twisting and turning as if trying to shake them, the track almost gone in parts, overgrown, the 4x4 struggling to navigate it.

'Could anyone come this way?' asked Rispoli as the vehicle jerked over another series of bumps.

'Not from this side,' said Emmaline, holding onto the handgrip. 'This track hasn't been used in a while.'

The Run lasted five kilometres that took nearly thirty minutes to navigate.

It eventually levelled out, widening at a patch of ground nestled close to a small bushy hill and fenced off by trees. There were, however, distinct tyre tracks in the dust, side by side as if two vehicles had recently parked there.

Emmaline got out of the 4x4 and looked around. There was nothing that would indicate a reason for anyone to be there. No posts, no cables, no water trough, nothing. There was barely room to turn.

'What are you thinking?' asked Rispoli, creeping around the edge of the site.

'I think one of these treads will match the crashed ute.'

'Assuming we get something from Forensics.'

'And the other set?' asked Anand.

'How far is it to Kallayee from here?' asked Emmaline.

A quick check of the tablet and Anand had an answer. 'Seven clicks. South-west.'

'And do you have to go through Hurton?'

'It doesn't say.'

'Let's try.'

Leaving Anand there, promising to contact Barker ASAP to collect both him and a cast of the tyre tracks, Rispoli and Emmaline navigated the rest of the Keenan Run. Around the hill, the scenery opened out. After a kilometre they came across the pleasure of hard, smooth tarmac. From there they steered west towards Hurton.

'Do I keep going?' asked Rispoli.

Then Emmaline saw it. A dirt road to the right.

'No, down there.'

Rispoli swung onto a road that went part way towards Hurton, before joining the broken tarmac of the once well-maintained road to Kallayee. From there it was a couple of kilometres to town past the TV trucks.

'What did that tell you?' asked Rispoli.

'One of those tracks will be the miners' transport. The other will match the Maguire's ute. If we ever find it.'

'But why meet all the way out there?'

Emmaline pursed her lips. 'A negotiation.'

'Over what?'

That she wasn't sure. 'Maybe over how to live in town together.'

'Again, why out there?'

'If the miners and the family knew of each other's presence then there would have been tension. They needed a neutral place. Away from prying eyes. They needed to negotiate to keep each other's secrets and keep the peace.'

Given the three bodies, however, it seemed that negotiations had broken down.

90

Lorcan

There was silence. Not even Dylan was talking. He was just staring. In silent judgement at his father letting his mother go. With Ian.

Lorcan toyed with following them. He could have tracked the dust cloud. But what if they veered onto the main road? That was harder to answer.

'Can we go?' pleaded Dylan.

'They might be gone,' said Lorcan, failing to hide his dejection at the situation. At his own ineptitude. He felt sick with shame.

'I only want to go out and play.'

Dylan didn't seem one bit concerned that his mother had left. She had gone and she would come back. The boy was living in perfect innocence and ignorance. But if he wasn't going to follow Nee then neither of them were leaving the house.

'We'll stay inside until Mum gets back,' said Lorcan, resting the gun on the floor beside him.

'When will that be?'

Lorcan squeezed his eyes shut to avoid a question he feared the answer to.

91

Mike Andrews

Like Pavlov's mutts they were cleaning the machines. Ian says jump, they say how high. The sweat that rolled off his forehead wasn't just from the sweltering heat. It was also from the anger.

'So he fucks up and we get stuck doing the heavy labour?' said Mike. Without the machines drowning out all and sundry, Stevie would be able to hear his invective. Not that he expected anything back other than some watered-down 'let's keep the peace' bullshit.

'Is this worth the hassle?' asked Stevie, his fingers oily from poking inside the grinder. 'We could go back home and find other jobs. They might be shit but the thrill of this has gone, hasn't it?'

It was accompanied by the same look of despondency Mike had last seen when they were given the heave-ho from Skyline. All lumped together as one. Stevie was a good employee. Not an agitator like he was. He was also a good friend.

'We shouldn't be kicked out of this, literal goldmine,

because of one guy, Stevie. If we were alone in this town . . .'

Mike glanced at his friend to see if he was receptive. Stevie shook his head.

'Ian isn't here to stop us,' said Mike. 'Neither is Naiyana. You could take care of the boy while I talk to that bastard father.'

92

Emmaline

The atmosphere in the caravan was as thick as the stench of cigarettes. She didn't dare leave the windows open during the day in case of scaly intruders or coming back to find everything layered in sand. Out the window a few TV lights still glared, reporters barking into microphones like dogs throughout the night, the outskirts of Kallayee remaining the defacto base for the press coverage. Still the town was roped off, a few trespassers forcibly removed and given a night in the cells. She considered going to Hurton and the Rack. She might not have been exactly welcomed but there was a chance of bumping into Matty and coming back here. Which wouldn't contravene the security of the scene. Nothing untoward had taken place in this caravan. It just smelled like it.

The temporary booster also meant phone coverage. Rispoli and the others had left twenty minutes ago. They would barely have made it to the main road. She could call Rispoli and get him to return. He was a police officer. That certainly wouldn't contravene security.

So she did. He didn't take much persuading.

Hearing the vehicle approach, she waited in the doorway of the caravan, striking what she hoped was a seductive pose, truly feeling like a black-and-white movie actress now, beckoning her strapping co-star into her on-set trailer. The movie was murder.

What happened between them wasn't acting.

The morning brought a search for clean clothes in the fetid air of the tiny caravan, then a trip to Hurton for breakfast, and reviewing a burst of new forensic information that was as exhilarating as the double espresso.

The lab had been working overnight. Fingerprints and DNA had been identified from the empty beer cans found at the crash site. Lorcan Maguire's. Putting him in the vicinity of two murders. Or at least the disposal of the bodies.

'So Lorcan killed them before he himself was killed?' said Rispoli, finishing off his breakfast. Not letting the morass of information affect his gut.

Emmaline was still trying to process the information. She had been expecting Ian Kinch's DNA on the tins. Even Mike Andrews or Stevie Amaranga. Nikos Iannis at a stretch.

She recalibrated the timeline. 'If it was Lorcan it means that he killed JDD and JDP, transported the bodies, prepped the truck and burnt it to destroy evidence.'

'Which is what you would expect from a career criminal. Like Ian Kinch.'

'Or Nikos Iannis. Or someone who could outsource it.'

'To professionals.'

'Yeah. But an amateur would make mistakes. Like leave his DNA near the site,' said Emmaline.

'Maybe he needed to have a few to calm his nerves. Before or after.'

'But someone helped him do this. He couldn't have done it alone.'

'The same person that then killed him and took his son?'

'It would seem to link.'

'But why?'

'I think something went badly wrong between the family and those miners. I also think that Nikos, and even Chester Grant, found out where the family were living,' said Emmaline. 'Plus the desert can do some crazy things to people.'

93

Naiyana

She stared across the seat at him as he veered off the road out of Kallayee, down the highway for a short spell before deviating again long before Hurton. He navigated a kilometre to a spot behind the hill, out of sight of anything but satellites and wild animals.

He looked serious and there was a smell of desperation in the dirty sweat that clung to his face. The relaxed cunning had gone. There was no playfulness in his voice, no overarching control. Lorcan was probably right in not volunteering to come. The coward.

'Something needs to be done about him,' said Ian, staring into the trees beyond.

'I'll try to keep him under control.'

'Try harder. As things stand *this* is beneficial to both of us. It needs to be kept that way.'

Naiyana nodded. Two kids to keep in order. And a set of unruly neighbours.

94

Mike Andrews

The heat and the pressure had become too much. He needed to get away from this dark prison cell. But on stepping into the searing air there was only one thing on his mind. Find Lorcan. Warn him. Make him leave.

Seeming to sense this, Stevie had followed him.

'Don't do anything stupid, Mike.'

'Like let them hang around here?'

'Let Ian do his bit.'

'By talking to her? We know she can't control him.'

'What are you going to do?'

'I don't know.'

'I'm not grabbing that kid,' warned Stevie.

'Maybe it won't come to that,' said Mike, as he approached the family's house. He didn't know exactly what he was going to do. Something. Anything. Lorcan had become the focus of all his anger and frustration.

Unexpectedly the front door opened. Lorcan was standing in the doorway, the kid nowhere to be seen. He looked pained and drawn, worried. Mike was determined to make him very worried. Using words only. Despite this self-assertion, he could feel his hands balling into fists. As Ian had said, 'Be prepared for anything.'

From the direction of the crossroads came the rattle of an engine. It pulled up outside the house, Ian and Naiyana exiting the vehicle.

'What's going on here?' asked Ian.

Mike stared at him, then Lorcan, before turning and marching back towards the crossroads without another word. Lorcan had earned a reprieve for the time being.

95

Emmaline

She drove everyone out of Kallayee for the rest of the morning. All distractions kept outside the caravan. She needed solace to feed her thinking.

Who were the bodies in the truck? The only people she could rule out were Lorcan and Dylan Maguire. So if it was two of the other people in Kallayee – likely, given the location of the scene and the fact that none of them had been seen since 30 December – then it was likely one of two groups. Mike Andrews and Stevie Amaranga, as they were friends before Ian Kinch became the third wheel, or Naiyana Maguire and Ian Kinch. Mike and Stevie might have developed some anger towards Ian over the gold, shot him, then went about killing the family. Naiyana first, then a fleeing Lorcan. But that was unlikely. They were scientists, not killers. And what would they want with Dylan? But the desert can do some crazy things, as she herself had said. Here she was debating with herself in the middle of a tiny caravan, being serenaded by dingoes and having to wash in a basin. She was one step away from becoming certifiable.

Her thinking edged towards the miners. Mike and Stevie. Both friends and both shot. Possibly at separate times. Then again possibly not. Ian could easily have killed both in the tunnel to carry on mining alone. But why drag them out and fake the crash? Or had he killed them and taken on Lorcan Maguire as his partner until something else went wrong?

They had worked the mine for at least three weeks. Three weeks trapped in the same confined space trying to avoid the Maguire family. Add to that the possibility that their gold return was dwindling. Her strong suspicion was that Ian had been fleecing Mike and Stevie and they had found out. After a confrontation Ian shot them. But the sound carried. The family heard. They tried to bolt but were hunted down.

But that still left Dylan and Naiyana. Did he not have the heart to shoot them? Was he swayed by her beauty? Or were their bodies still out there to be found?

She may have been taken along with Dylan. A contract put on her or her husband's head by Nikos Iannis or Chester Grant. Maybe the guy in the suit in the wrong place for an interview. Or the salesman who had come to Hurton. Used as cover to ask questions.

Emmaline rested her head against the thin lining of the seat, the plastic edge putting pressure on her skull, forcing her to stay alert. With all possibilities under careful consideration, she believed that the bodies in the truck would turn out to be Mike Andrews and Stevie Amaranga. In fact, she would stake her house on it. But given that this was currently a second-hand caravan with nicotine stains on the roof and a toilet door that didn't shut properly, she wasn't staking a lot.

Confirmation arrived in the early afternoon. The benefits of overtime and a now nationwide news story bearing fruit, everyone under pressure to produce results. The bodies in the truck had been identified.

Mike Andrews and Stevie Amaranga.

Emmaline called her team back to Kallayee. They convened outside the caravan, their lunches interrupted.

'Not a pleasant way to go,' said Barker, sipping coffee that Rispoli had brought back. He had dodged pulling sentry duty keeping the press back. Anand hadn't been so lucky. The disadvantage of being the junior member.

'No,' said Emmaline, 'but we're still not sure exactly how they did go.'

'Or why,' added Rispoli.

'What we do know is that of the six people in town, three are still missing, Naiyana Maguire, Dylan Maguire and Ian Kinch.'

'That I do have information on,' said Oily, making his way over from the huge Comms truck that had been added to their team, driven from Perth and now beached on the sand.

'We have confirmation that Ian Kinch left Queensland

at the same time as Mike Andrews and Stevie Amaranga. We even have photos of them together on the website for Deluxe. A nightclub in Brisbane.'

The high-quality photos showed Mike and Stevie, faces awash in drunken pleasure, some random girl wrapped around Stevie's slender waist. The only person who didn't look pleased was Ian, trying to hide his face from the lens but failing.

'He doesn't look happy,' said Barker.

'No,' said Oily. 'Given we found no pictures of the three together on Mike's or Stevie's social media outlets, this seems to have fallen outside the scope of his control.'

She looked closer. 'This is from the first of November. Anything more recent?'

Oily shook his head.

'Which suggests he is either dead himself, or he's gone to ground,' said Emmaline. 'And the only reason to go into hiding is . . . ?'

'Because he committed a crime,' said Rispoli.

'And he did. Mining without permits,' said Barker.

'True,' said Emmaline. 'But, if the murdered bodies of your mining partners and someone you were alone in a town with showed up, *and* you were innocent, you'd hand yourself in to clear your name.'

'So we think Ian Kinch killed these three people and then took Naiyana and Dylan?' said Rispoli.

'Or he took them hostage, before murdering them,' said Barker.

Emmaline added another twist to this supposition.

341

'Or, best-case scenario, he took them hostage and is keeping them alive somewhere.'

There was absolute silence at this being the best-case scenario. That a triple murderer still had two hostages alive after eleven days on the run.

Emmaline grasped for positivity. 'There's nothing in Ian Kinch's record that suggests he's willing or capable of killing someone. Let alone four or five people.'

'Unless things went awry,' said Oily. 'Whatever their original plan was it veered drastically when the Maguires arrived.'

'Maybe he just took her for some fun,' said Barker, raising an eyebrow. 'She's an attractive woman.'

That brought another hushed silence. Another scenario nobody wished to contemplate. But it gave Emmaline time to think.

'We're supposing that Ian Kinch would hand himself in if he was innocent,' said Emmaline. 'But what if you'd been threatened yourself, say by an associate with a criminal past like Nikos Iannis? Or by someone in power. Like Chester Grant.'

'The MP?' said Rispoli.

Emmaline nodded.

'How's he involved?'

Emmaline told them everything.

96

Mike Andrews

He despised being herded back to work like a dumb sheep. Using his penknife to work the dirt from underneath his fingernails helped ease his anger towards Lorcan. There was a wife and son – and Ian – to consider. He would see what Ian had come back with before contemplating a further move, though short of shackling and muzzling Lorcan Maguire he didn't know what would appease him.

'So what did you get?' asked Mike.

Ian paced to the far end of the room.

'She promised—'

'Promised! She can't deliver. Only handcuffs, a gag and a deep pit will stop that mutt!'

'It'll work,' said Ian. 'I know it.'

Mike enjoyed having Ian on the defensive. It was good to bark the orders rather than take them for once. At Skyline they shut up and did what they were told. And still got the boot.

'We've an agreement,' continued Ian. 'A few bucks and they provide cover should anyone come sniffing around.'

'I think we should call it quits and go,' said Stevie.

Ian raised his voice. 'No one goes. I don't need anyone out there running their mouths about what's going on here.'

'I wouldn't. I'm quiet.'

'Compared to me,' added Mike with a clack.

'We've made enough for six or nine months, right?' said Stevie. 'If we analyse the data for Murchison I'm sure there will be another sweet spot. Miles away from here.'

'But if we stay we can make more,' said Ian. 'We have the find right here. I have them under control. We stick together. We get all we can and then dump the hangers-on.'

'And if they have enough and decide to leave?'

'Then I'll deal with it.'

Ian stuck his hand into the middle like he wanted to initiate some schoolyard oath, hands on top of each other. Mike could see that Stevie was itching to leave. But Ian was right about one thing. Money was money. And Mike needed money. To start a company. To support himself. And his elderly parents. Plus he could rag Lorcan Maguire about the charity. He put his hand in the centre. He would play along for now. Stevie looked at them both, shaking his head even as he added his hand to the pile.

97

Naiyana

'What was that about?'

'What?'

'Why were those two at the house? What did you do?'

'What makes you think that I did anything?' said Lorcan, exiting their bedroom. Dylan was standing in the hallway between them.

'You didn't go see them again, did you?'

'I didn't leave the house. Did we Dyl?'

Dylan shook his head. A long, frantic shake that told Naiyana that he was telling the truth, no glance towards his dad to confirm the appropriate answer, no chance to distort the truth.

'What did Ian have to say?'

'Nothing much. Just to keep our heads low. For *you* to keep your head low.'

'I have to eat. We all have to eat.'

'This will help.' She under-armed the small bundle of notes towards him. 'Three hundred. To help with the house.'

She watched as Lorcan let it drop, bouncing across the floor and nestling in the corner.

'Why did he give you this?'

'I told you. To tide us over.'

'Charity?' spat Lorcan as Dylan fetched the money, waving the bundled notes around like a colourful fan.

'You were asking for it anyway,' said Naiyana, frustrated by his obtuseness. 'Isn't it better that I get it?'

'I offered to work with them, not get a handout.'

'Well, I'm sorry to tell you this,' she said, though not in the least bit sorry, 'but they don't want you working with them. I'm amazed they even care after what you did to their machine.'

Naiyana watched Lorcan's focus turn to Dylan as he rifled the edges of the bills. Even in the middle of the desert he was led by cash, greedy for profit. They had grown so far apart. She wanted to save her family. He wanted to save himself.

98

Emmaline

There was silence and shocked expressions around the table. Except for Barker who just nodded as if his suspicions had been verified. He always thought that there was something off about Chester Grant. That he looked and acted a little too poster-boy for a politician. Barker had never understood why anyone would fight for the rights of the constituents above their own. When Rispoli pointed out that he should be doing the same as a policeman, Barker shook his head disdainfully, as if his younger colleague was an idiot.

Emmaline got word from Zhao that their request to put Chester Grant and Nikos Iannis under watch had been cleared. Zhao would lead on this. Any suspicious movements or actions would be noted, even though they couldn't detain them. Not without solid evidence linking them to the deaths.

She returned to what they had.

'So we know that two trucks met on Keenan's Run. And from the number of tracks not just once.'

Then it clicked. She recalled the information she had got from Bobby Marley.

'A kid in town claimed he had spotted Naiyana west of Hurton meeting someone with a beard. We can assume that it wasn't anyone from town.'

'And why is that?' asked Oily.

'Because otherwise we would have a name, or the boy wouldn't have mentioned it at all.'

'Keenan's Run is west of the town too.'

'Yes, he claims to have seen them just off the road. But what if they had been heading to Keenan's Run and the quiet spot they had discovered? Around the back of that hill.'

'They didn't want anyone to see,' shrugged Barker. 'We know that because no one in Hurton seems to have known that the miners were even out there.'

'Yes,' said Emmaline. 'So why go all the way out there and risk being seen en route?'

'Because they were trying to hide something from those in Kallayee, *not* the people in Hurton,' said Rispoli, slapping his hand off the van, causing it to rattle.

'Exactly,' said Emmaline. 'Naiyana Maguire was meeting Ian Kinch out there. More than once.'

'As in having an affair?' said Oily.

Emmaline nodded. 'It looks it.'

'But how do we prove it?'

'We get a confession,' said Emmaline. 'If they're still alive.'

99

Lorcan

He had eventually wrenched the money from his son's hand. Neither of them were elated with this development but he couldn't afford for it to be lost down one of the holes in the yard.

The next day he woke up early and left for Hurton. He bought some bricks and cement dust, more to rub the money in Mallon's face than for any building plans. Show both him and his snide son that he didn't need credit. Despite his attempts to goad them, Mallon and his son remained in annoyingly good spirits. Cash was king after all.

When he had left Kallayee earlier he hadn't quite decided his next move. But handing over the money to the old vulture behind the register swung it for him. He wanted to be the one getting cash forced into his hand. And not just a measly few bucks either.

With the materials in the back of the ute he headed for Wisbech, hitting a hundred and forty and feeling like a lawbreaker, a man not to be messed with. He needed the swagger, he needed the backbone it supplied.

The meeting with Nikos had been arranged for the same place as before. Durston Park. Having charged down there, he parked up and watched from across the road. He didn't want to get there first. That would look desperate. Though the state of his unwashed clothes would probably give that away. He observed a swathe of people enter and leave the park, studying each one. None of them looked like Nikos. Lorcan was confident he wouldn't send an associate. Nikos wanted his slimy hands on the information. This was personal.

Eleven o'clock rolled around. Time to stick or twist. Stick with the trickle of charity money from Ian and maybe squeeze a little more if it came to it, or deal with Nikos, get rich but acquire an enemy for life. He knew all the rumours about who Nikos and Georgios were and what they had done. Which was fine when he was making them money. Now he was stealing it.

100

Lorcan

On the way back to Kallayee he called into a rest stop for a stiff one to calm his nerves. Nikos would be pissed that Lorcan had stood him up. Lorcan would get word to him through Phil that he had destroyed the evidence and that he wasn't looking to sell it. No hard feelings. He doubted it would work.

He was about to set off when another traveller pulled into the stop. Hitched to the back of his sedan was a trailer and a quad bike, a 'For Sale' sign looped around the handlebars.

Lorcan stared at it. It reminded him of an old quad his aunt and uncle had bought for him as a kid. His parents had hated it; too fast and too dangerous for their liking.

'What's wrong with it?' he asked.

The owner looked up, the nozzle of the pump stuck in the sedan, humming to himself as he filled it. He glanced at the quad then back.

'Nothing. Bought a new one, so don't need this one.'

Lorcan didn't need it either. But he was sick of denying himself luxuries. 'How much?'

'Couple of hundred and you can take it. Saves me dragging it up to Leonora.'

He unloaded the quad from the back of the ute as Nee glared at him. Dylan was jumping up and down in excitement that they had a motorbike. It was the happiest Lorcan had seen him since before Christmas.

'Cost me one-fifty,' said Lorcan, irritated that he felt the need to explain himself.

'And the stuff for the house?'

'I got that too. Cement dust and bricks. I can repair the roof beam myself.'

He could see that she wasn't impressed.

'And what do we use it for?'

'I can drag stuff behind it. Move things around. I can take it to town. Leave you the ute.'

'Really?' she said, perking up. Offered exclusive use of the family vehicle. 'Are you sure it runs?'

It had worked fine at the rest stop. But he decided to lie instead.

'I better make sure.'

Straddling the machine, he started it up. It was advanced in years and the drive chain was too noisy but he didn't care. It would be fun. Especially in a town all to himself.

Revving the engine, he sped towards the crossroads, hitching a left past the tunnel house. On the return journey, a nervous and angered Ian, Stevie and Mike emerged from the house to glare at him.

He zoomed back towards his own house, grinning at the speed and the warm air dashing through his hair. He felt alive and free. A kid again. Naiyana stood with her hands on her hips watching him with disdain. So distracted she didn't see Dylan dart for the middle of the road, past her before she could reach for him.

But Lorcan could see him, right in his path. Leaning his weight to the side he tried to steer the heavy quad away. Still he got closer, the bike refusing to change direction in a hurry, the steering old, lazy and stubborn.

At the last moment Dylan must have sensed the danger and paused, Nee dragging him away as Lorcan flew past.

Coming back, Lorcan's wide grin had transferred to his son who bounced from foot to foot with glee, in awe of his father. He was grasped firmly by Nee who shouted that he hadn't picked up anything to eat and that she would have to go to town. Ignoring her, he continued past.

As he sped towards the tunnel house again, Ian was standing in the middle of the road. Lorcan stood on the brakes, performing a controlled fishtail that released another pleasing burst of endorphins. He still had it. His youth. Today had been a good day.

'What are you doing?' shouted Ian over the shuddering engine.

In response Lorcan revved the bike. He didn't want

to stop. If Ian was going to get in his way, then he would flatten him.

Stevie and Mike watched from the side, equally frustrated. If it had been Mike not Ian in the middle of the road, Lorcan wondered if he would have stopped at all.

'That money was for the house.'

'I bought what I needed. This will help,' said Lorcan. 'I can move stuff with it.'

'Then get to work and quit messing around.'

'Everyone needs a break. Besides no one is going to think anything is wrong if we – me, Nee and Dylan – are happy and enjoying life. *We* are your best cover – keep us happy and you'll all be fine.'

'And if we don't?'

Lorcan revved the engine again and pulled away, swerving around Ian and off to the edge of town, whooping all the way.

101

Mike Andrews

As they watched the cloud of dust following Lorcan, Mike stared at Ian. Eventually he turned and caught his eye.

'I have to go,' said Ian, hoisting a canvas bag over his shoulder.

'Leaving us with him?' said Mike.

'Don't react.'

'He didn't listen to anything you said,' said Stevie.

'I'll insist tonight,' said Ian, 'but I've lined up another deal.'

'How will you insist?' asked Mike.

'You won't be seeing him on a bike for a while,' said Ian.

There was an undercurrent of malice that suggested Mike ask no questions. That was fine. The only thing he would insist was that Ian told him everything. Every bone-crunching detail. But not everyone was happy with this.

'You aren't going to run, are you?' asked Stevie.

It was something Mike hadn't considered, too eager to know what might befall Lorcan to think through the possibilities. This was what Stevie had brought to the lab as well, thoroughness and application.

'No,' said Ian.

'If you shaft us . . .' said Mike.

'There's one shaft you need to keep your mind on and it's that one,' said Ian, pointing to the tunnel. 'You've both seen the money. One security box each. One key each. Split evenly. Plus as usual, I'm selling half there and keeping half here.'

This had been the plan from the start. Keep half behind in Kallayee. Both as security in case Ian was arrested and as a commodity they could take should they need to leave in a hurry. They each had a burner phone too just in case.

'Let's see,' said Mike, spitting his used gum into a wrapper.

'You don't trust me?'

He tilted his head, then followed Stevie and Ian to the disused coal bunker, attached to the side of the house but minus the original sloping roof. Lifting up the board he shone the torch inside.

'Happy?' said Ian, dropping the board hurriedly, as Lorcan sped past again.

From the surly expressions it was obvious that no one was happy but it was good to know that should Ian unexpectedly decide enough was enough, their safety net was within reach.

Making his way to the ute Ian threw the canvas bag into the cab. Past the crossroads Mike watched as Naiyana got ready to leave at the same time. He and Stevie would be alone with Lorcan and his son for a while. He couldn't hold back the grin.

102

Mike Andrews

As they watched the two vehicles leave, he looked at Stevie.

Neither wanted to go back down the tunnel yet. There was a wall to pick and rubble to clear as well as installing netting above their heads to protect both them and the equipment from rockfalls, something that remained just as terrifying now as it did the first time he had been caught in one.

Lorcan passed again accompanied by the ripping buzz of an engine struggling in the heat and dust to escort its crazed cowboy through town.

'Just one dig,' said Mike, smearing the sweat from his brow as he clacked the gum. 'One dig to keep me going.'

Rather than the instant dismissal he was expecting, Stevie seemed to be considering it. Mike wanted to goad him about the charity. Some petty gratification.

'One dig?' said Stevie, doubt etched on his face.

Mike smiled, despite himself. One dig. Or maybe two. He might struggle to hold himself back.

'Some revenge for breaking our equipment.'

Stevie shook his head. 'Leave it. We'll make the money back, Mikey. The man has nothing but a broken house and broken dreams.'

It was delivered without glee, the honest truth from an honest friend. It was a persuasive argument. He shouldn't lower himself to Lorcan's level. Even if it would have felt good.

'Okay, let's get back to it,' said Mike with a smile, replacing the gum in his mouth with a new piece.

Two hours later and the rubble had been cleared, a couple of new stanchions in place, the netting affixed and some rock cracked by hand that had a few slim veins of gold striated through it. Maybe a couple of hundred once they put it through the machines. A tough but profitable couple of hours.

They made for the light. The sun was on the way down for the day. Nearly time to close up shop and head into Wisbech for a mini blowout.

The first thing that he noticed was the quiet. At first the endless silence of Kallayee had annoyed him but after suffering through the ear-splitting drone of the machines it was divine. But silence wasn't what he had been expecting this evening.

Stevie voiced his thoughts.

'You think he ran out of fuel?'

'Hopefully he crashed,' said Mike, smiling at the image. Insult and injury to Lorcan Maguire was the only thing that seemed to motivate him at present.

He sauntered out into the fading sun to stretch. The deep breath filled his lungs with air. And caught there. He spied the stationary quad. Parked beside the coal bunker.

103

Mike Andrews

He broke into a run, passing a confused Stevie.

'The bunker,' he shouted.

Stevie overtook him before they reached the coal bunker. Lorcan was there, a canvas bag on the ground beside him.

'Stop!' shouted Stevie as if calling out to a common thief.

'I'm going to kick the living shit out of you,' yelled Mike. And he would. Two against one. Even Ian couldn't complain about that once they told him what Lorcan had been attempting.

Then the rifle appeared from the bag.

Mike stopped as suddenly as he could, skidding in the dirt, all thoughts of attacking Lorcan as scattered as his nerves. The penknife in his pocket would be useless against a rifle. He glanced at Stevie. His friend sported the same frozen look of fear. A look that betrayed that he didn't know what to do. Their own rifle was in the tunnel, stashed by the steps. Too far away to be of any use.

'Put the gun down, Lorcan,' said Stevie, slowly.

There was an unsettling smile on Lorcan's face that Mike was trying to read. It looked demented. He hoped it wasn't.

'Kick the living shit out of me, eh?' he said, swinging the bag onto his shoulder and grabbing the rifle in two hands.

Mike found that he had nothing to say. Despite his bravado, now that shit was going down, he was lost.

Stevie inched closer to Lorcan. 'You can't take that,' he said, polite but firm.

'I am,' said Lorcan. 'And leaving with my family.'

'We can find a way,' said Stevie, his hand up, pleading for calm.

'We tried. You shut me out.'

Mike found his voice. It wasn't as strong as he had hoped. 'You can't rob us,' he said, the whimper diseasing the words.

Turning to him, Lorcan said loudly, 'I can and I am.'

Taking advantage of the momentary distraction, Stevie pounced.

Mike yelled at his friend to stop but the gunshot drowned it all out. Stevie slumped to the side, blood pouring out of a wound in his chest. There were no moans, no final, rasping gasps of air, no goodbyes. Just dead.

Mike stared at his friend. Just like words had failed him earlier, now his muscles failed him too. He couldn't move. He stared at Lorcan. The rifle was still pointed towards Stevie but lowered, aimed at the ground. If he attacked now he could disarm Lorcan. If he moved *right* now. But his feet felt glued to the earth.

In the end Lorcan moved first, the bag of gold slipping off his shoulder to the dirt. His face betrayed the shock of what he had done. Then he broke into a run, away from the scene, back in the direction of his house.

Mike's feet finally moved. He ran to his friend but could immediately see that there was no hope. All life had gone from the eyes, the blood seeping into the earth, creating a dark pool underneath him.

He looked up. Lorcan was still running, the coward fleeing the scene. The crippling fear left him. Revenge took over. Returning to the tunnel he grabbed the rifle. Checking it was loaded he made for the bastard's house.

Charging through town he stalked up to the front door still not quite aware of what he was doing. He had never fired a gun before, he'd had no need to in the quiet suburbs of Brisbane; nothing to shoot for there but the highest grades possible. Grades that give you an education. Grades that are meant to shield you from ever having to wield a rifle in anger.

Taking cover, he peeked in the living-room window. It was empty, the air quiet, prickling with tension. The kitchen was the same. Only a little more airy given the gap in the roof. He made a calculation. Lorcan was holed up in the back with the boy and the rifle. A firm press on the front door determined that it was closed, maybe even wedged shut. He wondered what to do. Climbing in the window was possible but left him a sitting duck. He wasn't built, designed or trained to stalk prey. Especially prey that could shoot back. And as much as he hated Lorcan Maguire's guts, he didn't want to shoot the boy by accident.

Feeling too exposed to think properly he retreated back to where Stevie lay. Anger boiled his blood. He needed to release it. To hurt Lorcan. Looking at the quad the bastard had just purchased, he pulled out his penknife and slashed the tyres, cursing Lorcan to hell as he crippled it.

It was time to consider his next move. He could return to the house and wait for an opportunity to shoot Lorcan, maybe even threaten him with the fact that he could testify to him killing Stevie to lure him out. Now, for the first time, he held all the cards. But the cost had been too great. His friend's death. He squeezed off the tear that leaked from his eye. This was no time to cry. It was time to decide.

Another option was to wait for Ian to return. Use their numerical advantage against Lorcan. But that had already failed once. Tragically.

In the end there was really only one choice: make a run for it. With the gold.

He glanced at Stevie's body in the bloody dirt, the sun already cooking his dead flesh. A tremendous guilt coursed through his veins for what had happened but there was something else. Something that had been brewing inside him ever since he agreed to this bloody scheme: a cold determination to profit from it. It was time for the living to stay alive.

Fishing the security box key from Stevie's pocket, he loaded up the rest of the gold into Lorcan's canvas bag. The three-way split was now two, half and half, so he didn't feel bad about taking it all. Fuck Ian. Where was his protection when they had needed it most? He was meant to stop the bullets. Or take them. But Stevie had instead.

He filled the bag, threw in the rifle and lugged it onto his back. It was manageable but awkward, the short straps biting into his shoulders. He needed to get out. Looking at the quad he cursed himself. He regretted slashing the tyres now. Another fuck-up in this town of fuck-ups.

104

Mike Andrews

He added some bottles of water to his haul of gold. And the rest of the Chunky Peanut Butter KitKats. His two-bars-a-day habit. He affixed the load until it was more comfortable on his back then climbed onto the quad and turned the engine. It spat into life, buzzing underneath him. If he took it steadily he might be able to use it to get out of Kallayee. Far enough so that he could swap it for another mode of transport. All that mattered right now was getting the fuck out of Dodge.

Using his foot to click it into gear he tried the throttle. The engine roared, trying to drag the bike like a donkey-owner at the seaside, but the flat tyres failed to rotate. He gave it more throttle but there was no progress, the engine spluttering frustration at being unable to go anywhere.

With the rising stench of burning oil, he shut it off. His rash temper had foiled his best chance of escape. Now he was wasting time. If the quad wasn't going to help him, he needed to set off on foot. He didn't know how much time until—

'What the fuck?'

The voice and the disruptive weight of the bag on his back almost caused him to fall off the quad. He turned towards it. Amidst the struggle and roar of the engine, Ian had returned, his truck and the Maguire's Toyota parked neatly on the road. Ian was staring at him; Naiyana was staring at Stevie's body.

He scrambled off the bike. From the bag he pulled out the rifle. Ian took up a defensive stance, his head cocked.

'Mike?'

'It wasn't me. It was Lorcan.'

Ian narrowed his eyes at this, glancing at Stevie's body.

'Lorcan wouldn't do this,' said Naiyana, shaking as she spoke.

'He did,' said Mike, hearing nothing but fear and guilt in his voice, his mouth drying up without gum, the companion that steadied his nerves.

'So what's in the bag?' asked Ian, flicking his eyes towards the coal bunker. 'Where were you going?'

Mike tried to straighten up and look threatening but still felt tiny compared to Ian.

'Fuck you! You were meant to be protecting us. You got Stevie killed!'

'Put down the gun, Mike. Let's talk.'

'Fuck talking!'

'That gold is ours. It's not yours to take.'

Mike laughed. A single, cold laugh that was as dead as the air. 'There's only two of us now. You were selling half this morning, weren't you? Take that money, I'll take this. I'm getting out,' he said, the rifle swinging towards Naiyana.

He didn't think that he squeezed the trigger. Maybe it was the waving of the gun that did it. Or the pressure. Or his fingers swelling up. Whatever it was, the rifle went off.

He heard the scream and the report, frozen to the spot as if all his momentum was consumed within the bullet. Then he felt the barrel being nudged out of the way and a fist strike his jaw, causing his world to deafen in shock and pain.

105

Naiyana

She heard the bullet. She even swore that she could see it in slow motion, but that was her eyes and brain adding falsities to the storyline, filling in the gaps. It zipped past her, the echo deafening her moments after.

She staggered back a couple of steps but watched Ian leap forward, punching Mike in the jaw. They both went down, fighting over the rifle.

In truth it wasn't much of a fight. Mike was too out of shape and looked as if he had never traded blows in his whole life. He took a catalogue of brutal punches as Ian tried to rip the rifle from his hands. A blow to the gut caused one of his hands to release its grip. Another forced the second away. Scrambling to his feet, Ian gasped for air, aiming the rifle at Mike who was wheezing in the dirt, coughing and moaning.

Ian glanced at her.

'Are you okay?'

She nodded. Her heart was thumping like a bass drum in her chest but yes, she was okay. There was even something else. A warmth, a glow that welled up inside her that someone had stood up for her in a time of crisis. Over the past week she had been standing up for Lorcan. He'd used her as a human shield. His own wife. Now the crucial decisions were in Ian's hands. It felt good to not be in charge. At least for the moment. She didn't know what would happen next. Things couldn't go back to how they were but she hoped he had a plan. Or that they could come up with one. A way out. Maybe Lorcan could fill in for Stevie, make as much money as they could and then she'd leave. With Ian. Not Lorcan. That ship had sailed.

Ian was now gazing at Stevie's body, the rifle still aimed at Mike. She watched as he squeezed his eyes tight as if coming to a decision, before squeezing the trigger and shooting Mike in the head.

He turned to her. Her brain went into scramble mode. Was he going to kill her next? Remove her from the equation. And then her family? Did she mean that little to him? Was she a fool to think she did?

He began to walk towards her. She glanced around but there was nowhere to go. She had made her choice. The wrong choice. A fatal choice.

'Please. Ian, I—'

But he just wrapped his arm around her, holding her close, drowning out everything that had happened in the last few minutes, enveloped in the damp darkness of his chest. He kissed the top of her head.

'It's okay, Nee. It's okay.'

106

Naiyana

13 Days Ago

Curiosity had briefly taken over but without the safety of the moonlight, the darkness made her tense. The brick-walled, tin-topped shack was in disrepair, the humming causing the roof to gently rattle like a one-note orchestra. Again she chided herself for prowling around alone at night. Whatever the noise was, Lorcan wasn't the cause. It would do until tomorrow. She put her hand out feeling for an inner wall to guide her way out but only found a wooden stanchion.

Which immediately gave way.

Followed by a terrible screech. From all around. The building was collapsing.

On her.

She dropped to her knees, throwing her arms over her head and neck. An instinctive reaction. And entirely useless. She squeezed her eyes shut, bracing for impact. Disjointed thoughts of Dylan alone in bed flashed through her mind; then Lorcan; then her family and her last bitter words to them. Love, hurt and anger bubbled around her skull as if trying to construct an emotional shell to shield her from the upcoming pain. It wouldn't help. She was going to die out here, alone, victim of her own stupidity.

Something caught hold of the back of her jumper. Suddenly she was in the air, dragged from the building and dumped with a thud on the ground outside.

Her eyes remained closed, absorbing the shock of the landing. She heard the squeal of tin against brick, twisting and bending as it fell, reaching a thunderous crescendo. Then silence. Only now did she dare open her eyes. The first thing she saw was dust, fluttering absently towards the moonlight. Then the building she'd just been inside – the front wall caved in, the tin roof broken and bent across the rotten wooden beams that had supported it for so long, resting at a low angle against the back wall. If she were still inside, she'd be dead. Crushed. She had no doubt about that.

'Are you okay?'

A breathy voice came from behind her, startling her. Heart still racing, she scrabbled away, back towards the collapsed building. A single thought arose; the house might have killed her, but whatever had saved her might be worse. At what she hoped was a safe distance, she turned to look back, arms reflexively held in front of her, to ward off attack.

The moonlight revealed a tall, bearded figure, not an ounce of fat on him, nothing left to waste, his angled jawbone set tight. Whereas she was petrified, he looked assured. As if this was his typical nightly gig. Saving unknown women from collapsed buildings. In the middle of nowhere. What was he doing here? In Kallayee. At night. Her thoughts, still adjusting to surviving the near-death experience, were scrambled. Was he someone from Hurton? One of Nikos's or Chester's buddies searching for her and Lorcan? Maybe someone who wanted to go off-radar like they were. Or someone on the run. He could be anyone.

He could be dangerous.

She needed to go back to the house, lock herself inside and wait for Lorcan to come home. Though she had lowered her hands, they were still shaking. Her legs too, as if the collapse of the building had generated some sort of mini-earthquake inside her. She made to stand up but although her heart was pumping furiously the oxygenated blood failed to reach the necessary muscles.

'Are you okay?' the stranger asked again, his voice soft, concerned.

He inched closer, as if approaching a wary animal. She finally caught sight of his full face: handsome, all angles as if cut from stone, his eyes blue but wondrously pale in the moonlight. She was drawn to something powerful in them. In him. Powerful enough to drag her from a collapsing building. A shiver ran through her as if by looking into them she had become caught in his trap, frozen into inaction.

'I'm okay,' she replied, though she felt far from it. 'You need to watch out in these buildings.'

That she agreed with. But the questions remained. Who was he and why he was here? Questions she wanted to voice but couldn't. As if some inner sense of survival was preventing her. The intractable fear that warned her that, if she asked, she would learn the horrible truth. That she hadn't escaped the building at all. That he was in fact Death, come to lead her away. The Grim Reaper in jeans and a shirt stained with dust.

He held his hand out to her. 'Can you stand?'

She looked at his hand, the tendons pronounced, crawling in the moonlight. She wanted to but felt unable to refuse.

She held out her own. After what seemed like for ever, their hands touched, sparking another wave of fear coursing through her that eventually settled deep in her stomach, hollowing her out.

The hand was not cold. It was warm and calloused. Very human.

Then suddenly she was on her feet, hoisted as if an expert puppeteer had brought a marionette to life. Though now upright, her legs felt wooden, the knees unable to lock, on the verge of collapse.

'I think we need to get you home. See to that cut shoulder,' said the stranger, wrapping his arm around her, practically holding her up now. Naiyana did nothing to prevent it. The fear that had invaded her stomach had suddenly turned to warmth. She suddenly

felt safe. In a way she hadn't felt since they'd come
to Kallayee.

And if she was honest, for a long time before that.

'Thank you for . . .' Naiyana felt her legs turn to
jelly again, his arm bearing her weight. She couldn't
finish the sentence. What she had been saved from
suddenly hit her hard.

'It's okay. You're just lucky I was there.'

'But why were you there?'

With her concentration focused on staying upright
and brainpower dealing with the near miss, the question slipped out.

The night turned silent again as if the whole world
was awaiting the answer.

None came. He looked away, back towards the
crossroads for a brief moment, the moonlight accenting
his high cheekbones, before his powerful gaze returned
to her, trapping her in its beam once more. Again her
heart began to pound, fear taking over, the fear of
knowing and not wanting to know, his arm tightly
clasped to her side, his entire body seeming to envelop
hers and arousing the warmth in the pit of her stomach
that she now recognized as having been alien to her
for years. Igniting a desire that she had considered a
lost teenage memory. His scent, a fusion of sweat and
a hint of bitter oil tingled her nostrils. It was earthy
and raw, imbued with a danger and desire that bound
itself to every atom of her being.

Still he stared at her, his answer conveyed by the
clarity in his eyes rather than words. She wondered

if it was mutual. She found herself hoping that he was experiencing the same rush, the same spark, she was. A spark that now raged within her, reawakening the memory of what it was like to be out of control, reawakening the yearning to rip up the rulebook and do what she wanted. Her mind cautioned her that maybe it was simply a high from having cheated death, basking in his protective hold, his urgent scent or the continued pounding of her heart, but she felt an inexorable pull towards him, complete and unmistakable and undeniable.

Once again she let herself get drawn into the magnetic pull of his eyes. She watched his gaze slide from her eyes to her mouth, then back. Locking onto hers. She knew that he felt it too.

Words couldn't express it.

They should never have met. It was in neither of their plans.

But they had met.

They came to an agreement. To see each other again.

107

Emmaline

An illicit affair between Naiyana Maguire and Ian Kinch was her preferred theory. But it was by no means proven. Oily found it hard to believe that someone like Naiyana would have involved herself with a petty criminal like Ian, whereas Barker thought that there was some other source of foul play involved that they hadn't yet discovered.

Over the video-conference DI Moore was adamant, her face too close to the camera, looming like a worried spectre of an old oak tree, that she wasn't to publicly accuse Naiyana Maguire of having an affair and of wittingly or unwittingly having a hand in the death of her husband. Certainly not without any solid evidence to back it up. She summed it up in a few sentences, the subtext being for them all to say nothing.

'Imagine you and your child have been kidnapped and put through hell, your husband murdered, only to find out that the police believe you were in on it. How would that make *you* feel?'

Emmaline understood her point. But she also understood what lay beneath it. Without a body, without any strong indication that she was dead – the blood on the mirror and traces on Lorcan's clothes wasn't considered strong enough evidence – then Naiyana Maguire could still be alive. And worse yet, she could sue for defamation. Nothing worried the boss more than the purse strings. Another reason for Emmaline not to seek promotion. The higher you climbed, defending the budget mattered more than defending against crime.

So they needed evidence that Naiyana Maguire was either dead or alive. Finding Ian Kinch might help in that.

To that end, the town of Hurton was interviewed again. Previous statements were re-examined for anything that might have been missed. A photograph of Ian Kinch was put in front of Bobby Marley but the kid couldn't say for certain that it was the man he'd seen with Naiyana.

Anand and Barker were sent out to Ulysses Hitchens for a second time but he had nothing to add aside from the extensive number of shooting stars he'd observed last night.

The net widened to include Leonora and Kalgoorlie but drew a blank there too. As if Naiyana, Dylan and Ian had disappeared into thin air.

Their former colleagues were re-interviewed but this added nothing other than more speculation, worry for Naiyana's and Dylan's well-being, and sympathy and shock at the murders.

Another major news story had broken overnight too, bumping the Kallayee Killings – as they were now known – to the bottom of the front page. The connection between Chester Grant's family and Brightside Foods had been revealed and plastered all over the papers, questions now being asked about his conduct in parliament, his lobbying record, his private life, with some even drawing tentative links around the disappearance of Naiyana and Dylan Maguire and the death of her husband.

Emmaline decided that it was a good time to question him again.

Chester Grant's office was under siege from reporters, a ring of security guards posted on the doors as if the prime minister himself was barricaded inside. Emmaline waved her credentials at the door. Zhao and Oily followed her in.

Chester Grant's secretary didn't even attempt to stop her from entering his office, too busy on the phone placating callers.

Inside, Chester stood facing the window like he was contemplating jumping while two men and a woman gabbled on mobile phones. All three dressed and spoke like lawyers.

'Mr Grant?' said Emmaline.

Chester turned and an already resigned face sunk even further. Then, as if suddenly plugged into a mains, he lit up.

'Is this your doing?' he said, pointing towards the

379

floor. Emmaline assumed he meant the palaver down-stairs.

'Nothing to do with me.'

'Only two people knew. You and—'

He suddenly shut up and looked to his lawyers who were abruptly ending their phone calls.

'Me and who, Mr Grant?'

'My client would like to say nothing at this time,' said the female lawyer, smoothing down her black dress as she stood.

'I know what he would like to do but he has questions to answer.' Emmaline stared at Chester Grant. 'You and who?'

Chester moved from the window, barricading himself behind his desk.

'I'm not going to help you. Leaking this—'

'I'm assuring you I didn't, Mr Grant. And if I didn't . . .'

Emmaline let this hang. If she wasn't the one who had leaked the details, then it might have been the other person who had known. Naiyana Maguire.

'She's still alive?' asked Chester, a mix of hope and regret on his harried face, the thick beard masking the paleness.

The female lawyer stepped in again. 'I must strongly advise you to not say anything at this time.'

But Chester Grant was focused on Emmaline, his eyes transformed from weary to wired.

'She's still missing. We both know she had information that was potentially damaging to you. And we know you met her on the thirtieth, don't we, Mr Grant?'

'You don't need to answer that here.' This was the eldest lawyer now, someone who looked as if they should have retired years ago. Probably a partner in the firm. The big boys drafted in.

'He doesn't, but it would be worse if it was later discovered that he didn't help with the investigation.'

Chester Grant slammed his hands on the desk, causing the plaque stating his name and many lettered qualifications to fall to the floor.

'Did you meet outside of Hurton too?' asked Emmaline. 'Was there ever something more between you? An affair?'

Emmaline asked because of the beard and white SUV. It was a long shot but worth ruling out.

Chester Grant froze, his mouth open.

'Well, Mr Grant?'

'No. I love my wife very much.'

'You look guilty.'

'Last time I checked, looking guilty wasn't a crime, Detective,' said the female lawyer, now standing beside her client in a show of support.

'No,' said Emmaline, 'but it is often an indication of wrongdoing.'

'I have a lot on my mind.'

'Like the disappearance of Naiyana Maguire?'

'Like all of this,' he said, his legs giving out and landing in his comfy office chair.

'So what really happened at this meeting on the thirtieth, Mr Grant?'

'I remind you that you don't—' offered his female lawyer.

'Just shut up will you,' shouted Chester Grant. 'I'm not guilty. I'm just going to tell them what I know.' He took a deep breath. 'We met once. In Wisbech.'

'When?'

'The thirtieth. We've been over this.'

'Let's go over it again.'

He sighed. 'We met, I asked her to help out Brightside with the photoshoot and she told me what she knew. It was a quick meeting. A few minutes. She kept glancing out the window as if she was in a hurry to get away.'

The story remained the same. There was something about the desperation in his voice that made Emmaline believe him. As if he had too many other lies to cover up to lie about this too.

Emmaline also had an inkling why Naiyana wanted to get away in a hurry. 'Did you see anyone else nearby?'

Chester winced a little. 'There was a guy hanging around outside. Leaning on his truck and staring in the window.'

'Waiting for Naiyana Maguire?'

'No. I thought he was nosy. Or just passing time.'

Pulling out her phone she flashed him a picture of Ian Kinch. 'Did he look like this?'

'Maybe. I wasn't paying attention. I had other things on my mind.'

'Do you remember what the truck looked like? A number plate?' asked Zhao.

'That was more distinctive. One of the old Ford Falcons you don't see much anymore. Rusted and not in great shape. A shame really. I remember because my grandad used to have one. He let us drive around his fields after harvest. It's where I learned to drive as a boy.'

In relating the story, Chester had finally become animated, a smile returning to his face. That he couldn't pick Ian Kinch out of a line-up wasn't helpful but at least the description of the truck matched what they had been expecting. It was the same type of Ford that had crashed with Mike Andrews and Stevie Amaranga inside. But in the end it only amounted to circumstantial evidence based on a witness statement from a few weeks ago. And given the latest events, not a very reliable witness.

After a few more questions, she left Chester Grant to clean up his mess. He had a lot of work to do.

The circumstantial evidence of the miners' ute being in Wisbech on the thirtieth led Emmaline to another theory. Naiyana Maguire and Ian Kinch had been in the same town on the same day. And if they were having a seedy affair, where best to continue it but at a seedy motel. She put Rispoli, Barker, Anand and whoever Zhao could rustle up onto it while she made her way back out east.

108

Naiyana

She broke off the hug. The dry air began to steal all moisture, giving her a prickly feeling that made her antsy, like maggots had already infested the recently deceased bodies and were now crawling all over her own skin. Assuming she would be next.

'I have to check on Dylan. On Lorcan.'

Ian stared at her. She could see that he was weighing up the new set of circumstances.

He shook his head. 'We have to move these first. Get them away from here.'

'But what if Lorcan and Dylan heard?' she countered.

'If they had they would be out here by now.'

'Unless they were terrified.'

'Good. We need them indoors. While we get rid of these bodies.'

Naiyana glanced in the direction of their house. She wanted to go and make sure Dylan was safe. Mike had claimed that Lorcan shot Stevie. Did he then go and shoot Dylan? The maggots that were crawling over her face now crawled down her body, her skin clammy and itchy.

'Nee!' Ian's voice was insistent. 'We have to do this.'

Backing his ute to the edge of the road, he carried Mike's upper torso while she struggled with his thick legs. Though she was facing the body she tried to look anywhere but at it, whimpering as she caught glimpses of the damage, one eyeball and socket caved in with the force of the bullet, the blood rapidly drying in the sun.

After he was loaded onto the flatbed, she wiped her hands on her dress, the essence of death rather than blood clinging to them.

Stevie was easier, about sixty pounds lighter. Again she refused to look at the fatal wound, the still-wet blood helping ease the slide onto the back of the ute. The friends reunited.

She wiped her hands frantically. Two dead bodies. One executed right in front of her. Ian had coldly and calmly shot a defenceless man. But wriggling amongst the stomach-curling disgust was an acceptance of what had to be done, as if some of Ian's steadfast demeanour was rubbing off on her. Only an hour ago they had been fucking in his dirty ute, her head scraping the roof as she straddled him on the front seat. And now this.

'We need to burn them,' he said as he clipped the back of the flatbed up. She held her stomach as he said this. He continued. 'It will remove the chance of ID-ing them quickly and break any DNA link we have to their bodies.'

'In the tunnel?'

'No. The smoke might only attract someone. We don't want them discovered until we are long gone.'

'We?'

Ian nodded. 'It's a "we" now.'

'What about my husband? My son?'

'Your boy won't talk, but Lorcan?'

She studied Ian. What was he implying? That Lorcan needed to be removed as well? She wondered if she could go that far.

'I want to make sure that they're okay,' she said.

'We need to get rid of these bodies, Nee.'

'And we will. But I want to make sure my son is okay.'

She offered what Lorcan called her puppy-dog eyes, an expression that was hard to conjure up under the circumstances. If he said no, she was likely to resist and go anyway. But Ian had shown that he was not someone to be messed with.

109

Naiyana

She made for the house. Ian had parked his ute a little further up the road out of sight. She spoke to him in a whisper.

'I'll tell him what's going on.'

'No,' said Ian. 'You can't—'

'Not the truth obviously. A cover story. To keep him calm.'

Ian twisted his lips tight and glanced towards his truck. She understood his trepidation. He wanted to get rid of the bodies immediately. But she had to see her son. He was the only thing that mattered right now.

She tried the door. It was forced shut. She called out for Lorcan and Dylan. It was her husband who came to the door and opened it, kicking a large iron pulley away from it.

He looked stressed, his face drawn. He was shaking.

'What's that for?' she asked, nodding towards the pulley.

'I thought it would make a good doorstop. An antique.'

She supposed it did. A tripping hazard too but she let that go. She was more anxious to see Dylan. But he wasn't at the door, buzzing around or running into her arms. She held her breath.

'Where's Dylan?'

Lorcan nodded back over his shoulder. 'Asleep. He was chasing around after the bike all morning. He's exhausted. Me too.'

She considered going to check on her son but if he was asleep that was good. It was better than coping with this mess.

'When did you get back in?' asked Ian, in the background. There was distrust in his voice.

Lorcan shrugged his shoulders. 'An hour, hour and a half ago.'

'Why are the tyres on the bike slashed?'

Confusion crossed her husband's face. 'Slashed? I don't know. I nearly totalled it earlier at the cross-roads. I abandoned it after that. It's left me a little . . .' He held his hand up to show how it was shaking.

'You didn't see any gold? Didn't try and take any?' asked Ian.

Lorcan reared back in the doorway as if he'd been punched by an invisible fist. 'Take the gold? I assumed you had it. To sell it. That's where *you* were, right?'

Naiyana flashed a panicked look at Ian. His lips grew thin, nodding deliberately in reply.

'I'm going back to lie down,' said Lorcan, squeezing his eyes shut as if in pain.

'You do that,' said Naiyana. 'I have to go to town to get something.'

She didn't elaborate on it and Lorcan didn't ask her to elaborate, giving a tired sigh and turning from the doorway as they left. It was every man for himself now and they all knew it.

110

Naiyana

She followed Ian across the back roads west of Hurton and up a dirt road she didn't know and didn't trust. He quickly left her behind, with only the blossoming dust cloud in front for directions.

She found him parked off the road, the rusted old Ford facing what looked like a deep gorge beyond. He was liberally dousing the inside of the cab with a jerrycan full of what she assumed was petrol. She could make out two heads propped up in the front seats ready to make their final trip.

'What took so long?' he asked, exertion making his T-shirt stick to his muscled body.

'I was being careful,' she responded, glaring at him.

'Good. We need that.'

She watched as he wiped down the surfaces with a cloth before striking a match. A whoosh of orange flame danced behind the glass screen, smoke beginning to eke out of a crack in the window as Mike and Stevie started to burn. She wanted to be long gone before the smell reached them.

Moving to the rear of the ute, Ian put his shoulder to it and pushed, the Ford inching slowly towards the edge, his feet planted in the sand. The front tyres reached the drop and in a flash the vehicle disappeared out of sight with a scream of metal and the crack of bushes being torn apart.

Ian tiptoed back to her, sweeping his tracks behind him with a branch, and got in.

'I've even buckled them in for safety,' he chuckled.

She wasn't in the mood to joke. All she wanted was to get away. Turning the car sharply across a nearby patch of hard-packed gibber plains, she headed back towards the road.

As she drove a slew of emotions overwhelmed her. Fear at what Ian had done, of what he might do to her and her family, regret at leaving Perth, at pushing things too far with BS Foods and Chester Grant, and disgust at where she now found herself. Only her love for Dylan and, even scarier, her singular love for Ian, fought against this. She knew why she was attracted to Ian. They were the same. She had come to realize that. Even now. He might be capable of more extreme acts to get what he wanted but she understood it. The need to win.

'We have to leave,' said Ian, as they scythed off the dirt road with a jolt and joined the once-paved road to Kallayee. 'Pack up the gold we have and run. I've copies of their security-box keys so I can get their cash too.'

'We can make it work,' she countered, scared of

how fast things were moving. They were like the truck now, the front tyres over the edge and barrelling out of control.

'Not here.'

'But I didn't kill them,' said Naiyana, immediately realizing that it was a stupid thing to say to a man who had just executed someone in front of her in cold blood.

111

Emmaline

By the time Emmaline reached Wisbech, her team had completed the search.

The Stay-Here motel on the outskirts of Wisbech was a flat-topped, two-storey block ringed in concrete pillars that hadn't been erected but left on the ground, partly hidden now by bushes and ready to rip the axle off some unsuspecting vehicle.

'We found it under his alias Ian King,' said Rispoli, meeting Emmaline outside. 'No plus one given. The owner says he was there alone.'

'Are they certain?'

Barker nodded. 'She said that she keeps an eye on comings and goings. That she is careful with her place. No riff-raff.'

'Even though she looks like the queen of riff-raff,' said Anand, with a smile.

If the outside screamed Siberian gulag, the inside wasn't any better, the decor a mustard yellow that looked like one massive stain, wood and beige coverings that had been an attempt to create synergy when it was first decorated but now looked tired and dowdy. Emmaline dreaded to think what the actual rooms were like. And she had just spent the last few days sleeping in a dead man's caravan.

She was introduced to Phyllis Trent, the owner and manager. Immediately she could see where Anand got his description from. With her neck tattoos and heavy-lidded eyes, she looked like she was no stranger to police questioning, calm but suspicious, waiting for a bone to chew on, almost snarling at their presence.

'Do you keep strict records?'

As Emmaline asked the question, Phyllis Trent shot her a look of contempt. 'Been doing this for more years than you've been shitting outside a nappy, love,' she said bluntly.

Emmaline ignored it. 'So he was here alone?'

'If that's what the log says.'

Emmaline took another look around.

'Do you get many men wanting a room for an afternoon?'

'How do you know he—?'

Emmaline was waiting for the question and pounced.

'The system notes his arrival at thirteen ten and the man we're after had things to do. Appointments to keep. So, is this the type of place that men use for an afternoon? Their partners kept off the books for reasons unasked?'

Phyllis remained schtum. The most risk-averse form of defence.

'Who else was working that day?'

Phyllis didn't need to answer that. Rispoli already had the information.

'Katie Yan,' he said. 'She's working today too, according to the rota.'

Phyllis sneered at being bypassed. And sneered even more when Emmaline requisitioned her office to speak to Katie.

Katie Yan was seventeen, with skin that looked perfect even close up, thick foundation and blusher giving her an almost Photoshopped look of perfection. Emmaline quickly learned that this job was a part-time earner on afternoons when she didn't have class. No way was this her career. Something she stated numerous times despite not being asked.

After confirming that she had indeed been working on 30 December, Emmaline showed her photos of Ian Kinch and Naiyana Maguire.

'Rings a bell.'

'How big a bell?'

'I keep to myself usually. Clean the rooms. Stock the ice machine. Sit on reception, sneak in some study. But she . . .' Katie then paused as if something had suddenly tugged at a memory.

Dragging her mobile from her pocket she started flicking through it. After a few moments she handed it over. 'Here. On the thirtieth.' She tapped the screen. 'I texted a mate that there was a fight in the parking lot.'

'A fight?'

395

'Okay, I exaggerated a little. A dispute.'

Emmaline didn't respond, keeping her face neutral. Letting Katie talk.

'Some arsewipe,' she said, rolling her eyes, 'was complaining about a ute parked in his space even though there were lots of empty spaces around. A girl came out of twenty-seven and moved it to another space. That's what she looked like,' said Katie, pointing to the picture of Naiyana Maguire.

'Are you certain?'

'I'd testify to it,' revealing that she had seen too many cop shows. 'And the guy with her looked like this guy,' she said, pointing to Ian Kinch.

'Why didn't you come forward earlier? Her photo's been on the news for weeks.'

'I don't watch the news. It's all fake.'

Emmaline left it at that. Visual confirmation of Ian Kinch and Naiyana Maguire at the motel together. The affair was real. And the consequences had been deadly.

Before leaving the motel, she had a final request. She checked the log for other visitors. Nikos Iannis. Chester Grant. Or three men staying for a night and checking in together. The mining crew couldn't live down the tunnel permanently. But none of them had stayed for a night. Not at the Stay-Here anyway.

112

Emmaline

Emmaline relocated her team to a restaurant in Wisbech. Having not stopped to eat all day she was starving. There she pieced together what she knew over a three-course meal that was minimal on quality but generous with portions. Barker's suggestion.

She started with the basics. 'On an unknown date but likely towards mid- to late November, Ian Kinch, Mike Andrews and Stevie Amaranga move into Kallayee on a mission to mine for gold.'

'And find some success as evidenced by the gold sales,' said Oily.

'It seems so. Then on thirteenth December the Maguire family move into Kallayee. Initially both parties are unaware of each other. Long enough for the family to settle a little and start to fix up the house. The mining likely explained the rumbling noises that Naiyana hinted at in their videos.'

'*The earth was growling as if ready to attack*,' said Rispoli, quoting Naiyana Maguire from the second of her vlogs.

'Then somehow they discover each other's presence. Or more precisely, the family discover the miners' presence. I'm sure the miners knew the family were there immediately.'

'When did they meet?'

'We can't be sure but the nineteenth is my guess. With Lorcan and Dylan out of town in Kalgoorlie, maybe the miners tried to make contact.'

'But we don't know this for sure,' said Anand.

'And we won't unless we find either the miners or the family,' said Emmaline before continuing. 'All we know is they meet. Maybe both sides try to co-exist or maybe there is tension from the start. Both know that the other is there illegally so maybe this allowed for a kind of unsteady truce between them.

'What it *didn't* do was interrupt their lives. Not at the start. Both Lorcan and Naiyana were seen in town, purchasing housing materials and groceries. The miners' movements are less known but we can assume they had to eat and drink too. But they probably ventured further afield or had a stash of goods to raid from.'

'So is the heat off Nikos Iannis and Chester Grant?' asked Anand.

Emmaline shook her head. 'I don't want to discount them entirely yet. We can't be certain that Lorcan met with Nikos Iannis, but we know Nikos was desperate to get that data back. Information that is still missing.'

'Or so he claims. It might be a cover story for the murder,' said Rispoli.

'But even if they did know where Lorcan was, why kill *him* but take Naiyana and the child?' said Barker.

'These things aren't necessarily concurrent,' said Emmaline. 'Lorcan did say in his message that Naiyana was *gone*. Maybe it was an accident. Maybe she was killed to put pressure on Lorcan, who then escaped with his son and was killed.'

To Emmaline this still seemed like the most obvious solution. Or would have if there weren't so many possibilities flying around.

'Chester Grant, however, admits to meeting Naiyana on the thirtieth. Briefly. She was privy to sensitive information he wanted desperately to keep secret.'

'Information that is now public,' said Anand. 'He's on the brink.'

'But back then keeping it secret was a priority.'

'And easier done if Naiyana was dead. Giving him motive,' said Rispoli.

'He didn't have time to follow her back to Kallayee and make his later meetings but he might have had someone else do it. An attempt to silence her that got out of control, killing Lorcan and then Mike Andrews and Stevie Amaranga as witnesses,' said Oily.

'But that's a big secret to keep. Even bigger than the one he was already hiding,' said Emmaline.

'So we can rule him out?'

'As a killer? I think so. But not as a co-conspirator for now.'

'But that still leaves Ian Kinch, Naiyana and Dylan Maguire unaccounted for,' said Rispoli. 'If they had fled to protect themselves, they would have made themselves known by now.'

'Yes. We know from Seamus Maguire that the house was in disrepair. That Lorcan was keen on leaving but she wasn't. Given that Naiyana had told her colleague, Leona Sanchez, on the twenty-first, that she missed Perth and wanted to go back means that something changed in those few days.'

'The affair,' said Anand, watching on like it was a soap opera.

'If they only have a short window of opportunity they meet on Keenan's Run where the tyre tracks are. Other times they meet further afield like the Stay-Here. A quickie in the afternoon, illicit and thrilling. Not a bad position to be in,' said Emmaline, with a smile she directed at everyone but which lingered on Rispoli.

'Until it is discovered,' said Oily, interrupting the moment.

Anand interrupted him. 'We can't be one hundred per cent sure it was discovered.'

Emmaline nodded. 'True. We can't know if either Lorcan or the miners were aware of it. What we do know is that there were some new housing materials that weren't paid for through the family's account or by Seamus Maguire. We can only suppose that Ian gave the family money. Perhaps to buy their silence, perhaps to keep Naiyana around.'

'Which wouldn't have gone down well with the other miners whether they knew about the affair or not,' said Rispoli. 'There would be a lot of anger.'

'Something is said. Anger spills over into violence,' said Emmaline.

'But who kills who?'

That remained the big unknown.

'What's certain is that Lorcan and Dylan were running away from someone when Lorcan was killed. Maybe the quad tyres were slashed to force them to flee on foot.'

'Maybe they were fleeing Mike Andrews and Stevie Amaranga,' said Barker.

'Then Naiyana and Ian return. Mike and Stevie confess and Naiyana orders her lover to take revenge,' said Anand.

'Or they decide they don't need Mike and Stevie any longer and kill them first. Lorcan then finds out about the affair and he is disposed of as well,' said Oily.

'All of which doesn't rule out a third party,' said Emmaline. 'A professional hired by Chester or Nikos who chases the father and son down and then kills the witnesses. Ian and Naiyana might have returned to find everyone gone. They spot the blood in the dirt and decide to flee themselves.'

There was silence around the table. They were going in circles, the affair only adding to the possibilities.

113

Lorcan

The buzzing noise could only mean one thing. Mike was trying to steal the quad. It also meant that he wouldn't hear him approach.

Leaving Dylan in the house, safe behind the overturned bed, he took the rifle and stalked back to the coal shed.

The two utes were already there and by the time he sneaked into position the quad bike had been switched off and only the sound of angry voices remained.

He considered heading back to the house and taking cover again but was worried Mike would feed Nee and Ian some bullshit – truthful bullshit – that he had shot Stevie.

Mike being around changed his plan. He had gambled on the arsehole scarpering, allowing Lorcan to blame him for killing Stevie in Ian's absence. By hightailing with the gold Mike would have looked even more guilty.

With the heightened tension having turned to

murder, Nee would surely agree to leave. And if she remained stubborn? He would leave on his own and take Dylan. That seemed the sensible course of action. Go to his relatives in Adelaide and lay low. Ian wouldn't have any problem if he laid low surely. Nee would follow. She would have to. To see Dylan. Then away from the strange draw of this place, they could talk.

But something held him back. He was glad to see Nee, glad that nothing had happened to her. But he realized something else: his lack of concern when she was away. He wondered if that told him something. To truly love someone surely you had to be concerned for their well-being. Especially letting her drive off for a meeting with a relative stranger in the middle of nowhere. But he had been more concerned for himself and Dylan. And yet he had left Dylan behind to do this. It was as if he was shedding parts of his life, subconsciously reverting back to being a free spirit, with no family or ties to be responsible for.

He watched the argument unfold, Mike getting off the quad and raising the rifle. Informing them that Lorcan had killed Stevie. The truth-telling bastard.

The argument moved on to protection. And the gold. Mike waved the rifle. Then a shot rang out.

The bullet clanged into the tin beside him, ricocheting off in a random direction. Had Mike spotted him? He gripped the rifle tighter, ready to pounce. But Ian was on top of Mike, wrestling for the weapon.

It was an unfair fight, two punches to the gut breaking Mike's resistance.

Ian climbed to his feet, holding the rifle. Lorcan knew he would be vindicated. There was no way that they would believe Mike now.

He considered coming out of hiding. Hands up. Without the rifle. Show that he was not the threat Mike insisted he was. As he considered his next move he watched Ian make sure that Nee was okay, something in the tenderness with which he said it, raising his suspicions.

Then Ian shot Mike in the head. Lorcan found himself unable to breathe. Stevie's death had been a tragic accident but this was an execution. Then Ian turned to Nee. Lorcan groped for his rifle as he watched on, hoping to fire at least a warning shot before Ian killed his wife.

But instead Ian wrapped his arm around Nee, holding her close, as if drowning out everything that had happened in the last few minutes. He delicately kissed the top of her head.

Blindly, he found the rifle. Still Ian and Naiyana held each other. Longer than just a reassuring hug. The truth dawned. They were together. Questions bounced around his skull. How long had they—? When did it start? Given that she was so resistant to living here at the beginning it must have developed here, when he was working on the house, or when she was out doing those pointless vlogs. When she was in town getting groceries and supposedly checking out that school. She'd had plenty of opportunities. He had been so blind. Betrayed. Taken for a fool. The rifle felt hot in his hand. He could kill both of them. He had already killed once. He could kill again, he tried to convince himself. Planned this time. Planned and executed. He could claim self-defence. His life threatened by Ian and his rifle. But would Nee back him up? Where did her loyalties stand now? With him or Ian?

As he contemplated his next move, he overheard the lovers – the thought made him snarl – discussing the bodies. About moving them. Ian was trying to get her to focus on getting rid of the evidence. But she wanted to check on her husband and her son. Now.

Lorcan knew that Nee would win the battle in the end. She always did. He also knew that he couldn't be caught out here. They couldn't be allowed to realize what he knew. He needed to get back to the house and plan his and Dylan's escape. There was no manual for that on YouTube.

114

Lorcan

He couldn't remember running that fast ever. He felt like Usain Bolt as he shot out from the rear of his hiding place and back to the house in two minutes flat. Charging in through the door, he didn't pause to catch his breath. There were things to do. Like act calm. Not easy to achieve as his lungs scrabbled for air, his heart pounding and his head full of new, horrifying images.

A narrow miss from a stray bullet.

Mike shot in cold blood.

And a loving embrace between his wife and another man.

Plus, on top of all that: Stevie's death by his hand.

None of it would be easily forgotten. It had all gone so wrong. He had only wanted the gold to start a new life for his family elsewhere. Ian, Mike and Stevie could always dig for more. He would have packed his family up – though now he suspected Nee might have stayed – and left for Adelaide. Or beyond. Not Kallayee. What had been simple robbery had become much more sinister. He had killed a man. But that had been a tragic accident. Ian had outright executed someone. Why stop there? Why not come after him and Dylan?

Despite his heart and brain working overtime his lungs began to recover. It was time to leave.

Lugging the pulley behind the door he made for the bedroom, yelling for Dylan to get ready to go on a trip. Entering the bedroom he looked behind the bed.

Dylan was not there.

Or in his own bedroom.

Or the kitchen. Or the living room. He wasn't even outside tending to his mining operation. Dylan was gone.

Had Naiyana and Ian beaten him here and taken him? Surely not. He would have heard the vehicles. So where had he disappeared to?

His thoughts were disturbed by the insistent shove at the front door. Dylan had come back. Lorcan felt a flood of relief. He had gone to find his father but had given up. There was still time to escape.

But the voice was Naiyana's, not Dylan's.

Lorcan took a couple of breaths and considered his next move. If he stayed quiet, she would force her way in and immediately wonder where Dylan was. Talking to her might buy him some time. If he could keep it together.

Removing the heavy doorstop, he put his hands in his pockets to mask the persistent shaking. She asked about the pulley and then Dylan. He explained that their son was asleep, exhausted from running after the quad all morning, trying to sell the lie, trying to control himself.

She took a step inside as if going to check. If so, he would have to tell the truth. That Dylan was gone. But she stopped, staring at him, accepting the explanation. Then Ian spoke. Wanting to know when he got back to the house and why the quad tyres were slashed, distrust oozing from every word.

Lorcan was confused himself as to why the tyres were slashed. So he played on it. Taking his quivering hands from his pockets he held them up and told them he had nearly crashed earlier so had given the quad up. By now he felt that he was running out of luck. He didn't know how long he could continue devising barely plausible stories. His mouth felt like the desert outside.

Then Ian accused him of trying to take the gold. Had he realized that Mike was telling the truth over Stevie's shooting? But Lorcan had one final play, reversing the accusation and questioning Ian's where-abouts and who he was with.

That bought a moment's silence, a flustered Nee glancing at her lover. He felt sick to the core.

Then they left, separately but together, Lorcan waiting until the vehicles disappeared from view before sliding down the wall to stop himself from collapsing. But he didn't have time to sit around. He needed to find his son.

115

Emmaline

On leaving the restaurant they caught a break. The family's white Toyota had been found. With a worrying amount of dried blood on the dashboard and in the footwell.

It had been discovered by police in the Northern Territory, off the road and half-torched. Emmaline wanted to get to the scene. The choice was a long drive up the Great Central Road or a bumpy flight from Leonora on a privately hired twin-prop. She chose the latter. Two hours of discomfort rather than fifteen.

Though the scene was technically out of state she was granted automatic authority from the Cross-border Justice Scheme, a partnership between the West, NT and South Australia. It had been designed for cases of this type, removing the territory borders to improve law enforcement, so that offenders couldn't escape justice by going interstate. The region it covered was known as the Ngaanyatjarra Pitjantjatjara Yankunytjatjara (NPY) lands. Something she was glad she didn't have to spell out on the forms.

On the flight she studied the details of the report. The officers who had found it noted that it looked like the fire had been started deliberately, the smell of accelerant lingering. It had failed to take hold though, so it was presumed that the occupants left before it did and were therefore unaware that it hadn't been destroyed. *Or they'd been spooked by something*, thought Emmaline, *possibly the worry over a national search for the vehicle.* The fugitive – or fugitives – had given themselves a two- or three-day head start until the family's disappearance might reasonably be noticed. After that they would have been piloting a ute that may as well have had a giant spotlight on it.

A trace amount of gold had also been found in the truck. Which suggested they had more to sell.

But it was the blood on the dashboard that was the most disturbing factor. An intensive search of the nearby area was already under way. Looking for a body. With the focus on Naiyana and Dylan Maguire.

Emmaline arrived at the scene in three hours. The ute was indeed off the road, hidden and half-torched, the white paint tarnished black and silvery in parts. She peered in the passenger window. A significant amount of blood coated the dashboard, still visible even though the interior was scorched.

'So he killed them?' said Oily, looking around the rest of the vehicle.

'Why bring them nearly two thousand kilometres if he was only going to kill them?' asked Emmaline. 'It would have been easier to do it back in Kallayee.'

'What's to say he didn't?'

'The missing bodies. If there had been an argument between them, there would be bodies nearby. Of either of them. We have to proceed on the assumption that all are alive. But one or more is injured.'

'There's no guarantee this is Naiyana's blood. It could be his. Or Dylan's.'

That was also true. She glanced at the officers patrolling the scene. Now outside of WA she was forced to ditch the local help, and felt a little lost without Rispoli's intelligence, Anand's humour and even Barker's no-nonsense approach. But such was a job with the MCS. Fly in, work with what you get, investigate and fly out.

She left the sweep of the area in the hands of the local sergeant advised by the inspector from Alice Springs. It was the onward progress of the group she was interested in.

From here it was assumed that Ian, Naiyana and Dylan had at least a week's head start. Bulletins had been issued around the state asking for people to come forward if they had been approached by either Ian or Naiyana. Or if anyone recalled seeing them in the area.

Emmaline was desperate to locate them. They might be the only people who could tell her what had happened in Kallayee. As witnesses or perpetrators. But for every hour that passed, the chance of the trail growing cold increased.

116

Lorcan

As he sat slumped against the wall, the urge to get out and look for Dylan made his whole body tingle, stinging with sweat and heat as if boiling from the inside out. He gave it five minutes, until he was sure Naiyana or Ian weren't coming back, before he left the house. Heading out of Kallayee was a great dust cloud, both vehicles gone.

He broke into a jog, which quickly became a run. He called out for his son as he peered into buildings and around the back of shacks that echoed the name back to him. He passed the spot where he had shot Stevie. And where Mike had been executed. The bodies were gone, all trace of them vanished apart from blood on the sand. They were being disposed of. His wife was helping with the disposal. He wondered if he was next. And then Dylan.

As he stood there another blood-curdling thought arose. What if Dylan had seen him murder Stevie like he himself had witnessed Ian murder Mike?

What would a six-year-old do after that? He'd be terrified. He'd run. So Lorcan ran too. Dylan was here somewhere.

117

Naiyana

The cab was as silent as it could possibly be given the condition of the road and the rocks chattering against the underside of the ute.

The enormity of what she had done filled the space. She might not have shot Mike and Stevie herself but she had assisted in disposing of their bodies. She was an accessory now, much like the hundreds of trinkets and ornaments held at the storage facility in Perth. Maybe she would never be back to collect them. But that didn't matter anymore. What mattered was what she might have to do next. Whether she wanted to or not.

She thought back to the rusty ute, Ian flicking the match inside, the flames bursting into life and Ian cynically making light of the whole thing. She found it both disturbing and reassuring. That resolute and absolute will to act. To see through to the end what was started. She was the same. Especially when there was an end goal. She had pursued Brightside Foods to the very end. And she would continue to pursue Chester Grant. She would make sure that he did the appropriate thing, vote the appropriate way, make the world a better place for as long as she was able.

But could she control Ian? Was this truly love or was this the dictionary definition of a torrid affair, a vicious storm that caused enormous upheaval? With the possibility of more to come. After all he had lied, cheated, stolen and killed. But was she any better?

She broke the silence as they approached Kallayee, manoeuvring around ruts that were now mapped into her subconscious.

'What happens next?'

She ushered the question into the open even though, like on the first night they met, she worried she might not be able to fully comprehend what was next. Ignorance wasn't just bliss. It was more than that. It was safe. Unless she was being led like a cow to the slaughter.

Ian didn't look at her as he spoke, eyes focused dead in front. In command or at least wanting it to appear that way.

'I want to be with you.'

Naiyana didn't respond. She didn't know what to respond.

'Since saving you from that building I haven't – I can't – stop thinking about you, Naiyana. Every day, every night.'

His sincere profession of love. At least in mere words. She had been consumed by it too but now she saw it for what it was. An infatuation – a chance to redeem himself – that had curdled his brain. And hers. For too long.

She repeated her question.

'So what happens next?'

'We leave town.'

She didn't respond to this immediately. She needed to find out what his plans were for Dylan. And Lorcan.

She glanced across to find that he was staring at her. The steely eyes bore into her. They wanted an answer. She told him the truth.

'Not without Dylan.'

That broke the eye contact, his drifting away. She sensed bad news.

'You'll have to leave him behind,' he said, coldly.

'I'm not doing that.'

'For the minute.'

'No – not for the minute.'

'We have to make a clean break. We'll come back for him later.' The coldness in his tone suggested he wasn't going to back down. She responded with fire in hers.

'He's not a bag of bloody laundry, Ian. Or a partner in crime you can dump – or dispose of – when they fulfil their purpose.'

They locked eyes again. She tried to read his face.

'If we take him, what do we do with Lorcan?' he asked.

'What do you mean, what do we do?'

416

'If we take the only thing he has left what do you expect him to do? Mike said he killed Stevie. He could do it again.'

'I don't believe that,' she replied, ignoring the doubts festering in her soul, all certainty evaporated from her psyche.

'He looked very nervous when we met him,' said Ian.

'He nearly fell off the bike.'

'Which we found close to where Stevie was shot. With the tyres slashed. Why would that be?'

Though Lorcan was above all a coward, access to the rifle meant that he was capable of something inhuman. But still . . . it was Lorcan. He wouldn't shoot someone to death.

'No. I know my husband. He doesn't have the guts. He sent me out to meet with you despite knowing *you* could be capable of anything.'

She looked across at her passenger wondering what exactly he was capable of.

'So what's the answer?' he asked.

'We need to secure his silence,' she said and looked at Ian. 'You should also know that he does have a rifle.'

'And you didn't tell me?'

'We all have secrets,' she said, as they entered the deserted streets of Kallayee. In the distance a small dust storm seemed to be forming. It was the last thing they needed.

Naiyana reached her house, Ian walking alongside

her, the rifle by his side. They exchanged a glance and he followed her in. The house was quiet, no sound other than the creak of their steps on the floorboards. She called out for her husband. Then her son. Receiving no answer, they searched the house. Lorcan and Dylan were gone.

'Dylan's backpack's missing,' she noted, running into the kitchen, opening a cupboard. It was almost empty. 'And some food.'

Ian nodded. 'Okay, they've legged it. Time for us to go too.'

She ignored the callousness in his voice. This was what he wanted after all. To run. Men were all the same in the end. They only wanted to run from trouble. Abandon everything and save themselves. But not this time.

'I want Dylan.'

'Later.'

'I'm not going anywhere without him,' she said as her eyes drifted to his rifle.

118

Emmaline

The blood on the dashboard was AB. Matching Naiyana Maguire's blood type. It would go through DNA analysis later but seemed to confirm she had been in the vehicle. The questions now were, how much blood had she lost? And how had it happened?

The search of the area surrounding the vehicle had uncovered no bodies and no blood trail.

'Do you think she was already dead? Blood dries quickly out here,' said Oily.

'Hauling a body, alive or dead, would be difficult in this heat and pretty damn conspicuous,' said Emmaline. 'Especially with Dylan too. It's not consistent with a desperate escape plan. So my guess is that she was alive when she left the ute. Injured, maybe even severely, but fit enough to support her own weight and comfort what was likely a distressed child. The question is where they went next. Anything from the hospitals?'

She directed this question to the local constable – Cooper – who had been attached to them like an intern shadowing on work experience. She was eager but overawed, dashing back and forth like a rabbit with the latest information.

'There have been no reports of an injured female matching Naiyana Maguire's description. Or a male matching Ian Kinch. Or a child—'

'Keep on them.'

'Will do, Detective Taylor.' Her standard response. Overly formal, maybe even needy for praise. Emmaline didn't have time for that.

She returned to the problem at hand. 'They must have accessed another mode of transport. And not public transport. Too risky with an injured partner. And given the trace of gold in the cab they must be carrying some too.'

'That's a lot for one person to shoulder.'

'Which indicates that they must like each other.'

'A true Bonnie and Clyde,' said Oily.

Emmaline couldn't decide if their acts were romantic or desperate. It was easy to confuse the two. With great desperation came moments of unbridled emotion that could be mistaken for love. She'd been there before. Another ten years and she might be there again. In that case she would remain single. No point in following convention if you actually detest it.

'Our best bet is to follow the money,' she said. 'In this case, gold. Have Cooper run a report on all gold dealers. We'll try those first.'

She stopped Oily before he ran after their intern, who in turn was running towards a squad car. 'Also any place that might accept gold in exchange for goods. Again, both legal and not-so-legal.'

119

Naiyana

Her eyes were still on the rifle. She had come to realize that a gun held a particularly grotesque knack of becoming the focus of a room, the ultimate scene-stealer. She waited for the barrel to rise and provide confirmation that she had made a terrible mistake, confirmation that she would lose everything, including her life out here. In a town she hated.

But the rifle stayed where it was. By his side. Instead he raised a question. 'Where could he run to?'

She didn't know. And in that she realized something. It was very unlike Lorcan to run. Especially with Dylan. Without means of transport. He wouldn't put his son in danger. Unless . . .

'Do you think he saw you killing Mike?' she said, the tide of panic rising again.

This tide transferred to Ian, who now understood that there might be a witness on the loose. 'He was nervous when he saw us. He could have sprinted back as we loaded the bodies.'

She nodded. 'I think the whole falling off the bike

thing was a lie. He was edgy because he saw you. He knew what you were capable of.'

The realization settled upon them like the dust that seeped through the busted gable wall.

'Shit! I should have checked on Dylan,' she said, angry at herself, hitting the wall and catching the edge of her mother's mirror, causing it to fall and shatter on the floor. But she didn't care about her broken heirloom or that she had nicked the side of her foot on a shard of glass. The only thing that mattered was her son.

'If I had seen him, he would have told me what was going on,' she said, aiming her vitriol at Ian. 'But you insisted we get rid of the bodies.'

'It was smart to focus on them. They had to be disposed of.'

'It would have been smarter to focus on the living. The dead weren't going anywhere. And we only had to dispose of them because you shot Mike!' she yelled, spit flying from the corners of her dry mouth. 'You better not have let anything happen to my child.'

She turned her eyes from him and looked around the kitchen. The broken kitchen in the broken house. She couldn't stay here any longer, the tension and the hatred was unbearable. She made for the front door with Ian's words stalking her.

'They can't have got far.'

He beat her to the car and climbed behind the wheel. When she tried to stop him, he told her that he needed her eyes. Which she could tell was a lie.

But focusing her concentration on finding her missing husband and son seemed a good idea.

'Would they go down the tunnel?' asked Ian as he started the ute.

'No, Dylan was afraid of it,' she replied. 'Lorcan would head for town.'

'We didn't meet them on the way in.'

'Minus a vehicle they would take the shortest route, across the bush. Plenty of places to hide as well if needed.'

Following her suggestion he hitched a left at the crossroads and made for a direct path off-road to Hurton.

They reached the sand and scrub quickly. She glanced around from window to window, the not knowing her son's whereabouts clawing at her insides.

'Do you think he could make it to Hurton?' asked Ian. 'Or contact the police?'

'That doesn't matter now,' she barked at him, briefly hopeful that a speck in the distance was Dylan but angered to find it was another worthless shrub.

'Of course it does. Even if they didn't believe him, it would bring heat onto us.'

She didn't care. They could bring all the heat they wanted. As long as she had Dylan.

'Let's run for it,' said Ian. 'If he has custody of Dylan, then he isn't going to mention any of this. To anyone. For his and Dylan's sake.'

For the briefest moment, she interrupted her scan of the outback to look her latest cowardly bastard of a partner dead in the eyes. 'I want to find Dylan.'

120

Lorcan

He found Dylan at the entrance to the tunnel. Staring into the dark abyss. Even when he grabbed his shoulders, the boy didn't flinch.

'Are you okay, son?' he asked. 'Why did you leave the house? Why are you here?'

'The tunnel is silent, Daddy. No arguments.'

'Did you see an argument?' he asked, nervous of what his son might say. If he had witnessed his father murder someone, then what? How do you silence your son?

'I heard it. And I heard shots.'

'And what did you see?'

'I saw Mummy leaving with Ian.'

'And nothing else?'

Dylan shook his head.

'Good. We have to go, son.'

'Where?'

'Away. For a while,' he said as he led Dylan outside, bumping into the door frame and stifling a grunt. As they made it into the fading sun, he looked around. There were no vehicles on the horizon, no dust clouds.

He had no idea how much time they had. Or how much time he had wasted searching for Dylan. Naiyana and Ian could be back at any time.

He started to jog, pulling Dylan along, his breathing constricted with the panic and the heat.

'Why are we going, Daddy?'

'We have to leave, Dylan. Before they come back. We'll go to town. Quick!'

He stepped up the pace. The sooner they were out of Kallayee the better.

'Where's Mummy?' asked Dylan, fear in his voice.

'She's gone,' he replied, looking back at his son and stumbling over the collapsed fence by the coal shed, his eyes drawn to the pool of blood in the sand.

In five minutes they were at the edge of town. He gazed at the bush and distant, rolling sand dunes. Making Hurton was doable but slower and more dangerous with the child in tow. Especially as Dylan was reluctant to go any further. Lorcan showed him his favourite dragon-patterned backpack of some cartoon character he had watched on endless repeat. Dak or Zak or something like that.

'We are going on a camping adventure,' he said, trying to sell it to his son. 'We might even camp out,' he added but hoped to get to Hurton by nightfall. Nee – and more worryingly Ian – would be on their tail as soon as they realized they were gone.

Hand in hand, father and son took their first steps into the unknown.

As he helped his son along, Lorcan kept glancing back at Kallayee. It very, very slowly began to disappear into the distance, like he was escaping from a monster in some sort of panicked fever dream. The town was to be their dream. How wrong they had been.

121

Emmaline

With information needed quickly it was all hands to the pump. Including Emmaline. She had never been to Alice Springs before and found it to be surprisingly green, like an oasis in the desert, Anzac Hill dominating the town, the buildings glowing white in the hot sun. In the distance lay the MacDonnell Ranges, red and flat-topped like a giant fence encompassing the south of the town, broken only by Heavitree Gap, all roads and rail south funnelled towards it.

The dealer she found herself at had a view of the Gap. With Cooper putting together the off-the-book list, they were checking out one of the registered dealers, his services luridly advertised on the picket sign hammered into his well-tended garden. He was welcoming as she introduced herself, a twinkle in his eye that suggested a certain admiration of her looks. Possibly in the expectation that there was not much behind them. A sadly typical reaction that she enjoyed shredding to pieces.

She showed him the photos of Ian and Naiyana.
'Seen them in here?'

The dealer was in his fifties, with neatly parted hair she supposed was meant to read as 'refined' but just came across as 'staid'. He tore his eyes away from her face and gazed over the top of his spectacles at the photos.

'I recognize him. He had a lot of gold on his hands. Nuggets, shavings, dust. Too much for me. He refused to provide a name or ID either. I'm no fool, miss.'

'Detective,' said Emmaline. 'And her?'

He shook his head. 'I would remember her. Not often I get two pretty women in my humble shop.'

'Usually you'd have to pay them,' she replied, unable to hold back.

The man's eyes darted towards Oily who stood in the background.

'Don't expect any help from me,' said Oily. 'You dug your own grave.'

'How much was he trying to sell?' asked Emmaline, refocusing the dealer's attention.

'Just under an ounce.'

'And how much would that get?'

'Fourteen hundred,' said the dealer, stuttering a little.

'And are you sure you didn't buy any?' asked Emmaline, her eyes boring into the washed-up letch's face.

'None. I wasn't buying.'

'But I bet you sent him to someone who was. I bet

429

I could find them on that computer of yours,' said Emmaline, nodding at it.

'That's private property.'

'And this man may be involved in a series of brutal murders. So, give me a name.'

The name they got was for a guy who worked out of a pub on Feldman's. Cooper warned them that the place was rough, frequented by bikers, hoods, anyone who was looking for action or trouble. Emmaline decided to test that.

Being late afternoon, it looked quiet, just a few bikes and cars dotted around outside.

Eyes turned to them as they entered. She asked the ham-faced barman to point her in the direction of Jeremiah Tung. The barman shook his head. As Emmaline tried to figure out if it was an outright refusal to help or that Jeremiah Tung wasn't in the building, Oily tapped her shoulder and directed her to a heavy-set man in a denim jacket with the initials JT stitched onto the back.

She and her undersized and slightly intimidated posse approached.

'Jeremiah Tung?'

The man in the denim jacket turned, eyebrow raised. His age was hard to determine, his face puffy with fat, smoothing any worry lines that might reveal his years, but she felt it was safe to say somewhere between thirty and forty.

'I need to ask you about some gold.'

The eyebrow remained up. 'I think you're mistaking me with Fort Knox,' he replied, a hint of Kiwi to the accent.

'I don't care if you bought it or what you did with it. You see something going at a good price why would I stop you? That's for the local cops,' said Emmaline, looking at Cooper who was a few steps behind her.

Jeremiah Tung didn't answer. But he didn't turn away either. She showed him Ian's photo.

'I just want to know how much he sold.'

Jeremiah Tung's mouth twisted in thought, nostrils flaring. 'I'll speak with you. Alone.'

Emmaline nodded for Oily and Cooper to stay put and followed Tung to a back corner, home to the eye-watering reek of the nearby toilets. Maybe this was the corner he always used to conduct deals, the stench an incentive to hasten business along.

'This gold. What's it to you?' he asked.

'The guy flogging it might have kidnapped a mother and son. As I said, I don't care about the deal, only how much he has.'

'And the local blue?'

'If they haven't made a move yet then you must be too small-fry for them.'

Jeremiah looked momentarily offended by this. Then he shot her a beaming smile. 'I bought the guts of an ounce. He wanted fifteen hundred. I gave him nine.'

Nine hundred. Enough for a week, maybe ten days at a stretch. There was a chance that Ian had then

431

moved on to other dealers, but she guessed he wouldn't want to hang around long. Especially with no guarantee that the next dealer wouldn't just get a friendly call from Jeremiah and be ready to mug him of the rest of it.

She was about to leave when Jeremiah called her back.

'He asked about buying a second-hand motor too. I directed him to my brother. On Trieste.'

Emmaline's rapid-fire tour of Alice Springs' lesser lights continued. Jeremiah Tung's brother – also heavy-set and wearing an excess of denim – confirmed that a man fitting Ian Kinch's description had bought a motor. An old Holden Commodore with two hundred thousand on the clock and no air con. For five hundred. Meaning he had four hundred left. Enough for a week, if he was sleeping in the car, which would be uncomfortable despite the Commodore's size. It had been purchased under a fake name – Ted Grant – but though he could hide his name, Ian couldn't hide his face. The licence plate number was immediately passed on to Cooper to run an ANPR check, though out here they would be lucky to get a positive.

Emmaline asked one final question. 'You see anyone with him?'

Jeremiah Tung's brother shook his head. 'Not that I saw.'

122

Naiyana

It was a rocky ride. Pretty soon she regretted complaining about the broken road out of Kallayee and the compacted dirt of Keenan's Run. They were like freshly laid tarmac compared to this, the ute being thrown up in the air before digging into the dirt and sand, almost burying the nose.

The rollercoaster nature of it also made it hard to see anything out of the window, the landscape rocking up and down like she was on a small boat on a choppy sea.

'Slow down,' she cried out as the seat belt bit into her shoulder.

'You want to find them, don't you?'

'I have to be able to see to find them,' she retorted, as the ute ploughed through a lonely mulga, shattering it into pieces.

'I want to find them too. I don't want to go back to prison. And lose you.'

She glanced over at him. His teeth were gritted, fighting the wheel. She wondered if he was fighting his emotions too. For the first time she wondered if the best decision was to let Lorcan and Dylan go. That way they would be safe. If Ian found them she couldn't be sure what he'd do. She felt another surge of regret. That she ever became involved with him. The brief infatuation had passed, a puddle dried up in the sun. She had tried to convince herself that they had the same desires but they did not. He could kill in cold blood. She could not.

She glanced at the rifle. It lay wedged between his seat and the central panel. She decided that if they found Lorcan and her son she would grab it. She would retain ultimate control. And if either Ian or Lorcan threatened her child she would use it.

Indeed the more she thought about it the more she edged towards grabbing it now. Both of Ian's hands were on the wheel, he was vulnerable. She resisted. For now.

She held onto the dashboard as the powerful ute fought through another dredge of sand, the engine revving briefly before being muted as the sand absorbed the noise.

An idea arose in her mind. A meeting in public. 'We could wait for them in Hurton.'

Ian shook his head. 'Too risky. We can't cover all the angles. One cry for help and we'd be surrounded. We don't need any outside interference. We don't need witnesses.'

'What do you mean?' she asked, hands inching towards the rifle.

'We don't need anyone outside the four of us knowing,' he said, taking his eyes off the road for an instant. 'I've got a record. I'd be the main suspect.'

'You did kill Mike.'

'But not Stevie. That was your husband.'

'We don't know that for sure.'

'Why are you sticking up for him?'

It was a good question. One she couldn't answer. Maybe she just wanted it to be clear in Ian's head. That he had killed someone.

'Keep your eyes on the road,' she shouted, thinking how ironic it would be if they 'drove off a cliff' like Mike and Stevie.

'Mike had it coming to him anyway,' said Ian. 'They both did. They knew what they were getting into. I told them that it wouldn't be easy but Mike was always a pain in the arse, unwilling to bend, that constant clack, clack of his fucking gum. He didn't understand that these things require flexibility.' He paused. 'Of course, there are limits. Sometimes resoluteness is required.'

Naiyana stared at him. She understood what he was getting at. One of those times of resoluteness was coming up. If they found Lorcan and Dylan, Ian would decide if there was to be another body. Or two. Or three. She was determined to make that her decision.

123

Lorcan

It hadn't taken long for him to grow impatient with Dylan's own impatience. Every two minutes he wanted a break or asked where his mum was or drifted off in a direction that wasn't conducive to reaching Hurton. And then Perth he had decided. Not Adelaide. Despite the menace of Nikos Iannis.

He had also ruled out going to a police station. There was no station in Hurton for starters and the police would only ask questions. And he wasn't sure if he had answers. Or if he would have answers to anything ever again given how clouded his brain was. There was only one certainty. That he had killed someone and that he would be killed if he stayed in Kallayee. Every step further from town helped confirm it a little more.

There was a second reason for not going to the police. They would attempt to contact Nee. Making it his word against the other two. His fingerprints were on the gold. And on the rifle in his hand. Stevie's murder weapon. He should dump it, but he couldn't let it go. It was his only protection.

Naiyana held the upper hand. She might have been an adulterer but that was not a crime. In a criminal sense she was merely a bystander, a witness, present when Ian had shot Mike. She could claim that she was forced to help him dispose of the bodies, a woman in love with a powerful criminal, under his spell, in fear of her life. Pure bullshit. But bullshit that could fly with a jury. So, he would go to jail. And she would get custody of Dylan.

So it was back to Perth and wait. If she did come for Dylan, then he would be surrounded by his family. He would go for her as hard as she went for him.

But given the current rate of progress, he and Dylan would be camped out here overnight amongst the dirt and the dingoes. He could try and sell it as a further adventure like before but Dylan was exhausted and emotional. His new complaint was that he wanted to go back and get his trucks. The only mine still oper-ating in town. The complaints quickly turned to tears and he grew concerned that the crying might draw unwanted attention. From people or animals. Worse yet, the wailing drowned out the possibility of hearing anyone approach.

As they made it over the sand dune, his feet going ankle deep in the boiling hot sand and scorching whatever hair remained on his ankles, he helped his son down the other side, acting as Dylan's eyes and ears now that his body was locked in tantrum.

At the bottom he paused. As they got closer to Hurton his chance of picking up a signal increased.

It was a faint hope, but phone signals were like magic sometimes. Maybe the earth would give him a helping hand. Maybe he was standing on a bed of iron ore that would boost the signal, if that was even a thing. He checked his pockets. And again. The phone was gone. He tried to recall when he had it last but . . .

Through the air came the sound of an engine. Faint, possibly distant, direction unknown. It seemed to fade and he wondered if he was imagining it. He looked ahead. They were over the massive dune and if it wasn't for the trees and scrub Hurton would have been visible in the distance. They were less than halfway there but reaching it by nightfall wasn't impossible. If they increased the pace.

The sound of the engine suddenly returned, roaring, drowning out everything else. He looked back as the white Toyota bounded over the crest, rearing into the air like a beast on the attack, its front wheels in the air, exposing the sand-clogged mechanics underneath.

It was coming straight for them.

124

Emmaline

With the licence number and description of the 1990 Commodore out across all states along with Ian Kinch's photo and alias, Emmaline and her team tried to narrow down his ultimate location.

Oily had put forward the option of a city, north to Darwin, east to Brisbane, or the long haul south to Sydney; but with their names and descriptions now on the daily news cycle it was a risk. The openness of the country was considered more likely, but didn't narrow down the options for investigation.

A break came. From a gas station north of Alice, about an hour up the Stuart Highway. The owner reported serving someone who looked a lot like Ian Kinch. Over a week ago.

Emmaline, Oily and Cooper made it out there in half an hour. It was a station that looked as if it was barely holding together, never mind barely scraping by. It consisted of two pumps that looked like relics from an old movie, a concourse where the white lines had been slowly scoured away by the sandpaper wind, and a main building that looked serviceable if unlovable.

The owner waved them inside, the air con whirring and the fridges fully stocked with everything a traveller would need.

The large man stuck out his equally large hand, his face open and friendly; a wide, beaming smile peeking from behind his dark lips. It was a smile that reminded Emmaline of her father, engaging and loving. She warmed to him immediately.

'Mr Atijabawal?' asked Emmaline.

'Call me Orad,' he said, as they convened at the counter. 'You want anything to drink? Coke? Orange? Grog?'

Given her dry throat, it was a tempting offer, but she put her hand up to decline. The others did the same.

'You said you thought Mr Kinch was here.'

'Or a boy that looked a lot like him anyway,' said Orad, in good cheer.

'More than a week ago,' said Cooper.

'Second of January.'

'How can you be so sure?'

Orad pointed to the small monitor behind the counter. 'CCTV. Just got it in. Lot of petrol thefts around here. People coming into the shop and distracting me while another yahoo fills up their ute and leaves. Then they chuck a U-ey up the road, come back and collect their partner. The police were doing nothing about it, so I did.'

Emmaline nodded. 'Has it helped?'

'Only been one try in the last week.'

'Ian Kinch?' said Oily, with a questioning glance.

Orad shook his head. 'Nah, mate, he paid. Another guy, sent his girl in but she clocked the CCTV, turned on her heels and left.'

He loaded up the footage. 2 January. A blurry image resembling Ian Kinch could be seen on the monitor filling a boxy Commodore at the pumps.

'Do you see anyone in the car?' asked Emmaline, the image dark on the screen.

'No,' said Cooper and Oily.

'That's the best shot I have,' said Orad. 'If it helps I didn't see anyone in the car. But they could have been lying down in the back seat.'

Because they were injured, thought Emmaline. *Or dead.*

After filling the car, CCTV captured him entering the store and approaching the counter. Even in black and white the dark stain on his shirt was visible.

'Was there blood on his shirt?'

Orad looked at the screen and nodded. 'A bit.'

'You didn't ask him about it?'

'Years of experience have told me that it's best not to. Could have hit a roo, a camel, anything.'

The self-preservation of the outback store owner, thought Emmaline.

'Did you see which way they went after?'

'Not from here,' said Orad, shaking his head. 'Can't see much out of these,' he said, pointing to the dusty windows. It was like peering through a sepia-tinted lens.

Without confirmation of the ute's onward direction she had to speculate on the options. *Ian might have been headed north to Darwin but just up the road was a turnoff for Route 12 and then the 76 heading east*, thought Emmaline as she watched Ian Kinch paying at the till. And grabbing something from beside it. Emmaline looked to her left. It was a display of insect repellent.

'Did he buy one of these?'

Orad looked at the small yellow and green cans, face twisted in thought. 'Yeah, he asked if it was good against mozzies. I told him it was so he bought five or six. Stuffed them in his pockets.'

'Thanks,' said Emmaline. 'You've been a great help, Orad.'

She bounded out of the petrol station. She now had an idea of where Ian Kinch was headed. And what had happened to Naiyana and Dylan Maguire.

They were back in the car before she revealed the importance of the repellent. She had Cooper bring up a map of the area on a tablet.

'We're here,' she said, pointing at the dot on the map. It was surrounded by a blanket of grey, one lonely line of yellow trickling up the middle. 'Up ahead are turnoffs that head towards Queensland. Now we know both Naiyana and Dylan Maguire were born and bred in Perth and what do we *not* get much of in Perth?'

There was a moment's pause.

'Mosquitoes,' said Oily.

Emmaline nodded. 'Ian Kinch though is from Cairns and so knows how bad they can get. Maybe he gets bitten himself, maybe he is taking them as a precaution for Naiyana and Dylan. What it means is that's where they were headed.'

'Are you sure?' asked Cooper.

'It's what he knows. It's where he has family.'

'It's also where he would expect we'd look,' said Oily.

'So, let's look.'

'We did,' said Cooper. 'We've tried his family and friends. They aren't talking.'

'Maybe they don't know,' said Emmaline. 'He's become proficient at staying under the radar.'

125

Emmaline

The Cross-border Justice Scheme provision had run out. It had before Emmaline had reached Alice Springs but she had pushed her luck in the hope that the trail ended there. But it hadn't. This meant getting clearance to pursue from the Queensland authorities and HQ.

She waited at Alice Springs airport for the go-ahead to fly to Cairns. Given that she suspected he was headed back home, she had suggested keeping tabs on social media. In case something was mentioned by a friend in passing. A slip-up. But the Cairns police were on it already. Thoroughly scoured. No leads forthcoming.

A call arrived. Zhao. It wasn't the go-ahead that she was eager for. It was a different update. Nikos Iannis had been arrested getting on a plane to Greece that afternoon. Using a fake passport.

She smiled as she hung up the call. So, Nikos had made a desperate attempt to flee. Which suggested he was planning, or had planned, something. Something that had gone wrong. She would have to trust Zhao could get him to talk.

Emmaline stared at the empty ticket desks. She turned to Oily. 'Would Ian try to get out of the country?'

'From Cairns?'

'He could have arranged something. Given as we weren't even looking for him until a few days ago.'

Oily pursed his lips. 'But Naiyana and Dylan Maguire's photos were everywhere.'

'Everywhere is a big place, Oily.'

An hour later they got the go-ahead. Two hours in the air and they were there. The temperature remained the same, but the humidity had cranked up to uncomfortable, clothes that stuck to flesh and refused to budge, growing ever and ever more like a second skin.

Ian Kinch's apartment had already been searched and surveillance confirmed no movement in or out. The stuffed-to-burst pigeonhole – post addressed to Ian King – suggested he hadn't been by in the last few months. The local dives had been checked and rechecked but all had drawn a blank. Ian Kinch and whoever was with him had become ghosts.

The local hospitals were questioned. A team in Queensland HQ had even taken to phoning all the local surgeries and health centres around the state to see if any had admitted or treated Naiyana Maguire, Dylan Maguire or someone fitting their descriptions.

Local gold dealers the same. All enquiries met with

the same silence. Leaving the possibility that Ian had run out of merch.

Tuesday flicked over to Wednesday. And Wednesday into Thursday.

Horizons that had been narrowed to concentrate on Queensland were broadened again. Budgets stretched and pledges given that this was the last time.

Calls were made to Darwin for the Top-Enders to make some enquiries. Brisbane and the Gold Coast too were put on alert. Even the Sydneysiders. The net was wide but with too many holes. A needle in a haystack.

Emmaline's frustrations grew. They had picked up the scent only to have the suspect shake them. The cranked humidity made her temper grow spectacularly short, snapping at the staff in the motel that somehow smelled worse than the caravan she had left behind.

She snapped at officers who weren't under her command. She missed being in command. She missed pursuing her own lines of enquiry and the freedom that working for the MCS back home provided. Out here she was a bystander watching on as Inspector Liang from Cairns QPS took over. She had no authority here. After driving the case all the way here that seemed wrong. She didn't enjoy taking a back seat. The views were restricted, the chance to steer remote and the journey only made her frustrated and bored.

With each tick of each minute her doubts solidified.

She had made a mistake. Ian Kinch and the Maguires were elsewhere. She had jumped on the logic of Ian returning home as some sort of security blanket but there had been no inkling of his presence.

He had managed to disappear off the grid once. But back then the full force of the law hadn't been looking for him. Now he had managed to stage another disappearance like he was David fucking Blaine.

It was 13 January now. Two weeks since Naiyana was last spotted alive. Two weeks since Dylan was last heard of. A month since they had entered Kallayee and now, even in this heat and oppressive humidity, the trail was quickly growing cold. Time was rapidly flowing against them and she was powerless.

After another meeting and another lack of positive sightings, she called up Zhao in case Ian had doubled back and ended up in the West. It was another dead end. And Nikos wasn't talking. Other than to say he had nothing to do with any killings.

After that she contacted Rispoli. This brought another dagger of frustration. How she could have done with him out here to take her mind off things for a while. A distraction was what she needed. His voice. His lips. Again she felt a pang of affection for that sweaty, dank caravan. She didn't say any of this to him. There was no point. They might meet again. Might even hook up again but right now all she could ask was for him to once again scour Kallayee for any clues. Check the tunnels again, check the house; look for a sign in the clouds, whispers in the air. She recognized what these were. Desperation measures to allow herself to exert some control.

That afternoon brought another visit to Ian's family, which she tagged along on. As another badge in a line. It was another attempt to cajole them into giving up anything they knew. Their pride regarding Ian was overtly apparent. Petty crime was the family business given the Kinch's lists of misdemeanours but Ian had broken through as the first nationwide Kinch villain, others merely local celebrities. The neighbours were canvassed again and again claimed not to have heard of Ian King or Ian Kinch even though his photo had been plastered all over the news. The wall of silence was tall and strong.

On leaving Emmaline pulled Inspector Liang aside. During the course of this blunt assault another angle of attack had occurred to her. They had tried relatives, neighbours and friends. But what about enemies? Surely not everyone was celebrating Ian's newfound fame? Inspector Liang studied her closely, sniffing persistently, something he seemed to do when mulling something over. Despite Emmaline being a drop-in, he had never once discouraged her or suggested she leave this to the QPS, the brush-off she had experienced before in other cases. Even when she outranked whoever was locally in charge. Inspector Liang stopped sniffing. He held his nose. And nodded.

HQ was quick to draw up a list of possibles and

it didn't take long for it to bear fruit. Toby 'Tubs' Wilkinson, a small-time local dealer, was happy to spill the beans in return for a petty theft charge being dropped.

After insisting that Ian Kinch was both not in town and a worthless piece of shit like all the other Kinches, Tubs eventually informed them that Ian had a lock-up out in Manoora, a southern suburb.

This was news to the team. A quick check revealed that the lock-up wasn't rented under Ian's name or any known alias and had been paid for in cash. The owner didn't know what was kept in it and didn't care as long as it wasn't illegal or flammable. Emmaline watched his face change from blasé to vexed when the police were unable to refute either.

Inspector Liang gave the command for the lock-up to be raided immediately by the Special Emergency Response Team. Emmaline and Oily rode with Liang in the backup truck. He didn't want either of them caught up in a gunfight. That was something Emmaline could abide by. As long as she was there when they caught Ian. She wanted to experience the satisfaction and thrill of the end of the hunt.

She waited in the third van back, tension mounting alongside the heat in the windowless vehicle. The SERT team readied themselves, weapons checked, masks adjusted, gloves pulled tight to fists. Breathing controlled. Waiting. After what seemed like an age the order was given. The three vans sped into the industrial park, down a double row of small garages

449

and skidded to a halt outside one with a red door and '41' graffitied on the front.

The forward team stalked up to the shutters before assuming defensive positions. Two members of the second team sprinted up to the lock with a drill, spearing through it in seconds. They then retreated and the officers poised at either side raised the door with a horrific, grinding squeak.

A call went up for those inside to come out with their hands up.

Emmaline peered into the darkness, looking for movement, looking for the barrel of a rifle to appear. Maybe even Naiyana's dead body sprawled on the floor.

But there was nothing, no movement aside from the newly disturbed dust. As her eyes adjusted to the gloom she could see that the garage was filled with scrap, old bikes and furniture, paint cans and general bric-a-brac. She watched as armed officers combed the inside but it was obvious no one was here.

After merely twenty seconds the cry of 'All clear' erupted. Emmaline and Oily joined Inspector Liang in entering. Her first impression was that the garage definitely hadn't been lived in, the air musty with inaction and lacking telltale remnants of scant meals or improvised sleeping arrangements. The floor and shelves were full of scrap she guessed was too busted for even Ian Kinch to fence. The only things of worth were stacked neatly in the corner. A pair of kayaks. Emmaline ran her hand across the fibreglass. A thin layer of dust but no scratches, suggesting they were prized possessions. Keeping them in the garage was probably more of a necessity than a desire, being too large to store in his small apartment. Behind the kayaks were a set of paddles and some rubber equipment she assumed was kayak related. This included a pair of helmets plastered with stickers. The same stickers covered the sides of the kayaks. For an adventure place in Cape Tribulation. A couple of hours' drive up the coast. A place she had only seen on television. A rainforest that backed onto beaches overlooked by the wonderfully named Mount Sorrow. It seemed the appropriate place for desperate runaways to flee to.

126

Emmaline

Cape Tribulation was much like Emmaline had seen on television. Only prettier. And hotter. The blue of the sky interrupted only by the dark clouds of mosquitoes that seemed to bite her en masse. Now she understood why Ian Kinch had purchased the repellent. She would sell a kidney for some right now.

On leaving the lock-up garage she had requisitioned a computer in District HQ and searched the adventure company stickered on the kayaks and helmets. Daintree Kayaks was based in Cape Tribulation and focused on sea kayaking around the coast, exploring the beaches, reefs and mangroves, offering 'great times' and 'wild, but safe tours for even the most inexperienced adventurers'.

Noticeably left out was the river itself. Even the bravest didn't kayak Daintree River for fear of meeting the giant saltwater crocodiles, or 'salties' as they were known.

What Daintree Kayaks did provide was training on proficiency badges. On a hunch, she checked them out.

Ian was listed as having a Sea Rescue endorsement, a Coastal Skills award and had last year begun a Sea Instructor badge, which would allow him to train individuals and groups to kayak at sea in moderate conditions. This was the other side to Ian Kinch. Even murderers needed hobbies. It also showed that he was serious about the sport. Minus any other leads on his whereabouts, this was the place to try.

Chaperoned by Cooper and Inspector Liang, who was taking great pleasure in conducting such a major operation, they first checked out her hunch that the pair would try and get out of Australia.

The docks were checked. Any boat that was going to Port Moresby in Papua New Guinea or to the Torres Strait Islands and then on to PNG. Passenger logs of boats that had departed in the last week were reviewed. Nothing was found to indicate that Ian, Naiyana or Dylan had been on them.

But that was only the official charters. They delved deeper. Skippers that needed no documents and asked no questions. Every one they quizzed returned the same answer. That they didn't go as far as PNG and that hopping from Thursday Island on to PNG was illegal. Unless you were a Torres Strait Islander. The official party line. The line that kept them out of trouble. A line that was almost too well rehearsed.

They had nearly run out of dock when Emmaline approached a guy who was polishing his boat, his hands a web of tendons as he scrubbed hard, the small vessel his livelihood, his prized possession.

He trotted out the same line. Didn't go there. Too far. Illegal.

'Has anyone asked?'

The guy stopped scrubbing and looked at her. 'People ask.'

'Any in the last few days?'

The guy paused, adjusting his stance to stand straight. A wince of pain. Back trouble from long days hunched over. 'Yeah. Someone asked. Friday, it was.' Four days ago.

'Did he look like this?' asked Emmaline, showing him the picture of Ian Kinch on her phone.

'Looks like the guy,' he said, returning to scrubbing as he talked, not wanting to waste any time. 'Fella was pretty nervous, looking around as if he expected to be jumped.'

'Why did he try you?'

The scrubber looked up. His hands continued to work as he nonchalantly shrugged. 'Must have thought I looked friendly.'

'But you weren't.'

'You couldn't pay me to go that far.'

'But he tried?'

'Said he had big bickies to make it worthwhile.'

'For one person?'

The guy shrugged, again almost nonchalantly. 'I guess so. Never mentioned anyone else and I never asked.'

Emmaline wondered what that meant for Naiyana and Dylan. Had she succumbed to her injuries? Dylan too? His blood was at the scene of his father's death after all.

'Fella also said that he would work to pay some off.'

'The travel?'

'Guess so.'

'Work for you?'

'Guess so.'

'And that was it?'

The scrubber shrugged again. 'Said he would be around for a few days if I changed my mind.'

'And you didn't?'

'Still here, ain't I?'

'Any idea where he might be staying?'

The scrubber thought about it. 'Fella didn't say.'

127

Emmaline

So, Ian Kinch had offered to work in return for passage abroad. And the suggestion, as far as she could tell from the boat scrubber, was that he was travelling alone.

The approach had been four days ago. Testing out the cost of transport. The offer to work some off meant he was running short of cash. Maybe he had looked for some short-term work to make the difference up. If so, his options were narrow.

Cape Tribulation wasn't really much of a town as such, named by Lieutenant James Cook when he ran the *Endeavour* onto the reef damaging the boat. It was a disparate series of eco lodges, tourist resorts, backpacker hostels and other accommodation tucked deeper into the rainforest. Supporting this were some cafes, restaurants and a couple of convenience stores. They scoured the local businesses for any trace of Ian Kinch, his name and photo presented to the staff.

The Daintree store was the only hit, the teller, a

bright-eyed guy with clumped brown dreadlocks, absolutely certain that he had served Ian Kinch.

'When?'

The guy shook his head as if this part was hazy. 'I want to say three, no four, days ago.'

Emmaline pressed on. 'How certain are you that it was him?'

'As certain as you are standing there.'

'And how much weed do you smoke?' asked Oily, who was checking the shelves as if Ian might be hiding amongst the tinned tomatoes.

The teller looked almost offended. 'None. You can call in your sniffer dogs if you want. I ain't got anything to hide,' he said, standing back and spreading his arms.

Emmaline glared at Oily, who returned to snooping around the store. This was an interview not a shake-down.

'So you're certain?'

'My head's clear, Detective.'

'Good. So you remember what he bought? Did he use card or cash?'

The teller looked up, staring at the tin roof for guidance.

'Some long-life,' he said, pointing towards the cartons of milk without opening his eyes. 'Cereal. Tim Tams. Beans. Bread. Bacon. Chocolate bars—'

'Peanut butter KitKats?'

The eyes flashed open, as if in wonder at her guess.

457

'Nah,' he shook his head, 'we don't sell them. Cherry Ripes. Mars bars.'

'Nothing else?'

The head shook again. 'Nothing.'

'Okay, thanks.'

'You don't want to search me for dope?'

'Not today,' said Emmaline. 'Bigger fish to fry.'

'Learn anything?' asked Oily, as they stepped outside. After the pleasant chill of the store, her skin started to prickle.

'The beans and bacon did.'

'Why?'

'They need cooking.'

'Which tells us?'

'Where they're staying there is a cooker. They can't afford catered accommodation so they must be in one of the self-catered lodges.'

'Or sleeping in the Holden,' said Oily, looking at Emmaline and shuddering. In this humidity, that would have been a nightmare.

128

Emmaline

With Ian sighted in the area the next stop were places of possible work. Knowing his area of expertise, Inspector Liang had swarmed the outdoor pursuits and adventure centres like the mosquitoes that seemed to follow Emmaline around. She reckoned she had swallowed about a million of them already. At a conservative estimate.

The business advertised on Ian's kayaks, Daintree Kayaks, wasn't listed, seemingly having gone out of business last year. Riley's Canoes hadn't seen or heard of Ian Kinch, but as Riley, married to the dreadlocked store assistant given the beach wedding photo on the wall, noted, she was new to the business this summer, as told by the brand new sign and fresh equipment that hung off her shelves.

Odion at Daintree Adventures had a group waiting to go out and was keen to get away as the daylight would be fading in a few hours. He had heard of Ian Kinch but hadn't seen him since last year.

Johnny, the owner of the Tribulation Experience

also knew of Ian Kinch. But again, hadn't seen him recently. Wondered how he was. Emmaline thought that odd as a visit from the police should have warned him how Ian was. Not good news. His vibe was one of a good-natured and sun-beaten old surfer in his late forties who seemed to have no care in the world. He even offered to take her and Oily out on the waves to look for Ian, but as bad as things might have been for him, Naiyana and Dylan, Emmaline doubted they were living on a kayak.

By 3 p.m. most of the businesses in the area had been questioned. Emmaline left Liang to check out the horse riding centre and the surfing canopy, which offered zipline experiences through the trees.

She tried Canyaks, a kayaking place at the far north end of town. It was run by an enthusiastic husband and wife team.

The wife fielded Emmaline's questions, her husband scrubbing down a kayak out the back behind the counter, the view looking out over the bay. She stood at the counter with a wide smile on her face, evidently content. *Someone who couldn't see themselves doing anything else, anywhere else*, thought Emmaline. Happy. The twinge of jealousy strangled her. That this woman had found a place she didn't feel the urge to escape from.

'I know Ian,' she said, not even looking at the photograph.

'When did you last see him?'

She appeared to glance over her shoulder at her

husband, the sun-bleached curls hiding her expression for a moment. Had something passed between them? A subtle warning to shut up?

She turned back. The smile had turned into a grimace.

'About three days ago.'

'Here?'

She shook her head. 'In town. Trying to hawk some work. He seemed desperate. I wanted to help but there's barely enough work for the two of us, never mind a third.' Again, she looked over her shoulder. Her voice hushed to a whisper. 'I like Ian. He's been up here for more years than I can remember but there was something about him this time, a desperation. I've seen it before. Like he had gone troppo.'

'Troppo?'

The woman smiled wanly. 'Spent too long hiding out from civilization and gone . . . a bit loopy. We've got caught out with it before. A guy we employed a few years back. He took a truck one evening with half our kayaks and gear. Drove off and flogged it down the coast. We lost a couple of grand. That's when I learned to pay attention to people. There are those who are desperate for work and those who are just desperate. Ian looked desperate. Troppo.'

Admitting this brought a sadness to her eyes. Emmaline could see that she cared. Maybe too much.

'And you haven't seen him since?'

'No, but try Tribulation. That's where I bumped into him. Coming out of it.'

Emmaline furrowed her brow. 'The Tribulation Experience?'

'That's the one. Used to be called Daintree Kayaks but Johnny wanted something snappier for his new location. He and Ian are pretty tight. He might have passed him a few hours, for old times' sake.'

Emmaline was out the door in a flash. Tribulation Johnny had said nothing about seeing Ian recently.

If Johnny was startled by the police arriving at his door for a second time, he didn't show it. He carried on taking an inventory of items in the shop, marking them down in his book.

'Change your mind about a tour of the coast?' he asked, with a cackled laugh.

'Have you changed your mind about when you last saw Ian Kinch?' replied Emmaline, hoping the directness would knock the dried bullshit from Johnny's demeanour.

Johnny paused briefly before returning to the shelves. 'I haven't seen him since last year.'

'That's not what we hear,' said Oily.

At this Johnny turned, his eyes narrowed as if waiting to hear what the police had before saying any more.

'He was spotted leaving this place, three days ago.'

Still Johnny didn't speak. So Emmaline decided to swing again.

'You do realize why we are after him, Mr McLaughlin?'

Emmaline watched some of Johnny's breezy disposition fade with the seriousness in her voice.

'He is a suspect in three murders, plus the disappearance of another two people.'

Johnny's mouth fell open as if to speak but shock prevented him.

'That's why we are keen to contact him.'

'Three murders?' asked a stunned Johnny.

Emmaline nodded. 'So I'll ask you again: have you seen Ian Kinch recently, Mr McLaughlin?'

There was a quick nod.

'Where and when?'

'He didn't say anything about . . .' Johnny trailed off. 'Here. He came in looking for work. A few hours, cash in hand. I've known Ian for years. He comes up here every summer . . . Three murders? And Ian killed them?'

'That's what we want to find out, Mr McLaughlin,' said Oily, inching towards the back exit to prevent any desperate attempt to escape.

'That's why we need to speak to him,' said Emmaline, covering the front door.

But it didn't look like Johnny McLaughlin was in any shape to flee, taken aback by the shocking revelations about his friend. He shook his head. 'Ian wouldn't . . . He's a nice guy.'

'There might be things about your friend that you don't know,' said Emmaline. 'Happens all the time. When was he in here?'

'Three days ago. I gave him a couple of hours' graft.

Haven't seen him since. I guessed he had gone out on the waves.'

'Did he say where he was staying?'

Johnny closed his eyes, thinking. 'Said it was a little around the coast. Not quite in town.'

'In his car?' asked Oily.

Johnny looked at him oddly. 'You don't sleep in your car here. You'll either boil to death with the windows up, or be bitten to death with the windows down.'

'Did you get a name of the place?' asked Emmaline.

'No, but there's only one place I can think of.'

129

Emmaline

All Tomorrow's was a business that hired out huts and cabins. It was based just off the beach and towered over by Mount Sorrow, the peak masked by a ring of low cloud as if shielding it from the horrors of the world below. The main office too was a hut, the one window peering through the trees for a beautiful, if obstructed view of the white sands beyond.

The owner was clad in a dress that was practically see-through, so much so that Emmaline struggled to keep Oily's attention focused on the case. Her name was Summer Haze. It suited her attire and her personality, bubbly and eager to help.

Emmaline asked if anyone by the name of Ian Kinch had rented out a property. Checking the records on the tablet, Summer shook her head.

'What about Ian King?' asked Inspector Liang, seemingly not bothered by the mosquitoes at all. In fact, of everyone in the room it only seemed to be Emmaline that they were targeting. Her and her sweet blood.

Again, Summer checked. Again a no. Followed by a half-smile that oozed pity. For herself. For not being able to help more.

'What about in the past?' asked Emmaline.

Re-energized, Summer set about getting an answer. A few taps later and her smile said it all.

'Yes, an Ian Kinch has been here before. For the last three years. Usually Ponting or Waugh. Good, quick access to the beach.'

It made sense that he would book under his real name. This was his getaway from any misdeeds. His separation of personal and public life.

'Are any of the cabins occupied at the minute?' asked Liang.

'They all are. It's summer!' said Summer with excitement.

'Did this guy rent one?' asked Emmaline, again passing her phone with Ian's photo on it. Her de facto screensaver at the moment.

Summer shook her head. Again disappointment washed over her face as if Mount Sorrow was wielding its malevolent influence again.

'But I only work day on, day off.'

'Who works—?' said Oily, finally getting the courage to speak. Emmaline cut him off.

'Anyone pay in cash?'

Summer looked it up. And nodded. 'A Mr and Mrs Jessop. In Waugh. I wasn't on shift. Come to think of it I haven't seen either of them leave the cabin.'

Two of them. Suggesting Naiyana was alive. But

no Dylan. Though Ian might have kept the boy's presence hidden. Emmaline looked at Liang but he was already halfway out the door. Everyone followed.

Summer shouted after them. 'Here's a map!'

Turning on his heels Oily waited behind to get it.

130

Emmaline

The same SERT teams that led the garage raid were put in place, the cabin surrounded.

Inspector Liang's confident mask had slipped as the day went on, ever more impatient as the threat of darkness began to intrude. Emmaline felt it too. An operation like this had a much greater chance of success with full visibility. Less opportunity for friendly fire. Stick to protocols, stick to your training. Something he had made clear to the SERT team.

Finally in position, they paused. There had been no movement from inside or outside, the small log cabin perched on the side of the slope, pillared at the front and surrounded by thick, canopied trees that shaded everything. Even the damn mosquitoes.

Emmaline was convinced that Ian and Naiyana were inside. Dylan too she hoped. This was the perfect place to hide out. At least until they could get away either by boat or island hopping. For enough cash someone would supply the service. Ian just hadn't hit the magic figure.

A call came through. Zhao. Emmaline grasped the phone, in two minds over whether to answer it or not. Shit was about to go down and she didn't want to miss it. First time had been a false alarm. This wasn't.

She answered it, keeping her voice low. 'Yeah?'

'It's about Dylan Maguire.'

'What about him?'

There was a pause.

'Some locals in Hurton rustled up a couple of dingoes that were worrying some livestock.'

'And?'

'They found pieces of clothing that had been ingested and had passed through their system. A name tag too.'

Emmaline knew what Zhao was going to say. She squeezed her eyes shut in preparation.

'Dylan Maguire. Nearby were a scattering of bones and a skull. The skull was fractured above the eye.'

Emmaline held her breath. Even with the machinations of Inspector Liang and the SERT teams nearby, everything grew still.

'It's been confirmed as cause of death,' said Zhao.

131

Naiyana

The crest caught them out, the down slope much steeper than the gradual approach. They were going too fast. Naiyana screamed as the ute reared up, her stomach suddenly feeling as if it had been ripped out, empty, her eyes closed and waiting for that butterfly-inducing lurch.

She put her palms on the roof to try and halt the sudden rise. There was a choked squeal from Ian as well, fighting for control. They were going to crash hard. The front of the Toyota pitched back towards the earth. There in front of them was Lorcan. And Dylan. Directly in their path.

Everything happened in slow motion. She wasn't sure if the scream she emitted was a continuation of the one that came from her when they launched over the crest, but it was as sharp and urgent. She watched Lorcan reach out for her son, trying to drag him away from the path of the vehicle. She felt the front of the ute slam into the sand, the tyres immediately burying into it. She hoped that it would arrest their progress but the vehicle didn't seem to slow one iota. She stared in horror as Lorcan yanked at Dylan's shirt. She lost sight of her child, nothing but scrub and sand in front of her. Then mercifully she could feel her progress arresting, the tyres biting, the brakes trying to halt them.

Then came the two sounds.

The first was hollow with a slight ring as if someone had cracked a shiny belt buckle off metal.

The second was harder. Her head whipped forward with a violent snap. The dull thud exploded in her ears, her skull ringing in shock. The ute came to a stop. She felt limp, her body thrown back in the seat, everything that had been so sharp now a blur. She squeezed her eyes shut. As if pressing the reset button. How she wished it so. Opening them, her eyes stung. A sudden cloying feeling wormed across every inch of her skin as if she was burning up. There was blood on the dashboard. And blood trickling off her chin into her lap. For a moment she sat there, her system trying to reboot. She could hear Ian asking how she was, his searing hot hand on her arm.

Outside the windows, all she could see was dust.

Dylan.

Grabbing the door handle she clicked her belt open and nearly fell out the door.

132

Lorcan

The pain was blurry but intense. He made it to his one good elbow, his other arm limp and useless. Broken. But that was a secondary concern. He looked at Dylan lying in the sand, at peace, almost idyllic. Reality struck like a hammer to his chest. He bolted forward, scrambling on his knees towards his son. From the side he could see Naiyana emerge from the Toyota, her face awash with blood, staggering towards them like an old-school movie monster.

As he lifted Dylan's head onto his knees, she knelt down beside him.

He put his hand to Dylan's mouth. There was no breath.

Putting him back onto the ground he began to pump his chest with one hand, the training he had undertaken years ago just a haze. Beside him Naiyana cried out for her son.

He pumped his chest as she stroked Dylan's face.

The body jerked each time as if still alive.

Each time Lorcan prayed for his eyes to open.

But there was no saving him.

Dylan was dead.

He placed Dylan's head back in his lap as Naiyana clasped her child's hand. He glanced over at her. They were finally united again. In grief.

From the background he heard a door opening. He turned to watch Ian get out of the truck, his rifle at the ready, like a farmer about to put down an injured dog.

Lorcan didn't move. His own rifle was only a few feet away behind Naiyana but there was no connection between his brain and limbs, his motor skills lost. The single abiding instruction tearing around his skull was not to leave Dylan. Not to let him go. Naiyana's tears arrived, bringing forth the vain hope that an outpouring of love could bring their son back. Or in futile competition over who loved him the most. A precursor to the inevitable accusations of who had killed him.

The inactivity of grief washed over him and anger filled the hole that it left.

He scowled at Ian, who stood watch over the proceedings. 'You killed him,' said Lorcan, searching for wrath but finding only a dry, reedy squeak, his arm in severe pain.

'I didn't see him,' said Ian, his voice also lacking power. 'I didn't mean to kill him.'

'You took him out here!' This was Naiyana, her tone fiercer than both of them. She had apportioned blame already. 'Why the hell were you running?'

'You both know why.'

She stared at him, reading his eyes. 'You saw it,' she said, her words faltering, the engine clogged, spluttering for power.

'I saw Ian,' said Lorcan, gritting his teeth when uttering his name, 'kill Mike. I assume he killed Stevie too.'

'No he didn't—' started Naiyana.

Ian half-nodded, half-shook his head as if confused. 'I wasn't there. Naiyana can back me up on that. Mike said you did it.'

'Lies. I saw you kill Mike, so you killed Stevie too.'

As Ian continued to twist his head in denial, Lorcan continued, 'I know something else too. Your affair. So, what I'm guessing is that Mike and Stevie found out, there was a scuffle and you killed them both.'

'No,' said Ian.

'Who are the police more likely to believe?'

He watched Ian raise the rifle. Lorcan knew he was testing him. He knew that it was a stupid thing to do given that Ian had already killed one person. But he realized something else. That he didn't care. He didn't care about anything anymore. Only Dylan. His beautiful son. Squeezing his eyes he fought back the tears. The pause allowed a shard of self-preservation to catch the light. He needed to stay alive. For Dylan's sake.

'But I don't want to go to them,' said Lorcan.

'What do you want?' asked Ian.

'We split the gold. And leave separately.'

He felt both their eyes on him. Weighing up if he was telling the truth. That he just wanted the money. Greed overwhelming grief for his murdered son. But Lorcan had a reason for wanting the gold.

'I want to take Dylan with me and bury him.'

Naiyana started shaking her head at this, holding her son's hand tighter. 'You're not taking him!'

'You don't have a choice,' said Lorcan. 'You're shacked up with the guy who killed him. *You* decided that.'

'It was an accident,' said Ian, shifting his gaze from Lorcan to Naiyana, trying to reassure her.

For all it mattered, Ian did seem genuinely distraught, but Lorcan didn't care. Naiyana could worry about his feelings. They could go screw each other and patch up their feelings. Fuck them.

'This was your fault,' he spat at Ian. 'And yours,' he said to Naiyana, right in her face, the tears streaked, drying on her bloodied cheeks.

'I'm taking Dylan,' he added, finding the strength to shout it across the barren landscape.

The first punch was weak but painful, her knuckles like knives as they rattled his teeth. Another followed, Naiyana attacking him as she let go of Dylan's hand. Trying to block her swinging fists, Lorcan fought beside his dead son, trying to give as good as he got despite having one arm. Scratching and biting in the sand and the dirt. All while Ian's rifle was pointed directly at them.

133

Naiyana

She fought with all her might. She fought dirty. She had to. The blood in her eyes had blinded her to all intent. She relied on wits that had been sharpened in the last year dealing with the shit she'd been through. She punched and when that didn't seem to make a difference, she scratched. Then bit. He was not taking her son from her.

She heard Ian shout at them to break it up. Like a teacher in a school playground. But this fight was for so much more than teenage pride. It was for Dylan. It was for everything they had been through. A fight to the death.

The punch rocked her. It caught her on the neck and caused one side of her body to suddenly go numb, her arm letting go of his shoulder.

There was no follow-up blow. Just a hard shove that forced her away from him.

It allowed her to clear some of the blood from her eyes. It felt like a thick, stinging molasses. Though the ache in her skull cried out for her to give up she put her hand out to lever herself back up. To go again. To attack. In doing so her hand brushed something hard. Metal. The rifle.

Grabbing it, Naiyana staggered to her feet. She raised the gun and aimed it at Lorcan. At the blur that was Lorcan, one arm hanging limp by his side.

She could hear Ian yelling for her to put it down. And Lorcan yelling that Ian had killed Dylan.

She needed to end this.

She would aim for his chest. The largest surface area. One half-decent shot would do it.

She tried to set her feet to do so but found she had little control of her limbs, as if the blow to the head had sheared the connections. The sand grabbed onto her feet, holding them in place as her body weight pitched forward. She stumbled towards her husband, falling pathetically.

Lorcan's one good hand grabbed for the rifle. She tried to squeeze the trigger but off-balance it was twisted from her hands, the butt swinging around and cracking into her forehead, spinning her to the side. More pain. More violent lullabies ringing around her skull.

The shot deafened her as she fell to the sand.

Blinking hard again, riding out the pain, she found Lorcan lying beside her, blood pumping from the hole in his chest. Her mouth opened but nothing came out. She rolled over and faced the sun, the savage evening heat and thick blood scalding her eyes, as if seeking to blind her completely.

Ian appeared into her blurred vision, standing over her. The rifle was in his hands. Now would be the time to kill her. She watched his finger tease the trigger. She tried to find the sparkling blue eyes that had drawn her into this mess. To plead with him. For what? For mercy? But what was mercy? Was it him finishing her off? Ending her misery?

She didn't find the answer, blinking furiously as the world washed away from her, leaving her in complete darkness.

134

Naiyana

She had spent most of the drive across the country in the back seat, fighting bouts of headaches, nausea and dizziness, but most of all she was besieged by the sheer weight of what had happened. Dylan was dead. Lorcan was dead. She was on the run with their murderer, dragged away from them as they lay in the sand. He had professed his love for her all the way out here. Every day if not every hour since. Probably because she was the only thing he had left. He blamed Lorcan for dragging Dylan into harm's way. Blamed Lorcan for causing all this. For making him shoot.

She only blamed one person. Him.

He had taken her to this place and this cabin. It was his retreat apparently. For a couple of months a year, if he had the money. He had warned her about the mosquitoes but not the sheer number. They swarmed around her like the plague but with the repellent coating her she was invisible to them. If only she could get an Ian repellent. Or a memory repellent.

He had been out today and purchased wigs for

both of them, but the blond wig he had picked for her was worthless. It would only make her stand out more given her Thai blood. The contact lenses too raised the same problem. She was small but hard to disguise. When he donned his blond wig and fake moustache it was hard to tell who he was. It was easy to think of him as someone else. And wish he was someone else.

The next day he brought her a black, short-haired wig. Wasting money on these disguises while they barely ate. Even if the mozzies could get to her there wouldn't be any blood to drain soon.

The new wig didn't help. She just saw herself in the mirror, blinded by familiarity. She was the cause of all this trouble, yet it hadn't been worth any of it. With her hatred of herself swollen to bursting, her hatred for him only grew every day. But she was weak from blood loss and the crippling pain of losing Dylan. He'd killed her child and she was stuck with him. He was her crutch.

But after a few days and a few meagre meals forced into a stomach that wanted to reject them, she had finally felt stronger. Strong enough to do what she had to.

135

Emmaline

'The presumption is that the animals dragged Dylan's body away post-mortem. Lorcan was too heavy to move so they returned to finish him later,' continued Zhao.

Emmaline stared at the cabin. Though a long shot she had been hoping to find Dylan alive and well. She supposed that there was still the slimmest of hopes. Forensics might have been wrong and it was another child's skull.

She waited by Liang's shoulder as he gave the signal. Two of the SERT team crept up to the front door of the cabin, their steps skilful and silent on the detritus. After a momentary pause and silent count they burst through the front door while another pair entered from the rear.

There was a sharp cry of 'Don't move!' All her muscles tensed as Emmaline wondered just what was in there.

The cry of 'Don't move' was quickly followed by a call of 'All clear'. There was no gunfire, no physical altercation. The occupants taken by surprise or fatigue.

Unable to resist, Emmaline broke away from Liang's short stride and ran, closing in on the door, twigs cracking under her urgent steps.

Up the front steps, she burst through the door, still unsure of what she was hoping or expecting to see.

Inside the atmosphere was fetid, the hut filthy. Food wrappers littering the floor, used medical gauze, wrappings, ointments and the intense aroma of two people cooped up in a small, humid room for too long. Accompanied by the ever-present tang of mosquito repellent.

Lying on the bamboo couch was Naiyana, covered by a thin blanket. She looked like she had lost weight, her cheeks gaunt, wearing an expression of haunted desperation. Beside her lay a clump of fur that at first Emmaline mistook for a small animal but which turned out to be a black wig. A blond wig lay on the floor in front of her. Streaked with red and loosely attached to Ian Kinch's dead body. A rifle and a bloodied knife lay on the floor beside the couch.

Naiyana Maguire broke down in tears, her spindly arms reaching out, the tendons in her neck pronounced as she screeched at those who had disturbed her resting place.

'He killed Dylan.'

Sucking in some air, the realization of where she was and what had happened seemed to hit her, her blinking pronounced as her voice fell away to a whisper. 'I had to kill him. He killed my son . . .'

Emmaline had a thousand questions to ask. Like,

what exactly had happened in Kallayee? To Lorcan Maguire. To Stevie Amaranga. To Mike Andrews. To her son. And what had happened after?

But Naiyana was babbling now, drowning in her grief.

The paramedics came bustling past Emmaline. Here to repair a mess that could never be rectified.

Acknowledgements

As I write this the whole world is in the middle of lockdown during this COVID-19 crisis. I have already mentioned it in the dedication but I just want to reiterate my thanks to all the hospital, post office and supermarket staff, and every one of the essential workers who put themselves at risk so the rest of us can shield indoors.

As for the book itself, again I have to thank West Australia for providing the inspiration for this story – with a nod to the Northern Territory and Queensland as well – for the sheer majesty and possibilities that lurk behind every town and rock and gully and for being such an inspiring place to write about.

The people I want to thank remain much the same as for the first book but I want to mention them again because they deserve praise for keeping me focused and sane at this time. Of these people one stands out most and that is my wife, Harpinder, for being honest about a story or a plot and as an inspiration for sheer hard work, drive and talent. And for not killing me during lockdown given she had to bear the brunt of my rubbish jokes.

I want to thank my family and friends, for being far away but always at the other end of a phone/video call. My wonderful agent, Marilia Savvides of 42 M&P, for expert guidance on what works, what doesn't, and for supporting me from the very beginning. Without her, this book wouldn't have seen the light of day. My editor, Anne Perry, was and is as amazing as ever, full of advice and ideas, helping me reshape this book to make it the best it can be. Kay Gale found many blatant errors my eyes overlooked. To Kim, Jack, Petros, Rhiannon, Alexandra and Gillian: thank you very much for your help behind the scenes. To Bethan, Harriett and Jess for their help, especially when I turn up at things unannounced. Also Jamie, Breanna, Sharon, Siobhan and everyone in S&S Australia who were so kind and helpful to me when I was out there last year – back when travel was a thing.

A special thanks must also go out to all the readers, tweeters and bloggers who take the time to read and review all the books out there and a thanks to all the bookshops that are going through a hard time at the moment and who I hope to be able to visit in the near future.

Finally – when I started out last year I didn't know another soul in the crime-writing community but I was lucky to fall into cahoots with a wonderful group of writers called Criminal Minds. They have been essential in keeping my spirits up through the long, slow process of writing a book and I hope to be able to meet up with them again soon.

And that's about it. Sorry if I left anyone out that deserves to be in this dedication. That is not because of a fault in your efforts but a fault in my memory. Any mistakes in this book are also mine rather than the fault of any contributor. For that I blame my memory also.

Also by James Delargy

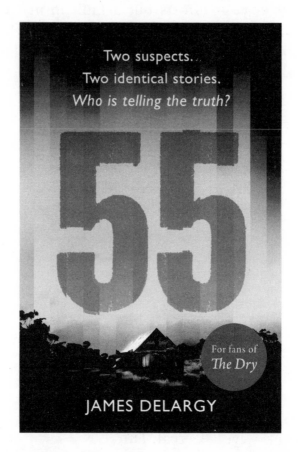

Two suspects.
Two identical stories.
Who is telling the truth?

55

For fans of
The Dry

JAMES DELARGY